of the Early Part of the Eighteenth Century.)

Whisper of Death

Also by Patricia Wynn

The Blue Satan Mystery Series in order of publication:
  The Birth of Blue Satan
  The Spider's Touch
  The Motive from the Deed
  A Killing Frost
  Acts of Faith

Regency Romances:
The Parson's Pleasure
Sophie's Halloo
Lord Tom
Jack on the Box
Mistletoe and Mischief
The Bumblebroth
A Country Affair
The Christmas Spirit
A Pair of Rogues

Historical Romance:
Capturing Annie

Whisper of Death

Patricia Wynn

PEMBERLEY PRESS
CORONA DEL MAR

PEMBERLEY PRESS
436 Begonia Avenue
Corona del Mar, CA 92625
www.pemberleypress.com

Jacket design by Kat & Dog Studios
Cover art: A Masquerade at the King's Theatre, Haymarket
Giuseppi Grisoni
Photo credit: V&A Images, London / Art Resource, NY

Library of Congress Cataloging-in-Publication Data

Names: Wynn, Patricia, author.
Title: Whisper of death / Patricia Wynn.
Description: First hardcover edition. | Corona del Mar : Pemberley Press,
    [2017] | Series: Blue Satan mystery series
Identifiers: LCCN 2017010640| ISBN 9781935421085 (hardcover : acid-free
    paper) | ISBN 1935421085 (hardcover : acid-free paper)
Subjects: LCSH: Great Britain--History--George I, 1714-1727--Fiction. |
    London (England)--History--18th century--Fiction. | Jacobite Rebellion,
    1715--Fiction. | Brigands and robbers--Fiction. | GSAFD: Historical
    fiction. | Mystery fiction.
Classification: LCC PS3573.Y6217 W48 2017 | DDC 813/.54--dc23 LC
record available at https://lccn.loc.gov/2017010640

❦

This book is dedicated to
my walking buddies:

Marilyn Alexander
Elizabeth Hoover
Marsha Nieto
Muff Tennyson
Stacey Von Berg

No one ever had more supportive friends.

Acknowledgements

After years of research, it is impossible for me to recall all the resources used to write this book, but it could not have been written without the following: *Hell-Fire Duke* by Mark Blackett-Ord for a detailed biography of Philip, Duke of Wharton; *Historical Newspaper Archives* for copies of the *Evening Post, The Weekly Journal or the British Gazetteer,* and the *Historical Register; Old and New London* by Walter Thornbury for descriptions and images of London, street by street, through the years; *British History Online* for many accurate details and primary accounts; the Victoria and Albert Museum for helpful images of period objects; *Royal St. James's* by E. J. Burford; *Ticket to Tyburn* by Kristine Hughes for information on Jonathan Wild; and many individual researchers for posting the fruits of their labors on the web.

A special thank you to the Stuart London Project, the British Library, The Leverhulme Trust, Motco Enterprises Limited, and the University of Sheffield for making available online the maps of John Strype's *Survey of London and Westminster* from 1720. These maps have never been republished in printed form, so after years of trying to extrapolate between the surveys of 1676 and 1738, I finally have a closer resource for the dates of my books.

The verses before every chapter of this book were culled from a number of Alexander Pope's *Epistles* and *Satires.* How lucky I am that one of history's most prolific and quotable writers was writing during the period of my novels!

Finally, thank you to Virginia Moore for her much-appreciated time and clear perspective in editing and proofing this book.

Historical Background

By the middle of 1716, King George I of Great Britain felt sufficiently confident that his throne was secure that he could safely leave England for Hanover, where he still ruled as a prince-elector of the Holy Roman Empire. Over the past year, his army had put down a rebellion intended to restore the throne to the Pretender, James Francis Edward Stuart, whose father James II had been overthrown in the Glorious Revolution of 1689. The rebels had either fled to France or been captured and put in prison. Many had been executed, and more awaited that fate. Working with Parliament, George had stationed troops around London to guarantee the peace and had enacted measures to silence the Jacobites (followers of James) by restrictions on speech and print.

The death of King Louis XIV of France, who had financed the Stuarts' invasions, and the desire of the new Regent, Philippe II Duc d'Orléans, for peace with Great Britain, made it appear that fears of a Jacobite invasion were a thing of the past. So, George took off for Hanover, leaving his son, the Prince of Wales, in temporary charge of the kingdom.

The political situation on the Continent was much more complicated than in England, and George had to address Hanover's interests. These did not always coincide with Great Britain's, and throughout his reign, George would be accused of overlooking one for the sake of the other. The complex politics of Europe with its ever-shifting alliances meant that he had to negotiate a torturous path, often concealing his agenda from his own ministers to achieve multiple objectives, but in 1717, his Hanoverian alliances had consequences for Great Britain.

Peace with France would be beneficial for both his domains and would strengthen his hand in restoring the balance of power in Europe, which was in jeopardy.

For years, Tsar Peter of Russia had been waging the Great Northern War against Sweden in an attempt to take back control of the Baltic Sea. His troops had ranged across the north of Europe from Holland to St. Petersburg, recovering the lands Russia had lost. The puppet-states the tsar had set up from the Baltics to Poland and Saxony raised alarms in Hanover. His plan to quarter his troops in the Duchy of Mecklenburg—the first step towards making it a client state—brought him too close to Hanover for comfort. George had "to divert the tsar from attempts which would immediately throw all Germany into a flame."

Meanwhile, having lost their champion, Louis XIV of France, the Jacobites courted Sweden for the support they so desperately needed to keep the Stuart cause alive.

King George's ministers back in London failed to grasp the severity of the Russian threat. Focused on the possibility that Sweden would support another Stuart uprising, Lord Townsend refused to adopt George's feelings of mistrust for the tsar, a position that cost him his office. Blissfully ignorant of their new king's concerns, the English courtiers attributed the changes in George's ministry to a combination of petty political intrigue and George's mistrust of his son, the Prince of Wales. The disaffection between the first two Georges would eventually lead to a major split in the Whig party that lasted for three years and establish the modern political concept of the loyal opposition.

Wharton, the scorn and wonder of our days,
Whose ruling Passion was the Lust of Praise:
Born with whate'er could win it from the Wise,
Women and Fools must like him or he dies . . . .

CHAPTER I

London, October 1716

After rounding another turn in the wide stone staircase, Hester Kean peered up and gasped with relief. Finally, the last of the two hundred fifty-seven steps up to the gallery in the dome of St. Paul's Cathedral was in sight. In her girlhood Hester might have scaled a comparable hill in the moors without so much effort, but today the lacings of her corset made it difficult to breathe. Too, for most of the past two years she had been away from those hills, and at the age of twenty-one she was no longer a girl. Her cousin Mary, sixteen, and freshly arrived from her brother's house in Yorkshire, had skipped up the stairs without struggling for breath. Hester could hear the girl's triumphant laugh up ahead as Mary celebrated her accomplishment.

"Just a bit farther, Mrs. Kean." Their guide, Mr. Christopher Wren, son of the great architect, took hold of Hester's elbow as she managed the final step.

She emerged from the stairwell to be greeted by a cacophony of strangely muted sounds, filling a vast domed space, the scale of which took her breath away. Far below, floor tiles were spread out in geometrical patterns. Huge gilded wrought-iron gates enclosed the quire, while a simple altar faced the immense circle where nave and transepts met.

Muffled voices, footsteps, and less-identifiable sounds echoed in Hester's ears as she gazed up at the ceiling, soaring hundreds of feet above her head. Scaffolding spanned the width of the giant dome, ascending from what must be a second gallery concealed within the curvature of the dome. The outline of a painting was starting to take shape on the ceiling, but too little had been completed for Hester to make out the story it would one day tell.

Suddenly, the ceiling swam before her eyes. As a wave of light-headedness seized her, she reached out for support. The muted din of noises confounded her bearings, but, with a firm grasp on her arm, Mr. Wren prevented her fall.

Her head still swimming, she gave an embarrassed laugh. "I beg your pardon, Mr. Wren. The magnificence of your father's creation appears to have overwhelmed me."

"I shall be happy to convey your compliment to my father, Mrs. Kean, but the demands of the climb are more likely the cause of your giddiness. You are not the first young lady to feel faint upon reaching the top. One is tempted to raise one's eyes immediately to the work taking place on the ceiling, which results in a disorienting effect. That is why I took the liberty of taking your arm."

Hester's vision was clearer now. She thanked him for the foresight, which had spared her an embarrassing tumble, if not worse, and nodded to advise him that she was ready to proceed on her own. He released her to check on Mary and James Henry, who had paused a few paces farther along the gallery.

Feeling cautious, Hester remained where she was a few moments longer. A careful gaze about the gallery informed her that they were not the only party visiting it today. A dozen or more men were scattered around the perimeter, walking in groups of two or three and pausing to gaze up at the unfinished ceiling or down at the cathedral floor below. Some were gentlemen in silks and shoulder-length perukes; others appeared to be merchants or prosperous tradesmen in wool and shorter bob wigs. A sprinkling of red uniforms attested to the presence of some of the soldiers encamped in Hyde Park.

Now that Hester had experienced the exertion of the climb to the gallery, she was not surprised to see no ladies besides Mary and herself. She had visited the new cathedral not long after first coming to London, but on that occasion her cousin Isabella, Countess of Hawkhurst, had been appalled by Hester's suggestion that they should climb the stairs. As Isabella's waiting woman, Hester had been obliged to stay with her mistress, so the pleasure of seeing the gallery had been denied her. Mary Mayfield—more intelligent and adventurous than her sister—would never hear of missing such a treat. Since Hester and she had arrived from Yorkshire scarcely a month ago, it had been Hester's pleasant task to show her cousin about London, more often than not accompanied by James Henry, Lord Hawkhurst's receiver-general, who insisted that the two ladies would be safer on the London streets with his escort.

He had taken quite a fancy to Mary during their four-day journey to London. With the suddenness of their departure and the shocks and losses accompanying it, Hester knew that she, herself, had been no companion for Mary on her first lengthy journey from home. Sensing this, perhaps, James Henry had taken it upon himself to entertain his lord's sister-in-law. The result was that Mary and he were now very easy in each other's company. Hester was amused by the way Mary looked to him for guidance and by the affectionate—almost proprietary—looks James Henry gave Mary.

He had taken her arm now, as she peered down from the gallery to see the great lectern Mr. Wren was indicating below. Still feeling too unsteady to lean over the railing, Hester moved backwards until she felt the support of the wall, before attempting to peer up at the ceiling again. Mr. James Thornhill, who had painted the hall at Greenwich, had been given the commission to paint the dome of St. Paul's with scenes from the life of St. Paul. The cathedral commissioners had taken the choice of artist away from Sir Christopher Wren to achieve a more economical rendering than the mosaics Mr. Wren said his father had planned.

Surer of her balance now and ready to join the others, Hester turned her head to see where they were. As she did, her ear lightly brushed the wall and in that instant, the gentle din that had filled the dome was pierced by a single hissing voice.

"I shall kill him with my bare hands."

The words came so suddenly and carried such venom that Hester jerked away from the wall. She looked left and right to see who had uttered the threat, but no one was standing closer to her than Mr. Wren and James Henry, whose conversation drifted to her as part of the general confusion of noise.

The voice she had heard had been unmistakably male, the words and the tone laden with anger and malice, despite being uttered in a whisper. It was impossible that she had imagined them, but there was no one near enough to make his voice heard. She looked down over the railing to see if the threat could have risen from the floor, but saw at once that this, too, was impossible. The noise from below merged into the din that again had filled her ears. Below her moved doll-sized figures, with the soldiers' red uniforms and ladies' dresses providing contrast to the more sombre hues.

"Are you well, Hester?" Mary came back along the gallery to fetch her. "Mr. Wren said that you were feeling a bit faint." Affectionate concern shone from her eyes.

Hester put the threat from her mind, though the mystery of how she had come to hear it still nagged. "I was taken by a fit of giddiness on reaching the top of the stairs, but as soon as I caught my breath, the moment passed. I am ready to go on."

"Good, for Mr. Wren says he has a surprise for us." Mary took Hester's hand and drew her to where the two men waited.

After receiving Hester's assurances that she was fully recovered, Mr. Wren continued the tour, describing the magnificent dome, the first structure of its kind in all of Great Britain. He explained that as impressive as the dome they saw here was, the exterior dome, a separate structure encasing this one, was larger still and proportioned to the exterior architecture, as this was to the interior. Then, he added, "Before we descend, I would like to demonstrate a curious phenomenon we have only recently discovered. I shall ask you to wait here until you see me reach a point half-way round the gallery from our current location. Then, as I turn to face that wall, I shall ask you to place your ears against this wall here."

Before they could ask any questions, he left them to hurry round to the opposite side of the gallery, bobbing hasty bows to the gentlemen he passed. Following his course around the inside of the dome, Hester espied an unwelcome group heading towards them, Lord Wragby with two of his friends. If Mr. Wren had not begged them to remain, she would have urged Mary to leave before the viscount spotted them. But it was too late now. Even as the notion of escape entered her mind, he glimpsed them and raised a hand in greeting.

Mary uttered a quiet groan, but there was nothing to be done. One could not slight the son of the powerful Marquess of Ireton, no matter how much one might wish to avoid him. He had recently noticed Mary at Hampton Court at a drawing-room held by the Princess of Wales and had demanded an introduction. Mary's mother, Mrs. Mayfield, had returned home in alt, convinced that her second daughter would make an even more splendid match than her first; but Mary was not as malleable as her sister Isabella and had made it clear that she found his lordship's attentions repugnant. That had not stopped her mother from encouraging the gentleman's pursuit or lecturing Mary on her duty to the family.

The only thing that had kept her from forcing Mary to accept his advances was the inescapable fact that Lord Wragby was already married.

Just two years ago, he had impulsively eloped with a general's daughter and presented her to his father as Lady Wragby. The fury of Lord Ireton had been such that Phillip had soon become disillusioned with his bride, loving the allowance that bought his horses and carriages and paid for his amusements more than a penniless wife. He had sent her to live at his country estate and had travelled the Continent with his tutor. Rumour had it that he had not laid eyes upon his wife since his return to England a month ago.

Hester saw that Mr. Wren had completed his walk, arriving at a spot across the great dome. He gestured for them to press close to the wall. Hester and Mary obediently put their ears to the stone, while James Henry, who had noted the viscount's approach, kept a jaundiced eye on his progress.

At first, Hester heard nothing but the usual echoes about the dome. Then, as she slightly turned her head, the voice of Mr. Wren rang clearly in her ear, "Can you hear me?"

Astonished, Hester raised her head to wave to Mr. Wren that she had received his whisper, but his face was still turned towards the wall. Then, as Mary evidently had not heard his voice, she helped the girl position her head so that she, too, might enjoy the marvel. After a few seconds, Mary gave a delighted cry and turned to tell James Henry what she had experienced. He listened with a distracted air, bracing himself for an unwelcome encounter with Lord Wragby and his friends.

As Mr. Wren turned to see if his surprise had met with success, Hester beckoned to him. With a beaming smile, he began the circular path back.

Before he could reach them, Lord Wragby brushed past James Henry to deliver a flourishing bow to Mary. Ignoring both of her companions, he greeted her in a reproachful voice. "Why, Mrs. Mary, you made no mention of visiting St. Paul's when I called at Hawkhurst House yesterday. If I had known you wished to see it, I would have escorted you here myself."

Mary completed her curtsy. "Thank you for your kindness, my lord, but we had a last moment change of plans."

With his arms tightly crossed, James Henry stood off to one side, glaring at Lord Wragby. His harsh, aquiline features reminded Hester of a hawk, eyeing its prey.

Hester hoped Lord Wragby would be too focused on Mary to notice James Henry's mien, for her brother-in-law Harrowby, the Earl of Hawkhurst, would be angry to learn that a servant of his had behaved with less than perfect courtesy to the son of the most powerful leader of the Whigs.

The Marquess of Ireton was a notorious rake and a member of the Kit Kat Club, neither of which circumstances had inhibited his political authority. He held an enviable position of favour with the Crown because it was due in part to his quick actions that the throne had been secured for King George after the death of Queen Anne. King George had rewarded him by elevating the once Earl of Ireton to a marquess.

Fortunately for James Henry, Lord Wragby seldom took notice of any persons beneath him. James Henry was a servant, a very trusted one who oversaw all his lord's estates and a landowner in his own right, but a servant nonetheless. He was the illegitimate son of the former Earl of Hawkhurst, but to Hester's knowledge, only three persons knew of this—herself, James Henry, and his half-brother, the outlawed Viscount St. Mars. She often wondered how James Henry managed to suppress what would be a natural resentment in his position, but except for expressing occasional loneliness, James Henry seemed to be content with his work. His father, though not acknowledging his paternity, had provided well for him, giving him a house and some acres of land, entrusting him with all his business, and paying him a generous wage. All he needed was a wife and heirs, and no one would find any reason to pity him.

Lord Wragby's companions had held back to give him access to Mary's side. As Hester's gaze lit upon them, the two gentlemen bowed politely, if coolly. She responded with a curtsy, hiding her surprise. She knew them to be Sir Francis Lichfield and Lord Charters, two young members of the Tory party. They had never accompanied Lord Wragby to Hawkhurst House, and seeing them with him here in St. Paul's astonished her. They gravely eyed their companion, evidently no more pleased to be caught in the encounter than James Henry was. Sir Francis darted furtive glances about the gallery, and Lord Charters' supercilious smile had an edge as sharp and as hard as steel.

Lord Wragby had now pressed so close to Mary that she was obliged to retreat a few steps. He giggled. "What? Do you fear that parson will scold us?" He looked about with an exaggerated air. "I do not spy any clerics about."

"I have done nothing to earn a scold, my lord. We are simply waiting here for Mr. Wren to re-join us. He has just showed us the most remarkable phenomenon, and we are eager to hear his explanation. Look, here he is now."

As Lord Wragby turned to glance behind him, Mary stepped closer to James Henry, who shifted to stand between her and her unwelcome suitor. The movement was accomplished so quickly that they had exchanged places before the viscount turned back around.

Mr. Wren reached them and made his bow to all the gentlemen. "My lords." Then addressing the ladies, he said, "I gather you heard my whisper?"

"Yes, indeed," Hester said, hoping to distract Lord Wragby. Mary concurred, saying that they were all in a quandary as to how his voice could reach them so clearly from the other side of the dome.

"It is a curiosity, which has only recently come to light, as I said. It seems that there is something in the shape of the dome which makes a whisper uttered by a person facing the wall travel across to the opposite side."

"What is this?" Lord Wragby glanced from Mr. Wren to Mary.

Mr. Wren patiently repeated his account, ending, "I wish I could explain the phenomenon, my lord. No doubt one of our scientific gentlemen in the Royal Society will discover the reason behind it, but for now it remains a mystery."

While Mr. Wren was speaking, Hester thought of the threat she had heard and realized that it must have travelled to her by this means. Now she knew why she had been unable to locate the speaker. She peered across the dome to see who could have uttered the words, but knew that she was searching too late. Whoever had spoken them, by now, would have changed his position. Since no one had gone past her to descend the stairs, however, the speaker must have been one of the men along the gallery now.

Hester scanned their faces, taking note of the few she recognized, but soon recognized the futility of this. The voice could have belonged to anyone of them, including the soldiers, none of whom she knew.

Lord Wragby had made a joke in response to Mr. Wren's explanation. "A mystery, sir, or a miracle?" He winked at Mary and gave an irritating giggle, then turned to address his friends. "We must hope that no one was listening to our conversation, eh? What do they say? Even the walls have ears?"

Their answering laughs looked forced, as if their conversation, whatever it was, was not something they wished to have discussed.

Hester took advantage of Lord Wragby's distraction to inform Mr. Wren that they were ready to descend. He did not urge them to make a complete circuit of the gallery—whether because he found Lord Wragby's jest about a miracle in his father's cathedral offensive or for his own convenience. By now, he must have escorted hundreds of visitors up to the "whispering gallery", so perhaps he was relieved to cut their visit short. He yielded to this adjustment to their plans with no sign of resentment.

They descended the stairs, Mary clutching James Henry's arm tightly as if afraid of falling, which, of course, she was not. Lord Wragby and his friends were obliged to trail behind them down the stairs and out onto the cathedral floor where they emerged beneath the great dome. Hester gazed up at the ceiling again to marvel at its soaring construction, which seemed to defy Mr. Newton's notions of gravity.

Lord Wragby quickly caught them up. Again, he used the privilege of rank to oust James Henry from Mary's side. He whispered words into her ear that made her blush. The sight of her irritation filled him with hilarity and his giggles echoed from all sides.

"Phillip! Remember where you are, sir!"

At the sharp voice, they turned as one to see the Marquess of Ireton exiting the stairwell. He was dressed with his customary perfection, from his expensive Parisian peruke to the diamond pin in his cravat and the sparkling jewelled buckles on his shoes. His long silk coat and matching vest were heavily embroidered with gold and silver thread. The Brussels lace at his neck and cuffs was of the finest quality.

Trailing behind him were a young black page in his master's scarlet and gold livery and two younger gentlemen whom Hester knew to be Whigs.

She bent into a deep curtsy and Mary hastily followed. The gentlemen made the proper obeisance for a peer of the marquess's rank. His censorious frown passed from his son, who sullenly glared back at him, to Mary and Lord Wragby's other companions. The two young Tories struck a defiant pose, while Mary guiltily lowered her eyes.

Hester wished that Lord Ireton's displeasure had not had this effect upon her cousin, who was not to blame for his son's attentions. A guilty demeanour would only confirm his suspicion that she would do anything to trap Lord Wragby into an imprudent marriage. Her mother's reputation was sufficiently fixed that no one would doubt her intentions in this respect. One had only to recall the machinations that had resulted in Harrowby's marriage to Isabella to suspect a similar scheme for the viscount.

Lord Ireton neither returned their bows nor acknowledged his son's friends with any greeting. Having delivered the reprimand for his son's boorish behaviour, he gestured to his page to follow and sauntered away, his companions in his wake.

The group about Lord Wragby stood frozen until he released a nervous giggle. Tension drained from them with an audible sigh.

"Trust my noble papa to spoil one's fun." Lord Wragby expressed his relief with a sneer. "He's just in a tiff because he won't be able to govern me much longer. I have seen to that."

Abruptly changing the subject, he offered his arm to Mary. "What say we escape this gloomy pile, eh?"

It was impossible for Mary to reject Lord Wragby's offer to escort her from St. Paul's, though it was made without so much as a glance at her companions. Clearly, he intended to sweep her away. James Henry could say nothing to keep him from walking away with her—he had no right—but Hester felt no such constraints. She would insist, as politely as she could, that Mary return to Hawkhurst House in the carriage in which her brother-in-law had sent them.

Unfortunately, yielding to Lord Wragby's rank would deprive them of a tour of the quire, carved with such magnificence by the Dutchman, Mr. Gibbons. They would have to return another day to see it. They had turned their steps to walk down the centre aisle—Mary on Lord Wragby's arm and Hester escorted by James Henry— when the organ burst into a soaring hymn.

The notes were so powerfully played that all voices ceased. Turning back with a cry, Mary halted their party in mid-stride, her face lit in radiance. Beside Hester, James Henry gave a quick intake of breath.

"Oh, may we listen? I have never heard anything so glorious." Mary directed her plea to James Henry, not to her noble escort.

Lord Wragby could not fail to notice the slight. His brow furrowed, as for once his gaze dwelt on James Henry. Finding nothing in those hawk-like features to please him, he said peevishly, "Well, remain here if you like, but my friends and I have no wish to dally." He relinquished Mary's arm, bowed coldly to her, and stormed off with an air of having dealt her a crushing blow.

It was all Mary could do not to laugh as she turned to Hester and

James Henry with arched brows and dimples in her cheeks. As Hester had foreseen, the polish she had taken on with new gowns and coiffures for Court had made her every bit as attractive as her sister Isabella. Her features might not be as perfect, but the intelligence in her eyes rendered her even more appealing.

Hester was not surprised that James Henry doted on the girl. He had always been more indulgent with Isabella than she deserved, swayed, Hester suspected, by Isabella's beauty. In Mary, he had found a worthier recipient of his regard.

"We can listen as long as you like. That is Mr. Handel playing the organ," James Henry said. " I have heard he likes to play the instrument here because it has pedals." They walked back towards the quire, James Henry explaining that both the extraordinary loudness and richness they heard was the result. Indeed, as they sat down in the quire, the music became so loud that it was pointless to speak. Hester closed her eyes and let the beauty of Mr. Handel's skill wash through her.

As her emotions were stirred by the powerful tones, her mind began to wander. She could not be alone with her thoughts for long before the pain of missing St. Mars filled her. They had last met in Yorkshire. He had asked her to marry him, and she had accepted, never truly believing that such happiness could be hers. Then before they could elope to France to live openly as husband and wife, James Henry had unexpectedly arrived to fetch Hester and Mary to London. His news, that Isabella's infant son had died, had dealt Hester a battering blow, hard on the heels of a terrifying experience. In the shock that ensued, Hester had barely been able to think. She had been only dimly aware of the hasty preparations for their journey, knowing still not only that her chance for happiness with St. Mars was slipping through her fingers, but that at all costs she must prevent James Henry from seeing him. For like everyone else, James Henry believed his half-brother Gideon Fitzsimmons, Viscount St. Mars, to be a murderer, and therefore, could not be trusted not to betray him.

Throughout the days of stupefaction, rocked by waves of shock and sorrow, Hester had wondered if St. Mars would forgive her for leaving. She had tried to send him a message explaining why she had been obliged to go, but she did not know if the message had been conveyed. Since arriving in London, she had frequently awakened in the middle of the night with the dread that he had come for her, had waited endlessly at midnight, and had left with his heart full of anger and hurt. It was now more than a month since they had said goodbye, expecting when next they were together that it should be for always, yet no word from St. Mars had reached her. Had he left for France without her, and if so, would he ever return? Would he be so hurt that he would never give her another chance?

Her brain argued this point with itself again and again. She tried to trust that St. Mars's love was strong enough to forgive her—that he would understand the duty that had driven her back to London and realize, too, that she had acted in part to shield him from discovery. But smaller voices inside her head whispered that he would realize how narrow his escape had been—that he had been on the point of eloping with a nameless, penniless woman when the *Vicomte de St. Mars* could marry a lady of his own station in France.

Hester was in the depth of these musings when the music stopped. They waited briefly for Mr. Handel to resume, but when he did not, they stood to leave.

Their coach with the Hawkhurst arms emblazoned on the door was waiting outside in Fleet Street. They had use of it for the day because Harrowby and Isabella had taken their newer carriage to Hampton Court to wait on the Prince and Princess of Wales. The weather through October had been trying with heavy rain nearly every day, which had dampened everyone's spirits. Finally, as the month was drawing to a close, there was a prospect of finer days.

It was not merely the weather that had put the Court and Londoners on edge. Hester had returned from Yorkshire to find regiments of soldiers encamped in Hyde Park, stationed there to prevent the kind of violence that could develop into another insurrection. King George had taken the steps he felt necessary to secure the kingdom he had inherited, while he visited his true home, the Electorate of Hanover.

The King had remained in Hanover since July, leaving his son to watch over Great Britain with limited powers. At Court it was said that the Prince still fretted over his father's refusal to name him Regent in his absence. Prince George also resented the changes the King had made to limit certain influences over him. Suspecting the Duke of Argyle of Jacobite sympathies, the King had dismissed him from his position as the Prince's Groom of the Stole. This had infuriated the Prince, and only a threat from the King to install his brother Ernst Augustus in his son's place had brought Prince George to heel.

Throughout the summer, the regiments of Foot Guards, Horse Guards, Horse Grenadiers, and Dragoons had discouraged rioters like those tried at the last sessions, but a few of the soldiers had fought duels and more than one had committed murder. That was the reason James Henry had given for escorting Hester and Mary about town.

Besides the physical danger of having so many idle soldiers in their midst, people were anxious because the jailing of suspected traitors continued. The slightest expression of disaffection with King George could lead to an arrest. Hardly a week went by, it seemed, that the *Evening Post* did not report that some person or another had been taken up by a King's Messenger. Publishers and printers were especially vulnerable to charges of producing treasonable material, but any baker, cordwainer, or cleric could be arrested for an ill-considered remark. Most of the latter were examined and released, but others were found guilty and sentenced to months or years in gaol or to being whipped through the streets.

The gaols of London were bursting at the seams, the rebels who had been sentenced to death awaiting an execution that had been postponed time and again, awaiting the King's return. The general hope was that his Majesty would pardon them in a spirit of reconciliation, but previously he had been immune to all such pleas.

Tomorrow, Hester and Mary would go to Hampton Court with their family to celebrate Coronation Day. The King whose crowning was to be fêted would not be present, but it was felt, though unexpressed, that his absence would scarcely be missed.

King George had little taste for court life. He rarely put on entertainments, preferring to spend his evenings quietly with his mistress, Madame Schulenburg, whom in July he had made Duchess of Kendall for life. The Prince and Princess of Wales, in contrast, entertained their courtiers with drawing rooms, balls, plays, and games of cards.

Now, as the Hawkhurst coach rattled down Fleet Street and Temple Bar came into view, Hester averted her eyes to avoid seeing the heads of traitors hanging there. Having just visited St. Paul's, she was struck by the irony of this other structure designed by Sir Christopher Wren. She wondered how the architect must feel to have his magnificent creation put to so gruesome a use. The last four prisoners to suffer the grisly punishment had been executed in July, so by now the rooks had picked their bones clean. Still, to see their skulls at the end of spikes on Temple Bar was a reminder that hundreds more might suffer the same fate. So many Londoners had lost their taste for blood that the executions, instead of acting as a deterrent, had raised sympathy for the Jacobites.

Surely, no one with any charity could stand to witness the drawing and quartering of a fellow human being, when the sentence was carried out in a way as to cause the person the greatest possible suffering. Just thinking of it made Hester cringe as the coach squeezed beneath the statues of the Stuart monarchs with the skulls of their most faithful adherents skewered above.

Mary had been happily chatting to James Henry, who listened to her with a fond look. The course of her speech faltered when the shadow of Temple Bar blocked the light through the small carriage window, leaving a chill behind. The first time Mary had seen the heads hanging above the gate she had shuddered and she grimaced now. James Henry leaned forward as if to take her hand, but, catching himself in time, he said instead, "You must not distress yourself over things beyond your power to prevent. Whatever else may be said, these men's sufferings are over now."

"I know, but I find it hard to believe that anyone could deserve such a miserable end."

"The penalty for treason has ever been harsh—a reminder to all who would contemplate it of the consequences of such a reckless step."

Mary emitted a huff. "Someone should warn Lord Wragby then. He does not hesitate to say the most scandalous things about King George."

"His father must never have heard him, for I'm certain Lord Ireton would be distressed."

James Henry's comment reminded Hester of something that had surprised her. "Lord Ireton cannot have been pleased to see his son in the company of Sir Francis and Lord Charters."

"Why not?" Mary turned to face her. "I have seen him in their company before."

"Because their Tory sympathies are well-known. In Lord Ireton's day, it was not often that Whigs and Tories could overcome their dislike of each other's politics to be on civil terms."

James Henry shook his head. "My late master certainly could not. What he would say if he knew his successor was a Whig, I should not like to contemplate." He said this with a teasing smile, to let Mary know that he did not share this bias against her family.

Hester recalled that St. Mars's father had been furious about his wish to marry Isabella. Their argument over her had led to St. Mars's arrest, costing him his title and lands, as well as his freedom. But, if it had not, she doubted that she and St. Mars would ever have become friends or that their friendship would have led to love.

She must not let her thoughts drift to him again, however, for the others were sure to notice her withdrawal and Mary might ask the cause of her melancholy. They had become used to her silence, believing it entirely due to grief over Georgie's death, which initially it was. But as the weeks went by, she had worried over the lack of any message from St. Mars.

The sight of the heads on Temple Bar had further depressed her, but it had also reminded her of the whisper she had heard in St. Paul's. She could not shake the sense that the threat had been real. The voice had sounded so cold.

While Mary and James Henry resumed their conversation, Hester thought about the men she had seen strolling around the gallery, including Lord Wragby and his friends. Anyone of them might have uttered the phrase before she had noticed them, but she found it hard to believe that Lord Wragby would conspire with a pair of Tories to kill anyone.

She had spied Lord Ireton pausing in his perambulation to greet a few acquaintances. His temperament certainly was fierce enough to spark a murderous intent. She believed he had killed his man in a duel, perhaps more than once. Perhaps, he was considering another challenge, but rumour was that his health was not sound. Surely a gentleman of his age should not contemplate a duel.

She had not known any of the merchants or tradesmen in the gallery. If one of them had spoken the hateful words, it was unlikely she would ever learn the cause.

Lord Ireton's friends, however, were another possibility. She had recognized both, for they were often to be seen at Court and even at Hawkhurst House. While not interested in government, Harrowby, nevertheless, counted himself a Whig, and careful always to stay on the Crown side of politics, he pursued most of his acquaintance within the Whig party. In consequence, he was waited upon by many a member interested in securing his vote.

Hester wished she had been able to make out the identity of the speaker, but there was seldom any distinguishing character to a whisper. Certainly not enough to recognize in a normal voice, if ever she should hear the speaker again.

It was an impossible puzzle, one that she and St. Mars might have tried to solve together if only he was with her.

Determined not to reveal her melancholy, she banished this thought, telling herself that the voice could as easily have come from one of the soldiers in the gallery.

This much I've said, I trust, without offence;
Let no Court Sycophant pervert my sense,
Nor sly informer watch these words to draw
Within the reach of Treason, or the Law.

CHAPTER II

"Does *monsieur* know when we may expect the pleasure of seeing him again?"

In his library at the Chateau de St. Mars, not far from the Loire, Gideon hesitated before replying to his *régisseur,* Jean-Luc. The two had been discussing the improvements Gideon wished made to his house while he was away.

Eventually he answered, "I cannot be certain." He could have added that he was never sure if he would make it safely back into France, but Jean-Luc was aware of his master's standing with the British Crown and understood the risk Gideon took each time he crossed the channel. Fortunately, Gideon could trust him not to alert the British authorities to his comings and goings. Jean-Luc had undoubtedly asked about his return because the improvements Gideon wished to make to his house suggested that he was planning for a more protracted stay— and that when he next came, he would not come alone.

He had not informed Jean-Luc of his intention to wed. The man carried out his duties as *régisseur* of Gideon's estate diligently and honestly, but he would never be the confidant that Gideon's groom Thomas Barnes was and had been since Gideon's infancy.

Gideon did not want anyone in his French household to know

of his disappointment, in case he returned again without Mrs. Kean. Their ignorance of it had made it possible for him to nurse his wounds in private. They must have noticed his dark mood, but at least he had not had to read sympathy or, worse, pity in their eyes.

He was giving Jean-Luc some final instructions when the sound of hooves on the gravel drive signalled the arrival of several horses. Gideon quickly moved to a window that looked onto the drive and saw a small troop of soldiers pulling up at his door.

The sight of armed men quickened his pulse. His instinct was to flee, but his horse was not saddled. Even if he managed to make it to the stables unseen, he would be captured before he left his property. Besides, if he was forced to flee from his estate at St. Mars, where could he find sanctuary?

Turning back to Jean-Luc and seeing the alarm in his eyes, Gideon dismissed him and sat down in the chair at his desk.

The officer who was shown into his library made a low bow before asking if he had the honour of addressing the *Vicomte de St. Mars.* When Gideon conceded this, the officer said, "My lord, I must ask you to accompany me to Paris."

"May I know upon whose orders?"

"By order of his Royal Highness, the Regent, the Duc d'Orléans."

"Did his Highness send any message for me?"

"No, my lord. My orders are simply to bring *monsieur le vicomte* to Paris to wait upon his Highness."

Gideon weighed his reply. At least he was not to be taken to the Bastille. That did not mean that he was not to be handed over to the English, however. Gideon was aware that an agreement was being negotiated between King George and the Regent of France, but he did not know its provisions. It would surprise him very much if it included anything calling for the arrest of English outlaws who had fled to France, but there would be no way of knowing until he presented himself before the Regent.

He stood. "I shall have my horse saddled and be ready to ride with you within the hour."

"Very well, my lord." The officer bowed again and returned to his men.

Gideon hid his misgivings as he instructed his servants to pack a bag and ready his horse for a journey to Paris. While the servants scurried to obey, unnerved by the presence of soldiers, he went back to his desk to pen a quick letter to Tom with a separate one for Hester, to be delivered only if he did not return. It would be the first letter he had written to Hester since they had parted in Yorkshire. He hoped it would not be his last, but in case it was, he had to tell her that he loved her.

He had fled England in a flurry of emotions. Anger at having his hopes so abruptly dashed. Frustration—for he had believed that his passion for Hester would soon be indulged. Hurt because she had chosen loyalty to her family—a family who abused her—over him and his love.

He had even been hurt to learn that she mourned the loss of the infant who would have inherited all that should be his.

He had been so consumed by angry feelings that it was days before he allowed himself to consider the trap in which she had found herself, and many days more before all his anger was gone. Then he told himself that he had not been angry with Hester, just with the circumstances that kept them apart. Still, he had not been able to bring himself to send a message that he would come again. He had never written her, because a letter might be opened by someone else and she would be forced to explain her relationship with an outlaw, but he could have sent her some word by Tom or Katy, Tom's wife.

It had taken him weeks to realize that what was keeping him from writing her was fear. He was afraid that she might make the same choice if he laid his heart at her feet again. He had asked her to leave England forever, to live the life of an exile with him in France when she had never once been out of England. What if the thought of leaving everyone and everything familiar behind was too overwhelming? What if his love was not enough to conquer her dread of the unknown?

He had been forced into exile when he had been named outlaw. Even having an estate in France and devoted to it had not assuaged his yearnings to live freely in England. It had not been enough to stem his

longing for home. How much harder would it be for Hester to commit herself to a life she had never experienced?

She said she loved him, and he believed her. He had assumed that
any life would be preferable to the one she lived now, as a servant to
her cousins, whom she could not possibly respect; but what if the
loneliness of living with him frightened her even more?

At last he had found the courage to face her again. He had made
his plans to return to England and put them in motion. Now, he regretted the delay that might mean he would never see her again.

He tried to calm his worries with the knowledge that he was a
member of the French aristocracy. He had done nothing wrong under
French law. He had been a welcome member of Louis XIV's court and
had met the pleasure-loving Duc d'Orléans on several occasions. There
was no denying, however, that the Regent had different aims from his
predecessor with respect to the English. The question was, how far
would he go to please them?

After three days of hard riding, Gideon and his escort rode into
Paris and directed their horses to the Palais Royal, the palace of the
House of Orléans. During their brief stops on the road, Gideon had
tried to pry more information from the officer in charge, but the man
seemed ignorant of his master's purpose. At an inn where they had
passed one night, Gideon had again thought about making his escape,
but until he knew the reason for his summons, biding his time seemed
the wisest course. He had no one in France to hide him. There was no
Tom here to rush to his aid. As much as he wanted to be on his way
to England to see Hester, if they were to be married, they would need
a home. His best course of action was to hear what the Regent had to
say and fight for his rights if he must.

Before arriving at the palace, Gideon requested a moment to make
himself presentable to the Regent. The guard waited for him at an inn
near the Louvre on the Rue de Rivoli, while he washed his face and
hands and changed out of his travelling clothes. Less than half an hour
later, at the Palais Royal, wearing a light brown, shoulder-length wig, a
satin justaucorps, silk stockings, and buckled shoes, he was taken past
the guarded gate into a side entrance and turned over to a footman

wearing the livery of the House of Orléans.

Though relieved to find himself in the palace and not on his way to the Bastille, he was still discomfited by the clicking of his heels on the parquet floor as he was ushered through a long enfilade of rooms to a library and instructed to wait.

The footman left, presumably to announce his arrival, and Gideon had nothing to do but look around. The grand reception rooms he had passed through, including this one, formed the west wing of the palace with tall, narrow windows looking out onto a courtyard. Beyond the courtyard and past the pillared gallery, he could see the garden laid out in parterres. The sumptuous furnishings of the rooms were equal to the richest he had ever seen. The walls were hung with masterpieces. Even in this relatively small chamber he spotted fine pieces by Dutch and Flemish masters.

The Palais Royal had been built by Cardinal Richelieu in the last century. Later, it had housed the Queen Mother, Anne of Austria, and her son who would become Louis XIV, as well as Henrietta Maria, the widow of Charles I, after she had fled from England. When her daughter, Henrietta Anne, had married King Louis's brother, Phillippe Duc d'Orléans, it had become the principal residence of the House of Orléans.

The palace was eventually deeded to the House of Orléans as dowry for the current *duchesse,* part of the price Louis XIV had paid to secure an illustrious marriage for his daughter by Madame de Montespan. Upon hearing that her son Phillippe II, then Duc de Chartres, had agreed to marry the King's bastard, his mother had slapped him across the face. The duke had never liked his wife, calling her Madame Lucifer, in spite of her having borne him eight children. He had been pleased, however, to bring the government of France back to Paris to house it in the Palais Royal, abandoning the Palais de Versailles and the town that had sprung up around it.

Gideon's wait seemed to take forever. He was tempted to leave the library by the tall narrow doors to walk around the courtyard, but he knew better than to offend the Regent of France. The King, Louis XV, who now lived in the Tuileries Palace just a short distance away, was only six years old, which meant that the Duc d' Orléans would hold the power in this kingdom for several years. If anything were to happen to the young King, the Regent's enemies whispered, he would hold it for much longer.

He was a man who preferred paintings to politics and beautiful women to war. He could not be more agreeable to King George of Great Britain if they had both been borne of the same mother.

Gideon's patience was finally rewarded when a door, concealed in the wall panelling, opened to admit the Abbé Dubois, Phillippe's recently appointed counsellor of state. He was the successor to Cardinals Richelieu and Mazarin, though it remained to be seen whether he would ever reach the heights of power his predecessors had. He was not an ordained priest and, therefore, could not achieve the rank of cardinal. His enemies, including the Duc de Saint Simon, despised him for his common roots and resented the fact that a man with no background had gained the Regent's confidence.

After the two men exchanged formal greetings, Gideon said, "I understood that the Regent wished to see me."

The Abbé answered in his provincial accent, "Ah, yes, as to that, my lord, my apologies. I may have given that impression to the guard, but in fact, it was I who wished to see you."

Waiting for Dubois to explain, Gideon studied his face. The Abbé had the high forehead and heavy eyebrows often seen in the French with a distinguished nose and an intelligent gaze. His skin was lined, many said, due to his debaucheries, it being no secret that he kept a mistress.

"Were you aware, my lord, that under the agreement we hope to secure with King George, all Jacobites are to be expelled from France?"

Gideon started, alarmed by what sounded like an accusation. "I am a French *vicomte,* monsieur, not a Jacobite. Whoever says that I am in the service of the Chevalier de St. George has given you false information." He used the title Louis XIV had granted to James Stuart.

The Abbé ignored him. "You must understand that this peace is important to France. We have every intention of honouring its terms."

"And I repeat to you, *monsieur l'abbé,* that I am no Jacobite! If you do not believe me, you can apply to the Chevalier himself." The truth was that the Pretender had been so annoyed with Gideon's assessment of his chances of succeeding with the rebellion that he had dismissed him from his service, making Gideon's decision not to work for his cause all the easier. The only reason he had agreed to perform even one task for James Stuart was to fulfil what he believed would have been his father's wish.

The Abbé studied him with a shrewd gaze. "Of course, his Highness the Regent sympathizes deeply with his cousin's plight. Nevertheless, another war with England would not be in his country's interest, so what concerns him now is whether the King of England regards you as a threat to the peace of his kingdom, not what the Chevalier de St. George believes you to be."

Gideon felt as if a trap had been laid for him, one that he was not clever enough to see. The Abbé must know that he was an outlaw in England. He seemed to be saying that Gideon had no way of proving his innocence of any involvement with the Jacobites. The only point in making such a statement that Gideon could see would be to gain something from him, something that, if he delivered it, would cause the Regent to overlook Gideon's guilt.

Better to say nothing than to take a step that might land him deeper in the trap.

When Gideon made no response, the Abbé's lips turned up in amusement. *"Ah, bon!"* he eventually said, "Perhaps *monsieur le vicomte* would be so good as to remain here a short while longer. There is someone who wishes to speak to you."

He turned and left the library through the same door he had used to enter, leaving Gideon in a quandary. He had not agreed to speak with this person, whoever it was. On the other hand, if he refused, if he used the opportunity to flee, he would surely be caught. He did not even know how to locate his horse, or whether a guard had been posted to keep him in the palace.

In the end, fretting over the forced wait, he chose a middle course, exiting by one of the tall doors to the courtyard. Passing a guard on his way out, he stopped and informed the man that if the Abbé Dubois returned and wished to speak to him, he could be found in the garden.

Rows and rows of plane trees had been planted to create shady walks in the summer. Now in autumn, their big leaves coated the gravel paths with yellow, brown, and touches of red. Busy gardeners were raking them into piles. They looked up and bowed, tipping their felt hats as Gideon strode by. He waved them back to their work, as he mulled over the strange conversation he had just had.

He was still in the dark as to Dubois's purpose. How could he even know if the Abbé was being truthful with him about the Regent's intentions? For decades, King Louis XIV had used his cousin James II, and then James's son, to annoy the English Crown, backing them with just enough money, men, and arms to mount a series of failed invasions. Who could say yet if the Regent truly wanted peace? There were people who suspected him of wanting the Crown of France for himself. What if his machinations involved using James Stuart again to draw England into another war?

Gideon failed to see what benefit war would bring unless it were to provide an enemy to justify the Regent's usurping the young Louis XV. Phillippe d'Orléans gave the impression of a man devoted to his pleasures, his mistresses, his paintings, his children, and his palaces. Abbé Dubois served to remove many, if not most, of the cares of state from his shoulders. But should Gideon forget that it was Orléans who had convinced the King's Council to overturn the old king's will—giving his bastard sons, the Duc de Maine and the Comte de Toulouse, power during the young king's childhood—and had seized the regency for himself? No lazy, unambitious man had accomplished that.

Could such ambition be as disinterested as Orléans pretended?

For the next half hour Gideon mused about what the Regent could possibly want. He was no closer to learning it when a servant came to inform him that the Abbé requested his presence again in the library.

Gideon took a deep breath and followed the footman back through the courtyard and to the door to the library, where the man stepped aside and gestured for him to pass.

In the library he found, not the Abbé Dubois, but King George's emissary to France.

Gideon paused just inside the door, reluctant to put any distance between himself and his escape route. "Lord Stair," he said, cautiously bowing.

"My Lord St. Mars." The elder gentleman acknowledged his bow with military politeness. The second earl of his line, John Dalrymple, Earl of Stair, had distinguished himself while serving under Marlborough in the last wars. For the past two years, he had been an able envoy to France, during which time his employment of spies had been so successful as to foil all the Pretender's attempts to retake his throne. Of course, his task had been made easier by the poor calibre of men who had flocked to join the Jacobites, men who apparently had never heard of the word discretion.

"Are you here to arrest me?" Gideon readied himself for a fight—or flight.

Lord Stair's expression gave nothing away. "That may depend upon the result of our conversation. For the moment, you are safe." He indicated the chair across from the Abbé's desk. When Gideon remained standing, he merely raised one shoulder in a shrug before taking his seat.

Before Gideon could remind him that he was not an outlaw in France, Lord Stair said, "We know you visited James Stuart last year."

In spite of what he had heard of the efficiency of George's spies, Gideon still was surprised. Clearly, someone close to James Stuart was informing the English government of the Jacobites' comings and goings if a visit as unimportant as his had been reported.

"Did your spy inform you of the object of my visit? If he did, then you know that my only purpose was to discourage the uprising. I gave the Pretender my sincere opinion that any invasion by him would fail. He obviously did not listen—why should he consider the opinion of a man he hardly knows? The result, however, was that many of my father's friends are now in gaol. That does not make me a Jacobite."

"I have long been aware of your father's sympathies."

"Then you also must know that he never gave any tangible support to the rebels. If you were to arrest everyone who simply sympathized with James, your gaols could never contain them all."

"You have not described your own sentiments. If you could not expect James to listen to you, why bother seeing him at all?"

Gideon refused to discuss with anyone the feelings of guilt he had about his father's murder. Even were they not too private and painful, he would not wish to give ammunition to his persecutors. He was already suspected of murder. Confessing to any feeling of guilt would tend to confirm their suspicions.

"I had hoped to avoid more bloodshed and hoped, against reason it turns out, that James could be made to admit the futility of another war in the Stuart name. If you still suspect me of treasonous intent, recall that, like so many others, I could have lied to him. I could have raised his hopes, and in exchange I would have received empty promises to restore me to my title and my lands."

The look that crossed Stair's face acknowledged the logic of what Gideon had said, but he merely gave another shrug.

Gideon wryly reflected that the earl's sojourn in Paris had been long enough for him to adopt the Gallic gesture.

"Why have you brought me here, my lord?" Gideon realized that Lord Stair had been behind his summons.

"I should imagine that the Pretender has had time to reconsider the wisdom of your advice."

"Perhaps, but why should that concern me? What bearing does it have on my presence here?"

"It may mean that he has learned to trust you. You said yourself that he has surrounded himself with liars or with men as desperate to believe in false hopes as he is, himself. The fact that you did not lie and proved to be correct might have raised you in his estimation."

Gideon did not like the direction Stair's remarks had taken. "To what purpose, my lord, when I have no intention of entering the Chevalier's service. I repeat, I am not a Jacobite, Lord Stair, in spite of the lack of justice I have received from King George."

As soon as the bitter words left his mouth, he regretted them. The change in Lord Stair's expression, a glimmer of satisfaction, hastily concealed, informed Gideon that he had given the man the opening he had wished.

"What if I were to tell you that his Majesty would be more favourably inclined to consider a petition of innocence from you, provided you could do him a service?"

A burst of wounded pride nearly made Gideon refuse to hear Stair's offer. He should not have to petition the King for clemency when, by now, George's spies should have informed him of Gideon's innocence.

It was impossible to believe that they could know of every visit to James Stuart and not know how his father had been killed.

But Parliament had already granted the title Earl of Hawkhurst to his cousin Harrowby, and Harrowby would never pose a threat to the Whigs. They would not be as sanguine about the son of the former earl, a Tory with Jacobite sympathies. Gideon knew that whatever King George would require of him before returning what was rightfully his would be no easy task.

It would be foolish not to hear what it was, however, so he nodded. "Go on."

"You may be aware of the alliances James is seeking?"

Gideon wearily shook his head. "I have told you, my lord. I am not in the Pretender's confidence. I have not even visited Saint Germain in several months." The Palace of Saint Germain was the seat of the Jacobite court of James's mother, the widow of James II. Although the Pretender had been banished from France under the terms of an earlier treaty with Great Britain, the community of exiles from his father's court still gathered at the palace Louis XIV had bestowed upon his father. Gideon had visited the former queen there on a few occasions.

"Not even that James is seeking a wife?"

At Gideon's impatient look, Stair waved this away. "'Tis no matter. What is important is that he hopes to marry the daughter of the Landgrave of Hesse. He tried to send one English emissary to Cassel with his proposal, but his emissary failed him." Disgust rolled over the earl's features. "Fortunately, the young gentleman proved to be a fool. Oh, he managed to meet James at Avignon without being stopped by our side, and he charmed James into giving him the commission. But he was more indiscreet than even the Pretender's other adherents. That was how we came to learn of the affair, and he was packed back off to England before he could carry out the task.

"We know that James has not given up hope for an alliance with Hesse, however. He will need someone else to be emissary, someone he thinks he can trust.

"It is vital to the security of the realm that the Pretender's aims to achieve this marriage be foiled. The Landgrave of Hesse is no friend to Hanover. We need a man of our own to undertake the negotiations for this or any proposed marriage to ensure that they never go through. It is imperative that James Stuart be denied the prospect of a Protestant bride, which might make his claim to the throne more palatable."

Gideon was incredulous. "And this is what you want of me? To insinuate myself into James's confidence, offer to negotiate his marriage, then make certain that the negotiations fail—and, presumably, keep you informed?" He did not try to hide his distaste.

"That would be one way in which you could serve his Majesty. I can promise you that all the charges against you will be cleared." Lord Stair gave Gideon a penetrating look. "There could be another, greater way, however." He tapped his fingers on the desk.

"We know that James's advisors are trying to create an alliance with the King of Sweden. If they manage to do this, Britain will be forced to make concessions to the Tsar of Russia. King George is very anxious not to disturb the balance in that conflict. Tsar Peter has already stated his intention to winter his troops in Mecklenburg, which is too close to Hanover for comfort. If he takes control of Mecklenburg, Bremen and Verden will surely be next. But, if Britain is forced into a greater role in the war against Sweden, it will be difficult diplomatically to keep him out of King George's dominions. You must see the importance of our knowing how James's negotiations are faring with the King of Sweden."

This was a much more vital issue than James's marriage. Gideon was astonished that Lord Stair would be so open with him. Why would they trust him with this information?

It occurred to Gideon that the Crown must already be convinced of his innocence, that their spies had informed them that he was not in the Pretender's service. Yet, knowing this, they would ask him to perform this dangerous mission before seeing that justice was done.

These were their conditions.

His guts had tied themselves into a knot. The prospect of recovering his title and his estates . . . then another thought . . . Hester in London. How long would she wait?

Lord Stair cleared his throat, urging his response.

Gideon steeled himself to settle his fate.

A Fool, with more of Wit than half mankind,
Too rash for Thought, for Action too refined:
A Tyrant to the wife his heart approves;
A Rebel to the very king he loves;

CHAPTER III

O n Coronation Day, Hester descended the grand staircase at Hawkhurst House and passed into the antechamber where the family would gather before taking carriage to Hampton Court. One of the housemaids had helped her into her finest gown, a cream silk mantua embroidered with flowers over a plainer pale blue brocade stomacher and petticoat. The maid had pinned up Hester's train in back after the newest fashion to add more width to her hips, careful that only the best side of the material showed. She carried the fine chicken-skin fan that St. Mars had given her, intending to keep it open in the hope that the exquisite painting on it would distract the guards from noticing her lack of jewellery.

It was the guards who decided who would be admitted to Court, based on how finely they were dressed, but since Isabella's cast-offs, one of which Hester wore now, were as extravagant as all her gowns, Hester's presence at Court assemblies had never been challenged.

She was the first of the female members of the family to descend. Only Harrowby Lord Hawkhurst had preceded her into the room, but it would never do to keep her aunt Mrs. Mayfield waiting, so Hester had learned to be prompt.

She found Harrowby in a pensive mood, staring down at the fire in the hearth, his long luxuriant wig brushing the back of the puce satin coat that reached to his knees. He returned her greeting absent-mindedly, one bejewelled hand supporting him as he leaned against the mantle. Suspecting the direction of his thoughts and not wishing to disturb them, Hester sat down on a high-backed chair and folded her hands in her lap await the others.

After a moment, Harrowby heaved a loud sigh. "Ah, Mrs. Kean, I was thinking of poor little Georgie. He did have a look of his papa, did he not?"

"Indeed, my lord. The likeness was unmistakable." Her own sadness whenever she thought of the child assured that her words were uttered in a sincere tone. Georgie *had* resembled his scapegrace father, so much so that Harrowby had doubted his paternity from the day of his birth. Time and affection had erased his suspicions, however, just as Mrs. Mayfield had predicted they would, so the memory he retained of Georgie grew more and more like himself every day.

"Ah, well. There is nothing for it. We shall have to try for another heir." He gave her a tentative look. "My lady has not said anything to you . . . ?"

"No, my lord, I am afraid she has not. If such good news does reach me, you shall be the first to hear."

"Of course, of course. It is simply that she has not looked her best of late. She appears rather wan."

It was true that Isabella did not look well, but Hester blamed this on her cousin's frantic pursuit of pleasure since the death of her son. She seemed determined not to deny herself one ounce of fun, as if chasing after every entertainment the Court had to offer, every opportunity to flirt, rich meals, and strong drink could ward off any future disaster.

When her mother had suggested that it was time for Isabella to conceive a new heir, her reaction had been to shriek that she would not be tricked into bearing any more infants. The pains of childbirth had been bad enough once. She refused to be put through that torture again, especially if the result was to lose the child.

Hester had advised her aunt to give Isabella more time. Surprisingly Mrs. Mayfield had heeded her advice—no doubt, frightened by her daughter's vehemence—though it was plain she fretted over the loss of power that Isabella, and by extension herself, could wield over her husband if she did not provide him with an heir.

After a brief wait, the ladies all descended, tricked out in their finery. Mary looked charming in green and gold brocade, but everyone was outshone by Isabella's costume of ivory silk, shot through with gold thread that matched the golden highlights in her hair. She was especially gay, as she led them out to the carriage, waiting in the courtyard.

They took their places in the coach, Harrowby and Isabella facing forward, and Mary and Mrs. Mayfield flanking Hester on the rear-facing seat.

"Inch over, Hester! You are taking more space than you deserve," Mrs. Mayfield fussed. "I do not see there is any need for you to accompany us."

Isabella reminded her mother that they would need Hester to keep an eye on Mary. "For I have no intention of curbing my own fun to play chaperone. And as I am certain you will wish to play at cards, who else can be depended upon to watch her?"

"I doubt anything terrible could happen to Mary at Court, not with so many courtiers around. If she would promise not to do anything to disgrace us, I am certain she would be perfectly looked after by one of her admirers."

"I had rather be in Hester's company." Hester was proud that Mary did not glower at her mother when she spoke, for she had cautioned her cousin that Harrowby would be more likely to give her a decent dowry if she spared him their petty squabbles.

Mrs. Mayfield was not so easily coached. She scoffed. "If you persist in that way of thinking, you shall never get a husband."

This was too much for Mary, who smiled her broadest, falsest smile and said, "Oh, is it a husband you want for me, Mama? I was under the impression that you wished me to become Lord Wragby's mistress."

Mrs. Mayfield swelled in outrage. "How dare you speak to your mama in that fashion! I have never suggested anything of the kind."

"But you have encouraged Lord Wragby to dangle after me, and he is married, Mama. So what else should I think?"

"There is talk that Lord Ireton will press the King for an annulment. Otherwise, I should never encourage him. I am certain his lordship is only waiting for the King's return to broach the subject, so it makes sense to be prepared."

"I refuse to hear another word on this subject, madam," Harrowby interjected at last. "We are tired of your incessant nagging on this point, when I have told you repeatedly that Lord Ireton will no more countenance a marriage between his son and your daughter—a girl without a penny to her name—than he did that thoughtless elopement. You have set your sights much too high."

Mrs. Mayfield did not dare incur her son-in-law's wrath by pursuing the subject, but the look she gave Hester and Mary told them that she had not abandoned her hopes. Since the only dowry Mary would have depended on Harrowby's generosity, Mrs. Mayfield had to tread warily before contradicting him.

Lord Wragby would reach his majority soon, at which point his father could do little to prevent him from marrying whomever he wished. He would still control his son's purse strings, but Phillip had an income that had been settled upon him by his late mother, which amounted to well over £1,000 per year, enough to live comfortably, if not extravagantly, until his father died. One of the problems Hester's aunt refused to acknowledge was that Phillip *did* live extravagantly and was unlikely to wish to share a limited income with a wife.

They had heard that when he lived at Paris, he had kept six footmen, one running footman, a *valet de chambre,* his Governor (whom he had insisted on calling his secretary), and two sets of coach-horses. Living in such magnificence, he could easily run through his fortune in a few years.

With Mrs. Mayfield sulking next to her and Harrowby moodily staring out the window, Hester did her best to keep up light conversation during the hour and a half it took them to travel more than ten miles to Hampton Court.

It was a journey Harrowby and Isabella had made several times since returning to Hawkhurst House after their summer in Royal Tunbridge Wells. Their frequent visits there kept the family apprised of the court news.

The Prince and Princess had lived in great splendour all summer at Hampton Court, where they had dined in the Princess's apartments every day in public after the fashion of French royalty, unlike King George who despised ceremony. The Princess's ladies-in-waiting had served them at table. Everyone said how well the Prince had behaved to his father's ministers, greeting them cordially and apparently eager to discuss state business. Lord Townsend, the King's Secretary of State, had called at the Palace nearly every day and, according to his enemies, had insinuated himself into the Prince's favour. The Tories who had hoped to take advantage of the spat between father and son were disappointed to see the Prince turning instead to a faction of the Whigs. The Duke of Argyle had spent the entire summer at his side despite being dismissed from the Prince's household. In short, the usual comings and goings and connivances had carried on all summer.

The Princess of Wales was due to be delivered of another child at any moment, so the revelries this Coronation Day were expected to be rather tame. She had spent the summer quietly, seeing company, reading and writing until evening, walking in the garden for sometimes two and three hours, and playing at cards in the Pavilion at the end of the Bowling Green. Now that her pregnancy was so advanced, she had moved the card games into the Green Gallery, and occasionally supped in the Countess of Buckenburgh's chamber with the Duchess of Monmouth, Lady Townsend, the Duchess of Shrewsbury, Lady Cowper, and others of her ladies.

When the Hawkhurst coach arrived at the palace, it had to wait its turn in the line of coaches to deliver its occupants to the red brick Trophy Gate, built for King William III. There, Lord Hawkhurst and his party descended, smoothed their rumpled silks after the long ride, and joined the crowd of finely dressed courtiers as they passed under the gatehouse and through the Base Court with its red brick wings. Then they passed through another gatehouse, built for the short-lived Queen Anne Boleyn by Henry VIII. As they emerged on the other side, Hester paused and told Mary to look back at the famous Astronomical Clock. Mary had been to the palace twice before, but with Mrs. Mayfield escorting her, Hester doubted she had been shown any of its more interesting features.

They moved forward with the crowd and Hester continued. "The wing on the right was designed by Sir Christopher Wren for King William when he rebuilt the Queen's apartments for Queen Mary."

"I know," Mary said. "The Prince and Princess are fitting out the Queen's apartments for themselves. Her Highness told me about the changes she is planning last time I was here."

Hester was impressed. Doubtless Mary knew more about the Palace now than she did, since she had not set foot in it for many months. At first, Mrs. Mayfield had been content to accompany her daughter to Court herself. The fact that Princess Caroline—who seldom addressed more than a few words either to Hester's aunt or to Isabella, neither of whom could converse with any intelligence—had bothered to speak kindly to Mary meant that she had recognized the girl as having more sense than either her mother or her sister.

They were ushered up the Queen's Staircase with its whitewashed, panelled walls and into the Queen's Guard Chamber, where Yeomen of the Guard in their flat hats and royal red tunics with purple facings and stripes and their antiquated white ruffs looked over each person's clothing to see that they were dressed richly enough to be admitted to the royal presence. Like the Guard Chamber at St. James's, the colourless walls and weapons displayed here were designed to intimidate even the most brazen visitor. As the courtiers filed through the room, they unconsciously subdued their voices.

Hester found this ritual of passing the Guard unnerving, but Lord and Lady Hawkhurst were well-known to the guards. Their party was waved on with scarcely a glance.

The Queen's Drawing Room was near to overflowing, with no space for chairs other than those set out for the Prince and Princess before the marble fireplace. Above this hung the painting of Prince George, the Consort of Queen Anne, as Lord Admiral before the Fleet. No changes had been made to the Drawing Room, for its walls were still hung with the allegorical paintings by Antonio Verrio, extolling the might of British naval power. Mary told Hester, however, that the Queen's State Bedchamber beyond had been fitted with a new bed for the royal couple, and that Sir James Thornhill had been commissioned to paint the ceiling.

They had no sooner crossed into the Drawing Room than, spying friends, Isabella and Harrowby left them to their own devices. When she saw that no tables had been set up for cards, Mrs. Mayfield gave a petulant, "Humph! Well, I wonder what entertainments have been planned for us after such a long journey. I hope we shall not be expected to stand in this stuffy room all evening! But perhaps something has been set up in one of the galleries." On that more hopeful note, she left Hester and Mary to go in search of a footman.

"Let us find a spot near one of the windows." With Mary in agreement, Hester cut a path for them through the crowd of courtiers: the gentlemen in long curled periwigs, lace cravats, and knee-length satin coats over fitted breeches and stockings tied up with garters; the ladies in small laced and frilled caps, tight bodices, pleated petticoats, and embroidered silk mantuas. A number of black pages accompanied them with fans, each in his master's livery. A blended odour of snuff, pomades, and strong perfumes overwhelmed Hester's nostrils in the crush of bodies, but if they could secure a place near the windows they might get to see the fireworks that had surely been planned for the occasion.

"Should we not make our curtsies to their Highnesses first?" Mary asked from behind her.

"I doubt we could get near them. The competition for their attention will be high." Hester knew that all the politicians would be paying court to the Prince and to his mistress, Mrs. Howard, one of the Princess's ladies.

They managed to squeeze into a corner by one of the central windows looking out onto the gardens, where a great parterre and avenues of trees extended as far as the eye could see. With this view before her, Hester breathed more easily, despite the fact that the windows were closed. Cooler air seeped in around them, dispelling the sense of being in a suffocating trap.

"Ah, Mrs. Kean, I see you have found my favourite spot."

Hester did her best to greet Lady Cowper with a curtsy in the confined space. She presented Mary to the pretty baroness, whose husband had been appointed Lord High Steward to sit in judgement over the Jacobite traitors. Lady Cowper, with whom Hester had formed an affinity, had confided to her what an unpleasant duty it had been, full of stresses, and one that had greatly diminished Lord Cowper's health.

"How fares her Highness?" Hester asked. Lady Cowper had been one of the Princess's ladies of the bedchamber since her arrival in England.

"She seems well. I am not in waiting this se'nnight, but I shall be with my mistress next week when the Court removes to St. James's. It is planned that we shall go by water, as the safest way in her condition. We should have been gone by now, but her Highness has enjoyed the tranquillity of this place."

"I doubt we will be able to get near her this evening to make our curtsies."

Lady Cowper ruefully shook her head. "Nor I."

A gentleman jostled Hester's elbow as the room became fuller still. He inclined his head by way of an apology, then turned back to address his friends. When Hester returned her gaze to Lady Cowper, she noted her expression. "You seem worried, my lady. Is it the Princess's health?"

"No . . . though none of her ladies are happy with her determination to be delivered by a German midwife. We have urged her to be laid by Sir David Hamilton, but she will not hear of it." She said this in a distracted manner, as if something else were on her mind. "You did not come to Court this summer, Mrs. Kean."

Hester explained that she had spent the summer in Yorkshire with her cousins. She noticed that one of Mary's suitors had found her and was speaking to her. Mary was listening politely, but with no great enthusiasm, which was just as well since Hester doubted the young gentleman's intentions were serious. Harrowby was correct when he said that Mrs. Mayfield had set her sights too high for Mary's husband, since a dowry of a thousand pounds or even two or three would not be enough to land a peer.

Hester kept one eye on her charge while giving her attention to Lady Cowper.

"What happened this summer that concerns you?"

Lady Cowper hesitated. Then she lowered her voice so much that Hester could barely hear her over the din in the room. "I cannot be easy with the scheming going on at Court. The Duke of Marlborough's friends have been intriguing to get Lord Townsend and Mr. Walpole turned out. Lord Townsend may suspect, for he and his family have been here all summer, paying court to his Highness and to Mrs. Howard and Mrs. Ballandine, too. He was foolishly ignoring the Princess until my lord and a few others advised him that he did so at his peril, and now he thanks my husband by insinuating things about him to the Prince! It was only due to the good offices of their Highnesses that peace has been kept among the Whigs.

"I have a great fear that the schemers will split the party and stir the animosity between his Majesty and the Prince, which will not be good for the kingdom. The Jacobites will be elated if that occurs. It has often been suspected that the Duke of Marlborough has Jacobite sympathies."

"But can he be behind this? I heard that he had a stroke of the palsy so severe that he has lost most of his reason and is unable to speak."

"That is true, and at first his palsy was a great check to the schemers. But he has spent the summer at the Bath and the Duchess has great hopes of his recovery. Whether or not he recovers, the Duchess still controls the power of his money and influence. And she has never been shy about using them. Everyone knows how devoted Lord Sunderland is to her, and he has been at his Majesty's side in Hanover for the past two months. When he left in August, he said he was going only to persuade the King to return soon, but you see how that promise has been fulfilled."

As she listened, Hester made sympathetic noises, while keeping an eye on Mary. In truth, the petty squabbles and jockeyings for power that went on in corners did not interest her. It would be different, she supposed, if she, like Lady Cowper, depended on the King for her living, but as it was, none of the scheming was likely to affect her. Nor could she influence any of the King's decisions, so she was happy to be spared Lady Cowper's cares.

She had turned the conversation to ask after the health of Lord

Cowper when a familiar, imbecilic laugh alerted her to the approach of Lord Wragby. She hastily excused herself and drew nearer to Mary, just as the viscount's gaze lit upon her.

"Ah, there you are, my dear," he said, sidling up to take her hand and raise it to his lips. "I feared I would have to search for you for hours in such a tight assembly as this. The fates must have guided me to you." Mary tried to disengage her hand, but he made a game out of holding on to it, giggling as she struggled as politely as she could.

"Will your wife be joining us for the celebration, my lord?" Hester asked, in a much louder voice than she usually employed.

As she had hoped, her question startled him into releasing Mary's hand. He turned and snarled, "No, she shall not." Something amusing occurred to him, and he turned back to Mary. "After I came back from France, she wrote and asked if she should join me in town. I wrote back and told her the smallpox was here, so she should come and get it. Then with luck, I should be rid of her. What do you think of that, Mrs. Mary?" He made a quick movement as if to grab her hand again and giggled when Mary snatched her hands away to hide them behind her.

She was flushed and shaking with disgust when she answered, "I cannot believe you would say anything so cruel, my lord. No one could."

He drew back in surprise. "Truly? I thought you would be pleased. You might assume that it was meant as a compliment to you."

"Please, my lord. You must believe me. I have no desire to be complimented in that fashion, not if it means being cruel to your wife."

"My wife be damned!" He waved his hand as if a fly had pestered him. "Do not waste your pity on her when you should have pity for me for being leg-shackled to her. But I shall not be forever. You shall see."

Hester was reminded of the threat she had overheard in the gallery of St. Paul's. Could it have been Lord Wragby who uttered it about his wife? She could have sworn the threat had been to a man, but either her hearing or her memory could have been at fault.

Two gentlemen appeared at Lord Wragby's side and demanded his attention. He scowled at the interruption, but the men were friends of his father's he dared not ignore. Lord William Silsbee, a younger son of the Earl of Rutherford, and Sir Horatio Allenby were members of Parliament and influential Whigs. They flanked Lord Wragby and bowed frostily to Hester and Mary, not asking to be presented to them.

Hester wondered if Lord Ireton had sent them to keep his son from doing anything foolish, including encouraging the aspirations of a penniless girl. If so, she could only be grateful.

She would have used the diversion to draw Mary away as quickly as possible, but Lord Wragby would not let the new arrivals rob him of her company. He forestalled Hester by taking Mary by the elbow and drawing her into the gentlemen's conversation. Since this consisted of nothing more than platitudes on the day's celebration, Hester's suspicions about Lord Ireton were confirmed.

She was as shocked as the two gentlemen when the viscount sneered. "Why should we celebrate the ascension of a German usurper to our throne?"

Lord William leapt nearer and hissed, "Careful, Wragby! Recall where you are!"

Lord Wragby ignored him and turned to Mary. "What say you, my dear? Should we drink the Pretender's health and death to the Whigs?"

Terrified—for the words alone could get them arrested—Mary abruptly freed her arm.

Lord William and Sir Horatio squeezed closer to Lord Wragby. "Have you not heard?" Sir Horatio rasped in his ear. "The Pretender is dead."

News of the Pretender's movements often appeared in the newssheets. Recently, the reports had mentioned that he was ill.

Lord Wragby stared at Lord William open-mouthed, then gave a disgusted smirk. "You are a fool if you believe it, no matter what you read in the newssheets. That will be a rumour put about by his enemies. I should know, for I saw him myself scarcely a month ago."

"Hush, fool! Do you want to lose your head!"

Though Lord William's voice had not been above a whisper, his agitated manner and Lord Wragby's louder voice had started to draw attention. Heads were turning and eyebrows were raised. Lord Ireton's friends stepped close to the viscount as if to silence him.

Hester took advantage of the situation to draw Mary aside. "We should pay our duty to her Highness, Mary. If you will pardon us, my lords . . ." Bobbing a curtsy to the gentlemen, none of whom noticed, she pulled Mary behind her to cut through the assembly, hoping that Lord Wragby's minders would keep him from following.

The crowd parted and closed just as quickly behind them. Hester did not begin to relax until they had put a good number of courtiers between them and the viscount. Then, they inched slowly towards the edge of the room where the Princess should be seated.

"Hester!" Mary's whisper was full of distress. "How will we manage to hide from Lord Wragby all evening?"

"I do not know, but if needs must, we shall attach ourselves to Cousin Harrowby or to someone else whose presence might be more discouraging than mine."

For the moment, at least, the danger was past. Lord Wragby would have to begin his search for Mary again, assuming his ardour was as strong as he pretended.

As they drew nearer to the Princess's chair, Hester caught a heavily accented voice, raised in a barking laugh. "But that is excellent! The English are so clever. We have nothing so fine in Hanover."

In that instant a parting in the crowd revealed the Prince of Wales, surrounded by a group of Whig gentlemen, laughing at all the appropriate moments. He knew how to please them better than his father did, extolling the virtues of the English over the Germans, when his father had so little time for his new subjects.

Well, it would be no bad thing if the next King of Great Britain admired its people. Still, in the Prince's tone, Hester thought she detected a note of flattery. Was he merely ingratiating himself to the Court at his father's expense?

The passing notion might not have occurred if Hester had not just been privy to Lady Cowper's worries; but she dismissed it as unimportant as she led Mary towards the fireplace in front of which the Princess's chair had been placed.

They arrived to learn that her Highness had retired to her closet. The closeness of the room must have been very trying to a lady in her condition.

"What shall we do now?" Mary asked.

Hester sighed. "If I did not fear that Lord Wragby would find us, I would suggest walking in the gardens, but if he were to discover us there, we could easily be trapped. I suppose we should keep moving until we find someone to act as a shield."

Mary nodded. The poor girl was looking nervously over her shoulder, as if fearing Lord Wragby might pop out of the crowd to surprise her.

Hester had never known her cousin to be afraid of anything. Mary would eagerly lead a horse over any hedge or ditch it could jump, and she stood up to her bully of a brother without so much as a blink. But this situation with Lord Wragby was delicate. Mary had no one but Harrowby to protect her from the unwelcome and improper advances of a gentleman of Lord Wragby's rank; and Harrowby was unlikely to bother if he thought that by speaking firmly to Lord Wragby, he might offend Lord Ireton. Hester cursed her aunt for placing the girl in this insufferable position. She resolved to beg Harrowby to take charge of what might end in a scandal for the family, if not a tragedy for Mary.

She wished she could dismiss the idea that Mrs. Mayfield would be willing to see her daughter become the mistress of a future marquess, but Mrs. Mayfield's ambition often overcame her sense of propriety. Hester had no doubt that if the King or Prince wished to make any child of hers his mistress, Mrs. Mayfield would be only too happy to profit from the honours such a connection could bestow. But the heir to a wealthy marquess? How high would the gentleman's rank have to be to tempt her?

Despite what Lord Wragby had said about his wife, it would not be easy to put his wife aside. If he did somehow manage it, Hester dreaded the pressure her aunt would bring to bear. As fickle as his lordship seemed to be, she could only hope that his fancy would light upon some other lady before a second marriage became possible.

For the rest of the celebration, until its conclusion with fireworks, Mary and Hester remained alert to avoid the viscount. The safety of the card tables was denied them, for neither had enough money to play for the high stakes the Germans had introduced at Court. A musical performance helped to pass one hour, and talking to acquaintances provided respites, but neither Hester nor Mary could be at ease until they were seated in the Hawkhurst coach and on their way home.

On 28th October, the Court moved back to St. James's, the Princess and her ladies conveyed by barge on a beautiful autumn day. Two evenings later, the Court gave a ball to celebrate the birthday of the Prince of Wales. Isabella, Harrowby, and Mrs. Mayfield attended, but Mary excused herself with a headache.

Her mother was incensed, asserting that she would never get a husband if she gave in to such a trifling complaint. Hester knew that Mary had fabricated the excuse. There was no mystery why. Lord Wragby could be expected to attend the ball, and his behaviour on Coronation Day had been enough to terrify the girl. Mary waited until her mother was gone before emerging from her chamber, her headache miraculously cured. She found Hester in the small parlour where she proposed spending the evening at cards.

They were taking tea when James Henry came into the house and found them.

He was surprised to find Mary at home and so deeply concerned about her headache that Mary finally had to admit her lie. A moment more and she had confessed her reason for avoiding the celebration at Court.

He listened with tightly compressed lips and a twitching jaw. When Mary repeated in a whisper the treasonous words Lord Wragby had uttered, James Henry did not try to conceal his fury.

"The man must be mad!"

Hester said, "I do not know if he is mad or simply foolish and rebellious. He behaves like a spoiled child whose will has been thwarted for the first time. I do not doubt he proclaims allegiance to the Pretender merely to annoy his father."

"That does not give him the right to endanger Mrs. Mary with his stupidity. You must see that he does not impose on her again, Mrs. Kean."

His tone was so accusing that Hester gaped, while Mary rushed to her defence. James Henry was obliged to beg her forgiveness, though she could see that he was far from satisfied. His agitation was so great, he started to pace.

In the end, she could do nothing but laugh. "We tried our best to stay away from him, but I assure you, sir, that it was no easy task. Mary and I were grateful for any protection we could find."

His troubled look only increased. Hester detected a feeling of impotence in the fists balled at his side. There was nothing James Henry could do to interfere with a gentleman of Lord Wragby's standing.

"I shall speak to my lord," he said. "If nothing else, Lord Wragby's treasonous remarks should make him wary of any closer association."

Hester sighed. "And I shall speak again to my aunt. I suppose I should have done so immediately after the celebration, but truth be told, I was so exhausted by the end of the evening, I had no energy left for a disagreement.

"But do let us change the subject. I have had quite enough of Lord Wragby for now." She invited James Henry to join their card game and the three spent a most pleasant evening. Hester believed she had never seen him so happy as he was in Mary's company.

Exactly one week after the Princess came back to town, she fell into labour. Word came to Hawkhurst House the next day that the Council had sat up at the palace all night, but there was still no sign of a delivery.

On the third day, when there was still no announcement, Mrs. Mayfield urged Isabella to go to the palace to demonstrate her concern for the Princess. Her nagging drove Isabella into a fit of hysterics.

"If you think someone should go, then you go yourself and take Hester with you! You know what a horror I have of such things! Hester will know what to say if you don't."

Suppressing her frustration, Mrs. Mayfield said that she would make her daughter's apologies. "I shall say that you are so unwell that you fear to add to the Court's concerns. But you had better remain within doors in case anyone should see you. I won't have you make me out to be a liar!

"Mary," she said, "stay with your sister and do your best to entertain her. Hester, I expect you to be ready to go with me in not a second longer than ten minutes."

Knowing how unreasonable her aunt could be, Hester fetched her cloak and gloves and was ready at the front door a full fifteen minutes before her aunt. Mrs. Mayfield insisted upon taking a chair the short distance from Piccadilly to the palace gate. Hester walked beside her, forced to hurry to keep up with the chairmen's pace.

If they had not gained admittance, they would have left a message for one of the Princess's ladies, but arriving just as Mrs. Howard stepped down from her chair, at her invitation they accompanied her inside. They followed her to the Princess's apartments, where a large gathering stood just outside the Princess's bedchamber, with everything in an uproar.

Members of the Council, their faces haggard, were arguing with Count Bothmar and the other Germans over their refusal to overrule the midwife and allow Dr. Hamilton to attend the Princess. The doctor stood to one side, nearly as frazzled as the Council gentlemen. He had been in attendance on the Princess at Hampton Court since early in October and now had to suffer the indignity of being excluded from her delivery.

The German midwife was standing in the doorway with her arms folded, an injured expression plastered to her face. Deeply offended, she was refusing to return to her mistress.

When Hester and Mrs. Mayfield asked for news of the Princess's condition, one of her ladies whispered that she had suffered from a violent shivering fit. Neither the midwife nor the Germans, including the Princess, seemed as frightened by this development as the English. The Council had begged the Countess of Buckenburgh to use her influence with the Prince to beseech him to call the doctor in.

The Prince arrived and listened to the midwife's complaint. She claimed that the English "fraus" were high dames who had threatened to hang her if the Princess miscarried. While her words were quickly translated and spread throughout the crowd, the Prince worked himself up into such a passion that his face turned red. He rounded on the Princess's ladies and shouted—just as the Duchesses of St. Albans and Bolton entered the room—that he would fling from the window anyone of them who pretended to meddle.

Instantly, the tone of the gathering changed, with everyone assuring the Prince of his wife's good labour and safety. Lord Townsend
went so far as to take the midwife by the hand and with ingratiating
smiles, try to convey his goodwill, for the woman understood no word
of English. With encouragement of this kind and the Prince's assurances, she was eventually persuaded to return to the Princess.

As soon as they could do so without drawing attention, Hester and
her aunt made their exits. Both subdued by the scene they had just
witnessed, they returned to Hawkhurst House to find another taking
place upstairs in the withdrawing room.

The moment they entered the front door, the sound of loud voices
reached them. A group of footmen were standing at the bottom of
the grand staircase, evidently paralyzed by indecision. As soon as Mrs.
Mayfield demanded to know what they were doing, they scattered.
The only one to stand his ground was Will, who had opened the door
to them, but it was clear from his pallor that he was as shaken as the
rest.

He quickly addressed himself to Hester, knowing she would not
blame him for something that was not his fault. "It's Mr. Henry and
Lord Wragby, Mrs. Kean. We didn't think we should do nothing to
interfere. My lord is away, and my lady is entertaining gentlemen at
her toilette."

With dread, Hester picked up her skirts to hurry up the stairs, with
her aunt emitting sounds of outrage close behind her. Mrs. Mayfield's
words did not have to reach her clearly for Hester to know whose side
of the argument she had already taken.

They found Mary standing between the two men, apparently trying to soothe Lord Wragby's wounded feelings while preventing any
violence between them. An angry James Henry, fists curled at his side,
was saying, "I shall be happy to meet you at any place you choose, my
lord, on any terms you choose to make."

Hester's gasp was echoed by Mary's, as straightening his rumpled
cravat, Lord Wragby sneered, "You dare to challenge me? A servant? I
will never condescend to meet you. I shall send my footmen to whip
you, instead."

"And a whipping you deserve!" Mrs. Mayfield pronounced, tossing James Henry a disdainful look. "How dare you insult a guest in your master's house? I shall know what to say to my lord, I assure you." She turned to Lord Wragby then, assuring him that she understood his position, and ignoring Mary, who immediately spoke up in James Henry's defence.

"You do not know what occurred here, Mama! You must not blame Mr. Henry. He was defending my honour."

"Your honour, mistress?" Lord Wragby's umbrage, though genuine, would have struck Hester as comical if the potential consequences were not so dire. "I have done nothing but honour you with my attentions!"

"Forgive me, my lord." Restraining herself, Mary wisely tried to make peace. "I hope you can see that your . . . handling of me must have led Mr. Henry to the wrong conclusion. It was very improper of me to receive you without my sister present."

"Indeed, it was!" her mother said, "and if my daughter's foolishness is in any way responsible, I beg you will forgive her, my lord."

Hester could hear James Henry seething beside her. She had taken a position at his side to aid Mary in keeping the two men apart. She could not blame him for being angry at her aunt's speech, which in the lack of affection it showed for her daughter had made Hester cringe. But like Mary, James Henry had realized that it would be better to appease Lord Wragby to a certain extent.

He maintained silence while Hester said, "This must have been some unfortunate misunderstanding. I suggest we retire and wait for cooler tempers to restore clearer thinking."

Lord Wragby was not mollified, but even he knew better than to prolong a fight in an earl's house. As he wavered, Hester noticed that both Will and John had followed her and her aunt into the room. Gratefully she turned to them and asked them to assist Lord Wragby to his horse.

She was relieved when the viscount did not persist, but allowed himself to be escorted to the door, a footman on either side. If he had stood his ground, she did not know if she would have had the nerve to have him seized and forcibly ejected. Besides which, her aunt would have been certain to countermand any such order.

He could not leave, however, without having the final word. He turned on the threshold and bowed to Mary. "I shall forgive you on this one occasion, my dear, but I trust you will not try my patience again."

Leaving them with a sense of foreboding, he turned and sauntered from the room.

Mrs. Mayfield rounded angrily on Mary and James Henry then, demanding to know what they were about to offend Lord Wragby.

"I found him in here, making rude and unwelcome advances to Mrs. Mary," James Henry said, clearly in the belief that even Mrs. Mayfield would bridle at the insult to her daughter.

"Fiddlesticks! I am certain he was doing no such thing! And who are you to decide what is unwelcome to Mary? You take an unhealthy interest in my daughter's affairs. I forbid you to speak to her again."

At this, James Henry paled. Then his cheeks burned red with a mixture of embarrassment and rage, before with a last glance at Mary, he turned and strode from the room. Hester assumed there was nothing else he could do to stop himself from giving her aunt the tongue-lashing she deserved. They could hear his heavy footfalls as he tore down the stairs.

Mary was no less stunned. Her mouth fell open and her eyes filled with tears. Then, with purpose and a great deal of dignity, she picked up her skirts and departed the room, heading in the direction of her bedchamber.

With no one left to lecture, Mrs. Mayfield rounded on Hester. "I blame you, Hester, for putting such squeamish notions into her head. I am certain Lord Wragby did nothing that any other gentleman wouldn't do if he found himself alone with a pretty girl."

"Then God help all pretty girls," Hester retorted, "if their mothers will not. Mary and I have both tried to warn you that Lord Wragby was not to be trusted."

"It is my business, not yours, who Mary should trust! But if she has gone too far this time, she has only herself to blame. Gentlemen will be gentlemen, and they are not to be called to account for every little thing. And I meant what I said about Mr. Henry. I do not like the interest he takes with Mary, and I shall have a word with Hawkhurst the moment he comes home."

"If you do, Aunt, please recall the number of times he has told you not to encourage Lord Wragby. I shall have my own version of these events with which to regale him."

Hester had the grim, but futile satisfaction of seeing a wary look spring into her aunt's eyes. Taking advantage of her silence, Hester left the room before their argument could recommence.

Not Fortune's worshipper, nor Fashion's fool,
Nor Lucre's madman, nor Ambition's tool,
Not proud, nor servile; Be one Poet's praise,
That, if he pleased, he pleased by manly ways . . . .

CHAPTER IV

As Hester went in search of Mary, she mused upon a new suspicion that James Henry had fallen in love with her cousin. The thought of the pain such an attachment could bring made her heart sink.

Mrs. Mayfield would never countenance such an inferior connection. She regarded James Henry as no more than a servant to her daughter Isabella, a man neither rich nor powerful enough to wed the sister of a countess. He owned a parcel of land with a house, given to him by his father, the former Lord Hawkhurst, but it was of too modest a size to elevate him into the gentry. His gentlemanly manners meant nothing to a person with Mrs. Mayfield's ambitions. Neither would the fact that Mary's brother was too impoverished to provide a dowry for his sister make her accept that marriage to a man of James Henry's condition might be as good as Mary should expect. Unaware that his father was the former Lord Hawkhurst, she believed he lacked the pedigree of a Mayfield, but, in truth, he was more prosperous than her family was now. If Isabella had not married Harrowby, her mother would have had no grounds for opposing the match.

Hester realized she had allowed her thoughts to leap too far ahead, anticipating trouble when she did not even know if Mary returned his affection. Certainly, she trusted and relied upon him. She was happy in his company. But James Henry was nearly twice Mary's age. She might regard him as the most admirable man she had ever known, but whether that respect would lead to the love a woman should feel for a husband, Hester had no idea.

For the moment, she needed to focus on the problems before her: how to protect Mary from Lord Wragby and how to keep Mrs. Mayfield from getting James Henry dismissed.

Hester found Mary standing in the middle of her bedchamber, staring at the foot of the bed as if she had forgotten her reason for being there.

Hester asked if she was well enough to tell her what had happened.

With a little shake of her head, Mary turned and gave an ironic laugh. "Thank you, Hester, for asking what my mother refused to hear." When her eyes filled, and Hester moved impulsively towards her, she angrily wiped the tears away, shaking her head more forcefully. "No, I am well enough, I assure you. He did not get the chance to harm me, but if Mr. Henry had not appeared when he did . . . ."

She shuddered involuntarily, alerting Hester that she had not, in truth, recovered from the incident. "I insist you get in bed, and I shall have some tea sent up." She helped Mary remove her gown, then leaving her to climb beneath the covers, she left to go in search of a footman. After giving him instructions to bring up a pot of tea, plenty of sugar, and a tray with two cups, she returned to Mary's side.

She waited until the tea was fetched and poured, the servant had departed, and they both had taken a few sips, to ask the girl, "How did you come to be alone with Lord Wragby? I know you would never have received him on purpose."

"No, of course not, but the footman showed him into the withdrawing room, and then missed me when he went to search for me. I cannot blame him for admitting Lord Wragby to the house when my mother has always welcomed his visits. I was in the parlour at the rear of the house when I heard a man's voice. I thought it was Mr. Henry, you see, for he had mentioned stopping by this morning, so I blundered into the room without checking first." The hand holding her teacup trembled slightly as she raised it to her mouth.

"Then, what?"

Mary shook her head as if to dismiss the incident. "You have seen him with me, Hester—how foolish and annoying he can be. This morning was no different, except that my arrival without a chaperone gave him the idea that I meant to encourage him. I tried to excuse myself on the grounds of propriety, but he would not allow it. He blocked me from leaving, giggling in that idiotic way of his, as if we were playing a game of fox and geese. He ignored every plea to be serious and to leave me alone.

"Once, when I nearly got past him, he grabbed me about the waist and refused to release me, no matter how violently I struggled. I must have kicked him in the shins quite hard a time or two, but he only laughed as if it were the greatest fun. He had started pawing at me and . . . and snatching at my skirts—I was about to scream—when Mr. Henry walked in and saw us.

"He did not hesitate for a moment, Hester." Mary turned to her with a wondering gaze. "He did not think of the risk to himself. He took hold of Lord Wragby by the scruff of his neck and threw him down to the floor." Mary smiled tenderly at the memory.

"Lord Wragby was so shocked, it was a moment before he gathered his wits to speak. He got up, cursing and spluttering threats, but Mr. Henry stood up to him as if he were of no more account than a dog. I do think Lord Wragby may be mad, Hester! What kind of person giggles like that, or behaves with so little regard for society?"

Encouraged by the outrage in Mary's voice, signalling a return of her spirits, Hester answered, "For all I know, he may be mad. Unfortunately, it is unlikely that he will ever be locked up, which means that we shall have to take our own measures to stay out of his way." His final words to Mary had suggested that he meant to pursue her still.

"The first thing I shall do is speak to Harrowby," Hester told her cousin. "If anyone can stop your mother from encouraging Lord Wragby, it will be him. I promise I shall not let her force you into Lord Wragby's company again."

She hesitated a moment before adding, "Whatever we do, we cannot allow James Henry to quarrel with Lord Wragby again. If he were to forget himself sufficiently to come to blows with the son of Lord Ireton, he would be utterly ruined. Lord Ireton is not the sort of man to tolerate an insult to his son, no matter how deserved it might be. He is too arrogant and vigilant of his position. He might even send his own footmen to punish James Henry if Harrowby refuses to dismiss him."

Mary sat up abruptly, worry on her face. "I will not permit Mr. Henry to suffer on my account. Whatever can we do, Hester?"

"Keep you away from Lord Wragby, even if it means staying away from Court until we go to Rotherham Abbey for Christmas. And I shall do my best to gain Harrowby's support, which may not be as difficult as you think. He is not so fond of your mother, you know, as to wish to please her."

This drew a slight smile from Mary, who must have noticed how much her mother annoyed him. Still, anxiety clouded her brow. "I can feign illness until Christmas if I have to, if that is the only way to keep Mr. Henry safe."

"Will you not miss the entertainments at Court?"

"In truth, I shall miss Mr. Henry more," Mary said in a forlorn tone. "Do you think my mother was serious, Hester? Will I not be allowed to go out with his escort now?"

The innocence in her tone persuaded Hester that Mary had no notion of being in love with James Henry yet, but the fact that she preferred his company to anyone else's might one day lead her to that conclusion. Her mother's opposition would only fuel Mary's affection. Perhaps it would be better if they were not to spend so much time in each other's company.

She begged Mary not to worry until she had spoken to Harrowby about the incident. Then, promising to look in on her later, she left her to her thoughts and went to discover if Harrowby's valet knew when his master might be expected home.

Her mission proved futile, for the valet was nowhere to be found. Asking a footman about his whereabouts turned up the information that, with no entertainment currently being offered at Court, Harrowby had left town to join friends at a card party, taking his valet with him. Hester did not know whether to be relieved that Mrs. Mayfield would be prevented from taking her grievances to him or to bemoan the opportunity of influencing him herself.

What Hester had not said to her cousin was that she was still afraid Lord Wragby might do precisely what he had threatened to do. The viscount was a man who tolerated no restraints, neither the bounds of decency nor the judgement of society. He had clearly been spoiled and was too accustomed to getting his own way, but added to that was a wilful, unpredictable streak. Perhaps he was mad, as Mary had suggested. In any case, Hester had no way of guessing how deeply he would nurse a grudge or how vengeful he might be. Recalling what he had said about his wife sent a shiver down her spine when she considered the cruelty of his thoughts, if not proof of his deeds. Had he merely been boasting, or was he truly capable of turning his most vicious thoughts into actions?

Again, she remembered the voice in the gallery of St. Paul's, the whisper with its murderous intent, wondering if Lord Wragby had uttered the words. Had they been only words or a serious threat, and if so, against whom? Was Lord Wragby capable of murder, if not at his own hands, then at the hands of his minions?

If only she could talk these things over with St. Mars, Hester knew she would feel better, but without his reassuring strength, she could not find the perspective with which to ease her mind. Oh, how she wished St. Mars were here! He would know what she ought to do, and, even though James Henry might believe him to be a murderer, St. Mars would do something to prevent his brother from being attacked.

The next day, word reached Hawkhurst House that the Princess of Wales was still languishing in bed, still undelivered of her child. With nothing to be done, and no amusements at Court, three of Isabella's current flirts came to watch her put the finishing touches to her toilette, offering her the benefit of their taste. Mrs. Mayfield, whose hair was getting noticeably thin, was awaiting a visit from her wigmaker.

Hester used the chance to gain her aunt's permission to take Mary to visit her brother Jeremy in the City. He had married the widow of a notorious bookseller, and the two operated a bookstall up against the

Church of St. Dunstan-in-the-West.

Such a connection was beneath Mrs. Mayfield's notice. She had always considered her nephew Jeremy to be a wastrel. She could not prevent Hester from occasionally visiting her own brother but until now, she had been unwilling to allow Mary to accompany her. Today, whether she was too vain for even her daughter to witness the session with the wigmaker, or she hoped that seeing how poorly Jeremy lived would shock Mary into compliance with her wishes, she finally gave her permission. It was accompanied by a warning that, if Mary did not do what was good for her, she might find herself selling books in Fleet Street, too.

Mary blushed for her mother's rudeness, but accustomed to Mrs. Mayfield's aspersions on her brother, Hester ignored them, glad only for permission to leave the house. She feared another visit from Lord Wragby, who was too conceited to be discouraged by yesterday's incident.

With two running footmen for escort, she and Mary secured the services of a hackney coachman to convey them to St. Dunstan's, in the shadow of which they found Jeremy and his wife Sally behind the counter of their bookstall, displaying folios to a few customers. Sally's beauty had attracted many hangers-on, but Hester could see that her sister-in-law had eyes for no one but her husband. They both looked happy as they greeted Hester and expressed pleasure in meeting Mary. Though several years her senior, Jeremy recalled seeing his cousin in the nursery once on a visit to his Uncle Mayfield's house.

They chatted briefly about Mary's sojourn in London. Jeremy urged her to go see the lions in the Tower. "I hear they are in the best of health, now that the Pretender has been defeated. You know, it is believed here in London that the lions are the best judges of who should properly wear the British crown."

Sally asked Hester about the summer she had spent in Yorkshire, and Hester gave her a brief account. She did not mention the murders that had been committed, or that she had received a proposal of marriage. Some things were better relayed in private, and as they were continuously interrupted by customers, now was not the time.

Hester did not wish to interfere with their commerce, so after a few futile attempts at conversation, she asked to be shown the newest items on their bookracks. The first that Jeremy brought forth raised her eyebrows:

Love's Perpetual Almanack, according to the Astronomical Observations of Cupid, calculated for the Meridian of the Heart, With Remarks on the several Months of the Year; Instructions how to manage Love's Orchard and Gardens; and how to make Love's Compass-Dial, shewing the Hour of Night and Day in a Receipt to make Love's Water of Health, and other valuable Curiosities. By Amorous Gay, Regious Professor in Love's Mathematicks. With a Key to the Whole.

Reading over Hester's shoulder, Mary smothered a laugh.

The second thing Jeremy brought them was no more impressive:

Court Poems. Containing, 1. *The Dream, or, Melesinda's Lamentation on the Burning of her Smock.* 2. *The Hyde-Park Ramble,* with some other Pieces. Written by a Lady of Quality. To which are added, *The Worms, a Satire.* Also, *A Version of the first Psalm, for the Use of a Young Lady.*

The Psalm notwithstanding, Hester was forced to doubt the quality of Jeremy's merchandise. When she gave him a speaking look, he leaned across the counter to whisper, "I know what you would say, Hester. Our father would be horrified to find that we are not publishing books of sermons, but it is these sorts of books that people want. And sermons can be risky these days. We daren't publish anything with even a hint of political or religious bias, for fear of being taken up by the Messengers, like Mr. Howell."

The nonjuring clergyman had been committed to Newgate for his involvement in printing a pamphlet entitled, *The Present State of the Schism in the Church of England, truly stated.*

"Believe me," Hester said with feeling, "I have no desire to see you in Newgate again. What else do you have?"

Jeremy reverently produced the first volume of Mr. Pope's translation of the *Iliad,* which he said had been a great success. Even unbound, though, Hester could not afford to purchase a copy, so he showed her a much lighter work by Mr. Gay, in three volumes, entitled *Trivia: or the Art of Walking the Streets of London.* On reading its first few verses, Hester decided it was just what was needed as a distraction for Mary.

She bought the first volume, promising to return for the others as soon as her purse would stretch to buy them.

She and Mary took their leave, then, with regret on both sides, Sally calling after them to come for dinner on a Sunday afternoon when they would have time for a better visit.

Having no wish to return to Hawkhurst House, instead of looking immediately for a hackney to drive them home, they walked east along Fleet Street to see what other shops might tempt them. Finding little but more bookstalls and Mr. Weekly's tobacconist shop, where the only product of interest was the Jerusalem Eye-Water for rheumatick eyes, they turned back to walk to Tom's Coffee House to carry out a special errand for Mrs. Dixon, the housekeeper. Hester sent one of the footmen ahead to purchase some tea. Tea had become so fashionable, that the owner, Mr. Twinings, was selling more dry tea than hot coffee, but it would not be proper for a lady to set foot inside a coffee-house.

Following more slowly, she and Mary were nearly to St. Dunstan's again when Hester spied a familiar figure rounding the old church, which jutted out into the street. She quickly seized Mary's arm and pulled her into the alley leading to Crane Court.

Before Mary could ask her why, Hester whispered, "I just saw Lord Wragby, heading in our direction. I do not think he saw us." Cautioning Mary to hang back, Hester crept to the corner for a peek.

There was no sign of the viscount. Hester peered carefully in all directions, but could not spot him again. She did not think he would have had time to get past the alley in which they were hiding, which suggested that he had turned into one of the streets between them, leaving her with the question of what to do next.

The worst thing that could happen would be for him to emerge from a side street just as they were attempting to sneak past. With no more protection than a footman, Hester did not want to expose Mary to another unpleasant encounter. Believing Lord Wragby capable of a serious affront to her cousin, Hester turned back and instructed Mary to wait out of sight with the footman, while she walked ahead to see where the viscount had gone.

Lord Wragby was so oblivious to anyone beneath his station, she doubted he would recognize her as Mary's cousin. Even if he did, she could claim to have come into the City alone. She could return for Mary after he had left.

Making her way again towards St. Dunstan's and peering warily into the shops she passed, she wondered what could have brought the viscount into the City alone. He was usually surrounded by friends or escorted by a host of footmen and pages—unless, of course, his plan called for privacy, as when he had made himself so obnoxious to Mary. In the glimpse she had caught, he had appeared unaccompanied by either friend or servant.

Hester arrived at the entrance to Fetter Lane and paused. It seemed most likely that Lord Wragby had disappeared up this thoroughfare to Holborn, but she could not see beyond the bend in the lane. Taking another look across the street and again over her shoulder without finding him, she turned into Fetter Lane and made her way north.

Fetter Lane was lined with wooden houses of three and four stories, crammed tightly together, each no more than one or two small rooms wide. The upper region of this street had survived the Great Fire. The lower had been hastily rebuilt with shoddy houses, the owners of the property unwilling to wait to comply with the new regulations calling for brick construction. The street had an interesting reputation, its inhabitants ranging from coal sellers and tavern-keepers to poets, lawyers, philosophers, and men of the cloth. Among the last were some leaders of dissenting sects. But the street had a more ancient reputation as the haunt of thieves and vagrants.

Hester saw nothing to warrant this aspersion, certainly no more vagrants than other streets boasted, and only one orange seller who had lured some apprentices into a game of chance. She had heard whispers, though, that the Jacobites had found a sympathetic ear in this quarter. Given Lord Wragby's apparent taste in friends, she wondered if he might be visiting one of them.

As she rounded the bend in the lane, she spotted him, emerging from one of the ancient houses on the right. She halted in mid-step; but she need not have worried, for instead of turning back the way he had come, he continued north towards Holborn. With the risk of running into him in Fleet Street past, it would have been reasonable for Hester to turn back. But something in his manner—he had looked oddly excited, as if embarked upon an adventure—had raised her curiosity. Too, it was odd that whatever his errand was, it had not taken longer, when if it had concerned just the delivery or retrieval of a message, he might have dispatched a servant.

Walking more slowly than before, so as not to risk overtaking him, Hester soon reached the door from which he had emerged and paused. The house was four stories high with a steeply pitched roof and green shutters. Bay windows jutted from its first and second floors. It was the kind of dwelling that a modestly successful, if not very prosperous, merchant might occupy. Indeed, the sign of a ship swayed on a rusting iron bar above the door. There was nothing remarkable about the house at all except that the heir to a marquisate had stopped there for a few moments.

Mary was waiting, however, and with nowhere to sit out of the cold. Hester went back to fetch her cousin, relegating her curiosity to the corner of her brain where unanswered questions were stored.

On Friday, after nearly a week of labour, the Princess of Wales gave birth to a dead prince, and a pall fell over the Court. No mourning was declared, for the death of a child was too commonplace. Still, the pain of losing their own child was too fresh for Isabella and Harrowby not to be affected by the Princess's loss. As were their customs, Isabella reacted by seeking amusement wherever she could find it, while Harrowby sat morosely at home and drank more deeply than had been his wont. In a rare demonstration of tact, Mrs. Mayfield refrained from filing her complaint against James Henry while their lord was in this humour.

With the King still in Hanover, Parliament was again prorogued, until 8th January, freeing its members to retreat to their country seats, where the gentlemen could enjoy stalking and shooting.

Since Harrowby was not as keen on sport as most aristocrats, and Isabella had no liking for country life, they lingered awhile longer in London. Both Hester and Mary would have preferred to escape to Rotherham Abbey, where Mary would be safe. Isabella and Harrowby could go to St. James's Park to see the Prince of Wales review the first Regiment of Foot Guards, but Mary did not dare go where she might encounter Lord Wragby.

She and Hester stayed quietly at home with their sewing and reading. This was hard for Mary, who was accustomed to a daily ride, and who, by nature, was more active than her cousin. She fretted at the inactivity, even more so when her boredom was not alleviated by the company of James Henry. They had not seen him since his confrontation with Lord Wragby in the withdrawing room. Mary had asked one of the footmen if Mr. Henry had left town and learned that although he had been gone for a few days, he had returned. She had not seen him because he had restricted his visits to the wing of the house where the business of the estate was conducted.

The *Evening Post* and the *Daily Courant* became Hester's sources of information, but there was little new. The Empire was still battling to drive the Turks from Belgrade. The Regent of France was still negotiating a peace with Great Britain, while defending himself from the faction that had sprung up around Louis XIV's bastards. Criminals condemned at the Old Bailey were being hanged, while the Jacobite rebels were either being discharged to the custody of a Messenger or having their punishments delayed, awaiting his Majesty's pleasure. Every so often, one managed to escape.

The only news that changed from day to day, it seemed, were the reports on the Duke of Marlborough's health. One day, he was dangerously ill, suffering from fainting fits, his daughters at his bedside, the next he had recovered enough to be expected in London at any moment.

In the fourth week of November, Isabella, Harrowby and Mrs. Mayfield rode out to Hyde Park to see the Prince review four troops of Horse Guards and two of Horse Grenadiers. It promised to be a splendid spectacle. As soon as they had gone, Mary, who was sitting with Hester in the small parlour at the back of the house working on a piece of embroidery, moaned over her imprisonment.

"Oh, when will we finally leave town? I have not sat on a horse for nearly two weeks!"

"How can you be bored with all the news I have related to you?" Hester said. "Why here is an item that should keep you enthralled for several minutes." In a dramatic voice, she read, "'The Duchess Dowager of Newcastle is reconcil'd to her Daughter the Lady Harley.'

"See." Hester set down the *Evening Post* to resume her sewing. "I could keep you entertained this way for hours."

Mary laughed and groaned at the same time. "I am serious, Hester. I do not know if I can tolerate much more of this confinement."

"It is not my favourite situation either, but another week or so and Harrowby will have no more excuses for putting off our journey. Isabella has invited a few guests to come down, and we must be there in time to receive them."

"Humph! Just her admirers. The rest of us will get to watch them fawning over her, the way they do here."

"I assure you, if Isabella is entertained, the whole household will be happier. As long as I am not made to play cards with them, I shall be content enough." Hester stifled a sigh. She knew that her words were not true.

It had taken all her fortitude to appear cheerful and engaged in her cousin's business. As long as Mary had been diverted by the sights of London, it had been easier, but now that she was often morose, Hester found it harder to conceal her own unhappiness. It had been nearly three months since she had seen St. Mars, and she had not had a single word from him. Even though it would be dangerous for him to write, he might have sent a message by Tom or Katy, if he had wanted to.

She had to suppose that he was either in France or that he had no desire to see her again. Knowing him and how impulsive he could be, she believed that he had crossed the Channel without her. Now, with winter on its way, the chances of his returning, risking a crossing at that season, were very remote, meaning that she should reconcile herself to no possibility of seeing him before spring, if then. Doubt and guilt depressed her spirits nearly as much as when she had believed he did not love her.

"Will Mr. Henry spend Christmas at Rotherham Abbey?" Mary's wistful voice interrupted her thoughts.

"He always has, so it would appear very strange if he did not. I suspect we shall see him there."

"But my mother will prevent it."

Hester shook her head and replied with all the patience she could muster, "She will not be able to prevent him from meeting with his lord or from being part of any household celebration. Besides, she seems to have refrained from taking her complaints to Harrowby. She must have realized how essential James Henry is to the running of the estate. Given a choice between him and your mother, Harrowby would likely choose the person who maintains the evenness of his life."

She was glad to see Mary's brow clear. They could not both be pining for things that could not be. Hester could only keep her misery in check if the people around her quelled theirs.

She was about to suggest a walk in the garden when Will the footman entered the parlour. Bowing to them both, he threw a nervous glance Mary's way, as if to warn Hester of something. "Mrs. Dixon would like a word with you, Mrs. Kean."

"Of course." Hester set down her sewing and stood to follow him.

"Shall I come with you?" Mary asked, as if she felt she should.

"No, thank you. It's likely to be something trivial. I shall be back presently."

As soon as she and Will had passed through the withdrawing room, leaving sufficient distance behind them, Hester asked, "What is it, Will?"

Will gave a worried glance over his shoulder. "You will see soon enough, mistress. Mr. Henry told me not to let on to Mrs. Mary that he asked for you."

"Mr. Henry!" Concern raised Hester's voice. It might be simply that he wished to have a word with her without disobeying Mrs. Mayfield's interdict, but Will's manner suggested that something more serious had occurred.

"Yes, he was brought here in a carriage by the gentleman who found him. He's in a right old state."

In dread, Hester followed him down the stairs to the ground floor and into the service wing of the house, saving her questions until she saw James Henry, who must be conscious, at least, if he had cautioned Will not to alert Mary to his condition.

She gasped when she saw him lying on a board in the butler's room with Mrs. Dixon, the butler, and Pierre, Harrowby's valet, in attendance. James Henry's coat and vest had been removed and laid across the back of a chair. His wig was gone, revealing a short growth of brown hair since his pate was last shaved. All about his face and scalp Hester saw the evidence of a beating. Bruises were forming around one eye, and his jaw was bruised and scraped. His upper lip was swollen beyond recognition, and blood oozed from a wound on his scalp. What looked like a quantity of blood had dried in streams on his shirt.

As Pierre dabbed at the wound on his head, a moan escaped him.

Hester's heart was racing. So Lord Wragby had carried out his threat. She approached the board quietly and asked Pierre, "How badly is he hurt?"

James Henry's eyes flew open. Pierre tsked. "I shall 'ave to remove 'is shirt to see, but I do not think that anything is broken. If nothing is broken, it will not be the fault of these villains who 'ave attacked Monsieur Henri!

"I am well enough. Just a bit bruised."

"You are bleeding."

He shook his head and winced in pain. "That is nothing. You know how badly scalp wounds bleed."

Mrs. Dixon said, "He will not tell us who did this to him, Mrs. Kean. And he's forbidden us to tell my lord or to call a constable!"

James Henry gave Hester a look, half-defiant, half-pleading.

"I daresay it was footpads or soldiers. If Mr. Henry cannot identify them, there is no point in calling in the authorities. I know he will inform Lord Hawkhurst if he should."

The anxious look in his eyes disappeared. "Yes, I shall do it myself, but not now. All I want now is to get cleaned up and be allowed to rest. But I would like a word with you first, Mrs. Kean."

The bleeding from his head had stopped, but he agreed to press a piece of lint to it, while Pierre went to find him a clean shirt. Mrs. Dixon and the butler left Hester alone with him, distress in the curious looks they sent over their shoulders.

When they were too far away to hear, Hester said in a gentle voice. "Lord Wragby's footmen?"

James Henry gritted his teeth and gave a slight nod. "It was entirely my fault." When Hester would have protested, he forestalled her. "No, truly it was. Since I got back to town, I have been following him, you see.

"I thought that if I could not protect Mary by escorting her, the best thing to do would be to follow her tormenter in case he tried to molest her again. But I wasn't as cautious as I should have been. He spotted me, and set his footmen on me." James Henry's jaw twitched. "He enjoyed watching the fight for a while. Then I suppose he grew bored, for he left them to do their work. I fought as long as I could, but there were four of them."

He broke through Hester's sounds of distress. "If Lord William Silsbee had not come along when he did, they would have done a much more thorough job of it."

"Lord William! Lord Ireton's friend? What did he do?"

James Henry looked mortified. "He drew his sword on them and had his own footmen chase them off. When I told him who I was, he called them back to help me into his carriage. He was kind enough to bring me here. I asked his groom to leave me at the stables, and he helped me inside. Lord William did ask, for Lord Ireton's sake, that I refrain from mentioning his son's part in the event.

"I gave him my word. So, you see, I cannot tell my lord, even if I wished to. And you must promise me never to tell Mrs. Mary! I feel enough of a fool already, without her discovering what a mess I've made of everything."

He had made a mess of things, but the bitterness in his voice prompted Hester to say, "If Mary knew, she would be very grateful. But she would, also, be terribly distressed to hear that you were injured on her account."

Hester continued, "If it helps your feelings, she and I have determined not to risk leaving the house until we all go down to Rotherham Abbey. And Lord Wragby will be denied if he tries to visit her here."

He closed his eyes with relief, telling Hester how anxious he had been for her cousin. She imagined that he had angrily set off from London, estate business as his excuse, but that worry over Mary had driven him back to town. Now that the muscles in his face had relaxed, she could see how heavily those fears had weighed upon him.

"I shall say nothing to my lord," she promised, "unless he hears of it by some other means. And not a word to Mary. If I am to avoid her questions, though, I should return to her now, and you should rest."

With a sheepish look, by way of thanks he took her hand for no more than a second, before laying his head back on the board. Hester left the room, wondering what repercussions were in store for them as a result of today's incident. She could only hope that Lord Wragby would be satisfied with his brutal retaliation for the insult he had felt. James Henry would suffer more from the humiliation of the beating than from his physical injuries. To anyone with a sense of pride, such treatment might rankle forever.

On her way back out of the service wing, Hester passed Pierre, returning with James Henry's fresh shirt. She stopped to ask him please to notify her if his patient took a turn for the worse. She also made him promise that he would say nothing to his master about the incident.

Pierre gave her his promise, but with a significant glance, he gave her to know that he was not unaware of its cause. "Monsieur Henri 'as developed a *tendre* for Mademoiselle Mary—*n'est pas?* —which Pierre is afraid will result in greater injury to 'im than a few bruises."

Hester refused to engage in gossip over his suspicions, but she could not suppress a sigh. That seemed to be confirmation enough for Pierre, who made a satisfied bow before returning to his patient.

He dies, sad outcast of each church and state,
And, harder still! Flagitious, yet not great.
Ask you why Wharton broke through every rule?
'Twas all for fear the Knaves should call him Fool.

CHAPTER V

The newssheets reported that the still-born Prince had been deposited in the vault with the children of the late Queen Anne. The Princess of Wales was said to be recovering as well as could possibly be expected. Now she was observing her period of confinement before going out in public again.

Mr. Walpole was still at The Hague, negotiating the peace with France, which continued to be undermined by the faction opposed to the regency of the Duke of Orleans. They spread rumours that any treaty with Great Britain would be against France's interest. King George remained in Hanover, addressing his concern with the Russian tsar, whose troops pressed dangerously close, and working towards a triple alliance with France and the Dutch Republic.

It was confirmed that under any peace treaty the Pretender would be forced to remove from Avignon beyond the Alps. A letter from him to his friends, encouraging them to hold fast to his interests, circulated about the city of Edinburgh, but the Jacobites there disowned it as counterfeit.

As December came and the days grew short, a lowering mood descended upon more than one person at Hawkhurst House. Bored with inactivity and worried about James Henry, Mary sulked. The lack of entertainments at Court made Isabella and her mother irritable and more demanding. Still mourning the loss of his son, Harrowby was drinking more deeply. And Hester found it harder and harder to conceal from everyone that she was pining for St. Mars.

On the morning of 2nd December, Hester was awakened from a fitful sleep by the sound of alarm bells. Parting her bed curtains, she found that her chamber was still dark. She fumbled for a candle and struggled to light it, but finally hearing shouts in the courtyard, she abandoned her attempts and felt her way to the window to peer out.

Whatever moon there was had been obscured by a thick covering of clouds. She could only guess at the hour, which judging from no light in the sky must be well before dawn. Still, she saw a number of servants with torches in hand milling about in the courtyard, and shouts of alarm came from out in the street. A voice she recognized as James Henry's issued some kind of order.

The bells, which were still ringing, carried the message that a fire had broken out. It had to be somewhere near for the sound to reach her so clearly. Nothing in the movements below suggested it could be in Hawkhurst House. Nevertheless, it was the responsibility of every able-bodied citizen to come to the aid of their neighbours.

Her eyes now more accustomed to the dark, Hester put on an old Indian gown and slipped on a pair of velvet mules. She managed to light her candle, before wrapping herself in a woollen cloak and going downstairs to investigate the cause for the alarm.

At the base of the stairs, she found Harrowby, wrapped in a striped banyan, his shaved head covered by turban, observing the activity of his servants. The front door was open, admitting a cold blast of air. The footmen were collecting the leather buckets that hung in the hall to be available at any moment. Hester joined Harrowby on the bottom step, where he informed her that a fire had broken out at Spring Garden near Charing Cross. She peered out in the direction he was pointing and could make out clouds of smoke rising from the spot where a source of flickering light relieved the darkness.

Just then, James Henry, who was dressed in woollen breeches and jacket but still in his night cap, approached, and with a hasty bow said, "The servants are all ready, my lord. With your permission, I shall take them to help."

Though the low light in the hall made them less obvious, Hester could still make out the bruises on his face. With luck, Harrowby might assume they were traces of smoke.

"Yes, away with you." Harrowby waved his hand. "If the fire spreads this way, you will bring them back to protect this house, of course."

"That is perfectly understood, my lord." James Henry made another slight inclination of his head, and with no more than a glance at Hester, set off into the night.

"There is nothing for us to do here, Mrs. Kean." With the door closed firmly behind them, Harrowby urged her back up the stairs. "We can return to our beds. Mr. Henry will alert us if there is any cause for concern."

"Yes, my lord." Hester bobbed a curtsy, happy to retire, but, with a sudden frown, Harrowby stopped her.

"Did you notice the marks on Mr. Henry's face? It appeared bruised."

"Yes, my lord." She would have to say something, but she kept the important information to herself. "I believe he was set upon by ruffians and suffered a great many blows. I am glad to find him as well as he is."

Harrowby angrily shook his head. "'Tis a scandal when a man cannot go about his lord's business without suffering an assault." He tsked. "I have some experience of that myself, Mrs. Kean, as you know."

Harrowby had never suffered a single blow, but his carriage had been stopped twice by his cousin St. Mars, disguised as the highwayman Blue Satan. The insult to his pride had never healed, even if his body had never experienced the slightest wound. Hester smothered a smile and merely nodded before bidding a yawning Harrowby goodnight.

Worrying about the fire made it hard to regain sleep, but she eventually fell into a deep repose and only awakened when the maid came in to shovel ashes out of the grate.

Parting her curtains, Hester asked, "Is there news of the fire?"

"Oh, yes, mistress!" The maid's tone was eager. "The fire was put out, but 'tis said the French Chapel and the Library was burnt to the ground, along wif some of the 'ouses. And you'll never guess what 'appened, miss—pardon me, Mrs. Kean—but the Prince of Wales came on foot all the way from St. James's wifout any of 'is Guards and 'e gave money to the firemen, and even to my lord's servants. What do you think of that, mistress?"

Hester made a suitable reply, praising the Prince for his generosity, while the maid stirred the coals, added more wood, and blew them into a flame. Then, when the worst of the chill was off, Hester got up, dressed, and went downstairs to breakfast.

The footmen who bid her good morning looked sleepy after their adventure. It was evident that they had got home too late to go back to bed; but, even had they not, the coins in their pockets would have excited them too much to sleep. Over the course of the morning, each one managed to find Hester to describe his part in fighting the fire and the surprise of being rewarded by the Prince.

The last to tell her his story was Will, who had been sent out again that morning by his master to gather more news.

What he had to tell her was disturbing. Some of the men who had fought the fire until dawn, on returning to their homes, had come across a corpse in Mermaid Court. Will had not heard any details about the death.

"They did say he was murdered." His sandy eyebrows were raised in excitement. "Somebody must've killed him while we were at the fire."

A shiver of foreboding ran down Hester's spine as she recalled the voice in the gallery of St. Paul's. "You did not hear who the victim was?"

"No, mistress. Do you want me to ask?"

"No." Hester shook her head abruptly then, realizing how sharp she must have sounded, smiled at Will. "I think we have had quite enough excitement for one day. I am certain the newssheets will report the poor man's name before long."

She did not have to wait for the newssheets. In the afternoon, after Harrowby had left for his coffee-house to see what he could learn about the cause of the fire, the ladies of the house were disturbed at their sewing by a visitor. The youngest footman came into the with-drawing room and informed them that a constable was waiting in the antechamber below and was insisting upon speaking with either James Henry or Lord Hawkhurst.

The sense of dread that had taken root in Hester's breast as soon as she had heard of the murder narrowed her throat.

Mrs. Mayfield was the first to speak. "A constable? Whatever can a constable wish with my lord?"

"Has it anything to do with the fire?" Isabella asked, unconcerned. "If it does, then you must tell him to come another time when my lord is home."

Sensing Hester's disquiet, Mary cast her a questioning look.

"Perhaps I should go down to see if it is anything worth disturbing him for."

"Nonsense!" Mrs. Mayfield said. "Let Mr. Henry take care of it."

The footman answered nervously, "I looked for Mr. Henry in his office, but he wasn't there."

Mrs. Mayfield snorted. "Of course not! Why should he be where he ought to be, when he had rather stick his nose where it's not want-ed?"

Quelling Mary's anger with a glance, Hester gently said, "He was up half the night, directing my lord's footmen at the fire. Perhaps he is recovering some of the sleep he missed. Have you looked in his bedchamber?"

"Yes, mistress." It was clear that the footman was agitated. "Shall I show the constable up? He says he won't go away till he's spoken to one of them. He's that persistent, my lady." He directed her this last in a pleading voice.

A terrible thought entered Hester's head. A jolt of fear passed through her, but before she could ask the footman if anyone had seen James Henry return safely from the fire, Isabella set down her crewel work and said, "Very well. You may show him up. I am bored with my pattern. Maybe he will have something diverting to say."

Mary had read the signs of alarm on Hester's face and seemed to catch her mood, even if she could not guess the thought that had run through Hester's head. What if the corpse that had been found was James Henry's? What if Lord Wragby's servants had attacked him again?

But, Hester reasoned with herself, would the constable have asked for James Henry if he knew he lay lifeless? Hester calmed her fears, telling herself she had more cause to believe him alive than dead. She gave Mary a reassuring glance before resuming her embroidery.

The constable soon appeared in a baker's apron, twisting his hat in his hands. Hester recognized him as the man who owned the bakery in Mary Bone Street. He bowed profoundly, darting glances about at the fine furnishings and peering at the ladies in alarm.

"Well, out with it, man!" Mrs. Mayfield peremptorily took charge. "What have you to say for yourself?"

He stammered, "I was to collect Mr. James 'Enry, my lady, and I daren't leave till I 'ave 'im."

"Collect Mr. Henry!" Mary repeated, startled. "Whatever for?"

"For the killin' of my Lord Wragby, mistress. Mr. Stanley—that's the Justice of the Peace—it's 'im what sent me. 'E wants to examine this Mr. 'Enry."

Everyone gasped. Mary and her mother blurted questions, the answers to which the constable could not supply. Feeling the blood drain from her face, Hester remained silent. Her relief at hearing the corpse was not James Henry's had been immediately overturned by the news that he was wanted for questioning in Viscount Wragby's death. The dread she had felt for the past few hours had been warranted; but if any scene had formed in her mind, it would have cast Lord Wragby as the villain, never as the victim of murder.

She heard Mary's voice raised in protest. "What information could Mr. Henry possibly give Mr. Stanley about Lord Wragby's death?"

"What information, indeed?" Mrs. Mayfield exclaimed triumphantly. "I make no doubt that he'll have something to say!"

Mary rounded on her, "That is not true and you know it!" Stamping her foot in frustration, she burst into tears.

Mrs. Mayfield's voice rose to a screech. "How dare you speak like that to your mother!"

"Mama! Mary!" Isabella covered her ears. "I will not have all this shouting!"

The constable stared, goggle-eyed at the excitement he had raised. Then, gazing around for someone calm enough to deal with the situation, his eyes lit upon Hester. "I just fetch the people Mr. Stanley tells me to collect, my lady. 'E don't tell me the whys and wherefores."

Hester got instantly to her feet. "I am certain this will all be quickly settled. We shall find Mr. Henry, who will be eager to clear up any misunderstanding. Meanwhile, a servant will accompany you to the kitchen where the cook will be happy to supply you with some food and a mug of beer while you wait." She motioned to the footman, who had stayed hovering near the door, and, after giving him orders for the cook, she waited until the two men had walked out.

Mary, who had long been suffering under a sense of injustice, had not stopped railing at her mother. Ignoring Isabella's warning, Mrs. Mayfield was pleading with her to take her side. Upset with both, Isabella, who had not seemed very well since Hester's return to London, and had pushed her constitution to the limit with ceaseless revelries, launched into a fit of hysterics and threatened to send them both back to Yorkshire.

"There, there," Hester said, coming to Isabella's side in the silence that greeted this threat. "No one will have to go anywhere if we just stay calm. Mary, go call your sister's maid to take her to her bedchamber for a rest. Aunt, we should send one of the footmen to inform my lord and bring him home."

It was Hester's intention to send other servants to search for James Henry. She would not entrust this mission to her aunt, who was likely to provoke an even worse situation with her wild accusations.

Fortunately, Mrs. Mayfield was eager to put her own views before Harrowby before anyone else could, so with a smirk of triumph for Mary's benefit, she hurried from the room. Fearful of what her mother might say, Mary turned to Hester with a protest on her lips and would have balked, if Hester had not forestalled her. "Let us, please, get your sister settled in bed before we decide what is best to do. I have something important to tell you."

With a glance at Isabella's tear-streaked face, Mary swallowed what she had wanted to say, and left to do Hester's bidding. Hester had coaxed Isabella only a third of the way to her bedchamber before the maid arrived and took over from her, cooing to her mistress. She promised Hester that she would soothe her lady with cordial water and a few drops of laudanum.

Leaving Isabella in the maid's capable hands, Hester turned to Mary, who had followed the servant, and said, "We must move quickly before your mother catches on." Taking Mary by the hand, she led her down to the hall, where she found her two most trusted footmen, Will and John, and charged them with the task of finding James Henry.

"Tell him, he must return to the house on the most urgent business, but ask him to wait for me in his office. He must not go near the kitchens until after we have spoken. And as soon as you do find him, please come tell me at once. I shall be in Mrs. Mary's chamber.

"Come with me, Mary," she said, drawing her cousin back upstairs. Mary's bedchamber was nearer to the staircase, so it would take the servants less time to fetch Hester there. She did not speak again until they were safely inside Mary's room and the door was closed. Then she told her about James Henry's beating by Lord Wragby's footmen.

Mary clapped both hands to her cheeks. "Oh, how monstrous! And how cowardly—to make others do his wicked work for him! Poor Mr. Henry!"

"Yes, it was both those things, but you must see how bad it will look if the J.P. finds out — if he has not learned of it already."

"Why didn't you tell me?"

"Mr. Henry made me promise not to do it. He did not wish you to be upset." Hester withheld the information that James Henry had been watching Lord Wragby to keep him from bothering Mary. The fewer people who knew that, the better. Besides, Mary might blame herself for what had happened or make James Henry's action into a chivalrous fancy, neither of which would serve any useful purpose.

Hester spent the next few minutes assuring her cousin that none of his injuries were grave and that she had seen him active and well since then. She told her about his taking the footmen to fight the fire and about the corpse that had been found in Mermaid Court. "I cannot be sure if that was Lord Wragby's body, but if so, he was discovered very near to where James Henry was fighting the fire."

Mary stared at her in horror. "What are you saying, Hester? You cannot believe that Mr. Henry killed him!"

"No, of course not, but when it is learned where he was, someone may draw that conclusion. All I do say, Mary, is that you must be very careful not to defend Mr. Henry too loudly. If you are perceived to have strong feelings for him, that could add to their suspicions. You must not give your mother any more reason to slander him. I have seen her do it to someone before and the result was great harm. Having her as an enemy will not do him any good."

Just then, there was a knock at the door and, praying it was one of the footmen, Hester went to answer it. It did prove to be John, who whispered that Mr. Henry had returned and was now awaiting her in his office.

"We didn't have to search for 'im, Mrs. Kean. We ran into 'im out in the street as he was making his way home."

"Good. I shall go directly."

"I must see him, too!" Mary said from behind her.

"No." Hester turned. "Please think about what I just said. I will convey your concern, I promise, and you will be able to speak to him soon, when we go down to Rotherham Abbey."

She left Mary discontented, but resigned, and made her way to the wing off the courtyard where James Henry had an office. When she entered the relatively unadorned room with its massive desk and shelves of bound ledgers, she found him anxiously pacing the floor.

The moment he saw her, he came quickly to meet her. "What is this I hear about a constable sent to fetch me? And Lord Wragby has been murdered? How? They cannot possibly think that I killed him!"

"I do not know anything more than what the constable said, which was very little indeed," Hester replied, as calmly as she could. "He said only that he was to take you to be examined by Mr. Stanley, the Justice of the Peace. I thought you should have a moment to compose yourself before you accompany him. I sent him to the kitchens to wait, and someone has gone in search of my lord."

James Henry fingered his forehead, distress clouding his visage. "He must be summoned, of course, but I cringe to think what he will say. You know how much he hates the very thought of a scandal."

This drew a smile from Hester. "Indeed, I do, but he has weathered a few. There are more important considerations to worry about."

His head shot up and he fixed her with a stare. "Do you think I shall be arrested?"

"I believe the J.P. would have sent two constables if that were his intention. Undoubtedly, someone has informed him of the hostility between you and Lord Wragby or he would never have sent for you.

"I doubt it was anyone in this household," she added, noting the question on his face. "It is far more likely that a servant of Lord Wragby's mentioned it, which should mean that the cause of it is not yet known." She hesitated, then said, "Unfortunately, my aunt is quite capable of informing the authorities of your defence of Mary, and if she does, she will cast it in the worst possible light."

"Why? Why would she wish to do me harm?"

Hester helplessly shook her head. "Because she is a selfish, vicious person and does not care whom she hurts. Because her plans to wed Mary to Lord Wragby, if his marriage could be overturned, were thwarted, and you were conveniently at hand to blame. . . . Because you appear to have more influence over her daughter than she has herself."

His head gave a jerk, then he lowered his eyes as if wishing to conceal whatever they contained.

"Who can understand the wicked things she does?" Hester continued. "The point is that you must speak to Mr. Stanley and assure him that you had nothing to do with Lord Wragby's death before my aunt has a chance to spread her calumny."

"And Mrs. Mary? What does she think?" He turned away and straightened the few papers on his desk.

"She is very concerned about your welfare and would have accompanied me, but I thought it safer for you if she did not."

He looked up quickly. "She does not believe me guilty, then?"

"Of course, not."

This bolstered his spirits, and he took a deep breath. "Then I should not keep the J.P. waiting any longer." He gave a twisted smile and squared his broad shoulders. "I thank you, Mrs. Kean, for coming to warn me."

Hester bowed her head by way of reply and curtsied, wishing she could thank him for all his many kindnesses to her, but she did not wish to give him the impression that she feared never seeing him again. "As soon as my lord is come home," she promised, "I shall tell him where you have gone and do my best to assuage his worries."

This proved to take more than a simple effort on Hester's part. Harrowby came home from the coffee-house, already alarmed by Mrs. Mayfield's message, conveyed by the footman. Arriving at Hawkhurst House in a state of perturbation, he summoned the ladies of his household to the library to demand an account.

Isabella sent word by her maid that she knew nothing of the affair and refused to be burdened with it. That left Mary, Mrs. Mayfield, and Hester to explain to Harrowby why James Henry would have anything to do with the murder of a viscount.

"I have never been so shocked as I was to hear of Lord Wragby's death," Harrowby began, as they converged in the room. "When I got to the coffee-house, the talk was of nothing else. Then, to be informed that a servant of mine had been arrested for his murder! What can you all have been doing to bring this infamy to my house?"

Hester hurried to speak before her aunt could poison his mind. "Mr. Henry was not arrested, Cousin. He was merely asked to attend the Justice of the Peace, presumably to satisfy some questions that had been raised."

Mrs. Mayfield snorted. "I make no doubt but that he will be arrested once he opens his mouth!"

Mary cried out in protest, and Harrowby raised his voice. "Then, why was I informed of an arrest? I demand to know what has been going on! What on earth has James Henry had to do with Lord Wragby?"

"He insinuated himself into my daughter's affairs, that's what! And most improperly, as I told him. What right had he to discourage Lord Wragby's attentions? I am sorry, my lord, but I fear you will find that your servant took leave of his senses and murdered the viscount to keep him away from my Mary."

"Mr. Henry only defended me, when you would not do it," Mary retorted. A flood of tears nearly choked her. "Do not try to blame him for a problem you caused yourself."

"Does that mean that Henry did kill him?" Harrowby's voice wavered as he fell into a chair. "Zounds! What a catastrophe! My name will be ruined—Lord Ireton will see to that. And he has the King's ear. We shall all be banished from Court and forced to end our days at Rotherham Abbey. My lady will fall down in a fit when I tell her that she has to spend the rest of her life in the country."

Before Hester could get in a word, he rounded furiously on Mrs. Mayfield. "And I shall know who to blame for this, madam! I ordered you to stop encouraging Lord Wragby to dangle after your daughter. Now you see where your ambition has landed us! And do not think that you shall be coming with us into Kent. I shall insist upon that oaf of a son of yours taking you back into Yorkshire where you belong!"

His unexpected tirade silenced Mrs. Mayfield. Her mouth gaped, and Hester took advantage of the silence to say, "I am strongly of the opinion that it is much too early to despair, my lord. When Lord Wragby was killed, Mr. Henry was busy fighting the fire. You saw him go yourself. I am certain his responses will be enough to satisfy any suspicion that has been raised."

Harrowby turned to her as if clinging to a branch in a storm. "Do you honestly believe so? Then, tell me for God's sake why anyone should suspect him?"

"I do not know who laid information against him, my lord, or indeed, what was said, but someone in Lord Wragby's household must have been aware of at least one incident between them."

"What incident? And there was more than one? Where?"

Mrs. Mayfield tried to speak, but he hushed her with a glare. "Go ahead, Mrs. Kean. I insist upon knowing, though I had much rather not!"

"I am afraid that the last time he called here, Lord Wragby forgot himself so far as to behave in a very insulting manner to Mary. Fortunately, Mr. Henry arrived in time to prevent his lordship from doing something he surely would have regretted, and which certainly would have displeased his father. Mr. Henry's intention was to spare both Mary from injury and Lord Wragby from irreparable scandal, I am certain. Lord Wragby did not thank him for his interference, however.

"I do not know if this was the information imparted to Mr. Stanley, so I would advise no one to raise it. There may have been some later friction between them, but as to that, I cannot say."

Harrowby scowled at Mary, who blanched as if struck. He refrained from accusing her of causing the trouble, though, perhaps softened by her reaction into recalling that she had never wanted Lord Wragby's attention. In his heart, he knew who was responsible.

"May I suggest, my lord, that we await Mr. Henry's return before agitating ourselves further? He may be able to lay all our worries to rest."

Harrowby acquiesced. He begged them to leave him alone, but shook his head and added, "He may put some of them to rest, Mrs. Kean, but I still dread what Lord Ireton will say. I do not know how I shall meet him."

"Perhaps, it would be as well to remove the family to Rotherham Abbey for Christmas, my lord. Then, when the King is returned and Parliament opens again, at least some few weeks will have passed."

She left him with this thought and followed the other two out. No sooner had they exited the library than Mrs. Mayfield took Mary roughly by the arm and hissed, "How dare you take that man's part against me, and in front of my lord! Have you no respect for your mama?"

Before Mary could reply—invitation though it was—Hester said, "If we are not to displease him further, I suggest we forego argument. He is incensed enough as it is."

Mrs. Mayfield cast her a resentful glance but, perhaps realizing that to continue might only harm herself, she released Mary and stormed off.

She had not come out of the exchange any higher in Harrowby 's favour. Now, she would have to weigh the possibility of angering him further against the value of her quarrel with James Henry, the result of her desire to please Lord Wragby. With the viscount dead, her animosity could serve no purpose, unless she was sincerely worried that James Henry and Mary had become too fond of each other. If that were the case, as Mary's mother, she could put barriers between them without falsely accusing him and getting him hanged. Harrowby was unlikely to be grateful if she robbed him of his trusted receiver-general. Hester could only hope her aunt would choose self-interest over a simple vicious wish.

To be forced to wait for James Henry's return tried both Hester's and Mary's patience. Hester asked for tea to be carried to Mary's bedchamber, where they retired to avoid any more scenes with Mrs. Mayfield and to talk over the shocking news of Lord Wragby's death. They sat close to the fire, clinging to their cups for comfort. Seeing how anxious her cousin was, Hester did try a few times to change the subject, but found that impossible when only one thing was on their minds.

Without any details, however, not even about the manner in which the viscount had been killed, they could do nothing but guess at the circumstances. Hester was hoping that James Henry would bring some information to them when, and if, he was free to return.

"I suppose we should not be surprised to learn that someone took such a violent dislike to Lord Wragby," Mary said. "I cannot be the only person who found his society intolerable."

"No, indeed. But we should not be quick to dismiss the possibility that a footpad was responsible. He might simply have been the victim of a robbery. But, if he was, then where were his servants, and why did they not protect him?"

"You said the corpse was in Mermaid Court? Why would he be there in the early hours of the morning?"

At a loss to answer, Hester shook her head. Then, raising her eyebrows in a significant gesture, she said, "I wonder if he might not have been visiting a mistress, or even searching for a woman on the street. I am not conversant with such situations, but would a gentleman want his servants to accompany him, if that is what he was doing?"

Mary giggled and threw her a look of mock reproach. Then she sobered, "Oh, I know it is wrong to make light of anyone's death, but I confess that when the constable said Lord Wragby had been killed, I felt nothing but relief. Is that shameful of me, Hester, and shall I be punished for such wickedness?"

"I cannot believe it, my dear. And if we are confessing, then I must admit to feeling the same. But you see, when James Henry could not be located, and the constable arrived, I was so afraid that something else dreadful had happened to him. Will had already informed me that a corpse was discovered this morning, you see."

Mary's cheeks turned pale. She spoke in a breathless voice. "Oh, dear . . . oh, no. How glad I am that that did not occur to me. I should never have borne it."

Hester regretted the image she had raised and did what she could to erase it. Reaching for Mary's cup to pour her more tea, she said briskly, "As miserable as Lord Wragby made you, I think it quite natural to feel a touch of relief. And you must not feel guilty for such thoughts. You would not have had them if Lord Wragby had not made himself so unpleasant. I daresay he offended a great many people."

"But enough for one of them to murder him? Oh, Hester, you do not think Mr. Henry could have done it to protect me!"

Hester stared at her open-mouthed. For the briefest of moments, Mary's question shook her faith—could she possibly have been wrong? But before Mary could notice her hesitation, her confidence in James Henry's character reasserted itself. "I do not believe it for one moment, and if that is what you fear, I beg you will banish it from your mind. Mr. Henry is not a murderer. And no matter how highly you figure in his esteem, it would take a great deal more to provoke him to kill than Lord Wragby did."

Mary's relief came out in a rush of breath, and she briefly closed her eyes. "Of course, you are correct. You must think me very vain to suspect that he might do such a thing for me. But after you told me about the beating he had suffered, I had to wonder whether he might not force Lord Wragby to accept his challenge."

"If Mr. Stanley has been told of the beating, he must suspect the same, but James Henry was busy at the fire, and I have never heard of a duel taking place in Mermaid Court."

Mary gave her a grateful look, but before she could say anything more, a knock sounded at the door. It was a footman there to let them know that James Henry had returned to the house and was closeted with his master.

Long, as to him who works for debt, the day,
Long as the Night to her whose Love's away,
Long as the Year's dull circle seems to run,
When the brisk Minor pants for twenty-one:
So slow th' unprofitable moments roll,
That lock up all the Functions of my soul;
That keep me from myself; and still delay
Life's instant business to a future day . . . .

CHAPTER VI

After promising to return with a report of everything she learned, Hester left Mary and went to stand outside Harrowby's rooms to waylay James Henry. The wait was uncomfortably long, and her worry was increased by the sound of Harrowby's voice raised in anger. She could not make out his words, but knew him well enough to guess that fear over his standing with the King would figure more strongly than any concern for his loyal servant.

Finally, after Harrowby had exhausted himself, or else had grown hoarse, silence settled over the rooms. In a few moments the door opened and James Henry appeared, looking pale and anxious, but showing signs of disgruntlement, too. When he perceived Hester, he started, then checked over his shoulder to make certain no one was following him out, before quietly closing the door. He gestured for her to remain silent as he led her downstairs to the small antechamber, where they each took a chair.

Hester did not need to ask him what had transpired, for rubbing his forehead as if it ached, he began, "Thank you again, Mrs. Kean, for giving me a few moments to prepare myself. I do not know how well I would have acquitted myself, else."

When Hester said nothing, he continued, "You were correct.

Someone notified Mr. Stanley that Lord Wragby held some animosity towards me. It could have been Lord William Silsbee, who, you'll recall, chased off Lord Wragby's footmen and helped me home. Mr. Stanley was aware of the beating I had received. The marks on my face confirmed it. He wished to know why Lord Wragby had treated me thusly."

"What did you tell him?"

James Henry gave a wry smile. "From what he said, I gathered that he had no information about what had transpired between Lord Wragby and me here at Hawkhurst House or, indeed, of his lordship's pursuit of Mrs. Mary. I put him off with a tale of some perceived, though unintended, insult. I told him, as humbly as I could—" his voice took on a note of bitterness— "that as I was not of his lordship's rank, he chose to set his footmen upon me instead of giving me the honour of challenging me to a duel."

"Did he believe you?"

James Henry sighed. "He seemed satisfied for the moment, but if he should learn of my defence of Mrs. Mary, I misdoubt I shall be examined again."

"What did he say about Lord Wragby's death? How was he killed?"

"He was throttled." James Henry's jaw twitched. "So, you see, it was the sort of thing that a brute like me might do."

The first part of his statement startled Hester so much that she ignored the last. "Strangled? With what? Did Mr. Stanley say?"

He looked at her queerly. "As far as I know, no instrument was used. According to Mr. Stanley, the murderer used his bare hands."

Hester parted from James Henry after hearing what Harrowby had said to him. As she had imagined, Harrowby's greatest concern was for the damage Lord Ireton could do to him if he believed a member of the Hawkhurst household had murdered his heir. They had agreed that Mrs. Mayfield must somehow be prevented from speaking to anyone about the contretemps at Hawkhurst House. James Henry, however, had not been able to understand why Mary's mother would wish to tell anyone of the incident, which would only give rise to gossip about her daughter.

Hester had explained that her aunt had a penchant for boasting of her daughters' suitors, and the fact that two men had come to blows over Mary was precisely the kind of fodder she used to feed her vanity. She had not added that resentment of James Henry alone would give her aunt reason enough to betray him if she thought it would serve her interests.

Hester was determined to use all her powers of persuasion to make her aunt understand that Harrowby would be furious if she drew more attention to the conflict between his receiver-general and the murdered viscount.

She had not told James Henry the reason for her question about the manner of the strangling. His answer had sent a chill down her spine, reminding her of the words she had heard in St. Paul's. The recollection of that malevolent hiss and its promise had paralyzed her thoughts.

She had little doubt that the speaker of those words had uttered them with Lord Wragby in mind. But who had spoken them? And why? What had Lord Wragby done to elicit such fury and hatred? He was self-centred and cruel, foolish and indiscreet. She supposed that any of these qualities could have inspired distaste or revulsion; but to provoke anyone to murder, surely he must have done something unforgivable, to the murderer, at least.

Hester tried again to recall the faces she had seen in the gallery that day. Lord Ireton was there, of course. Before he had reprimanded his son, she had spotted him with two of his friends, Lord William Silsbee and Sir Horatio Allenbee, two Whigs who could not have been pleased to see Lord Wragby's Tory companions, Sir Francis Lichfield and Lord Charters. The treasonous comments Lord Wragby had made at Hampton Court on Coronation Day had greatly alarmed the first two. Had the motive for the murder been political? It had not been long since the Tories and Whigs had settled their quarrels with swords.

No other familiar faces came to her mind from that day in St. Paul's. Those were the only gentlemen she had recognized. She thought she could dismiss the soldiers, merchants, and tradesmen who had been visiting the gallery, for none of them should have known Lord Wragby well enough to develop such a determined hatred for him. It was far more likely that one of the gentlemen who had been either with him or with his father had committed the crime.

But how was she to discover if any one of them had committed murder?

If St. Mars were here, he could help her sort through their motives. He would surely want to clear his brother James Henry from suspicion, no matter how bitter and contentious their relationship had been. She knew him well enough to know that he would not let resentment stop him from seeking the truth.

St. Mars, however, was not here, and she would not have his help. She tried to shake off the despair that filled her every time she faced that prospect. Sooner or later, she promised herself, she would learn to accept it and the pain would grow less intense.

She thought of discussing the crime with Mary, but Mary was young and her thoughts were clouded with worry for James Henry. Besides, she was no better placed than Hester to investigate gentlemen's affairs. James Henry had a cool head, but the farther he was kept from Lord Wragby's and Lord Ireton's associates the better.

A thought entered in her head, telling her that perhaps there was one possible source of help. She did not know if her request would be welcomed, but it was certainly worth a try.

Two days later, while everyone in Hawkhurst House was busily preparing to move the household into Kent, Hester took a chair to the Strand and asked to be put down at the entrance to Old Round Court. She paid the chairmen then took a look about.

On the south side of the Strand, no more than two hundred yards away, the New Exchange bustled with customers exploring its shops, for everything from fine hoods and linen caps to penknives and scissors. Their counters would be alive with the flirting that went on between the shop girls and the beaus and fops who came to ogle them. Lately, the custom in the Exchange had seemed to fall off, as more shops opened west of the City, but Hester still was wary of encountering someone she knew among the customers.

That was why she had taken the trouble to invent an errand that would take her a safe distance from its crowds. It had been all too easy to convince Mrs. Mayfield that the celebrated Anodyne Necklace invented by Dr. Chamberlen for children's teeth might have some curative properties for her frequent tooth pain. Advertisements for the necklace had appeared in nearly every newssheet for months, and the most recent in the *Evening Post* had promised its effectiveness against not only teething pains, but a score of other ailments. Afraid of being trapped with a toothache in the Weald of Kent without this miraculous treatment, Mrs. Mayfield had ordered her niece to obtain it at once.

Shivering from the cold, as well as anticipation, Hester made certain that her friends were not yet in sight before directing herself towards the door under the sign of the Sugar Loaf. She entered the house and, as instructed in the advertisement, climbed one flight of stairs above the confectioner's shop and knocked upon the door. It was opened by a woman in a neat linen cap and apron, who identified herself as the doctor's wife. After inquiring after Hester's business, she invited her into a parlour which had been fitted out for business. She asked for the five shillings quoted in the newssheet and made up a parcel with paper and string, containing the "admirable" necklace with instructions in English and French for wearing it, the philosophical essay upon it, and the *17th Edition in English, French, and High German of the Practical Scheme of Secret Injuries and Broken Constitutions by Fast Living, Etc.*

The latter had been offered gratis with a purchase of the necklace and urged upon the public by the doctor himself, but Hester doubted that her aunt would wish to read it. In spite of her fast living, she seemed to have escaped the risk of "secret injuries," or if she had not, she had managed to overcome them without Dr. Chamberlen's advice.

Hester thanked the doctor's wife and descended the stairs with her parcel to enter the confectioner's shop. Her nose was instantly greeted by the welcome aroma of fruit, spices, and chocolate, and the warmth of the baking oven. Jars and pots of raspberry, apple, and gooseberry preserves shared the shelves with currant jelly and orange marmalade. Boxes of candied flowers, quince paste, and dried pears and apples were stacked near the fire to keep dry. On the counter, an array of plates piled high with chocolate almonds, almond loaves, and lemon puffs tempted the customers.

The shop was crowded. Hester searched among the people in front of her for a familiar face, but neither of St. Mars's servants was in sight. Nerves fluttered in her stomach at the thought that perhaps they had not received her message, or worse, that they had, but had decided not to come.

She took her turn in the shop and bought a dozen lemon biskets for Mary and a few ounces of chocolate almonds to console herself. Then, turning to go out, she was met at the door by Tom, just entering with Katy on his arm.

They were dressed for a day in town, Tom sporting his best breeches, a well-pressed coat, and a neatly brushed felt hat, Katy finer in a woollen skirt, cape, and hood that revealed the skill of her needle. On seeing Hester, they broke out in smiles, before stepping in out of the cold. Hester led them to a corner of the shop out of the way of customers before turning to greet them warmly as Tom bowed and Katy curtsied.

It was easy to see that marriage was suiting them both. Hester had not seen Katy since her wedding some nine months ago, but her radiance had not diminished one whit since that day. When her eyes lit on Tom, they glowed with love. For his part, Tom seemed contented and proud beneath his apparent eagerness. Hester looked for other changes and wondered if she saw evidence of thickening around Katy's waist.

After the greetings and inquiries after health had been exchanged, Hester was startled when Tom blurted out, "So you've heard from my lord? Did he say when he's coming home?"

A pang of disappointment, tinged with fear, shot through Hester. A knot formed in her throat. "He has not been in touch with you, then? In all this time?"

All eagerness fading, Tom stared at her, dumbfounded. "But I thought—" He looked to Katy for help. "That is, we reckoned . . ."

"No, I'm very sorry, Tom. I have not heard from your master. I had hoped—I had assumed—that you would have news of him."

Tom shook his head, staring down at the floor as if unwilling for her to see how worried he was. Either that or he did not wish her to detect the other thoughts that must be turning through his head. If St. Mars had not written to her, surely he must be angry with her, and if that was the case, should his servants be waiting on her now?

In the confectioner's shop, the customers were merry, as who should not be merry with so many treats in front of them? They took no notice of the three in the corner whose hearts had been struck with an indefinable concern.

"No, mistress," Tom finally said, stiffness straightening his back. "He usually just writes to let me know when he's coming home."

"I see . . ." With the government reading the mail, that made sense, although Hester had assumed that the use of an alias would protect both St. Mars and Tom from the law.

"It hasn't been that long since he left." Katy tried to console them. "Just a few months, and he's been gone that long before."

Neither Hester nor Tom took up her remark. They both knew that, this time, St. Mars's departure for France had been different. Tom must have seen St. Mars return after Hester's failure to meet him. He would have known that something was wrong, even if St. Mars had not confided in him. Knowing how devoted Tom was to the master he had served for more than twenty years—the master he had helped to escape from the law—Hester knew that Tom would be privy to most of the intimate details of St. Mars's life.

The stiffness of his posture, his continued reluctance to meet Hester's gaze, confirmed that her suspicions were correct. How could Tom know how to treat her, when the last he had heard of Hester was the blow she had dealt to St. Mars? And what if her own worst fears came true? What if St. Mars's absence was the result of some accident or capture and not merely disappointment? If it were, would that not also be her fault?

The silence between Hester and Tom threatened to go on indefinitely. Recalling why she had summoned him, Hester suppressed her hurt and self-pity, and forced herself to speak. "I suspect that Katy is correct. You will either be hearing of his arrival soon, or we must wait until spring for news. I doubt he will wish to cross the Channel once the winter is upon us.

"But something has occurred that perhaps he would wish to know," she continued. "Mr. Henry is in trouble. It is possible that he may even be arrested for murder."

Tom reacted with a jerk. He raised his head and greeted this information with a look that was at once troubled and relieved. With a problem to address, he could put questions of loyalty aside, for now at least. "Mr. Henry, kill someone? That don't sound like him."

"I have no doubt of his innocence, but there are circumstances that raised the magistrate's suspicions, and until the real murderer is caught, I am afraid that he will be the strongest suspect."

She told him a portion of the story: how Lord Wragby had made himself a nuisance to her cousin, how James Henry had confronted him, and how the viscount had repaid him with a beating at the hands of his footmen. "The latter incident was reported to the magistrate, who does not know the reason for their quarrel. If he discovers it, he will surely examine Mr. Henry again."

Tom looked puzzled. "What was Mr. Henry doing meddling in your cousin's affairs? That don't sound like him neither."

Hester kept her real suspicions to herself. "I'm afraid that neither my aunt nor Cousin Harrowby was willing to take Lord Wragby on. You must know that his father is the powerful Lord Ireton."

Tom gave a snort, whether at her mention of Harrowby or out of disgust, she did not know. Then, he nodded slowly. "That do seem more like. I've never known Mr. Henry do anything dishonourable—'cept in that business with my lord." The recollection made him frown.

Hester could see that he was troubled. James Henry was another person who had let his master down, if not actually done him harm. Tom must be trying to imagine what St. Mars would wish him to do.

"Do you think you could write to my Lord St. Mars and tell him of the danger Mr. Henry is in? I believe he would wish to know."

This speech made him recollect that he was not sure how much he should trust her. Withdrawal entered his eyes. Finally, he said, "I suppose I could write to his lordship."

Hester had summoned Tom as the only person to whom she could turn. He had always helped her in the past. But it was clear from his demeanour that until he knew how severely she had wounded his master, he would not overlook the harm she had done. There was nothing more she could ask of him now.

"When you do write to him, will you please say how much I look forward to seeing him?" The rush of blood to her face as she spoke these words nearly choked her, as desperation overcame humiliation.

Katy sent her a look of pity mixed with understanding, as Tom nodded in acquiescence.

Hester took her leave as he and Katy turned to await their turn for service at the counter. In all her life Hester had never felt so dejected and friendless as she did now.

Two days later, Hester set out with the entire Hawkhurst household on their journey into Kent. The family travelled together in one coach, while Isabella's maid and Harrowby's valet shared the other. Both were laden down with boxes, trunks, and portmanteaus, full of every possible garment, piece of bedding, or toy that their master and mistress might need for a few weeks' stay in the country. A full complement of guards, armed with blunderbusses, sat atop the two coaches. Harrowby was wary of another assault by the highwayman Blue Satan, who had waylaid him twice on his journeys to and from his estate.

James Henry had preceded them by a few days. His escape from London without further examination by the magistrate had afforded Mary, Hester, and Harrowby no little relief. Isabella gave no more thought to the danger he faced than she did to anything that did not affect her comfort and, while Mrs. Mayfield would have loved to see him put soundly in his place, she seemed content to bide her time until she could best profit from an attack.

Mary and Hester were the only travellers whose spirits had been raised by the prospect of time in the country. The others dreaded the tedium they were sure to face without the diversions of Court, and the assemblies, tea parties, and afternoon calls of aristocratic society. A promised visit from two of their friends was the only consolation they could look forward to.

Hester was obliged to ride in the middle of the rear-facing seat as they lurched mile after mile towards Harrowby's country seat, Rotherham Abbey. She did her best to ignore Mrs. Mayfield's complaints that she was taking up more than her share of the bench. With each one, Mary did her best to squeeze more tightly towards the window to give Hester room to breathe. Mary spent most of the early part of the trip looking out at the vast woods that covered the county, contrasting it with the open aspect of the Yorkshire moors, but after hours of looking out at impenetrable forest, she tired of it and fell into a gloom to match Hester's other companions'.

Hester did not make her usual efforts at conversation to pass the time. For once, they seemed beyond her powers of dissimilation, when every shred of her composure was required to conceal her sense of hopelessness. She focused on the peace and quiet that awaited her in the walks about Rotherham Abbey, counting on the restfulness of the views, even in the midst of winter, to make up for the discomforts she was enduring now.

Their progress was so slow down the rutted and muddy roads that, with the shortness of December days, they were obliged to put up for one night at the inn at Tunbridge Wells. In the morning, while the servants packed up the sheets they had put on the beds the night before, the family took breakfast, with Mrs. Mayfield and Isabella fussing over the earliness of the hour. Then, still aching from the rattling they had suffered on the previous day, they resumed their uncomfortable seats and rode on. They passed through the village of Hawkhurst near dark, and arrived at Rotherham Abbey to be greeted by anxious servants, warm fires, and a filling meal.

It was while they were at table that Hester took note of someone's absence. The Reverend Mr. Bramwell had been resident at Rotherham Abbey for many years, first as tutor to St. Mars, then as chaplain to the former Lord Hawkhurst and his household. She would have expected him to greet the family upon arrival and to share their meal.

When she remarked on this, however, Harrowby frowned. "Mr. Bramwell is no longer dwelling here. I could not permit a non-juring priest to be a member of this household. What would his Majesty think if I were to shelter an enemy of his?"

Mrs. Mayfield was quick to commend his action, but Hester was horrified to discover that a faithful old servant had been turned out. She pitied the aging priest, but said nothing about it now, aware of the futility of any argument. Still, she resolved to ask James Henry what had become of St. Mars's old tutor in case something could be done for him.

James Henry might also have supped with them, but no doubt he was stopping in his own house nearby. Hester assumed that he and Harrowby would conduct some business while here and only hoped that Mrs. Mayfield would not try to exert her influence against him to keep him away from their table.

Later, after they had all visited their rooms and as the others settled down to a game of cards, Hester conducted Mary through the house to acquaint her with it. Mary was delighted with everything, from the splendour of the chambers that had been built to host monarchs to Hester's much smaller bedchamber, which was distinguished by a wall that was panelled in elaborately carved wood.

Hester did not share the secret of that wall: that the carvings of vines and pineapples concealed a mechanism by which one of the panels could be opened to give access to a tunnel, leading from the house to the ruins of the original abbey buildings a hundred yards away. It was a secret known only to herself, St. Mars, and his trusted groom Tom. Hester fended off the memory of the night she had first learned of the tunnel, promising herself the pleasure of dwelling on it later, when she would be alone.

Their exploration of the house ended in the Long Gallery, where a wall of multi-paned windows faced a row of portraits of members of the Fitzsimmons family, as well as paintings that had been bestowed upon them by grateful monarchs. As they strolled along the gallery, carrying candles to illuminate the dark, Hester was so weighed down by low spirits, and the effort needed to hide them, that she did not perceive danger coming until it was full upon her.

They had just passed a handsome portrait of King Charles II, when gazing ahead, Mary stopped. "Hester, who is that gentleman in the blue coat?" She raised her candle to shed more light on the portrait.

Hester's heart leapt into her throat as she stared up at the portrait of St. Mars. She had forgotten that Mary was the only member of the family here at Rotherham Abbey who had seen him when he had not troubled himself with a disguise. He had believed himself safe from recognition in Yorkshire and, against Hester's better judgement, had spent the summer in her company with no more concealment than an alias.

For a second she was dumbstruck. It would do no good to lie, for anyone of the servants might tell Mary who was represented in the portrait. "That is the former Lord Hawkhurst's son, the Viscount St. Mars." She hoped her voice was steady.

Mary approached the painting and peered closely at it. "He looks just like Sir Robert! You remember—the gentleman we met last summer!"

Hester moved to stand beside her. She tried to hold her candle so that its glare would reflect off the paint to distort Mary's view. "Yes, I do see some resemblance."

"Some? Why, Hester, how can you say such a thing? He is the very image of Sir Robert!"

Hester struggled between the need to lie and a strong urge to confide. "Could your memory be confused? The resemblance is quite striking, but one must allow for the artist's flaws. I've seen very few portraits that accurately represent their subjects."

When Mary turned to stare at her, Hester's gaze faltered. "Hester, I know perfectly well that this is a portrait of Sir Robert. Was that not his real name? What mischief is afoot?"

Hester had failed to pull the wool over Mary's eyes, but she believed she could trust her. A worse danger would be to let her speculate and, perhaps, to speak of her suspicions to someone else.

She took hold of Mary's free hand. "I must ask you, if you love me, never to let on that you have seen him before. Will you promise me?"

Mary said, "Of course! I would never betray any confidence of yours."

"I beg you earnestly, Mary. If you were to betray us—even to James Henry—it could mean St. Mars's life. And, if he were to die, I fear I might die, too."

Mary repeated her assurances, though it was apparent that the notion of keeping a secret from James Henry was unpalatable to her.

"Let us retire to my bedchamber. I cannot feel easy speaking of this anywhere we might be overheard."

They returned to Hester's chamber where, perched on the bed, over the course of an hour Hester haltingly imparted the story of her friendship with St. Mars. It was difficult to know how much to reveal or conceal, but for the moment, she kept to herself the knowledge that St. Mars occasionally assumed the character of a highwayman known as Blue Satan.

Mary was puzzled by some aspects of the history, which could not be fully explained without that important fact, but for now, she had enough to ponder. What she did not understand, and insisted upon knowing, was why she must not admit James Henry into her confidence.

"I cannot be certain that Mr. Henry is convinced of St. Mars's innocence. He was very devoted to the former Lord Hawkhurst, and the evidence implicated St. Mars. We were able to uncover the killer, but most of the evidence against him died with him. There was a letter he sent to Isabella, which might have helped to clear St. Mars, but I fear it was destroyed."

"Could not Isabella testify to its contents?" Mary looked anxious about the answer she would receive.

Hester gave her a rueful smile. "I would not blame your sister. I doubt she could recall it, not when so many gentlemen were courting her at the time. You know her as well as I do."

Hester could see that Mary was hesitant to ask what part her mother had played in these events, but had her suspicions that Mrs. Mayfield's role had not been slight.

"The letter has disappeared, so please do not concern yourself with it. I only mention it so you know that we tried to set everything right. But I never could find it. And now, I believe that St. Mars is reconciled to the loss of his estate. He is not without other resources. He has a smaller estate in France, and that is where he will live." She paused, then added, "That is where I believe him to be now."

She did not add that, if she had not returned with Mary to London, she would have gone with him. Someday, perhaps, she would confide those plans to her cousin, but the disappointment was too recent, her feelings too raw.

"That is all you need to know, and all I am prepared to tell. I just beg you again to guard the secret. I may never see St. Mars again, but if he were to come into England, his life would still be at risk."

Mary repeated her promise, and sensing how tired Hester's confession had made her, kissed her gently on the cheek and bid her goodnight.

Hester undressed and went to bed, exhausted as much by her outpouring of the truth as she had been by the long day of travel. She fell asleep, not knowing whether sharing her burden with Mary had helped to relieve it or not.

So much the Fury still outran the Wit,
The Pleasure missed her, and the Scandal hit.
Who breaks with her, provokes Revenge from Hell,
But he's a bolder man who dares be well.

CHAPTER VII

During the following week, Hester occupied herself with long walks and decorating the house with greenery. Mary kept her company in these pursuits, but she also took advantage of Harrowby's stable for the rides she had missed. Occasionally Isabella, also an excellent horsewoman, joined her, less for the exercise than for the pleasure of wearing her new habit, fashioned after a gentleman's coat and topped by a tricorn hat. Hester had no doubt that once Lord Kirkland came to visit, Isabella's rides would become a daily event.

Occasionally, while walking, they ran into James Henry, who always dismounted and accompanied them on their ramble. The first time this occurred, he was visibly uneasy—embarrassed, Hester suspected, to be reminded of his behaviour on the last occasion Mary had seen him. She was so plainly happy to see him, however, that his reserve soon disappeared, and, despite his efforts to maintain a respectful distance, his joy in her presence was as evident as ever.

Hester took advantage of the first such meeting to ask him about the Reverend Mr. Bramwell. The moment she mentioned his name, James Henry's smile changed into a rueful grimace.

"Yes, that is correct," he said. "My lord did insist that Mr. Bramwell be removed; however, it was not as cruel as it sounds. When I ventured my opinion that the former Lord Hawkhurst would have been very distressed to hear of it, he did consent to make a provision for Mr. Bramwell by offering him different lodgings."

"What sort of lodgings?"

Though always loath to criticize his lord, James Henry gave her a speaking look. "He would have removed him to his property in Northamptonshire; but, eventually, he agreed that the house would be unsuitable for a clergyman of his advanced years."

"I should say it would, if I am correct in assuming that it is little more than a hunting lodge, chilly at best, and unequipped with any comforts! I cannot imagine a frail person like Mr.Bramwell surviving one winter in such a place, especially if it has no library."

"That is more or less what I said to his lordship. He allowed me to inquire among my former lord's acquaintances to see if any would be willing to accept Mr. Bramwell into their homes as long as he received an allowance. Fortunately, on being applied to, Mr. Bramwell himself was able to suggest a possibility, due to the death of one of his clerical colleagues, a correspondent of many years. He wrote the man's patron to propose himself as a replacement and was accepted."

Hester did not need to ask to know that this patron would be a Tory with Stuart sympathies, like the former Lord Hawkhurst. "That was a lucky turn. I hope he has found a sympathetic situation, but a change such as that, after so many years, could not have been easy for him."

"No, I confess, it was painful to see."

By this time, their steps had taken them as far as the old abbey ruins. James Henry amused Mary by pointing out where the various parts of the abbey would have stood. Hester was holding her breath in fear that he had discovered the entrance to the tunnel on his own, but he did not mention it, and the shrubs and vines that hid it were enough to discourage further exploration.

"I suppose I should get one of the men to clear these branches away."

"No!" Hester said. "Please leave them as they are. The ruins are much more romantic for being impenetrable."

James Henry laughed, and his gaze dwelt on Mary, who was petting his horse. "By all means, then, we shall let them remain romantic."

After this first encounter, he met them nearly every day, and from some of the things he and Mary said, Hester gathered that they occasionally met on horseback.

Mrs. Mayfield was kept in the dark about these events. Hester dreaded the moment her aunt would learn of them, but she could not bring herself to put a halt to her cousin's happiness. She was much too fond of Mary, and of James Henry, too. She owed him for many past kindnesses. She also feared that if she tried to stop them from seeing each other, she might spur the feelings that were plainly growing between them. Mary had been infatuated once before and had had the good sense to recognize an unsuitable match. James Henry was as sensible a man as Hester had ever known. She could only hope that the good sense of both would protect them from feelings that could only result in disappointment.

Twice during the first week of their stay, after completing his business with Harrowby, James Henry did sit to dinner with the family. As he was Harrowby's guest, as well as his servant, Mrs. Mayfield was obliged to keep silent on these occasions, but she watched him like a hawk whenever he spoke to Mary. He did not join the family at night, when they had no other entertainment than conversation, games, needlework and reading, though Hester was the only one who applied herself to the last.

The December nights were long and tedious. At Rotherham Abbey, the family kept country hours, wearied by one another's company and the dullness of amusements. Until bedtime every evening, Hester and Mary took turns making the fourth at the card table for Ombre or Whist. The only passionate player was Mrs. Mayfield, but her passion was for gambling, not the strategy of the game. With neither Mary nor Hester possessed of any money to wager, the rest could only play for pennies or pins, which robbed Mrs. Mayfield of any enjoyment. Over the course of a week, she became so tired of the meagre stakes that her temper began to fray.

It erupted one evening shortly after a footman brought Harrowby the post, which had just arrived from London. He interrupted their game to break the seal on a letter.

He perused it first, then before reading it again, exclaimed, "Of all the impertinence! Egad! Who does he think he is to address me in such a fashion?"

Awakened from a state of impassivity, Isabella asked, "Who's the letter from, my love?"

"It is from Sir Horatio Allenby, who has had the impudence to send me a warning!"

"Has he threatened you?" Aware of Sir Horatio's relationship to Lord Ireton, Hester was sincerely alarmed.

"No, it's not a threat. He says, the warning is meant to alert me to Lord Ireton's displeasure.

"Just listen to this: 'My dear Lord Hawkhurst'—Humph! His dear, indeed!—'I am writing to alert you to a private concern, which I fear you may develop after reading the newssheets of this week. You will wonder why you were not invited by my Lord Ireton to the funeral of his recently deceased son, Lord Wragby, as were most of the Whig peers. My lord is aware of the suspicions concerning your servant, Mr. James Henry, in regard to the murder of his son. Although he does not blame you personally for the violence done Lord Wragby, he cannot find it in himself to invite the man giving shelter to his enemy.

"'Let this be a warning that your friendship with my Lord Ireton may be damaged if you persist in harbouring this criminal, which would be a shameful misfortune for your family and any friends who may be seen to sympathize with you in this very grave matter.

"'I assure you that my intentions in the conveyance of this information are both selfless and well-meaning.

"'Yours truly, Sir Horatio Allenby, Bart.'

"There!" Harrowby held out the letter and gave it an indignant shake. "Have you ever heard a greater piece of impertinence?" Despite his brave words, Harrowby looked rattled.

"I tried to tell you, my lord!" Mrs. Mayfield leapt into the conflict, eyes blazing. "I said that you should rid yourself of that ill-mannered servant. Now look at what has happened. Not only will you be shunned by your peers, but the rest of us will suffer a loss of standing as well. Now, who will wed my daughter Mary with Lord Ireton set against her?"

"I do not need Lord Ireton's goodwill to find husband," Mary said with her teeth clenched. "And I suspect that few of his cronies have as fond memories of his son as he does himself. If they do attend Lord Wragby's funeral, it will be with a sense of relief, not of mourning."

"How dare you refer to poor Lord Wragby in that disrespectful tone! Have you no shame for the way you treated him? As devoted to you as he was! Why, there is nothing, I daresay, he would not have done for you. And, instead, you showed favour to a man who was not fit to wipe his boots!"

"Mr. Henry is a hundred times the gentleman Lord Wragby was!" Mary spoke in his defence.

Harrowby cut in, "I do not give a fig for either your or your daughter's standing, madam! Not when you bedevil me with your arguing. All I ask is for a little peace in my house, yet I am continually plagued by pique."

"But, my lord, if you do not care for me or the prospects of my poor daughter, still you must think of yourself and the reputation of your house. Surely you cannot wish to incur the wrath of so powerful a gentleman as Lord Ireton! Why, what if he should challenge you to a duel? How horrible it would be for all of us to lose you, and all for a servant!"

Hester saw that this argument carried weight with Harrowby, especially the prospect of a duel. Lord Ireton was rumoured to have disposed of more than one enemy at the point of a sword.

To redirect his thinking, Hester said, "My lord, Mr. Henry was examined by the magistrate and given leave to go home. In his grief, Lord Ireton may be nourishing an erroneous assumption, which, once reason has reasserted itself, he will reject as the magistrate has."

Ignoring the sounds of disgust coming from her aunt, Hester pressed on, "You know Mr. Henry, my lord. Have you ever known him to err in any way? Is he not the most reasonable and cool-headed of men? Where would we all be without his superior management? Who could you ever trust to take his place?"

Harrowby was wavering between the reassurance in her words and the dire image Mrs. Mayfield had drawn, when his mother-in-law went one step too far. She snorted, "Why, as to who could take his place, I am sure my son Dudley could do at least as well as your Mr. Henry. You have only to summon him, my lord, and he will come to your assistance."

Mary blurted out a most unladylike laugh. Hester did not roll her eyes, but the look she directed at Harrowby was clear enough to convey what she thought of her aunt's suggestion.

Since Harrowby had hosted his brother-in-law for several months in London and had witnessed Dudley's boorishness and temper first hand, his eyes widened in horror. "I forbid you to write to him or to any other of your relations concerning this matter, madam. I shall take care of the problem myself. As Mrs. Kean says, James Henry is more likely to be innocent than not, in which case, if I were to discharge him, I should only do myself harm."

A frown of confusion came over his face. "What I do not understand, however, is why Lord Ireton should suspect James Henry of the murder. How would Ireton have heard of any contretemps in my house?" He glared at his mother-in-law. "You did not speak of it to him, did you?"

Defeated for the moment, Mrs. Mayfield shot a look of loathing at her niece. "No, of course not, my lord. How could I have approached Lord Ireton? He is scarcely aware of my existence."

"Then, pray he stays that way," Harrowby said firmly. "I shall see what his humour is once we are back in London. Till then, I do not wish to be troubled with this subject again."

Mary had remained silent, allowing Hester to defend James Henry after a look from Hester reminded her not to burden her brother-in-law with squabbles. When Harrowby soon retired to bed, fatigued with worry, she sighed and silently gave Hester's hand a grateful squeeze.

They were not to be left in peace. As soon as Harrowby was safely out of earshot, Mrs. Mayfield rounded on them and berated them for a quarter of an hour, listing all their sins from disobedience and disrespect for their elders to arrogance, wilfulness, and deceit.

"And I had better not discover that you have been conversing with that man!" Mrs. Mayfield added as her parting shot. "If I do, I shall marry you off to the first imbecile who can be tricked into offering for you, and Mr. Henry shall see what happens to those who defy me."

She left the room with that threat, the first part of which was not as outrageous as it seemed. Girls had been married off to imbeciles and worse if their families could benefit in any way from the connection.

It was the last statement in her threat that worried Mary, however. She turned to Hester and in a terrified whisper said, "How can we keep her from slandering him? I am so afraid she will do him harm." Tears welled in Mary eyes. "He is so good and kind and selfless, Hester. I have never known anyone like him." She certainly had not, with just her immediate family for examples.

Hester led Mary to her room, where she spent an hour comforting the girl with every fact she knew that would weigh in James Henry's favour. She reminded her that Harrowby had no wish to lose his excellent receiver-general, and that he had repeatedly forbidden her mother to speak disparagingly of him to anyone else.

By the time she bid Mary goodnight and sought her bed, she was exhausted. The bickering and emotion were not the only things that had taken a toll. She was also worried that Harrowby might change his mind when he discovered that Lord Wragby's footmen had been responsible for James Henry's beating. His last question that evening had concerned how Lord Ireton had become aware of the conflict between James Henry and his son. If Harrowby were to pose that question to Lord Ireton or to one of his friends, he would be certain to learn of the beating, and he might leap to the conclusion that either James Henry or Hester—or both— had purposely concealed the fact.

Immersed in these thoughts, Hester was scarcely aware of the steps she took to her bedchamber. Finding herself outside it, she raised the latch then placed her candle safely on the stand just inside, before closing the door behind her. The emotional turmoil of the evening, her concern for James Henry and Mary, and her loneliness overwhelmed her with a sense of despair. Too tired to cover the remaining distance to her bed, she rested her forehead against the wooden door and prayed silently for the strength to carry on. A minute later, she opened her eyes and sighed. She removed the lace cap from her head and reached to unfasten the hooks of her bodice.

"I shouldn't finish that—unless you are willing to let me help."

With a cry, she whirled to see a dark figure stepping out from behind the curtains of her bed. Her hands flew to her mouth to smother a sob. Then she flew across the room to throw herself into St. Mars's arms.

"My love," he whispered. "My dearest love!"

"I was so afraid that I should never see you again." With his arms tightly squeezing her, she raised her hands to his face to gaze upon his beloved features. Even in the dim candlelight, she could see that his eyes were gleaming.

"If I had been assured of such a welcome, I would have come much sooner."

Hester could not help the rush of tears that came. She buried her face in his neck cloth and let the fears of the past few months drain out of her in sobs.

"But what is this? Have I made you unhappy? I am so sorry, my love."

She shook her head, but refused to look up. "How could you forgive me? You must have been furious."

"Yes, I was, but never at you, just at my accursed bad luck. But that is all over now, unless you tell me you cannot be my wife."

Hester felt him hold his breath, as if all his hopes rested upon her answer.

"I shall be your wife the instant we can manage it—" she raised her eyes to meet his— "even if it means a Fleet wedding."

His response was to kiss her longingly and deeply. Hester's fatigue fell away as her senses awakened with lust. With her eyes closed, she was dimly aware of the route his hands travelled, caressing first her neck and then her breasts, before finding their way beneath her skirts. He deftly loosened her petticoat and let it drop to the floor. He held her steady as she stepped out of its hoop. Then, with a moan of desire, he lifted her and laid her on the bed. He quickly stripped off his coat and vest, before lying down beside her,. Then, he pulled her back into his arms and pressed her the length of his body, until they were both breathless and vexed by the layers of cloth between them.

Hester fought for air, certain that her ribs would break. "My lord," she gasped. "I cannot breathe."

He released her, rolling onto his back to cover his face with his hands. He spent a few seconds catching his breath. Then, he said huskily, "My apologies, my dear. I fear, I lost control for a moment."

"No, you mistake me, my lord," she spoke shyly. "I merely require your help with my stays."

St. Mars stilled. Then, with a growing smile, he slowly rolled onto one elbow to search her face. "Are you perfectly certain?"

"As certain as I can be of anything. I believe we are both tired of waiting."

With a growl of pleasure, he gathered her close again, and whispered in her ear, "Well, let me have at these laces of yours. I promise you will never regret it."

Sometime later, long after the candle on the table had burned itself out, they lay entwined with only a glimmer of moonlight peeking through the curtains to illuminate their features. St. Mars had fulfilled his promise, leaving Hester floating in a lazy glow of satiation. As St. Mars slept, his vigour temporarily spent, her eyes traced the contours of his face. She felt happier than she had ever been or, indeed, ever hoped to be. She and her love had become one, and nothing would ever be the same.

After a while, he stirred. He turned on his side and pulled her close to nestle with her back against his chest. His breath tickled the nape of her neck. His hand began to roam, and the hardness between his legs made her gasp.

"Did you know—" his voice was low and sultry in her ear—"it is a proven fact that a woman's need for sex is even greater than a man's?"

"Is that true?" She suppressed a giggle. In her limited experience, St. Mars's needs were clearly a match for hers.

"Um mm, it is an established medical fact. It shall be my duty and pleasure to see that yours are always met."

She couldn't help it. The hum of his voice on her neck tickled too much. Her laughter erupted as she squirmed in his arms.

The moan that issued from him, then, gave her a delicious thrill of power. He clasped her firmly to him until he brought himself under control. "Careful . . . careful, and your patience will be rewarded."

"I have been so rewarded, my dear, that I doubt I shall be able to walk in the morning."

"My poor love! Have I been such a brute?" He loosened his hold to put a few inches between them.

"No, you were gentleness itself, but, remember, I am a novice. It must be like riding a horse. I will have to develop the strength for it."

"Then I shall dedicate myself to training you."

She snorted and would have rapped him with her fan if she had one. "I said *like* riding a horse, not being a horse."

"The same principles apply. The more one exercises, the stronger one grows. We should put my theory to a test."

Laughing, she rolled over to face him. "Agreed, though not just this instant. There is so much I want to know. So Tom sent my message to you? That is why you finally came home?"

She felt more than saw his jerk of surprise. "What message? I came here directly from the coast. I haven't yet been to London. I hoped to find you here to sort everything out between us before another moment passed."

Hester raised a hand to cradle his face. "I am so very happy that you did." She kissed him gently, then said, "I was so miserable without you. I finally arranged a meeting with Tom to learn what news he had of you. And we were both shocked to discover that the other had no news at all."

"I couldn't bring myself to write. But I would have been here a few weeks ago, if the French had not waylaid me."

That startled her. She begged to know what had happened.

He told her that the Regent had sent a small troop to escort him to Paris. "I was afraid they meant to arrest me, but I had to accompany them or risk becoming an outlaw in France, too. It came as a great relief when they conducted me to the Palais Royal and not the Bastille. I was received by the Abbé Dubois, who informed me that under the treaty King George is negotiating, all Jacobites are to be expelled from France."

"But you are not a Jacobite . . . are you?" Hester had never felt that she had the right to ask before, but as his future wife, she thought she ought to know. It would not change how she felt about him, but it would raise a few qualms.

He laughed and squeezed her. "No, my love. Many months ago, I made the decision not to embroil myself in the Pretender's affairs, but that has not stopped his chief supporters from trying to involve me in his plots. Fortunately, James himself decided that I was unworthy to serve him. He did not like it when I tried to discourage him from mounting the rebellion."

Hester thought of teasing him about his prescience, but then she thought of all the men who had lost their lives, the others who had lost their liberty and homes. Something in his voice said that he was thinking of them, too.

"In any case," he continued, "George's spies knew of our meeting. When the Abbé left me to face Lord Stair, I had to tell him the purpose of my journey to Bar-le-Duc and defend myself against his accusations.

"I needn't have wasted my breath, for it became apparent that the threats they had both dangled over me were merely to encourage me to accept a mission of theirs. Lord Stair wanted me to spy on the Pretender in exchange—possibly—for a pardon from King George."

Hester felt as if the air had been sucked from her lungs. She did not know what to say. "Oh . . . ." was the only syllable she could manage. Then, when it seemed he needed more, she asked, "So what reply did you give?"

He reached to tuck a lock of hair behind her ear. "Will you be terribly disappointed to hear that I refused? The offer was tempting, but although I do not think that James Stuart would make a good King of Great Britain, I could not betray him. Not when the right is surely his.

"Besides," he added, "how can I trust George and his ministers when it is clear that they are aware of my innocence, yet they continue to persecute me? I have no doubt it is because they can be assured of Harrowby's complete loyalty and acquiescence. He would never challenge any motion that came from the Crown, whereas my positions are unknown."

Hester answered by snuggling closer to his chest and kissing him on the neck. "I shall never be disappointed when you have made an honourable decision. And I should hate to think of you as a spy! There is something repugnant about the occupation."

"Like lying and deceiving? I doubt I should be convincing in any case. I only manage to lie when I am wearing a mask, and since everyone knows never to trust a masked man, there is a certain honesty in the exchange."

She chuckled. "Well stated, my dear."

"In truth, when I thought of what I have asked you to do, to leave England for a life in a strange country with me, I did consider it. But then I realized how long it might be before I saw you again if I did undertake the commission, and there was only one answer I could give. I was about to leave for England when the soldiers arrived and I was terrified they would keep me from you."

He kissed the top of her head and squeezed her, and she hugged him back, understanding the greatness of his sacrifice, for it was unlikely that the Crown would restore his title now that he had refused to do their bidding.

They lay comfortably in each other's arms before something else occurred to her. She raised her head and found that he was still awake.

"If you came here without speaking to Tom, then you know nothing of the trouble we are having."

"What trouble, my love?"

"I fear that James Henry may be arrested for murder."

He was silent for a moment before responding, "And this distresses you?" His tone was halfway between amusement and resentment.

"Yes, of course it does! Mr. Henry has been very kind to me, so you must listen." Hester pushed herself up and leaned against the bolster to emphasize her seriousness.

"If it means your pulling away from me, I can hardly be expected to sympathize with him." St. Mars sighed and rolled over to prop himself on both elbows. "But you may tell me what he has done."

"Or not done, more like." Hester did her best to explain how James Henry had become Mary's knight in shining armour, when no one else would defend her from Lord Wragby's unwelcome advances. She told him about the incidents between them, one of which had led the magistrate to question him after Lord Wragby was found murdered. And she remembered to add the story of the threat she had heard in the gallery of St. Paul's and her belief that the threat had been intended for Lord Wragby.

St. Mars listened to her at first with a distracted air as if he would have preferred to resume their lovemaking, but she had not got far into her tale before he gave her his full attention. Once she had concluded, he turned himself over again and moved up to sit beside her. He took her hand in his, kissed it lightly then rested it on his leg.

"Do you have any notion of who the real murderer is?"

"Only that it might have been one of the gentlemen I saw in the gallery that day." Hester listed the men she had espied there: Lord Wragby's two companions and Lord Ireton and his friends, adding, "Lord Ireton was not at all pleased to see his son in the company of two Tories." She told St. Mars of her and Mary's subsequent encounter with Lord Wragby on Coronation Day, and repeated the disloyal remarks he had made. "Lord William Silsbee and Sir Horatio were there, too. They tried to hush him. I had the distinct impression that Lord Ireton had sent them to keep a watch on his son."

"He must certainly have been an embarrassment. I can imagine what my father would have felt if I had praised King George at a Stuart court." St. Mars tilted towards her and traced her breasts with his finger. "Very well, my love, if it is important to you and to Mary to spare my half-brother from the gallows, I shall help you discover the murderer. But I will be doing this for you and not for him."

"If I truly believed that, you would not find it so easy to seduce me." She sank down onto the feather mattress and gave herself over to his caresses, leaving more sober matters to another day.

St. Mars left her an hour before dawn, with the promise that he would return every night. He told her to light a candle and to move it back and forth in her window after the servant had made up the fire and there was no longer any risk of their being interrupted. He would await her signal in the ruins before entering the tunnel.

"I hate to think of your waiting out in the cold. I may not be able to leave the drawing room early on many nights without arousing suspicion."

He kissed her lingeringly before pushing himself off the bed. "Thoughts of you will keep me warm."

Then he was gone, and before she could have believed possible, Hester fell into a deep sleep from which she did not awaken until a maid came in to see if she was ill. The fire in her hearth had long ago died out, and since Hester was always one of the first members of the household to rise of a morning, Mary had worried when she had not come down to breakfast.

If not for a distinct ache between her legs, Hester might have believed she had dreamed it all. The deep sense of wellbeing that filled her could have been the result of a dream, but St. Mars's lovemaking had left evidence of his passion. Hester told the maid that she had simply overslept and asked her to bring a pitcher of hot water as soon as she had remade the fire. Then, when the water had been fetched, she bathed, wondering how she would hide her feelings of immense joy from the family.

She found that most of them, even Mary, were too absorbed with their own concerns to notice her dreamy state. She felt so languid that it was hard to move. Every word that was uttered, every object she rested her eyes upon made its impression through the screen of her blissful night with St. Mars.

When, at dinner, Mrs. Mayfield remarked in her peevish way that Hester was more than usually stupid, she felt only a desire to laugh. Her aunt would never have the power to reduce her to despair again, for her life with St. Mars had begun. Hester understood now what it meant for two people to become one. She would never have to face anything alone again.

In the afternoon, when she and Mary were out walking and she was not attending, Mary did ask her impatiently once, "Are you quite all right?"

Hester shook the wool from her head. "Yes, I just feel a bit slow today. It must have been the scene before bed last night. I did not get as much sleep as usual."

Even with the trees bare of their leaves and the lawns and park grey, Hester found the countryside beautiful. She had to pinch herself to believe that St. Mars had given up a chance to regain not only Rotherham Abbey, but all his father's other estates, in his haste to come to her.

"I was saying how worried I am that Lord Ireton will prevail upon Harrowby to dismiss Mr. Henry. Harrowby seems so afraid of Lord Ireton."

Hester had worried about this, too, but today nothing looked as grim as it had the day before. Turning to Mary, she took hold of both her hands and gave them an encouraging shake. "Yes, Harrowby is a bit of a coward, but I promise to use all my influence with him to avoid such an outcome, not only for Mr. Henry's sake, but for the Hawkhurst estates. What we need to do is discover who really killed Lord Wragby, so Mr. Henry can be cleared of suspicion."

"But how can we do that?" Frustrated and angry, Mary was near tears.

"I do not know precisely, but if we keep our eyes and ears open, I am sure we shall learn of others who had a motive for killing him."

Mary laughed ruefully. "Of course we shall! I had one myself. But how are two females supposed to prove anything?"

Hester took her arm and drew her back towards the house. "Somehow we will do it. You must promise not to despair, and I promise, we shall not be as helpless as you think."

Superiors? death! and Equals? what a curse!
But an Inferior not dependent? worse!
Offend her, and she knows not to forgive;
Oblige her, and she'll hate you while you live:
But die, and she'll adore you—Then the Bust
And Temple rise—then fall again to dust.
Last night, her Lord was all that's good and great;
A Knave this morning, and his Will, a Cheat.
Strange! by the Means defeated of the Ends,
By Spirit robbed of Power, by Warmth of Friends . . . .

CHAPTER VIII

That evening, Hester could hardly wait for the others to go to bed. She would have left the drawing room earlier, if not for the need to protect Mary from her mother's tongue. It would have been cruel to leave the girl with no one to defend her, so she waited until Isabella's yawning put an end to the evening before seeking her chamber. To avoid suspicion, she asked the maid to help with her laces, before carrying her candle to the window and moving it left and right to alert St. Mars that his passage was clear.

His caresses were even more tender and giving than the night before. Under this treatment, Hester's passion reached new heights, and she lay against him afterwards in a daze of wonder.

He was the first to break into their contented silence. "It has occurred to me, my love, that these activities, as pleasurable as they are, could lead to consequences. I should like for us to marry as soon as possible."

She was grateful for his consideration, and chastised herself for being so much in love that she had neglected every practicality. She realized that even now she could be carrying his child. "I am happy to go with you at any time. You have only to tell me when."

"Even with James Henry's troubles unresolved?"

Hester winced. She had just that day made a promise to Mary, and she had never reneged on a promise. She told him what she had said to her cousin, then said, "But I will never again put another's happiness before yours. If you wish to leave for France tonight, I will do it, and you need not fear that I shall rue the decision."

He laughed, but she knew her answer had pleased him. "I would gladly ride off with you this instant, but for now we are quite comfortable here. In honesty, I would not like to subject you to a winter crossing. The seas are much too dangerous. Lately, the winds have been so fierce that several ships have been lost along the coast." He enveloped her in his arms. "And I am not willing to lose you, now that I have you."

"And I had rather not drown." She raised her gaze to his face. "But if I should fall pregnant?"

"Then we shall make our way to the Fleet to say our vows. It is not the most appealing place, but it is much nearer than Scotland, and the winter would make it difficult for us to travel so far without the risk of being stopped."

Hester felt a thrill of excitement. He felt her shake and mistook it for a shiver of disgust. "It would be just a temporary solution. We can repeat our vows as soon as we are in France. Or, if necessary, we could travel to Holland."

"I should hope so! But I was not at all offended. I was just thinking how scandalized my father would have been. He always believed Jeremy to be his reprobate child, but even Jeremy got married in a church.

"But," she added, "I have just thought of something . . . an alternative, perhaps." She told him about the Reverend Mr. Bramwell and how he had been sent to live with one of the former Lord Hawkhurst's friends. "Even if he marries us without a license, at least we shall know we are married in the sight of God. Nothing else matters to me."

He approved the notion, and moments passed before they spoke again. St. Mars was still propped atop her, applying kisses to her breasts, when he said, "When you return to London, I will follow. I shall need to see Tom." Seriousness had entered his voice. "He will never come to France, you know. I shall need to make some provision for him and

Katy to live here. He will need employment."

Hester gently stroked St. Mars's head, conveying the sympathy she felt with her touch. It would be as hard for him to leave his faithful servant, as it would be for Tom to see him go. Tom had stuck by his master through all his trials. If not for his aid, St. Mars might have been hanged. "It is good that he has Katy," she said. "When I saw them, it was clear that they are very happy together."

Changing the subject, she said, "And while you are taking care of Tom, I shall do what I can to discover Lord Wragby's murderer."

"I do intend to help you. Our only difficulty now will be in finding a satisfying place to meet. Somehow, I cannot see us being quite as content with a church pew as we were before." He teased one of her nipples with his teeth.

She giggled. "No, my dearest lord, I, too, find it hard to imagine. You may have to take new lodgings next to Hawkhurst House."

"Now, there is a notion I like!"

For the next few weeks, Hester led a double life, trying to maintain peace in her family during the day and delighting in her time with St. Mars at night. Mindful of the risk of pregnancy, she used a sponge soaked in vinegar, a trick that Isabella had confided to her when she needed Hester to pick up sponges at the shop. She was obliged to sneak them from Isabella's supply and hoped she would not notice that any were missing.

St. Mars employed his own methods. When she asked him where he had learned them, he teased her awhile before assuring her that the information was widely spread at the Court of France.

The late winter dawn gave Hester a few hours each day to catch up on her sleep. Mary always took an early ride, and in the morning no one else in the family attended to anything except the clothes they would wear that day.

The newssheets from London arrived with the post, informing them of which Jacobite prisoners had been released, which had died in Newgate of gaol fever, and which had been tried for treason. Three printers had been found guilty of printing the Jacobite newssheet, *The Shift Shifted,* but as they had only printed it and the publisher could not be proven, two were punished only with a fine. One Mr. Isaac Dalton, however, was so defiant during his trial, insisting that there was no harm in the papers, that he was sentenced to the pillory and a year of gaol in addition to the fine.

The news that Mr. Charles Radcliffe, Esq., brother to the late Earl of Derwentwater who had been executed for treason, had escaped from Newgate led Harrowby to surmise that someone in the government must have helped him.

The most shocking news they received, however, was that Viscount Townsend had been asked to resign the Seals as his Majesty's principal Secretary of State. He had been given the post of Lord Lieutenant of Ireland, a clear indication that the King was displeased. He was to be replaced by Mr. Stanhope, who would be made Earl of Sussex.

The change gave the family something to gossip about. Clearly the intrigues that had worried Lady Cowper, confided to Hester on Coronation Day, had produced this result. The ministry was certain to be divided before the King returned from Hanover.

The first day of Christmas came with the exchange of gifts. Hester gave her aunt a new deck of playing cards, decorated and printed with illustrations of the glorious victories of the reign of her late Majesty Queen Anne. She received a grim collection of sermons in return. The author was a clergyman who often preached on the duties of servants to their masters.

Isabella admired the lace that Hester had obtained for her in York, and Hester was grateful for the fur-lined hood from Isabella and Harrowby. A box of Harrowby's favourite snuff and a chicken-skin fan for Mary were Hester's other gifts. Mary gave her the second volume of Mr. Gay's *Trivia,* explaining that she had got it several weeks ago by asking James Henry to purchase it from Jeremy.

It distressed Hester that she had no present for St. Mars, but even in her dreams, the last thing she had expected was to see him at Rotherham Abbey. That night, he persuaded her that the love she had given him made him happier than any mere object, and since she felt the same about his, she was easily convinced.

The next day, Isabella's guests arrived to enliven their solitude— Lord Kirkland, the first of their friends to adopt new fashions, who appeared in a new looped wig, white with powder, and his cousin, Sir Marmaduke Ensley, a rotund fop. They came with the intention of staying for the remainder of their hosts' sojourn in Kent, bringing a book just published entitled, *Twenty-Four New Country Dances for the Year 1717,* and promising to teach them all the steps before their return to Court. They also carried the news from London that the Princess of Wales had appeared at the Royal Chapel at St. James's for the first time since her lying-in and that she had dined in public with the Prince, also that Mr. Secretary Stanhope, though still in Hanover, had purchased the estate of the former Earl of Sussex.

Lord Kirkland relieved Mary and Hester of the obligation of making the fourth at cards, raising the wagers to a level that satisfied even Hester's aunt. Sir Marmaduke, who declared himself hopeless at cards, proved to be an entertaining guest. While the others played for exorbitant amounts, he amused Hester and Mary with children's games and gossip. If Hester had not been so eager to see St. Mars, she would have enjoyed his chatter without reservation. The presence of guests made it difficult for the family to squabble, but it also made it hard for her to retire as early as she would like.

The daily newssheets supplied them with topics of conversation. Since her voice was so clear, Hester was appointed to read them aloud every evening. The negotiations for peace with France and Holland went on at The Hague, with the Abbé Dubois and Lord Stair representing their respective monarchs. The Swedes were poised to invade Norway as soon as the winds became favourable to their fleet. Europe was still at war with the Turks. And the Russian tsar had shown signs of relaxing his hold on Mecklenburg. These developments did not inspire much discussion, but matters of more immediate interest to the company did.

The Court at Hanover was reported to be numerous, and King George had postponed his return to England until the middle of January. As a consequence, Parliament would not sit until the seventeenth of that month. While Hester secretly delighted in the time this would give her with St. Mars, other members of the family were displeased. Though not truly interested in political debate, Harrowby did enjoy the social life that Parliament gave rise to. He complained that now many peers would not return to town until duty summoned them, though he could not imagine what they found to do in the country beyond a little shooting.

With guests, he was obliged to ride out every day, but as he took little pleasure in hunting, he relied upon his gamekeeper to fill the pot. Lord Kirkland and his cousin were of a similar bent. The principal charm the country afforded the first was a chance to carry on a flirtation with Isabella.

Not long after the two gentlemen arrived, one newssheet carried a report from Avignon, where the Pretender still lived, refusing to leave that city until the Pope demanded it. The Pope had written to the Chevalier de St. George, James Stuart, that the most recent funds he had sent to support him and his court had been retrenched from the fund established for his Holiness's own table. While this spoke of the Pope's devotion to the Chevalier, it was taken as a sign that his followers would soon be reduced to poverty if they continued there. Many were leaving Avignon to seek their fortunes in some other monarch's service.

Only a few days later, in the evening as they sat in the drawing room, Hester read that the Chevalier's mother, the Queen Dowager of England, was to be given an eight-month pension by the Court of France in exchange for her agreement to depart the kingdom. It was predicted that she would return to her own country of Modena, at which time her dowry to King James would be returned to her. Already eight waggon loads of her furnishings had been taken to Avignon from St. Germain, where she had held court since her husband's ouster, including the rich tapestries given to her by King Louis XIV of France.

The four at the card table, Harrowby, Isabella, Lord Kirkland and Mrs. Mayfield continued to play, while Sir Marmaduke and Mary listened more attentively.

Hester read on, "'They say here, that notwithstanding the Opposition of the Court of Rome, the said Chevalier must depart from Avignon in the Spring.'"

"Aha!" Sir Marmaduke sprang up and clapped his hands. He turned to address the card players. "That means, the peace will soon be concluded. Now, we can all make our plans to journey to Paris this summer. Who will go with me?"

"I will!" Isabella declared from the table, "as long as it is not too far. I cannot abide a long carriage ride, but I should love to see the fashions in Paris before everyone else at Court."

"It is not as far as from here to York, my dear," Harrowby said, cheered by the prospect. He laid down a card and took the trick. "At least, I do not think so. And some of the journey is by boat, of course. We could rest as long as you like in Calais before making the latter half."

A conversation about the new hairpieces that ladies were wearing in Paris followed, while Hester silently read on, skipping over news of the Dutch lottery, which would soon be drawn. Then her eyes lit upon the following: *This Morning, the Corps of the Viscount Wragby, son of the Marquess of Ireton, was carried out of Town to be interr'd at Kineton Castle in Warwickshire.*

Hester was grateful for the banter floating about her while she weighed whether or not to convey the news to the company. In the end she did, thinking it safer to raise Lord Wragby's name while guests were present to moderate her aunt's reaction. As soon as she was begged to resume her reading, therefore, she imparted it.

Sir Marmaduke tut-tutted. "His father must be grieved to lose his only son, but one knew that something like this was bound to occur with the company Lord Wragby kept."

Mary blanched. In a touchy voice, Harrowby asked, "Whatever do you mean?"

Alarmed, Sir Marmaduke sent Mary a pleading look, then recovered. "Oh, present company excluded, my lord, of course! I was referring to the viscount's more questionable connections. He would associate with Sir Francis Lichfield, which must have caused his father no end of despair. You must have heard of their most recent exploit?"

His pride assuaged, Harrowby said, "Do you mean that business of the club? What did they call it? 'The Brotherhood of the Damned' or some such nonsense?"

"Yes, and it is hard to imagine a more unsavoury name." Sir Marmaduke turned coy. "One has heard of such scandalous proceedings."

"What sort of scandalous proceedings?" Mary glanced pointedly at her mother.

Sir Marmaduke eagerly returned to sit beside her on the settee and lowered his voice. "Well, this is just rumour, you know, but I have heard of things like mock religious ceremonies with harlots robed like nuns."

"For shame!" Mrs. Mayfield spoke up. "You should not speak so ill of the dead!"

Sir Marmaduke gave Mary a wink. "My apologies, madam! If you prefer, I shall confine my subject to Sir Francis, who has a certain reputation with the female sex."

His mind still half on his play, Harrowby snorted. "A fine companion for a Whig gentleman!"

"As to that, my lord, are you certain Lord Wragby was of the same political persuasion as his father? There are more than just rumours to the contrary."

As one, the players turned to look at Sir Marmaduke, except for Isabella, who continued to frown over her hand, clearly too confused by it to pay any attention to their gossip.

"Nonsense!" Mrs. Mayfield said. "I am certain his poor lordship was a loyal Whig. This will be gossip put about by Lord Ireton's enemies. You are seeing their influence now at Court."

"But it is true, is it not, Hester?" Mary said. "You recall the disloyal comments he made at the Coronation Day celebration? He was praising the Pretender and denouncing King George."

"Mary, you shall not lie about Lord Wragby in my presence!"

Harrowby glared at his mother-in-law. "What have I said about this endless argument? Madam, you are blind where that gentleman is concerned. I have heard of his disloyalty myself. Will you now accuse me of lying?"

Reddening, Mrs. Mayfield bit her tongue. "Of course not, my lord! Anything you say must be the truth. My only concern is as a mother. I would not have Mary speak on matters that do not concern a girl of her age." She gritted her teeth, sending Mary a venomous look. Then turning to Lord Kirkland with a honeyed smile, she said, "I believe it is your turn to play, my lord."

Sir Marmaduke took the hint that Lord Wragby was not a welcome subject of conversation in his hosts' house, and deftly introduced another by challenging Hester and Mary to a game of spillikins.

Hester begged to be excused, claiming that reading by candlelight had strained her eyes. She bid the company goodnight and retired to her chamber to signal to St. Mars.

He came with his usual alacrity, but Hester noticed hints of fatigue. His blue eyes were tinged with red, and he suppressed a number of yawns. When they had made their way into the bed, she challenged him. "I believe you have worn yourself out, coming here every night, my lord." She knew that the journey from the inn near Smarden, where he stayed, took him nearly an hour in the dark and an equal time to return.

He waved off her concern. "I am never too tired to lie with you. Nothing could make me happier."

She coaxed him to rest his head on her breast. "How much sleep are you getting?"

He chuckled. "Not much, I admit. Lade's inn is not the quietest place during the day. He has a tendency to yell at his servants."

"Well, I should be very glad this evening if you will get some sleep." He relaxed against her, content to use her breast for his pillow. Before he nodded off, however, she told him what Sir Marmaduke had said about the Brotherhood of the Damned. "With such frivolities, there might have been someone else with a motive to kill Lord Wragby."

"Like half the clergy in the Church of England?" His yawn alerted her that he would not be awake much longer.

"We shall put them on our list of suspects." She smiled as his weight increased.

"Excellent idea, my dear. I shall trust you to do it."

That was the last she heard from him until several hours later when his stirring woke her. He got out of bed and lit a candle to check his watch for the time.

"I should leave in another hour." He climbed back in with her and pulled the covers snug around them. "I should inform you first that my energy is fully restored."

She laughed and invited him to put it to use, however he saw fit.

He complied and when they were done, she said, "How I wish you did not have to go!"

"I know, my love. It is hard for me, too, but in a few months we should have all our business sorted and be able to go for good. You will not regret it?"

"Regret leaving my aunt? Of course, that may break my heart, but I shall strive never to reproach you for forcing me to do it."

"Seriously now!"

"Then, seriously, I expect to live in such bliss that I shall forget that I was ever born in England."

"I suppose I shall have to be satisfied with that answer." He kissed her before sitting up on the edge of the bed. "We do not have many days left before you'll be taking the road to London."

"No, very few in fact." This idyll of theirs was coming to an end, but it should not be for long. "I hope you will be careful when you follow. I read that a regiment is being sent to the coast to await the King's return. You must not run into them."

"I shall be alert, as always." She heard the smile in his voice. He always teased that she worried about him too much.

Gideon left her later than usual that morning, reluctant to forfeit even a second of their precious time together. Eventually, however, Hester's anxiety that he would be seen overcame his reluctance, and he started his journey through the tunnel to the old abbey ruins. As he reached the bottom of the narrow stairs behind the carved wooden wall, the light from her candle disappeared and he heard the click of the latch. As always, she had insisted on waiting until he was safely down before extinguishing her candle, though the light from his own would have sufficed.

He paused for a moment to allow his eyes to adjust to the fainter illumination before making his way down the dank corridor, but his steps along it were confident. After using it for a fortnight, he was familiar with every stone in the floor. The earthen walls, though damp, provided shelter from the wind and the temperature below ground was warmer than the outside air.

In a few minutes, he emerged from behind the growth of vines that concealed the other entrance. From here, he would set off on foot to the spot where he had hobbled his horse. He was mildly alarmed to find that dawn had already broken and congratulated himself on the foresight that had made him conceal his mount in a thicket. If any of the servants or labourers were about, they would notice the presence of a strange horse and investigate. As it was, if he had not known the Abbey lands like the palm of his hand, he would have had trouble concealing it from the gamekeeper.

Gideon was about to step past one of the damaged walls when he heard a voice say sharply, "What was that?"

He froze, as a second person responded, "What?"

"Did you not hear the stirring of leaves?"

He held his breath. It seemed the others did, too, as they listened for more noise.

Finally, the second voice Gideon had a heard—a woman's, and somehow familiar—said teasingly, "It must have been the Hawkhurst ghost."

More cautious, her companion hesitated, before replying in a voice that revealed him to be James Henry, "I thought I had assured you that there are no ghosts in these ruins."

Gideon was astonished by the tenderness and indulgence in his tone. He had never thought James Henry capable of such emotions. He exhaled quietly, fearfully of being discovered, but as the woman spoke, he recognized the voice of Mrs. Mary Mayfield and realized that he was not the only person here dreading discovery.

"How can I be sure that you did not say that just to lure me here?"

The minx! Gideon thought, smiling. What would her mama say?

He was surprised again by James Henry's laugh. "I suppose I *would* tell a fib to get you to myself."

"If it were necessary, I hope you would," Mary teased. Then her tone turned serious. "But you must know that it is not."

Gideon squirmed. He did not like listening to such an intimate conversation and hoped he would not have to much longer, but he dared not move. He did not know how James Henry would react if he saw him. He might alert the law that the escaped Viscount St. Mars, accused of murder, and with a price on his head, had dared return to the scene of his crime.

Even if he managed to escape James Henry, it would not be without wounding him, which would not help his case. And Mary knew him as Sir Robert Mavors, the gentleman who had visited her family in Yorkshire. If she and James Henry compared stories, which they surely would, his real and his false identities would be linked, and he might lose his refuge in Lambeth and the freedom to move about London.

But it seemed that the two on the other side of the wall were so entranced with each other that the likelihood of his being discovered was slight. He just had to be patient until they moved away. He heard the jingle of a bridle, which told him that at least one of them had ridden to their rendezvous. He tried not to listen to their words, but he heard enough to learn that they were in love and that neither had any hope that Mrs. Mayfield would countenance a match between them.

He tried to recall Mary's age and knew that it would be several years before she could assert any control over her choice. No parent could force a child to marry against her will, but intolerable pressures were often brought to bear and usually the offspring of unmovable people were persuaded to give in.

Gideon wondered if Hester knew of the attraction between them. Surely she would have told him if she did. As he listened to the two lovers in the dawn and heard the same yearning in their voices that he and Hester had felt, he could sympathize. He certainly bore Mary no ill will, and he found, that in spite of his resentment towards James Henry, something made him hope that Mrs. Mayfield could be thwarted. Perhaps it was simply that his resentment towards her was even greater, but his heart was so full now with love that he suspected it was something else.

Eventually, after saying their goodbyes and promising to meet again on the morrow, the two rode off. Gideon waited awhile before emerging from his hiding place and used all the cover he could find to conceal his progress towards his horse.

It was with relief that he left all sight of Rotherham Abbey behind and made his way to the ramshackle inn under the sign of the Fox and Goose in the Weald near Smarden. The stable-boy, Avis, came out to take charge of his horse.

"I thought mebbe you wasn't gonna make it back," the boy said, with a curious look.

"Yes, I'm a bit later today." Gideon handed him the reins. "He was hobbled half the night and the grazing was poor, so you should feed him some oats."

"'Sir. Will you be takin' 'im out again tonight?"

Gideon nodded, hiding a smile. Both Avis and his master Lade lived in hope that he would tell them of his adventures. They both believed him to be a highwayman, but he paid them enough to keep them quiet. They would be disappointed to hear how he had spent the past fortnight.

"See that he rests, and have him saddled at the usual hour."

Gideon managed to avoid Lade on the way up to his chamber, where he threw off his clothes and caught a few hours of sleep. When he was awakened by hunger, it was past noon, The smell of stewing mutton was seeping beneath his door, and he heard Lade moving about in the taproom downstairs. At the thought of mutton again for breakfast, he groaned, but he dragged himself to his feet and, after splashing cold water on his face—left in the pitcher from yesterday—he dressed to go down. The icy feel of the water, the empty grate in his room, and the sad condition of his clothes had him—not for the first time—bemoaning Tom's absence.

He would have to get used to living without Tom; but in France, at least, he could be assured of competent servants. It was Tom, himself, he would miss. If he would not be gaining Hester's companionship, he doubted he could have given up his groom.

In the taproom Lade was brooding over a tankard of beer. He looked up when Gideon walked through the door. "Thought ye was goin' to sleep till the cows come home. What'll it be?"

"Some bread and cheese first with my beer. Then we'll see about the mutton stew."

"Ye're goin' to waste away, ridin' all night, if ye don't put some o' that stew down." Lade yelled for the new wench he had hired to bring

Gideon his breakfast, while he drew a tankard of small beer. "Have any luck last night?"

Gideon tried not to smile. "It was a good night, yes."

Lade slapped the beer on the bar and slid it Gideon's way. "Then, 'ow come I don't 'ear nothin' 'bout any excitement round 'ere?"

Gideon picked up his drink and carried it to a table near the fire. As usual, the room was empty, which made him wonder how Lade would support himself without his tenancy. "I conduct my business as far from here as I can get. And what does it matter what you hear, as long as I pay you? You should be grateful that I do not draw attention to your house."

Lade thought for a second, then shrugged. "'Ave it your way."

He went back to his brooding, leaving Gideon to enjoy his breakfast in peace. While he digested the cheese and bread, he thought about the task that he had promised Hester to undertake. They would both be back in town soon, and it would be time to discover what he could about the murder of Lord Wragby. He hoped to resolve the puzzle shortly so they could make the journey to France in the spring. He would like to take her to his estate of St. Mars in time to enjoy their first summer together there.

Finding a boat to take them across the Channel even in springtime was not going to be as easy as he had led her to believe. The newssheets had reported that an owler, a smuggler, had shot and killed one of the King's excise men. Gideon had no doubt that the watch along the coast would have been doubled, at least temporarily. He had been forced to rely on owlers to take him into France, for he did not have the passport one needed to travel lawfully, but he knew how desperately smugglers could behave. When the laws prescribed death for even appearing to be a smuggler—for blackening one's face to avoid being spotted at night—an owler would always kill rather than be caught.

Gideon would have to find a safer way to take Hester across. He hoped he could do that while searching for Lord Wragby's murderer.

"'Ow much longer are ye goin' to drag yer 'eels 'ere this time, eh?" Lade asked sullenly. "Don't 'is Majesty 'ave anythin' better fer ye to do?"

By 'his Majesty', Lade meant James Stuart. He had convinced

himself that he was a warrior in the Pretender's cause and that Gideon was a Jacobite, too. Gideon had used Lade's fantasy more than once to elicit his aid.

"I'll be going up to London in a couple of days."

"Oh, yeh?" Lade looked up, his gloom forgotten in the hope of being useful to the cause. "Goin' up to recruit some soldiers for 'im, are ye?"

Finishing his beer, Gideon did not reply. He refused to lie outright to Lade, finding it easier to let Lade answer his own questions. But the suggestion that he might be going to London to recruit troops for the Pretender sparked an idea. Gideon put his tankard down and turned on his stool to face the innkeeper.

"With so many Jacobites in prison, it's getting hard to find good recruits. One must be careful. George's spies are everywhere."

Lade took up his tankard to come eagerly round from the bar. Without asking for permission, he sat himself down at Gideon's table and leaned close to whisper, "That's 'cause ye don't know the best places to look, see?"

Gideon eased back on his stool to avoid Lade's bad breath, which reeked of stale beer. "If you mean Ozinda's coffee house, none of James's men will go there since Ozinda was arrested."

Lade barked a laugh. "If ye think that's the only place to find men loyal to 'is Majesty, then it's no wonder ye've been 'angin' round 'ere. Why, when I were in London, I knew 'eaps o' places where they were's thick as thieves."

Putting on a dubious face, Gideon shook his head. "I don't know, Lade. It's been a few years since you were up in London." He did not want to appear too eager for the innkeeper's information or he would surely have to pay for it.

Lade scoffed. "But I knows the keepers of all them taverns, don't I? I used to work in one of 'em. The King's 'Ead, weren't it, in Ivy Lane. Why, Mr. Barradell, he's as loyal as you or me! And the master of the Duke of Albemarle's 'Ead in St. John's Square, he used to pass notes fer 'is Majesty's spies. Just ye go and 'ave a look at them ale-houses. They'll be far enough away from St. James's to be safe. And ye'll find 'is Majesty some soldiers or my name's not Percival Lade."

Keeping his expression sceptical, Gideon thanked him all the same. If two of Lord Wragby's friends were Jacobites, he would need to work his way into their confidence to find out how deeply Lord Wragby had been involved in the cause. It would be better to approach them where Jacobites gathered. As yet, he did not know where they lodged, and it would be awkward for Hester to inquire about the addresses of two gentlemen.

Discovering where they lived and what they were up to must necessarily fall to him.

Or shall we every Decency confound,
Through Taverns, Stews, and Bagnios take our round,
Go dine with Chartres, in each Vice outdo
K—l's lewd Cargo, or Ty—y's Crew,
From Latian Syrens, French Circean Feasts,
Return well travelled, and transformed into Beasts,
Or for a Titled Punk, or foreign Flame,
Renounce our Country, and degrade our Name?

CHAPTER IX

Before the Hawkhurst household left for London, news that the great peace had been signed reached Rotherham Abbey. Hester celebrated with her family and their guests, drinking toasts to King George and the Regent of France. Hester would always be glad for peace. There would be some opposition to the treaty on both sides of the channel, but for now, at least, the threat of another rebellion in Great Britain, financed by the French, was no longer a concern. She did not know what it would mean for St. Mars or the crossing they would soon make, but it seemed to her that the King's navy would not have to be as vigilant in the channel as before.

Parting from St. Mars was achingly painful, but this time she knew that it would not be forever. They said their goodbyes, longingly and lovingly, until Hester's fear that St. Mars would be caught out by the dawn outweighed her regret at his leaving.

The bustle of packing up their belongings for a return to Hawkhurst House kept her very busy, and memories of her long nights with St. Mars filled her mind. So it was not until they were seated in the carriage and on their way that she noticed something different about Mary.

For the first several minutes of the journey, Mary looked out of the window at the retreating view of the house. When it was entirely out of sight, she heaved a big sigh. "How I hate having to return to London. I much prefer the country, and Kent must be the most beautiful county of all."

She displayed a strange sort of melancholy for a place she had only visited for a few weeks. At times, she looked as dreamy as Hester felt, and occasionally a secretive smile touched her lips. Catching herself on occasion, she looked guiltily about as if to see if anyone had noticed. Fortunately, Mrs. Mayfield's view was blocked by Hester, who had to occupy the middle seat, and Harrowby and Isabella were engrossed in discussing the new wig Harrowby was determined to order before the next drawing room at St. James's.

Once, she did catch Hester eyeing her curiously and blushed. Hester felt her heart sink when she guessed at the reason. She was almost certain that James Henry had made Mary a declaration of love, and if she read Mary's emotions correctly, then it appeared that his love was returned. She dreaded the scenes that would ensue when Mrs. Mayfield found out, and it might not be long before she did. As soon as they arrived in London, she was certain to start scheming again for her daughter to make a brilliant match. Knowing her cousin as well as she did, Hester had no doubt that Mary would inform her mother of her wishes in no uncertain terms.

Though she would support Mary in her choice, Hester did fear her aunt's reaction for the toll it would exact from James Henry. She must be prevented from doing him harm until the real murderer could be found. The only way Hester saw to do this was to prevail upon Mary to keep her secret awhile longer. Surely, if she feared for James Henry's safety, she would agree.

⅌

Having left the Fox and Goose earlier that morning, Gideon rode to his house at Lambeth, reminding himself occasionally to keep an eye out for troops on the road. King George's coaches and carriages had been sent to Harwich and Margate to await his arrival. He would only stop in Holland until the winds were favourable, so his appearance was looked for any time after the middle of the month.

Gideon made it to Lambeth without incident. He turned his mount through the gate to his small holding with its modest house and outbuildings, which overlooked the Thames with a view of the Millbank. He briefly paused his horse to see what changes Tom had made during his absence and noted repairs to the stables and brew house. The place looked neat and tidy, though the kitchen garden was bare for now.

A large greyhound dog came out of the stable, ready to chase an intruder off, but as soon as Gideon greeted Argos by name, the dog's tail began to wag. He gambolled about Gideon's horse, barking for joy to announce the return of his master, then came to be petted the moment Gideon dismounted. In the next instant, Tom and Katy rushed out of the house to greet him. Tom's face was overcome with relief and Katy beamed as she curtsied. Gideon suspected that Tom had fretted so constantly as to drive her to distraction.

Gideon had smiled the entire length of his journey, feeling a deep contentment he had never known before, and the pleasure of being welcomed so warmly stretched his lips even further. In the first few moments of their greeting, he did not notice the smaller figure hidden behind Katy's skirts, but eventually a slight movement caught his eye.

Seeing the direction of his gaze, Katy turned and wrapped her arm about a frightened boy to draw him forward.

"Go on. It's all right," she said. "But you must make your bow. 'Tis the master, but he won't hurt you."

The child's eyes were round with fear, two circles of white in a black face. Without thinking, Gideon fell to one knee and took the boy by the hand. He was dressed in a new homespun suit with good leather shoes.

"Of course, I won't hurt you," Gideon said, in his gentlest voice. Turning to Tom with a questioning look, he said, "Who is this? How did he come here?"

Tom looked uncomfortable. "Well, y'see, it was Katy, my lord. When we found him by the river—freezing he was—she said we couldn't leave him there to starve. So we brung him back here and gave him a bit to eat and a place to sleep, and he slept as if he'd been awake for three days straight. I didn't think you'd mind."

Gideon turned back to the boy with a smile. "I do not mind in the least. That was the right thing to do." He reached to pat the boy on the head, but the child flinched as if afraid of being struck.

"It's all right, boy." With a hint of exasperation, Tom echoed his wife's words. "The master won't never hit you. Now be a good boy and run back inside. I expect Mrs. Barnes's got a treat for you in her kitchen."

Katy wrapped her arm around the boy again and, with a grateful look at Gideon, ushered him back inside the house.

Gideon stood and grimaced ruefully at Tom. "He's somebody's servant, you know. You will have to return him."

Tom nodded. "I told her the same, my lord, and she didn't like it one bit. It's plain, the boy's been beaten—you saw how he flinched. And he's like that all the time. Believe me, it took a good fortnight before he could be brung to trust me. And he's such a little thing that her heart just aches at the thought of him being hurt."

"If you are caught keeping him, you could be tried for a thief. Katy, too."

Tom shrugged, but his face betrayed his fears. "I told her that, my lord. She says we can watch the advertisements to see if anybody posts about a runaway boy, but we shouldn't go looking for his owner. We've been reading the newssheets, but we haven't seen nothing yet. She doesn't say what she's going to do if anybody does advertise for him."

"Well, we can see about buying him in that case. Tell her that. Meanwhile, what does the boy say about his master?"

As he turned to walk to the stables, Tom followed, leading his horse. It would have to be returned to the livery where Gideon had hired it. He was eager to see his own horses, especially Penny, his Arabian mare.

"Well, see. That's just it, my lord. The boy don't talk. I think he may be a mute."

Gideon sighed. "Well, keep your eyes open, and we'll deal with it when the time comes."

A neigh from inside the stable alerted him that Penny had heard his voice. As soon as he entered the building she put her head over the stall door. Then she bobbed it up and down and snorted as if chastising him for leaving her behind.

"I missed you, too, girl, but you would not have enjoyed the voyage."

"Why didn't you write me, my lord? I would've met you at the coast with her."

A smile pulled at the corners of Gideon's mouth. "I had some business to attend to first. I rode to Rotherham Abbey, Tom."

"Were the family there, my lord? And Mrs. Kean?" Tom's voice was even, but his hopeful eyes gave him away.

Gideon laughed and touched his forehead to Penny's muzzle. "You know she was, or I would not have this foolish grin on my face. We are to be married, just as soon as possible, and I am to get ready to return to France in the spring."

"I'm happy to hear it, my lord." Though Tom's words were sincere, they were spoken with unease. He knew that Gideon's next departure would be for a long time.

Gideon kept his gaze fixed on his horse. "I wish you and Katy would come with us, but I won't ask it of you, Tom."

Tom bowed his head, knitting his fingers in the reins he still held. "I don't think I could live with all them foreigners, Master Gideon. You know I would follow you anywhere else."

Gideon nodded. He gave Penny a final pat, then said, "Well." He turned and clapped Tom on the shoulder. "We can discuss what you and Katy would like to do, but for now Mrs. Kean has a job for us. I understand she spoke to you about it."

Tom looked grateful for the change of subject, but as he turned to follow Gideon, his words were anxious again. "If you mean that business with Mr. Henry, my lord, yes, she did. But I didn't see what I could do, or even if your lordship would want me to. I did write you about it, my lord, but you wouldn't've received the letter."

"That's all right, Tom. I'm not sure there was anything you could have done, but now that I'm home, we shall have to get busy. You'll have to return the horse. Then, we can discuss it."

Gideon told him where he had hired the hack, and Tom saddled his own horse to lead the other on the road to Bromley.

Before he left, Gideon went into the house and climbed the stairs to his rooms. Katy must have rushed to make up the fire because flames were leaping in the grate. Instead of getting right to work on James Henry's problem, Gideon removed his hat, cloak, and boots and fell backwards on the bed.

He had floated all the way back from Smarden, scarcely aware of his surroundings in spite of the need for caution, still basking in the warmth of a fortnight of making love. He could still smell Hester's essence on his skin. With his eyes closed, he could recall every inch of her body, every expression on her face, and the perfect smile which had first drawn him to her. Thinking of her now made him want her again. He would have to brace himself not to miss her every minute of every day.

He could not believe his luck to have found the perfect woman with whom to share his life. It was worth losing nearly everything he owned to discover her, for he knew that if not for his misfortunes, he might now be married to her cousin Isabella, and miserable. And with Hester as Isabella's companion, sooner or later he would have realized his mistake, and he would never have been able to correct it.

Now he would do anything to make her happy, even work to protect the half-brother who had turned against him. Their father had trusted James Henry and had given him a position of importance and material support to make up for his illegitimate birth. Unaware of the connection between them, Gideon had been jealous of their relationship, even as he had acknowledged James Henry's worthy qualities. He had wondered why James had been consulted on all matters concerning the estate, while he himself had been excluded. Now he thought he understood. Their father had wanted to give his older son some part of himself when only Gideon would inherit his name.

He wondered whether, if they had been raised as brothers, their jealousy of each other would have been as strong, for surely jealousy was in part to blame for why James had accused him of their father's murder. That mistrust, which had stung, had turned Gideon's own jealousy into resentment, which in his bitterest moments he had nursed. It would not be easy to forget, but if Hester wished him to forgive his brother, then he would try.

The fact that James had been kind to her, when no member of her own family had bestirred himself to care, was a mark in his favour. If he could see Hester's worth, if he had done all he could to ease the misery of her situation, then something was owed to him.

Gideon prodded himself to keep that fact in the forefront of his mind as he went about investigating the death of Lord Wragby. And, he decided, he had better get started if he and Hester were to sail for France in the spring.

He stood and crossed to his desk, where he found paper, ink, and a quill pen. Making a few notes might focus his mind. He recalled the names of the four gentlemen Hester thought might have killed Lord Wragby and scratched them down with plenty of space between them for whatever information he might cull.

Then, he tried to collect all he had ever heard about Phillip, Lord Wragby.

He recalled the scandal over the viscount's marriage, which had taken place at about the same time that Gideon had been courting Isabella. Lord Ireton's fury when he had learned of their elopement had been widely reported, the impression being that those who had not witnessed his reaction were fortunate to have been spared. The marquess was known as a person who would not tolerate defiance or disobedience from anyone, especially his son and heir. But the new Lady Wragby's family was respectable enough that nothing could be done to annul the match.

Hester had related Lord Wragby's cruel remarks about his wife one night as they had lain quietly together to let Gideon catch his breath. The memory of that night brought an unbefitting smile to his lips, which he did his best to erase while pondering the significance of the viscount's hatred for his wife. Since Wragby had been throttled, it was inconceivable that a woman had murdered him, no matter how justly provoked, but if her father was still alive, might he not also be a suspect?

Hester was persuaded that the killer must be one of the men who had been in the gallery of St. Paul's dome at the time of her visit. The rasped words had made a forceful impression on her. Gideon trust-ed her judgement on this, as on everything, but still he would keep the thought of Lady Wragby's father, the General, at the back of his mind.

What else did he know about Lord Wragby? Rumours of his preposterous behaviour in France had reached Gideon, even at St. Mars. The viscount's pomp, his arrogance, and his extravagance had made an absurd impression on many of the French, a people not known for their restraint in these matters. One of Gideon's friends at the Regent's court had written him, describing the viscount's appearance in Paris, certain that Gideon would find the story amusing. He had included the information that Wragby was strutting about Paris spouting Jacobite sympathies to the dismay of Lord Stair and that, by his own account, he had attempted to visit the Pretender at Avignon.

Gideon had forgotten all this when Lord Stair had mentioned the English gentleman who had undertaken the commission to negotiate a marriage between the Pretender and the daughter of the Landgrave of Hesse. Now, reminded of their conversation, he wondered if the "fool" of whom Lord Stair had spoken could have been Lord Wragby. If he was, the circumstances seemed irrelevant to his murder, except as proof of how deeply he had been involved in the Stuart cause.

Gideon looked down at the four names he had written on his sheet. Two of the men were known to have Jacobite sympathies. The other two were Whigs who supported King George. It would be his task and Hester's to discover which party in the struggle for the throne had been so offended by Lord Wragby as to want him dead.

Over the next week, with Tom's help, Gideon attempted to discover where the four gentlemen lived. He wished to have something useful to report when he next met Hester.

He knew three of the gentlemen by sight, as well as by reputation, since they were of a similar age to his. The exception, Sir Horatio Allenby, was an older gentleman, who, as a Whig, would never have been permitted to cross his father's threshold, but as a minion of Lord Ireton's, he would easily be found.

Gideon entrusted the search for Lord Ireton's friends to Tom, who could hang about the marquess's house and chat with the servants. Lord Ireton occupied one of the grander houses in St. James's Square.

Tom had only to appear on the square with Beau, the former Lord Hawkhurst's hunter, and it would not be long before the residents' grooms struck up a conversation.

Finding the other two men would take a bit more connivance, but Gideon knew that he should study their habits before making any attempt to approach them. They were Tories and Jacobites, which meant that they would frequent different coffee-houses and taverns than Lord Ireton's friends. The Tories claimed the Cocoa Tree, the coffee-house his father had favoured, and his friend Lord Peterborough could often be found at Smyrna's, but Gideon could not risk being seen in any of the establishments in Pall Mall. He thought it more likely that with all the recent arrests any Jacobite scheming on behalf of James Stuart would prefer to conduct his business in a London tavern than within view of St. James's Palace. If this were true, the information he had coaxed out of Lade might prove to be invaluable. With a black wig, a deal of white paint on face, and a plethora of patches, he would defy anyone at a London tavern to know him.

Late the next evening, dressed and painted to look like a fop, with a dozen patches on his face, he hired a boat from Lambeth Stairs to row him to Paul's Wharf, where he paid the waterman and set out on foot to explore the taverns between St. Paul's Cathedral and Clerkenwell. Chances were that, by now, the inns Lade had mentioned had changed hands, but at least Gideon was armed with a few places to start.

He strode quickly from the boat to Thames Street to avoid any trouble near the wharf. While he had chosen one of the quieter pathways into the City, all manner of men from all over the world worked and scavenged along the Thames. It paid to be cautious.

Crossing Thames Street led him into a more respectable quarter with schools, colleges, trade guild halls, and one of the churches rebuilt by Sir Christopher Wren after the Great Fire, but Gideon was unprepared for the silence of its streets this late at night. As he made his way up St. Bennet's Hill, the great nave of St. Paul's loomed black in the darkness. Massive, it blocked any light that might have shone from the houses to its north. At this hour, little candlelight came from the College of Arms or from Doctors' Commons as he passed. Windows were shuttered tight against the cold. Gideon's path grew even more obscured the closer he got to the cathedral. Clutching the hilt of his sword in one hand, he stumbled over a body, which yelped like a dog. Mercifully, no cur leapt up to bite him, but he found himself wishing he had hired a linkboy to light his way through this sleeping part of the City.

After feeling his way towards the dark building ahead, he knew the instant he had arrived at St. Paul's Churchyard for an even larger object rose up to his right. The great dome of the cathedral was outlined by the starlight beyond. The booksellers' shops that clustered round the churchyard, which thrummed so busily during the day, were all closed. There was still no place of business open here to cast even the faintest beam. He edged his way past them with one hand on his sword the other out to steady himself until he rounded the massive cathedral. Then, since his eyes were used to total darkness, the streets beyond it seemed to glow.

Lade had given him the name of an ale-house in Ivy Lane, so Gideon found the Chapter House to St. Paul's on a corner and, directing his steps northward, searched for the sign of the King's Head. The lane became livelier the nearer he came to Newgate Street. Men moved in and out of the ale-house, which he spotted up ahead, while drunkards staggered from a distilling shop where Geneva must be sold. The laws about distilling had been changed to encourage the consumption of corn. As a result, anyone could set up a distillery for gin, as it was called for short, though some tried to pass theirs off as brandy.

Gideon had to hug the wall to avoid a collision with two drunkards, who staggered out in front of him and teetered indecisively before recalling the direction they wanted to take. He did not envy them the headache they would suffer in the morning, for gin was becoming known for this unpleasant effect.

After letting them pass, he made his way to the other source of noise, and entered the public room of the King's Head. There was a momentary lull in the conversation, the kind that naturally arose whenever a stranger appeared. Affecting not to notice, Gideon called for a pint of his host's best and chose a table near which two gentlemen were sitting.

The drawer soon brought his mug of ale. Gideon took a sip as his eyes roamed the room, but neither of the two gentlemen he was looking for was among the company. The wariness with which he was still being observed lent some credence to Lade's claim that the King's Head was a gathering place for Jacobites, but that very caution on the part of its patrons would make it difficult for Gideon to earn their trust.

He was about to move on to the next ale-house when an urchin laden with a stack of broadsides entered the room. The boy made a tour, hawking his papers. A couple of patrons shooed him off, but most, including the two gentlemen to Gideon's right, handed the boy a halfpenny for a copy.

Gideon reached into his purse and, signaling his willingness, produced a coin. He had noted that the host of the ale-house had purchased one, too.

The broadside was too small to be intended for posting and printed only on one side. There was no heading to say who had published it, and at a half-penny it must have escaped paying the new duty that had been levied on newssheets. Its only content was the reproduction of a Jacobite song.

Gideon saw no purpose in its printing, unless the intent was to keep up the spirits of the faithful. He pocketed the paper and stood to go, tipping his hat to the host before heading outside. Behind him, the scrape of stool legs announced that the two gentlemen were leaving the ale-house, too.

Out in the street he passed a few officers, two in the company of lewd women. With the rebels defeated, the Land Forces had been cut, including officers. The danger from France having been eliminated by the peace, no further executions for treason had taken place. The newssheets had reported that after the King's arrival from Hanover, several of the prisoners in Newgate were expected to be discharged. The mariners on the men-of-war were being paid off as soon as their ships docked. The officers who were still stationed in London and other towns had nothing to do but get themselves into trouble.

Some soldiers had been whipped in St. James's Park for offenses ranging from desertion to speaking ill of the government. With so many men being turned out with no pay, the streets would soon be riddled with beggars and thieves. It would not be wise to cross Smithfield alone at this time of night, so Gideon hired a hackney coach to take him past the empty cattle market and up St. John's Street. This wider street became the Islington road farther north, so it was lined with inns and bustled with coach and cart traffic, even at midnight,

Gideon told the driver to set him down at Hicks Hall at the entrance to St. John's Lane. He stepped down across the street from the sessions house, the first one built in the County of Middlesex, where some of the regicides who had signed the death warrant for King Charles I had been tried. It stood in the middle of a wider section of the street, forcing traffic to move to both sides around it. Gideon skirted the hall to cross to the entrance of St. John's Lane and made his way along it towards St. John's Square.

From an alleyway a few yards up, two figures emerged, an elderly captain in his Majesty's forces, clearly the worse for drink, leaning for support on a woman of doubtful virtue. She was trying to persuade him to take a chair, but he insisted that they should walk. Gideon paused to let them stagger past, but two men, coming up behind him refused to cede the path. Passing Gideon, one on each side, they shoved the officer, knocking him down and causing the woman to utter an angry curse.

"Here! Who the devil!" With the woman's help the captain struggled to his feet. "Just you watch where you are going, sir, or I shall be forced to teach you some manners!"

Instead of begging his pardon, the two younger men laughed. One of them said, "I dare you to try, you common old sot! Make way for your betters."

"And, while you are at it"— the other, who wore a sword, made a grab for the woman—"I'll relieve you of your companion, since you are in no fit state to entertain her."

"Why, you—you impudent cur!" The captain lunged to drag her back.

She shrieked and scolded, pulled in two directions like a pullet bone.

"Here, give me your sword!" Not waiting for permission, the unarmed man yanked the weapon from his friend's waist. Inebriated himself, he waved it over his head like a lunatic, ignoring his friend's protests, then swept it in a wide, dangerous arc and caught the captain across the neck.

His friend had already dropped the woman's arm to make a grab for his sword. Together, they had taken a hasty step backward to escape the sweep of the blade, but the captain's drunkenness had made him slower. Blood spurted from his neck. He fell to the pavement, with a sickening, gurgling sound.

It had all happened so fast that Gideon had not reacted in time. Nor had any passers-by had the chance to intervene, but now, a number of them converged on the spot, As Gideon fell to one knee to assess the captain's injury, the others grabbed hold of the men who had assaulted him.

The captain's wound had bled so violently that the street beneath him was already soaked. Within a matter of seconds, only a weak trickle came from the slit at this throat. His eyes were fixed open in astonishment. Gideon could not find a pulse. Still, he unknotted the man's cravat and tied it about his wound to staunch whatever flow was left.

When he had finished, he looked angrily up at the swordsman, who looked shocked by what he had done. "You have killed him," Gideon said.

The people around them gasped. The woman burst into tears. With a look of horror, she turned and scurried away. The crowd let her flee, as cries went up for the Watch. The murderer, who seemed younger now, stammered that he had never meant to kill the old man, just to scare him.

Gideon knew that he must not wait for the Watch. He could not afford to give testimony, for he would be asked to appear in court at the young man's trial. There were a goodly number of witnesses in the street, a few of whom seemed outraged enough to see that justice was done.

Gideon bent over the officer again to make certain he was dead. Then he stood and asked the men who had gathered to carry the captain's corpse to Hicks Hall for the inquest. A few agreed, and Gideon

stepped aside to allow them to collect the body. He made as if to accompany them down St. John's Lane to the sessions house, but instead
remained, watching them walk away with their burden, too busy to
notice who followed.

By now, the Watch had come upon the scene, and several witnesses took it upon themselves to describe the crime, while others looked
on. One man, in gentlemen's clothing, arriving from the direction of
St. John's Gate, stopped and stood aloof. The offenders were pleading
with the Watch for mercy, trying to portray the killing as an unfortunate accident. The voices of the witnesses and pleaders grew louder, as
each tried to make himself heard over the rest.

Taking advantage of the disturbance, Gideon stole away, in the
direction in which he had started out. He had reached the opening to
Pissing Alley, which connected the lane to St. John's Street, when he
heard footsteps behind him. He did not turn to see who was following, but took the precaution of withdrawing his sword partially from
its sheath.

To his left, all along the lane, stood the shells of partly built houses
in the place where fashionable mansions had once stood. One of the
greatest, Berkeley House, had been sacked in the anti-Catholic riots of
the last century and subsequently abandoned. The nobility had nearly
all deserted this quarter in favour of the West End, which put them
closer to Court. Taverns and inns had moved into the former houses of
the rich, from the Queen's Head at the bottom of the lane to the Old
Baptist's Head farther on. Political enmity had now replaced religious
strife. Last year, one of the Whig mug houses in St. John's Lane had
been attacked by a mob of Tories.

The only aristocratic dwelling Gideon knew to remain in the area
was Newcastle House, which had been occupied by the mad former
Duchess of Albemarle until she was tricked into marrying the Earl of
Montague. He had presented himself to her as the Emperor of China
and the ruse had gained him her fortune.

Ahead of Gideon stood St. John's Gate, a remnant of the old Priory of St. John, once the property of the Knights Hospitallers, who had
lived in the houses along the lane. Since the dissolution of the mon-
asteries, the gate had been in private hands, its chambers rented to a

succession of tradesmen who wished to escape control of the London guilds. Its stones had been charred in yet another riot, reminding him again of the violence this lane had seen.

A wooden wall had been built to block the great crenelated gate with two openings cut through it to allow pedestrians to pass. Still not overtaken by his pursuers, whose footsteps were coming closer, Gideon walked through one of these passages. Then, drawing his sword, he stepped quickly to one side and pressed his back to the wall, hoping that the shadow of the gate had concealed his movement.

In less than thirty seconds, the first of his pursuers passed through the narrow door, followed immediately by the second. Before they could see that he was no longer in front of them, Gideon moved quietly behind the latter and laid the tip of his sword on the back of the man's neck.

The man gave a startled cry and tried to turn, but he quickly stilled when Gideon said, "I should hate to have to wound you, but if you move, I may be forced to act."

Whipping round at his friend's cry, the first man drew his weapon and would have attacked, if the second had not yelled, "Put that down, you fool, or he'll skewer me!"

His friend hesitated, but at a gesture from Gideon, he lowered his sword. "What do you want, damn you? Money? If that is it, you shall have to let me reach into my pocket."

"Where you may keep a pistol? Not if you value your friend's life. Please do me the favour of showing me both your hands."

Gideon waited until the man had complied, then said, "Besides, I have no intention of robbing you. Rather, I should like to know why you have been following me." Now that the two men were near, even in the dark, he thought he recognized the men who had been sitting at the table next to his at the King's Head.

He sensed, more than saw, the surprised looks they exchanged. Then the man with the sword at his throat finally said, "You have not been seen in the King's Head before. We wondered what your business was."

"Is that a matter of concern to you? I was given the name of that ale-house by someone who knew it before he found it prudent to leave the city."

This silenced the two, until the man facing him gave the other a nod. "Perhaps, we mistook your purpose. It would help if you could tell us your destination now."

Gideon's pulse gave a leap. He sensed a chance that the night had not been entirely wasted. "I was on my way to have a drink at another ale-house in St. John's Square, the Duke of Albemarle's Head. Do you know it?"

This time, the men's reactions were palpable. The man with the sword at his throat emitted a loud exhale, and the shoulders of the other relaxed.

"We know it well," the latter man said, "and if your business is for the gentleman we think it is, put down your sword and we'll take you there, ourselves."

This could have been a trick to make him let down his guard, but the signs the two had given were subtle enough to convince Gideon that they were genuine. He took a big step backwards, and when neither made an attempt at his weapon, he slid his sword back into its sheath.

"I should be grateful for the introduction, and perhaps you will assist me further. I have not been in England for some while, so my acquaintance is sadly out of date."

This pleased the two men even more. "Let us first have a drink." The man he had held at sword point rubbed the spot on his neck. "Then you can tell us how we may be of help."

⌀

Hester's family arrived at Hawkhurst House, sore and crumpled from the slow, jostling ride. Not even the ample cushions in Harrowby's new coach could brace them from the deep ruts produced by winter rains. The moods of most, however, were high, Harrowby, Isabella, and Mrs. Mayfield, looking keenly forward to entertainments at Court, and Hester eager to see St. Mars. Only Mary was downcast at the prospect of her mother's new attempts to marry her off to a man of fortune.

The newssheets had reported that King George had finally left Hanover to return to England, leaving behind his grandson, Prince Frederick—aged ten, and third in line to the throne of Great Britain—to represent him. The moment Isabella and her mother entered Hawkhurst House, they set about shopping for new finery to welcome the King's return. Hester was kept busy running between them to lend her skill with a needle to new purchases of satin and lace. She was grateful that their anticipation of pleasure was keeping both in good cheer, while she looked forward to her first reunion with St. Mars. Harrowby's French valet, Pierre, happy to be within reach of the shops, was preparing his lord not only to greet the King, but also for the opening of Parliament.

One morning not long after their arrival, Lord Kirkland and Sir Marmaduke attended Isabella's *levée* to advise her on the latest fashions and to opine on the placement of her patches. They lounged upon chairs in her dressing room, while her hairdresser arranged her hair. Hester, Mrs. Mayfield, and Mary, with needlework in their laps, occupied other chairs, which soon would be filled with other admirers when they learned that the beautiful Countess of Hawkhurst was back in town. For now, with so much to finish before the King's return, it was more convenient to do their sewing here.

Having arrived in London a few days earlier, the gentlemen regaled the ladies with the gossip they had managed to collect, as well as news of other members of the nobility who had arrived in town. Both had seen the Duke of Marlborough taking the air in Hyde Park. Sir Marmaduke ventured his opinion that his Grace would not last the year. "It is evident that he has lost the use of his arm, and one side of his face droops, no matter how skilfully his valet tries to hide it."

"The Duchess will parade him in public as long as she hopes to gain any power from it." Mrs. Mayfield said in a huff. She sat near her daughter, needle in hand, pretending to be of use.

"That may be true. Still, I believe her sincerely devoted to her husband."

Craning his neck to regard himself in Isabella's looking glass, Lord Kirkland volunteered, "Lord and Lady Bolton have set out from their estate and should be here in time to greet the King."

"Lady Bolton will not miss any opportunity to ingratiate herself with the Duchess of Munster." The spite in Mrs. Mayfield's voice belied the fact that she, herself, had bribed the King's mistress in the interest of her son.

The gentlemen took her gibe in good part, knowing that the best way to the King's purse was either through his mistress or Madame Kielmansegge, whose relationship to the King was less understood. Some believed she was his mistress, others his half-sister, and the Jacobites put it about that she was both.

"Perhaps the new duchess will be more approachable, now that she has the title she coveted,"

"What? An Irish peerage? I doubt she will settle for anything less than an English one." Sir Marmaduke's coy remark made the others laugh.

Hester, busy with her needle and trying to stay focused on her work instead of her next rendezvous with St. Mars, barely registered his comment; but the sound of their laughter made her raise her head in time to catch Mary's wince. Following the direction of her gaze, Hester realized it was a reaction to a new gleam in Mrs. Mayfield's eye. It would not be long, she thought, before her aunt nagged Harrowby again to bribe her Grace of Munster to give Mary a place at Court, when no one could be less suited to a life in waiting. Mary, with her love for riding and her vibrant energy, would be miserable standing for hours at the whim of a princess, but Mrs. Mayfield would see the post as an opportunity for Mary to capture the eye of a wealthy nobleman.

Sir Marmaduke ventured another bit of news, his gaze shifting curiously from one lady's face to another, "The Marquis of Ireton is, also, expected shortly."

Mrs. Mayfield and Mary both stiffened, but not for the same reason. Mrs. Mayfield said haughtily, "The movements of that gentleman are of no interest to me."

Mary, whose concern must all be for James Henry, said nothing, but she sent Hester a pleading glance. Hester gathered up her needlework and excused herself from the company, adding, "The light in here has dimmed. Mary, shall we take our work into the small parlour where it should be brighter by now?"

They curtsied to the two gentlemen, who stood and bowed at their departure. Mrs. Mayfield looked torn between following them to begin her next campaign against Mary's wishes and staying to hear more gossip. In the end, her taste for gossip prevailed, so she remained in the dressing room, equally unwelcome to Isabella's company.

"I know my mother is plotting some other horrible future for me," Mary said, as soon as they were safely out of earshot.

"She undoubtedly is. But do not fret too much over the notion that she'll press the idea of your going into waiting. She may be enticed by the prospect of getting the Duchess of Munster to exercise her influence on the King, but she forgets how much it will cost. She can plot all she likes, but you can be certain that Harrowby will refuse to part with the ten thousand pounds or more to make it happen. He did that once for Dudley and it came to nought. He is not likely to throw good money after bad."

As they made their way to the small parlour, Hester was glad to see that Mary seemed comforted by her words. The girl even smiled. "And as penniless as I am, none of her other prospects are likely to offer for me."

Hester laughed. "This may be the only time that I hear a lack of fortune being celebrated. It is true," she said, as they reached the parlour and sat where the light from a window could illuminate their work. "There are few gentlemen who will marry without the need to fatten their pockets. Few seem to see the prospect of a wife and children as a blessing when they had rather spend their fortunes on themselves. But there are exceptions, of course. Love has been known to overcome selfishness at times."

"Then I shall take special care not to let anyone at Court fall in love with me."

"Are you certain you can manage it? You are young and pretty, and for some that will suffice, especially if they have need of an heir more than a need for money." Hester spread out the stomacher she was embroidering with silver thread for Isabella and avoided looking at Mary while she took up her needle. She would not ask Mary about her feelings for James Henry, but thought the girl might confide in her.

"I shall make myself as unattractive as it takes. Mama will be furious, but there will not be much she can do to stop me."

Hester grimaced at the thought of the rows that were sure to result, but she did not try to dissuade her. She applied herself to her embroidery and Mary did as well. Neither raised the spectre of Lord Ireton's return. It was better not to tempt fate.

SHUT, shut the door, good John! fatigued, I said,
Tie up the knocker, say I'm sick, I'm dead.
The Dog Star rages! nay 'tis past a doubt,
All Bedlam, or Parnassus, is let out:
Fire in each eye, and papers in each hand,
They rave, recited, and madden round the land.

CHAPTER X

The next day, while Mary and Isabella were out riding in the park, Hester went downstairs to speak to the housekeeper, Mrs. Dixon. On her way back, she passed through the hall and happened to hear a gentleman's raised voice, coming from the antechamber where Harrowby's visitors were asked to wait. She peered into the room and found Sir Horatio Allenby, scolding one of the footmen.

"Does your master know that I am here at the request of Lord Ireton?" he demanded.

"Ay, he does, sir, but his valet says he is too busy to receive company. He said, perhaps it would be better to return another day later in the week."

"Return? When I have been sitting here for hours already?" Sir Horatio could barely contain his fury. He must know as well as anyone that a mere baronet could not demand to see a personage as illustrious as an earl, but his vanity was apparently too great to accept it.

"As I told you before, sir, my lord is unable to receive visitors today." The footman was trying to be firm, but it seemed to Hester that the gentleman's indignation was wearing him down. He stammered, "Maybe I should ask one of the other servants to explain the matter to you."

He was not used to turning gentlemen away. Harrowby was fond of company, especially at his *levée.* He was flattered by attention from anyone with even a hint of gentility. Hester was not aware of any appointments that would have kept Harrowby from receiving anyone he wished to see. She suspected he simply did not wish to hear the message Sir Horatio had brought from Lord Ireton.

She did wish to know what it was, however. It was better to be forewarned of any threat Lord Ireton might still pose to James Henry.

"That will not be necessary, John." Taking pity on the footman, she stepped into the room. It was furnished with four armchairs upholstered in silk, so the earl's visitors could wait in comfort. "I shall carry this gentleman's message to my lord."

With a look of profound relief, John bowed himself out of the antechamber.

Hester curtsied to Sir Horatio and gave him her name. His eyes narrowing, he made her the sketchiest of bows, before saying, "Mrs. Kean, is it? You are some sort of cousin to Lady Hawkhurst, I understand. I have seen you before, have I not?"

"You have, sir. At the celebration on Coronation Day, I believe. We were standing quite near to each other, though we were never introduced."

As he recalled the occasion, his eyes widened, perhaps at the memory of Lord Wragby's treasonous speech. He recovered, however, to look down his nose at her. "Yes, of course, you were there as Mrs. Mary Mayfield's chaperone."

Hester smiled slightly. "I was there as her cousin, that is correct." She was not willing to let this gentleman degrade her status to that of a servant. Not a servant to Mary, at least.

"That is of scant importance now." Sir Horatio's indignation was rising again. "I have been waiting to see Lord Hawkhurst for upwards of an hour, and I wish to speak with him as soon as possible."

Hester noted that the length of his wait had been reduced from untold hours to just one. At least, he knew better than to exaggerate for her.

"My cousin will be distressed to hear that you have been so terribly inconvenienced." She delivered this with a polite smile, but in a tone that left no doubt that Harrowby would not care one whit for his discomfiture.

Sir Horatio flushed at the just rebuke. "It is not for myself that I demand to see him, but for Lord Ireton whom I have the honour to serve as messenger."

Hester inclined her head. "That will distress Lord Hawkhurst, undoubtedly, but perhaps I may be of assistance? I shall be happy to convey his lordship's message as soon as my cousin can lend me an ear."

Sir Horatio drew himself up. His nostrils flared. "It is not the sort of message that a lady should convey."

Hester raised her brow. "Dear me! That sounds ominous! I trust Lord Ireton has not sent you here to call my lord out?"

"No, of course not!" He was getting red in the face. "If a challenge needs to be issued, Lord Ireton will deliver it himself."

"My lord will be relieved to hear it. Still, even the mention of a challenge is bound to unsettle him. I doubt he is aware of any conflict between himself and Lord Ireton. Are you certain, there is nothing I can tell him to allay his fears?"

Sir Horatio had finally had enough. He took up the tricorn hat he had deposited on a chair and beat it against his leg. "Yes, very well, mistress. You may tell him that Lord Ireton desires to know whether he has dismissed his receiver-general, as Lord Ireton requested. Tell him, too, that it will be in his best interest to do as Lord Ireton asks."

Hester did not promise to relay this last message. She curtsied to indicate that their exchange was at an end. Sir Horatio nodded curtly, before putting on his hat and storming from the room.

Hester took in a deep breath. So, Lord Ireton had not given up his quarrel. He must believe that James Henry had murdered his son, in which case it was understandable that he would refuse to let the matter drop. Recalling the beating that James Henry had suffered at the hands of Lord Wragby's footmen, she shuddered, wondering what sort of vengeance Lord Ireton would take. Getting him dismissed from Harrowby's service might be only the first step, in that it would not befit a marquess to thrash an earl's highly-valued servant, perhaps even to have him killed.

With this fear in mind, Hester climbed the stairs and made her way to Harrowby's suite. She knocked at his dressing room, and in a few minutes it was answered by Pierre, who opened the door scarcely more than a crack.

"*Oui, mademoiselle?*" As usual, Pierre gave no sign that he recalled the escapades they had shared with St. Mars. Before St. Mars's arrest, Pierre had served happily as his valet. Harrowby had envied his cousin the possession of such a skilled servant and, on assuming the title Earl of Hawkhurst, had employed Pierre immediately. With such a vain master, Pierre was given greater license to explore his sartorial whims, but he had aided St. Mars on a few occasions without any pangs of conscience, even fashioning for him the disguise that transformed him into the highwayman Blue Satan.

Though Hester did not often have occasion to speak to Pierre, she was glad to have one ally in the house who knew of her relationship with St. Mars. Today, she asked him in a low voice, "Is it true that your master is unable to receive visitors?"

With a furtive look over his shoulder, Pierre replied in a conspiratorial whisper, "Milord has returned to his bed. There is a gentleman downstairs who he desires not to see."

"Yes, I have just spoken to Sir Horatio and have persuaded him to leave. He did give me a message for my cousin, however."

Pierre approvingly raised his brows. "In that case, one moment, mademoiselle, while I see if milord will receive you." He left her standing outside the room, but returned in an instant. "Milord would speak with you now."

He opened the door all the way to usher her into the splendid apartment where Harrowby held his *levées*. Like Isabella's dressing room, it was magnificently furnished with paintings in gilded frames and armchairs covered in embroidered silk. Its plaster ceiling had been painted with cupids and garlands of flowers. The only difference between the two rooms was that Harrowby's dressing table, in addition to being covered with pots for make-up and patches, held a stand for his shoulder-length wig, which awaited his use, combed and brushed to a lustrous shine. More wigs for riding and hunting rested on stands placed about the room.

Hester barely glanced at these things as she followed Pierre to the adjoining bedchamber, where he bowed to his master and announced his visitor.

Harrowby was reclining in a great bed with a red velvet canopy, beneath a painted plaster ceiling, surrounded by walls covered in colourful Flemish tapestries. He was dressed in an elegant banyan and sipping chocolate from a cup, his shaved pate concealed by a red and gold turban. A few newssheets lay scattered on the counterpane covering his legs, but the expression on his face spoke of petulance and tedium.

He sat up anxiously at the sight of her and waved her to a chair, too impatient to acknowledge her curtsy. "Mrs. Kean, is it true? Sir Horatio has gone?"

"Yes, my lord, not more than five minutes ago." She sat down in a chair near the bed. "However, he seemed most determined to speak with you. John was doing his best to discourage him, but Sir Horatio was behaving so stubbornly, I thought it best to intervene."

"Excellent woman! I had no desire to see him. Now, perhaps I shall be permitted to leave this confounded bed!" He gave it a look of loathing as if the bed itself had held him prisoner.

"I should think it reasonable, my lord, as long as the servants all know to deny him. He is very persistent."

"Yes, curse him!" Harrowby's cheer was short-lived. He cast her a fretful look. "You say that he left a message for me?"

"Yes, my lord. Or at least he said that he was delivering a message on Lord Ireton's behalf."

Harrowby groaned. "Very well, then. I suppose I shall have to hear it."

In spite of the seriousness of her errand, Hester was forced to hide a smile. She thought of giving him the news that Lord Ireton had not sent an envoy to call him out, but would do so himself if the situation demanded. But, this was no time for levity, and she would need Harrowby's compliance to keep James Henry safe.

"I am afraid to say that he came to discover if Mr. Henry is still in your employ, and he implied that Lord Ireton would be angry to learn that he was."

"Is that what you told him?" Harrowby's eyes grew round.

"No, my lord. I made him no reply at all. I simply made it clear, I hope, that he should not expect to be given an audience with you merely on the strength of demanding it."

She was glad to see the effect of these words. Harrowby sat up straighter, his nostrils widening. "Did he demand to see me, by gad! The nerve of him! Well, in that case, he deserved to be sent on his way."

"So I thought, my lord. I would not have him think that he could dictate to the Earl of Hawkhurst in matters that affect his own household."

"Indeed, not!" Harrowby agreed, before it occurred to him what Hester really meant. He looked at her askance. "At least . . . you do not think the prudent thing would be to dismiss James Henry? I cannot be at outs with Lord Ireton, you know. He has the King's ear, and he is a difficult man to cross. He has killed his man in a duel more than once, you know."

"Yes, I have heard that he can be most unaccommodating. But, if you will forgive me, my lord, I doubt that he means to call you out. There is no evidence linking Mr. Henry to his son's murder, so he could hardly justify such a course. If there were any evidence, Mr. Henry would have been taken into custody. I think rather that his lordship's intention is to get Mr. Henry dismissed from your protection, so that he can punish him—perhaps even kill him—without causing a rift between you."

Harrowby looked a bit sick at this thought. "You mean, that if I dismiss him, Henry is likely to be killed?" He gave a weak laugh. "Surely, not?"

"We know that Lord Ireton is too conscious of his dignity to confront Mr. Henry in a fair fight, so if he is serious about seeking vengeance for his son, in this entirely erroneous belief that Mr. Henry murdered Lord Wragby, is it impossible to think that he might have him killed?"

He looked sicker still, but he mustered a protest. "I can tell you, Mrs. Kean, that if given the choice between fighting Lord Ireton in a duel and letting Mr. Henry fend for himself, I would be foolish to choose the first!"

"I do not believe that to be the only choice, my lord. If you will permit me, I have a suggestion to make."

She waited for his permission, until he said petulantly, "Go on! Go on! Out with it."

Hester gave him a smile of gratitude, as if he had already agreed to her proposal. "I believe that if you send Mr. Henry to your estate that lies the farthest away and order him to remain until this matter is resolved, you will not be obliged to do anything else. If Lord Ireton asks you where he is, you can truthfully say that you sent him away. You do not have to elaborate."

"But if I do not replace him, who will collect my rents?"

"Lady Day is more than two months away. I hope the real murderer will be caught in that time. If not, another stratagem may have to be employed, but perhaps by that time, Lord Ireton will have other things to occupy his mind. The King will be here, and Parliament will be in session. He might send his minions to search for Mr. Henry, but he is unlikely to send them as far away as Northumberland."

Harrowby weighed her words, but he was not entirely convinced. "What if he presses me on the question of where Henry has gone? He can be very intimidating, you know."

"Then, perhaps you could give the impression that Mr. Henry may have fled for France?"

"Lie to him, you mean?" Instead of being outraged, Harrowby looked hopeful.

Hester tried to sound sympathetic. "As repugnant as the notion may be to a man of your probity, it would be merciful in this situation. Mr. Henry has loyally served the Fitzsimmons family for many years. It will be hard to manage without him, and if we are fortunate and the real killer is caught, he can resume his duties."

"Er . . . yes. It would be distasteful to lie, of course. But I suppose it could be done, for mercy's sake, as you say." He breathed more easily, then gave her an ingenuous look. "If truth be told, Mrs. Kean, I shall be just as happy to avoid him."

Hester rose from her seat and curtsied deeply to him. "Then, if it pleases you, I shall send a footman with paper and pen so you can write Mr. Henry directly, and I shall inform the servants that if Lord

Ireton or one of his friends calls, you will not be at home to them."

"That is fine for here at Hawkhurst House, but I shan't be able to avoid him at Court!"

"No, my lord, I quite see that." She moved towards the door and ended with her most soothing voice, "But I have no doubt at all that you will manage."

Hester was not as confident of this as she let on. Still, the immediate danger had been averted. She hastened to find John to send him to his master with his Bible box, ink well, and pen. She was afraid to wait for Harrowby to get out of bed to write the letter, for fear he would think better of her idea and not do it.

She would write James Henry herself to make sure he understood the risks if he should decide to ignore Harrowby's instructions and come to London.

Better yet, she would get Mary to do it.

℘

A few days later, King George returned to his Kingdom of Great Britain, accompanied by great ceremony the length of his route. He had embarked at Helvoetslys and, with favourable winds, landed at Margate the next day, where his ships fired their cannons and were greeted by cannons on shore. Three of his yachts arrived at Greenwich the next morning, carrying on one the Earl of Sunderland and Mr. Secretary Stanhope, on another the Duchess of Munster, and on the third Baron Bernsdorff of Hanover, each with their households. At noon, Prince George rode through the City of London to greet his father at Blackheath, where the King descended from his coach, embraced his son with open arms, and carried him in his own coach to town, where the cannons in the Tower were fired.

That night, celebrations and formal demonstrations of joy were carried out across the land. The people of London were entertained on the occasion by a royal procession all the way from Cheapside to St. James's. Members of the mughouses carried effigies of the Pope, the Pretender James Stuart, and vanquished Jacobites—the former Earl of Mar, Colonel Forster, and others—in a cart to be burnt in a great bonfire at Charing Cross. Mr. Bravant, a French pastry-cook created lanterns out of egg shells and arranged them into the letters G and R with a crown placed overhead. Other rows spelled out loyal mottos, such as, "God bless King George, our Faith's Defender, Who keeps us from a Popish Pretender."

The *British Gazeteer* assured its readers that the procession had been carried out without the slightest disorder or damage. It ended with drinks to the health of his Majesty, the Prince and Princess of Wales, and others, encouraged and prolonged by loyal gentlemen from the Young Man's Coffee House and other windows in the street.

There was some dispute the next morning over whether the Lord Mayor of London had refused permission to burn the effigies in Cheapside out of disloyalty to his Majesty, but it was finally settled that his decision had been made out of respect for the Sabbath, the celebration starting so late in the evening and the next day being Sunday. Not everyone was happy to see the King safely returned, however. Throughout the celebrations, in towns like Stamford where Jacobite sympathies were strong, men ran up and down the streets, crying, "Down with the Rump! Down with Roundheads! Damn the Whigs!" and "High church and Ormonde forever!"

One of the first things King George did upon reaching St. James was to offer a reward for information leading to the capture of the smugglers who had murdered one of his Riding Officers. But it was rumoured that all the rebels still imprisoned would be pardoned and set free in an act of amnesty to restore goodwill.

At Hawkhurst House on Friday, Hester and her family had heard the cannons firing in St. James's Park, announcing that the King had safely landed. He arrived at the Palace Saturday night, and on Sunday, Isabella and Harrowby attended service in the Royal Chapel where the aristocracy would have the privilege of seeing him for the first time in more than six months.

No drawing-room was held to welcome him home. The King was too busy, receiving dignitaries who made official expressions of gratitude for his return, opening Parliament, and catching up on matters of governance, which had been postponed during his absence. The peace that had been negotiated with France could not be ratified until the article demanding that the Pretender leave French soil was fulfilled. Report said that the Regent had dispatched Lt. General Dillon to Avignon with instructions to make use of menaces if fair words failed, but again James Stuart refused to budge as long as the Pope was content with his occupation of the Papal Palace there. So far, the Pope was disinclined to comply with the demands of the Court of France, which put the two states at odds.

James Henry had written back to his lord, thanking him for his support and promising to comply with his wishes. If Mary received an answer to her letter, she did not share it with Hester.

With James Henry safely on his way north, Hester's main worry now was how to get to the meeting she had arranged with St. Mars. Isabella, Harrowby, and Mrs. Mayfield were often out in the afternoons and evenings. While the Court might not be hosting entertainments at the moment, the aristocracy was flooding back into town, creating its own amusements from rides in the park and tea and card parties to dinner parties and balls. And there were always plays and musical performances to pass the time.

Mary might wish to avoid attending any of these where her mother could introduce her to more gentlemen, but Mrs. Mayfield would not allow her to remain at home. If she did, Hester could not think of an excuse for leaving the house without taking her along. And if Mary were made to attend the function, Hester was required to go as chaperone.

Not knowing how free she would find herself, she had promised St. Mars to meet him at St. Martin-in-the-Fields on the first Friday morning after the King's return. Walking to the church in the cold winter air, wrapped in a woolen cloak, Hester smiled at the memory of his response.

He had shaken his head in disbelief. "My dearest love, can you not agree that we have progressed so far in our intimacy that sanctuary is no longer an option?"

She had laughed hard, blushing at the same time. "I shall be happy to meet you elsewhere, if you can find a place where no one will see us. Somewhere closer to Piccadilly than your house at Lambeth, too, if you please." She had reminded him of the difficulty she faced escaping from her family unless she told them that she wished to go to church. "If my father had not been a clergyman, I doubt they would have indulged such assiduous devotions, but they excuse them as a peculiar habit I have inherited."

He had eventually accepted her reasoning, but pledged that he would make it his solemn duty to find a better place for their trysts. "Fortunately, it shall not be needed for long, for in a few months' time, we shall be gone."

As Hester made her way down Hemmings Row past St. Martin's Churchyard, her pulse quickened at the prospect of seeing him. It seemed an age since they had been together.

They had met in this ancient church before. The building had been declared unsound and would be replaced as soon as the funds were raised for construction. Meanwhile, no services were held in it, and there was no incumbent. For the most part it remained deserted, so except for the risk of being crushed if its aged walls fell, it was as safe as anywhere they could meet.

As on the last occasion of their coming there, a group of whores had taken shelter in the nave to escape the cold. Some drowsed, while others nibbled on crusts of bread. St. Mars must have paid them to leave him alone, for he stood looking out for her at the door to one of the high-backed pews. Hester was taken aback to see him again in his long black periwig, heavy white paint, and patches, after all the nights they had spent together without any disguise, but when he smiled on seeing her walk towards him down the aisle, her heart gave a skip of joy.

He took hold of her hands to draw her into the pew, saying, "Take care of your skirts. The wood is splintered. And I had better hold onto you tightly in case the bench collapses from rot."

Hester laughed, but allowed him to draw her into the circle of his arms. "We should be ashamed of such conduct, but if those poor creatures behind us are welcome here, I suppose we are, too."

His brow creased. "Do you feel shame about what we have done? If so, then we must be married at once." He spoke in just above a whisper, for sound had a tendency to reverberate within these aged walls.

"No, my love." Hester whispered back, gazing up over her shoulder at him. "There cannot be anything sinful about our love for each other. No matter what doctrine says, I find I cannot believe it. I was just teasing. But let us not waste our time on things that cannot be helped. You know I shall not be able to tarry long."

She told him how difficult it had been to escape the family, even more so with Mary at Hawkhurst House. They talked about ways to meet each other regularly and concluded that the best chance would be in the mornings when Mary often took a ride in the park, and the others were either still abed or dressing—a process which could take up to a few hours.

Then, careful to keep her voice low, for the matters they had to discuss could attract unwanted attention, Hester told St. Mars about Sir Horatio's visit, concluding with the information that Harrowby had sent James Henry into Northumberland to avoid Lord Ireton's wrath.

"Indeed?" He raised his brows. "I had not thought him capable of such good judgement."

Hester tried to hide her smile, but he saw it. "Ah, I should have known. It was you who suggested it." He pulled her to him and planted a kiss on the top of her head. "You will be glad to hear that I have not been entirely idle, myself. Tom has discovered where both Sir Horatio and Lord William Silsbee live, and I have been rubbing elbows with Jacobites."

He told her about being followed from the King's Head and introduced to a Jacobite circle at the Duke of Albemarle's Head. "They believe I was sent from Avignon to recruit soldiers for the Pretender."

"Is that what you told them? Is that not a risky thing to do?"

"I have never been explicit as to the purpose of my 'mission.' It was an idea I got from Lade, if you can believe it. He told me about two alehouses where Jacobites were known to meet and exchange messages, and it was he who made the assumption that I was going to London to recruit. I have found that Lade is always happy to invent roles for me in the conspiracy without any suggestion from me, and the same strategy seems to work with my new confederates. A nod here and a wink there, and they are ready to jump to all sorts of conclusions."

"But if they are in communication with the Pretender, might they not mention your name?"

"I doubt they would put anyone's name into writing. It is far too dangerous. But, yes, eventually my deception will be discovered, at which time they will assume that I've been sent by the government to spy on them. So, whatever I am to find out about Lord Wragby, it had better be soon."

Hester had turned to face him in the pew. "Were either Sir Francis Lichfield or Lord Charters present?"

"No, and they were all very careful not to use names, at least of the living. But when I asked about Lord Wragby and said that I had met him at Avignon, that seemed to put the seal on my impersonation. They knew that he had visited the Pretender there. He told them so himself. I had guessed it from a remark that Lord Stair made during our conversation at the Palais Royal, so I mentioned it both to enhance my credentials and to discover whether this circle had any connection to his friends."

"Was that not even riskier?" She could not help fearing for his safety. If Lord Wragby had been murdered by one of the Jacobites, the killer would not hesitate to kill again.

"How, my love, when Lord Wragby can never deny that we have met?" His blue eyes twinkled out at her from the abominable paint on his face. "As a witness, he is a priceless asset."

She conceded this, pursing her lips to suppress a smile.

He looked at her mouth as if he would like to devour it, and Hester's stomach gave a flip. She had to clear her throat before speaking again. "What will you do next? How will you learn more about our suspects?"

A grimace let her know how hard he was finding it to maintain decorum when they were sitting so close. Tearing his eyes from her face, he stared at the back of the worn pew in front and concentrated on a response. This provoked a frown. "I confess, I do not know, but I suppose I shall have to use the contacts I have made. I could say that Lord Wragby gave me the names of his friends who were loyal and that perhaps I should call on them."

"That sounds like an excellent plan. I wish I could think of a way to help. My biggest concern has been to prevent your cousin from dismissing James Henry to avoid crossing swords with Lord Ireton; but now that a temporary solution to that problem has been reached, I shall put my mind to the murder itself.

"Did you get the sense that Lord Wragby had angered any of the Jacobites you met? He had a talent for giving offense, and his temper was so volatile, I would not be surprised if he made enemies in that quarter, as well."

"On the contrary, I got the impression that they took him at his own valuation. He was known for boasting of his allegiance to the Pretender."

"Yes, Mary and I were both witnesses to that. But if he was that indiscreet, mightn't someone have felt threatened enough to need to silence him?"

St. Mars was about to reply when the door behind them opened, letting in a blast of cold air. It closed with a bang that echoed off the walls. As St. Mars turned to see who had entered, Hester straightened, but it was only another poor woman seeking refuge. She must have spotted the top of St. Mars's head, for she immediately shuffled up the aisle. By the time she reached their pew and put her hand out to beg, St. Mars had already reached into his pocket and held out a silver two-penny coin.

She expressed her gratitude with a toothless grin before shuffling off to find a pew to sleep in, and St. Mars turned his attention back to Hester.

"That was very generous," Hester said. "Is that how much you gave to each of those women?"

He grinned and nodded. "After last time, I came better supplied with coins, the object being enough to pacify them, but not so much as to cause a riot."

"If this is where we keep having to meet, you shall soon be reduced to begging, yourself!"

This made him laugh aloud. "Hardly. But if this is what it costs to see you, I consider the money well-spent. Still, if we must meet like this for more than a few weeks, I shall have to think of something better."

"The weather should improve soon. We might go for walks in a park."

The look he gave her told her just how much he thought of this idea. "We will not be able to do what I have in mind in a park."

It was Hester's turn to laugh, as a wave of heat flooded her. She lowered her voice again. "Well, if we wish to shorten the time," she said, her voice quivering, "we should concentrate on finding our murderer. What were we discussing when that poor woman interrupted us?"

As they both tried to recall where their conversation had broken off, an unrelated thought entered Hester's brain. "I do know something that could be relevant, another avenue to pursue, perhaps."

He abandoned his thoughts to listen.

"Mary and I once spied Lord Wragby down in the City. He was alone, which in itself aroused my curiosity for I had never seen him unaccompanied by either friends or servants. At the time, I was chiefly concerned with keeping him away from Mary—he had not caught sight of us yet, but he had been pestering her mercilessly, you know, and his attentions had been growing more insolent. So, I asked her to remain out of sight, while I watched to make certain that our paths would not cross.

"I followed him a little way down Fleet Street and then up Fetter Lane, where he entered a house. He could not have been inside more than a minute before he emerged again. I thought it very odd at the time, for if he simply had something to leave—a note or a parcel—he would have sent a servant."

"Unless the note could have implicated him in treason."

"That was my thinking at the time, yes. I had already heard him speak against King George, you see."

"A reasonable conclusion." St. Mars pondered the information. "It is hard to think of any other explanation for it. Lord Wragby seems the kind of man who would insist upon all the privilege and trappings of his position, unless doing so would interfere with his image of himself. He made a spectacle of his wealth in Paris, but to visit the Pretender in Avignon, he had to disguise himself as a commoner. The role of spy would require a departure from his habitual deportment, and he undoubtedly relished the importance of the role. If he had not, he would not have boasted so loosely about it."

"I agree, although I do think an element of his political behaviour may have been calculated to annoy his father as much as possible."

St. Mars grinned at her wry tone. "That would certainly be the case with most young men, and some never grow out of the tendency." He returned to the subject of Lord Wragby's mysterious visit to the house. "But I should find out who lives there and if the inhabitants have a connection to any of our suspects. Can you describe it for me?"

"Yes, it is on the east side of the street, several houses up from Fleet Street around a slight bend, and it has green shutters and—oh, the sign of the ship!"

He gave her a teasing smile. "That should be enough to help me find it. What a shame your memory is so poor!"

She returned his smile. The bells in the church tower tolled, filling her with a powerful ache. "My love, I fear that is the signal that I must go."

She saw the same longing in his eyes, but he nodded and embraced her once before helping her to her feet. They arranged to meet there again in one week, agreeing that as slowly as the time would pass, it would hardly be enough for progress to be made on the mystery, the solution of which would allow them to leave for France with no regrets.

Your Plea is good; but still I say, beware!
Laws are explained by Men—so have a care.
It stands on record, that in Richard's times
A man was hanged for very honest rhymes.

CHAPTER XI

Gideon wasted no time in searching out the house in Fetter Lane. From St. Martin's-in-the-Fields, he walked directly up the Strand, past the New Exchange, bustling with shoppers, and the old hospital founded by Henry VII on the site of the Savoy Palace, which had been closed these fifteen years. For a while, its aged buildings had been turned into barracks. Now they were rented out for a host of dubious purposes. By contrast, Somerset House, refurbished by Sir Christopher Wren, with its sprawling buildings and gardens, still retained an air of magnificence. A property of the Crown, it was used for grace-and-favour residences.

Gideon noted that the King's benevolence had not extended to making repairs to the property, so even its buildings, once the residence of queens, were showing signs of decay. But after all the wars with France, there was no money in the Treasury for such luxuries.

With the exception of Northumberland House, hard by Charing Cross, it was the only one of the magnificent residences that had once lined the bank of the Thames still standing.

At Temple Bar, Gideon left the town of Westminster to enter the City of London by one of the arched passages designed into the city gate by Sir Christopher Wren to separate pedestrians from horse traffic. He reflected, as he always did, that few men on earth had left a greater impression on any city than the great architect and genius. And with the dozens of buildings he had built in London and outside it, he had designed even more. Only a lack of money had prevented them from being built. Temple Bar was greatly appreciated by those who did not wish to soil their shoes in the dust of the unpaved street, even if it was already too small to admit all the carriages that used it without constant discord between their drivers.

Gideon had walked this far with no fear of being recognized. He had learned that his disguise was good enough to conceal his identity in most situations, but he had used it more than once to visit the bookstall owned by Hester's brother and his wife. So, he took greater care when passing the Bell and Bible, glancing only to see that both were busily occupied serving customers—surely a good sign.

Only a few more steps took him to the bottom of Fetter Lane. He turned up the street and started searching for the house Hester had described. Following a curve in the lane, he spied the sign of the ship just beyond. Then, noting that the house was half-way between two inns, the Red Hart and the White Horse, and espying a tavern between them, he crossed over to it in hopes of securing a vantage-point from which to observe comings and goings.

Like most taverns, this one had a low ceiling supported by dark oak beams with a fire in the hearth and a bar behind which the owner served his customers. What was unusual about it was a large collection of silver tankards, displayed on shelves about the room. Gideon approached the bar, ordered a mug of ale, and asked the owner, who proceeded to serve him, about the rare display. He learned that his host was possessed of an extraordinary sense of patriotism and had had a tankard hammered out in honour of each of the battles the English had won during the war with France. He proudly took each one down to show Gideon its legend, beginning with Englesfield and ending with Malplaquet, the Duke of Marlborough's head stamped onto each.

Gideon congratulated him on his fine collection. Then, having established a rapport with his host, he settled down to drink his ale. Most of the tavern's patrons sat huddled close to the fire, so it was easy to find a spot near the window from which he could study the door across the street.

The house, he noted, was just three doors from where the Great Fire of 1666 had burned to a halt. This was easy to see because of its age. Instead of the brick that had been prescribed for new construction, it was built of wood and plaster, its great timber frame suggesting a width of two rooms. The upper two floors had been jettied out for more space and loomed over the street, the highest floor crowned with a pitched roof. It was a typical tradesman's house in this part of London, if there could be said to be anything typical in these ancient streets. It appeared to consist of a kitchen, a shop, two chambers above, a garret, and possibly a cellar.

The inhabitants of Fetter Lane included a wide variety of tradesmen. From his seat, he spied the premises of a leather-seller, an apothecary, and a tailor. At the bottom of the street he had passed a coal shed and a sign indicating the home of a midwife, while nearer the Holborn end he knew there was a school. Gideon recalled being told that the poet Dryden and the philosopher Hobbes had both been residents of the lane. And he was aware of its reputation for heterodoxy.

The Moravian Chapel, one of the original eight conventicles where Divine worship was permitted, stood near here along with another Independent chapel. The leader of the Puritans, Praise-God Barebone, who had railed against plum-porridge, theatres, dances, and Christmas pudding, had retired from Parliament to a house somewhere in this lane, but it had also housed one of the leaders of the Waller Plot, an attempt by a group of dissenters, royalists, and Cavaliers to overthrow the radicals in Parliament to restore King Charles. Two of the plotters had been executed just north of where Gideon sat.

If the inhabitant of the house he was watching was involved in political intrigue, he would not be the first of his sort in Fetter Lane.

A boy entered the tavern with copies of the *Post Boy* for sale. Gideon paid him for one, then divided his time between reading and keeping an eye out for activity across the street. When he got down to the advertisements, among the several announcing new books just published, lost dogs, stolen horses, houses to let, and the usual patent medicines, one in particular caught his eye.

"Found the 3rd December last, near Spring Garden at Charing Cross, a Gold Snuff Box with Enamel and Brilliants. The Person that lost it giving a Description of it in Writing to Jonathan Wild, Thief-Taker General of Great Britain & Ireland at the Blue Boar Inn in Little Old Bailey Street and leaving Word at the Bar what time he'll call again, may have it return'd, paying the Charge of this Advertisement and other Charges."

Gideon had heard of Jonathan Wild, who styled himself Chief Thief-Taker of Great Britain, a scoundrel who had outsmarted the law by conspiring with most of the thieves in London to sell stolen property back to its owners instead of fencing it to the public market. Usually, Wild would place advertisements inviting persons who had been robbed to describe their lost possession, which he would endeavour to locate in exchange for a fee of a few shillings plus half the value of the item returned. In this way he positioned himself as an investigator, not a fence. The person who had lost something valuable was usually too relieved to have it back to refuse to pay the reward, which would be split between Wild and the thief.

More often, one would see advertisements placed by the person robbed, describing a lost item with the promise of a reward "and no questions asked." Wild had gained so firm a control over the criminal fraternity in London that none dared operate without him. If anyone did, Wild was likely to testify against the thief in court in exchange for the forty pounds offered for such service. It was generally understood that if a stolen object was wanted back, the best thing to do was to contact Jonathan Wild.

To announce an object that had been "found" must mean that no one had advertised its loss. For something as valuable as a gold and diamond snuffbox, this seemed odd.

The tavern-keeper came to see if he could draw Gideon another mug of ale. When he brought the mug back brimming, Gideon said, "I am looking for a friend of my father's, a man by the name of Wilkins. Can you tell me if that is his house?" He pointed to the door at the sign of the ship.

His host stooped to see which house he had indicated, then straightened with a look of disapproval. "I don't know of nobody round 'ere by that name, but I will say, you're not likely to find any friend of yours in that 'ouse over there."

When Gideon asked how he could be so certain, the man replied, "I don't think any gen'leman like yerself would want to take up with the sort I've seen going in there. Why, I've even seen Frenchies pass through that door!"

Gideon arched his brows in amazement, as he assumed he was meant to do. "Frenchmen, eh? Do you know why they come?"

His host glowered. "No, but stands to reason, they've got to be up to no good."

"To whom does the house belong?"

The tavern-keeper gave a grudging shrug. "That would be Mr. Burchet. 'E's a Frenchie hisself. 'Born in France' is the way I've always 'eard it, then moved 'ere to run 'is trading business."

"Has he been there long?"

Another shrug. "S'long as I 'ave, and I came on me marriage, near fifteen year ago."

Gideon thanked him for the information and changed the subject to ask whether the White Horse or the Red Hart was more likely to give him a good dinner. Directed to the White Horse, he downed his ale, paid his bill, and went in search of a meal.

The White Horse was filled with the lawyers from Barnard's Inn, one of the lesser Inns of Chancery. Gideon found himself a seat amongst them and devoted himself to a dinner of mutton, bread and cheese. The meal was good enough to explain the presence of so many pleaders of the law, and it would sate him before he made his way home.

He had decided that it would be pointless to watch the house now. A more active approach was clearly called for. He might have excused the visits of Frenchmen to a house that was occupied by another, had Hester not seen Lord Wragby enter it; but, the combination of Lord Wragby's visits and the owner's nationality was enough to raise his suspicions that some kind of treasonous business had gone on between them.

There was one thing he had not mentioned to Hester, and that was the sense he had got from his evening with the Jacobites that something new was afoot. Their reaction to his presence in London had been one of anticipations met, not at all what one would expect from a defeated faction. Their excitement had appeared to be founded in the validation his arrival had given to their hopes.

Lord Stair had, also, suggested that the agents of James Stuart were still at work. The peace with France had made it clear that the next support for his endeavours would not come from the Regent, but King George had other enemies on the Continent who might be willing to take up the fight that the ruler of France had abandoned.

Gideon had not mentioned his suspicions to Hester because they were merely that. Her interest was in finding Lord Wragby's murderer, which might have nothing to do with the Jacobite cause. On the other hand, if there was a government spy in their midst, and Lord Wragby had discovered him, would not that have been sufficient reason for murder? And the exposure of a government agent was only one of the possible motives for violence that he could imagine when treason was in play.

Gideon made his way to Lambeth at dusk, arriving home to find that Tom had grown anxious over his absence. He greeted his master at the front door in a tone of reproach. "I thought you was going to give Penny a run this afternoon. I had her all saddled and waitin', but in the end, I had to take her out myself."

"It's as well you did, but I hope you did not tire her, for you and I have an errand this evening." Tom listened with a frown as Gideon told him of the house he needed to search and how long the night might be. "It would be better if we rode and took a room at the Red Hart. We may find ourselves waiting for days before an opportunity presents itself."

Tom sighed, not bothering to conceal his displeasure. He had never hidden his disapproval from his master, but he had learned to obey without voicing his complaints. The only thing he said was, "What should I pack, my lord?"

Gideon told him to pack a few clean shirts and fresh underclothes, as well as the paint and patches he would need to maintain his disguise. "I may wish to visit the new friends I've made at the Duke of Albemarle's Head. It makes no sense to go back and forth across the river every night. And this way, if one of them doubts my loyalty and decides to follow me, he will see that I am putting up at an inn, as a traveller would."

While Tom was collecting their belongings for a few nights' stay in town and then saddling the horses, Gideon went upstairs to get his mask and cape. He reckoned that if he were seen breaking into Burchet's house, it would be better if he could not be recognized as the traveller in the long black wig who had stopped at the Red Hart.

After resting for an hour, he went downstairs to find Tom saying goodbye to his wife. Gideon begged her forgiveness for taking her new husband away again, which made Katy smile and erased some of the worry clouding her brow. Gideon knew that Tom's role in their adventure would not be the riskier part, but Katy could not know that, and Gideon would not embarrass Tom in front of his wife by assuring her that he would be perfectly safe. He promised to return him in good order, and left them alone to put his highwayman's disguise in the hiding place Katy had created in his saddle blanket.

Argos followed him from the house and into the stables, eagerly wagging his tail. As Gideon reached Penny's stall, he was taken aback to find the little black boy inside, petting Penny, and apparently unafraid. In truth, he had forgotten about the boy, his mind taken up with his own business. He paused now outside the door, amazed to see his horse, usually all fire and drama, being soothed nearly to sleep by the boy's small hands. He was afraid to speak for fear that he might startle Penny and cause her to lash out.

The boy, however, soon sensed his presence. He stopped petting the horse and turned. His eyes widened with fear at the sight of Gideon, but he must have been expecting him for all he did was dart past him out the door to run into the house.

Penny was a bit startled, but she reacted as calmly as Gideon had ever seen. He greeted her, gently rubbing her muzzle, then put his cape and mask away, wondering at the boy's instinctive harmony with the horse.

When Tom caught him up just a minute later, Gideon told him what he had seen. "There is a future for that child as a groom." He stepped into his stirrup and lifted himself into the saddle. "That, of course, will be if he is not put to some other sort of work.

"You still have not seen an advertisement reporting his loss?"

"No, my lord." Tom mounted and followed Gideon out of the yard on their way to the horse ferry. "I've checked the papers every day, but I swear there's been nothing. I know Katy would like to keep him—she fair dotes on the boy— and you've seen how good he is with horses." A note of pride had entered Tom's voice, which made Gideon smile. It was the same note he had heard as a child whenever his skill in riding had pleased Tom.

"We shall simply have to see who claims him. That is all I can say for now. He still is not talking?"

"No sign that he can talk, my lord. But he understands most things well enough."

"Well, please, see if you can get him to understand that I have no intention whatsoever of harming him."

Tom heaved a sigh with little hope. "I'll try, my lord."

By nine o'clock that evening, they were installed in the Red Hart, up against Mag Pye Alley, Gideon in a room of his own and Tom over the stable where he could take care of his master's horses. Leaving the inn to return to the tavern up the street, Gideon pointed out the Frenchman's house. The only light shining from it came from a single room on the first floor. No candle would ever be left to burn in an empty house, so either Burchet or another member of his household was certain to be in.

No one emerged from the house that night, so they retired, hoping for greater success on the morrow.

Late the next day, just before sunset, leaving Tom to watch the front door, Gideon crossed Fetter Lane to explore how to break in. Burchet's house formed part of a short row between Dean Street and Plough Yard. He turned up Dean Street, but finding no outlet there that would bring him near enough, he retraced his steps and went along to the entrance to Plough Yard. There he found a turning into an alley that ran not only behind Dean Street but also behind Burchet's house. A wooden gate to the property provided access for the night-soil men to the cesspool for the house.

With no one about to notice his suspicious behaviour, Gideon examined the wall at the back of the dwelling to search for footholds. There were no horses in the tiny stable, which meant that Burchet did not keep a horse of his own. Most Londoners found animals too expensive to feed, and, if a horse was needed, one could always be hired. A faint smell of hay and some shuffling sounds farther along the alley told Gideon that a few of the neighbouring stables were occupied, but he suspected that the mews was generally quiet at night.

Satisfied that he had found the best access into Burchet's house, Gideon walked to the end of Plough Yard and wove his way through the gardens of Thavie's Inn, having to scale one wall, before arriving at St. Andrew's Churchyard and emerging on Holborn Hill. He wanted to acquaint himself with another exit to Plough Yard in case someone in Burchet's house called for the Watch.

In short order, he had crossed Holborn Bridge over the New Canal, a widening of the Fleet River, up which barges from Newcastle brought their loads of coal to the warehouses that lined it. Then, he followed Cow Lane up to Smithfield and made his way to St. John's Gate, a journey of little more than a mile, before heading for the Duke of Albemarle's Head.

This time he was in luck. The men he had met at St. John's Gate were sitting at a table with Sir Francis Lichfield, whom he recognized from his school days. They had never been friends, but still there was a risk Sir Francis would identify him if he let his disguise slip. Gideon had cultivated a different air and a voice to suit his painted guise, and he had learned that confidence was the key to any deception.

The gentlemen spotted him as soon as he entered and waved him over to join them. Gideon placed his order at the bar before drawing up a stool to their table. He pretended not to know Sir Francis while the two from his previous encounter introduced them, giving the name that he told them he had assumed for his purpose here in London—O'Brien.

Gideon was grateful for the darkness of the room and the smoke from pipes being puffed around him, for Sir Francis fixed his eyes upon Gideon's face to study his features before a steady return of his gaze made him turn away. After that, he resumed the nervous, shifting glances Gideon recalled as being his characteristic habit.

"We were hoping to find you here," his friend in the dark green coat said. "Have you brought us any news?"

Gideon shook his head. "I was not sent here to carry news. You must have other friends for that. My purpose here is different."

They were clearly disappointed, so Gideon offered, "The death of our friend Lord Wragby has left a vacancy. A missing link, if you will, which I have been sent to repair, and I shall need your help."

Taking a risk, he added, "As I am sure you know, Lord Wragby was in contact with our friends over the water, sending useful information. Who will take his place?" He turned to face Sir Francis, as if he should be the logical choice.

Looking anywhere but back at "O'Brien", Sir Francis shifted on his stool. "That is not something I can do. Phillip—Lord Wragby—enjoyed a degree of protection through his father that few of us have."

"It does not appear to have protected him for long. He returned from seeing his Majesty less than three months ago, and now he is dead."

"That is not the sort of protection I meant. The government here would have thought twice before arresting any son of Lord Ireton's. He's much too powerful and his support for the Crown is vital." Sir Francis's tone turned bitter. "Phillip could say things that would have had anyone of us taken up for treason—and often did."

"Who do you think killed him? Would someone loyal to the usurper George have done it to put a halt to his activities?"

The three men looked at one another. Gideon's friend in the brown coat offered him snuff from a silver box, and Gideon took a pinch, placed it on his coat sleeve, and sniffed while they considered their response.

Eventually, Green Coat broke their silence. "It is something we've discussed. But if a person in the government were responsible, he would have had to be very careful not to leave any trace, or Lord Ireton would have punished him, himself. Besides, it could just as easily have been that servant of Lord Hawkhurst's. That is what Lord Ireton believes, at any rate."

"A servant? Do you mean that Lord Hawkhurst might have sent a servant to kill him? We know he is a Whig."

Gideon had posed the question to appear ignorant of his cousin's character, but he was amused by the laughter it drew. Brown Coat scoffed, "You must not know Lord Hawkhurst, even by reputation, for a greater coward never lived. Nor anyone less engaged in politics."

Gideon acknowledged this with a nod. "So, who is this servant? And what would have been his motive?"

Brown Coat shrugged. "He's a steward or some such."

Sir Francis scoffed. "A dog in the manger if ever I saw one. Phillip had his eye on Lady Hawkhurst's sister and made his intentions abundantly clear. The fellow was clearly besotted with her—fancied himself her guard dog—but we knew who was going to get her in the end. Her lady mother would have seen to that. But something must have occurred between the two because Phillip sent his footmen to punish the dog for his insolence."

Gideon could not resist asking, "So, the girl preferred Lord Wragby?"

Sir Francis squirmed beneath his fixed stare. "What would that have to say to anything?"

Remembering the voice Hester had heard in St. Paul's, Gideon asked, "Did you ever hear Lord Wragby threaten to throttle this fellow?"

An impatient look came over Sir Francis's face. "Didn't I just say that Phillip sent his footmen to beat him? He would never have touched him himself. Phillip was proud like his father. He would never have lowered himself to fight with anyone so far beneath him."

Gideon let the matter drop. He signalled to the tavern-keeper to bring another round of drinks. After the drawer served them and moved away, he returned to the subject of who might take Lord Wragby's place in the conspiracy. It was a good pretence to meet the other suspect Hester had identified among the viscount's friends, so he asked if Lord Charters was sufficiently committed to the cause to fill his dead friend's shoes.

"You will have to ask him yourself." Sir Francis's hesitation betrayed his doubts. "I can arrange for you to meet him, if you like."

"The sooner you can arrange it, the better. Send word to me at the

Red Hart in Fetter Lane."

At the mention of his lodging place, Gideon thought he saw a flicker of recognition in Sir Francis's eyes. It was possible that Sir Francis knew of the connection between Lord Wragby and Burchet. Neither of the other two betrayed any knowledge of it, however, so Gideon did not mention the Frenchman.

Having discovered all he could for now, he took his leave, repeating his desire to meet Lord Charters as soon as possible. No one questioned the need for urgency, which confirmed his suspicion that another Jacobite plot might be imminent.

Gideon returned to the tavern to hear Tom's news. He had watched Burchet's house until the candle in the upstairs window had been extinguished. No one had left the house since, so Tom assumed that Burchet had simply retired for the night.

There was nothing more to be done tonight. Tomorrow, they would watch the house again to see how well it was guarded and to spot the Frenchman.

Oft have you hinted to your brother Peer,
A certain truth, which many buy too dear:
Something there is more needful than Expense,
And something previous even to Taste—'tis Sense:
Good Sense, which only is the gift of Heaven,
And though no Science, fairly worth the seven:
A Light, which in yourself you must perceive;
Jones and Le Nôtre have it not to give.

CHAPTER XII

Hester was having more difficuly investigating Lord Ireton's friends. With few gatherings at Court since the King's return, she had no opportunity to pose questions, and since Harrowby wished to avoid Lord Ireton, it was highly unlikely that she would encounter them at Hawkhurst House.

Under these circumstances, she found that the best source of information was Sir Marmaduke, who loved to gossip and who could be counted upon to know everything about anyone of consequence or even a passing interest. One morning, at Isabella's *levée,* a chance remark of his and a few questions on Hester's part elicited the information that Lord Wragby's young widow, Lady Wragby, had come to London and was once again residing with her father in Theobald's Row.

"She was left without a *sou,* you know. Lord Ireton never sanctioned their marriage and without a contract, she received no widow's portion."

"Is it possible that Lord Ireton will be moved by their shared grief to make a small provision for her, at least?"

Sir Marmaduke gave Hester a pitying look for her *naïveté* and shook his head. "She was fortunate that the General forgave her enough to offer her a home. Do not forget that she eloped, thereby earning her father's ire, as well as the marquess's."

"Poor child—for she must have been little more than that, surely."

"Old enough to know what it means to obey. But I am told Lord Wragby could be very persuasive when he wished."

Hester ignored the unspoken invitation to gossip about Mary. "He certainly could be persistent," was all she said.

Their conversation, however, gave her an idea, which she mentioned to Mary that very afternoon. After telling her what Sir Marmaduke had said, Hester added, "What would you say to the idea of paying Lady Wragby a visit? If she is as destitute as Sir Marmaduke says, she may be very glad to receive one, even from two complete strangers."

Mary looked stricken. "Oh, Hester! How could I face her when her husband pursued me so scandalously? She may have heard, and blames me for their estrangement."

"All the more reason to show how blameless you are. We might not learn anything of importance, but if she is virtually friendless, we shall at least have done a good deed. I can go alone if you prefer."

"No . . . I shall go with you. If she doesn't wish to speak to me, she can always deny us at the door."

Now, with Mary's agreement, Hester had to choose the most auspicious moment, not only to beg Mrs. Mayfield's permission, but to request the use of the carriage. She did not know how to get to Theobald's Row, but she believed it was too far away to be certain of securing a hackney coach. According to Sir Marmaduke, it was north of Red Lyon Square, for all intents and purposes out in the country.

The opportunity arose just two days later when Harrowby was summoned to Court to kiss the King's hand. Isabella and her mother accompanied him to the Palace in chairs to pay their addresses to Lady Hinchinbrook, who had been made Lady of the Bedchamber to the Princess of Wales in the place of the Countess of Berkeley, who had died. Since their visit was a private audience, they did not invite Hester and Mary to go with them; so with a little manoeuvring on Hester's part, the carriage was put at their disposal.

As soon as the three had departed in chairs for St. James's, Hester and Mary set off in Lord Hawkhurst's coach with the earl's coat of arms emblazoned on both doors. Hester had asked permission just to take Mary out for fresh air, claiming that her lack of spirits and pallor were likely due to the soot in the air, to which she was not yet accustomed. Her request had been made so reasonably that Mrs. Mayfield could not complain, and since the use of his coach posed not the least inconvenience to Harrowby, he did not much care where it took them. Beyond cautioning them not to let the coachman take them out onto the heath—for reports of highwaymen had appeared in the newssheets, one being so audicious as to rob the Bristol mail—no one put up any resistance to their plan.

After a brief discussion of their route, the coachman drove them down Piccadilly. At Hester's request, he turned north to the Tyburn Road, so that later she could honestly say that they had driven by pastures, though the prospect of fields in January offered nothing but greys and browns. Still, both young ladies felt a sense of adventure at having the coach to themselves and escaping the confines of Hawkhurst House. They shared a love for clean air and the view of open ground.

Soon, rolling and bumping along Great Russell Street, Hester pointed out the two great mansions, Montague House and Southampton House. The first stood behind a pair of ornate gilt gates. Hester was able to describe a few of its rooms, for she had attended a masked ball there. She relished the memory of that adventure with St. Mars and their stroll back to Hawkhurst House, the exhilarating freedom of being out alone with him at night, the danger they had encountered, and the excitement of their closeness.

A smile must have betrayed the nature of her thoughts, for Mary broke into them, asking curiously, "Did you dance with someone in particular?"

"No, I did not dance at all, but it was a grand occasion all the same."

"I think I should like to attend a masked ball, but I would be sad not to dance."

"I should not be surprised if an opportunity to attend one were to arise very soon." The nobility were pouring into town with the opening of Parliament and the social season. "Invitations will begin filling the house in the next week, I suspect."

The coachman had turned just beyond Southampton House. Now, he turned left into another thoroughfare and slowed the horses to a stop. Hester had informed him that she would have to ask directions to the house they meant to visit.

"This is Theobald's Row, mistress," he called back.

Hester let down the window and beckoned to a boy sweeping the street. She asked him to discover which house was General Green's and promised him a penny for his effort.

He answered promptly by pointing out a new brick house with a red door on the south side of the street. "No need to find it, mistress. The Gen'ral lives there."

Hester thanked him, gave him his penny, and called up to the coachman to deposit them at the house with the red door. He drove to the corner and turned the coach around to pull up on the proper side of the street. As they turned, Hester glimpsed open ground ahead. She had never been north of Holborn in this area, but she guessed that both Lincoln's Inn and Gray's Inn must be near.

The coachman climbed down from his box, let down the step, and handed Hester and Mary down.

"We should not be long, if you wish to walk the horses," Hester said, "but please wait to see if we are admitted before you drive away."

The coachman tipped his felt hat before climbing back up to his seat. Hester glanced at the surrounding buildings and noted that several new ones were being built across the street. This must once have been the very outskirts of town, but it seemed that everywhere she went, the city was growing.

Mary and she nervously eyed each other, and with a bracing breath, Hester said, "Well, let us see if Lady Wragby or her father will receive us."

They knocked, and the door was soon opened by a manservant with a military bearing. Inviting them in out of the cold, he took their names and asked them to wait while he searched for his mistress. He returned from a brief trip upstairs to inform them that Lady Wragby would see them. It was evident that having the widow of a viscount living in his master's house gave him a sense of importance, even if no fortune had come with the title.

They were shown into a withdrawing room that had been fitted for a military gentleman. The furnishings were plain, and there were no trimmings or flourishes to indicate the taste of a woman, just sensible wooden chairs.

A young lady dressed in black bombazine stood to greet them, polite confusion on her face. She was a very pretty girl with English roses in her cheeks, fair hair, and large blue eyes. She appeared to be no older than Mary, though she must be eighteen by now. All three made their curtsies before Hester informed her that they had come to express their sympathy on the loss of her husband.

Having first given her own name, Hester indicated Mary with a slight movement of her head. "My cousin, Mrs. Mary Mayfield, and I were briefly acquainted with Lord Wragby, and having heard that you were recently come up to London, we wished to pay our respects."

Lady Wragby turned to study Mary and tears filled her eyes. "I see," she said, in a dignified tone. "It was kind of you to bother."

Moved by pity, and anxious to erase any misunderstanding, Mary impulsively seized their hostess's hand. "I assure you that our motive in coming was just that. We were only slightly acquainted with your husband, but we knew of your devotion to him. We hoped that some company might offer you a bit of comfort, but if we are intruding, I pray you will tell us and we will leave."

She spoke so warmly that no one could doubt her sincerity, least of all a young lady who must be finding herself in need of friends. With a shaky smile, Lady Wragby invited them to sit and asked the servant who had ushered them in and still waited by the door to bring them some tea.

"Yes, my lady," he said proudly. Before leaving on his errand, he moved a tall, round table into the space between their chairs, then bowed at the door.

Lady Wragby looked a bit embarrassed to be the object of such deference, but she did not comment on it. "Pray tell me how you came to know my husband," she said.

To spare Mary the necessity of inventing a story, Hester piped up with an explanation of their relationship to Lord and Lady Hawkhurst, which had brought them both to Court not long after Lord Wragby's return from France. "We met a few times at Hampton Court, and Lord Wragby was kind enough to call upon us at Hawkhurst House. We could not have met him much more than half a dozen times—" which was true, Hester thought— "but he always condescended to chat with us when we did."

She held her breath, exhausted by the need to fudge the truth. It was the information she was obliged to leave out that had tested her.

Mary did not give their hostess any time to respond. "You must have met him when you were very young, yourself," she interjected. "How did you make his acquaintance?"

A wistful look came over Lady Wragby's face, but she blushed when she said, "I was shopping at the New Exchange when Phillip saw me. I did not know who he was, and it was very improper to speak to him, I know, but he insisted on learning my name. He told me his, and at first I did not believe him, but then I noticed the footmen attending him and realized he must be the nobleman he claimed to be.

"He followed me home and called again the next day. My father was alarmed by the attention Phillip paid me. He doubted the seriousness of his intentions, but Phillip truly did love me, and I soon returned his affection. It was impossible to resist such devotion." A longing filled her voice. "My poor father tried to keep us apart, but Phillip refused to be defeated. I should be ashamed to tell you that we eloped." She sent both her visitors a challenging look, and for an instant, Hester caught a glimpse of a wilful streak—she was, after all, a general's daughter. "But we loved each other so intensely that we had to be married, and I cannot regret anything that brought me such happiness . . . even if only for a very short time."

She did not say when that happiness had ended, but they knew that Lord Wragby had left her just a few months after their elopement. Her gaze fell to the black-gloved hands in her lap, and they heard her sigh. Being witness to such undeserved grief was painful.

Fortunately, they were interrupted by the servant who carried in a tray with three cups and the accoutrements for making and serving tea. He placed them on the table and asked if everything was in order before leaving his mistress to fulfil her role.

Lady Wragby took a key from the chatelaine at her waist and opened the tea caddy. She carefully measured some leaves into the pot, already filled with hot water. Her motions were quaint, like a child performing a grown-up task.

Once the tea had been served, Hester returned to their topic. "Of course, you could not resist such an ardent courtship. I hope your father realized he was mistaken about Lord Wragby's intentions, as soon as it became evident that they were honourable."

"Yes . . . ." Lady Wragby sounded as if she had more to say, and eventually added, "He was never quite reconciled to our marriage, though. He was troubled by the unequalness of our stations and by the knowledge that my husband's father disapproved of the match."

Hester was surprised by her candor, but she supposed that it was a relief to Lady Wragby to unburden herself, even to two strangers. Her father, being a military man, might not offer the most sympathetic ear, and there was no evidence of another female in the house.

"Has Lord Ireton come round? We know how grieved he is by his son's death."

Lady Wragby swallowed her tears and attempted a smile. "No, I fear he has not. He has made it clear that my marriage to his son was unacceptable and that I am not to regard him in the light of a father. That is why you find me here instead of in my husband's house. Lord Ireton sent a messenger with a letter immediately upon Phillip's death, saying that I was to remove from his son's house in Norfolk as soon as possible, which he trusted would be within a fortnight."

Hester and Mary expressed their dismay, murmuring sympathetic noises. Though they had already been informed of Lord Ireton's heartless treatment of his son's widow, the abruptness of his cruelty still came as a shock.

"How did you contrive?"

Their hostess threw a nervous glance at the door, as if afraid that someone might enter and overhear. Then, after a brief hesitation, her need for comfort overcame her reticence. "At first, I was in such despair, I did not know where to turn. My father had not yet forgiven me for eloping, you see. But with no other recourse, I wrote to him and he immediately agreed to help. He sent Josiah to fetch me and my clothes. I had little else in the way of belongings."

Hester indicated the door with a slight tilt of her head. "Is Josiah the servant we've seen?"

A glimmer of affection lit Lady Wragby's eyes. "Yes, Josiah has been my father's sergeant for years. I have known him all my life, and he has always taken the best care of me."

"It must be a comfort to have such a devoted servant."

"Yes, I was very glad to see him. And it is a comfort, too, that he never scolds."

Her tone suggested that her father had not been quite so forbearing. It would be a rare father, Hester thought, who could forget the hurt that his only daughter's elopement must have caused. She knew from experience how some men could nurse a grievance. After her brother Jeremy had left home, their father had never mentioned his name again.

"Well, I hope that Lord Ireton will regret the way he has treated you. Has he made no provision for you at all?" Again, she knew the answer, but she prolonged the conversation to see what other information she might glean.

"Lord Ireton made it plain from the start that he would never support me in any way. It was his uncompromising hostility to me that destroyed my husband's affection. He made Phillip choose between us, and I cannot blame my husband for his choice. But I shall never forgive Lord Ireton for doing it. Never!"

That hint of a martial element in her nature appeared again. It should help her recover from her loss, Hester thought, and the resentment she felt for Lord Ireton had certainly been earned.

"Have none of Lord Ireton's friends been of any service to you?"

She made a scoffing sound. "No, in fact, it was a friend of Lord Ireton's who brought the letter ordering me to leave our house."

"Sir Horatio Allenby?" At Lady Wragby's look of surprise, Hester explained, "I have known him to be Lord Ireton's messenger in another unpleasant business. He has an officious character, and I believe Lord Ireton's patronage elevates his sense of importance."

"No, it was Lord William Silsbee."

"Really? I had heard that he was capable of greater kindness."

Lady Wragby sighed. "I did receive the impression that the errand made him uncomfortable and he was very polite, but Phillip told me once that Lord William has great political ambitions, and his best way to achieve them is to court Lord Ireton's favour. His family's fortune has dwindled and his father cannot afford to advance his prospects."

That much was understandable, Hester supposed, but she had to wonder how far Lord William would go to please his patron. As the son of an earl, even the youngest in a numerous family, surely it must have been galling to be sent on such an errand. But if Lord William were so eager to curry Lord Ireton's favour, that would seem to absolve him from suspicion in Lord Wragby's murder.

"But what about Lord Wragby's friends? I know I have seen him with Sir Francis Lichfield and Lord Charters."

Lady Wragby recoiled on hearing the two names. After a moment's hesitation, all she said was, "I fear that my husband was not always prudent in his choice of friends. I would be reluctant to accept the friendship of those two gentlemen, even should they offer it."

There was something in her manner that discouraged Hester from pursuing the topic. Lady Wragby's objection to the two men could have been their politics, but it felt like something else. Something morally repugnant? Hester had seen a hint of revulsion on the widow's face.

The spirit of trust that had slowly developed between them seemed to have been broken. Lady Wragby looked as if she regretted how forthcoming she had been. In truth, the spilling of such confidences to two strangers was extremely imprudent. She had no way of knowing if Hester and Mary would keep them or repeat what she had said to every person at Court.

When they soon stood to leave, Hester was moved to reassure the young widow. She took her by the hand and said, "It was kind of you to receive us today. I hope our visit has not added to your distress. That was certainly not our intention. And, if there is anything we can do to ease your grief, I hope you will advise us."

Though Hester had not promised to keep their conversation private, Lady Wragby's obvious relief told her that she had understood the words as a pledge of discretion. With a lightened demeanour, she bid Hester and Mary farewell and expressed the hope that they would visit again.

∅

On the third evening of their watch on Burchet's house, Tom noticed that the last candle had been extinguished, and a few moments later, the Frenchman left by the front door, bundled in a dark wool cloak and cocked felt hat. Tom followed him down Fetter Lane until he climbed into a hackney coach. Then, Tom returned to the Red Hart, where his master was waiting.

Earlier in the day, Tom had observed the comings and goings at the house and had determined that none of the servants that Burchet employed slept on the premises. The last servant had quitted the place just after eight o'clock, leaving his master alone in the room where the single candle shone.

Tom reported all this to Gideon, who immediately sprang from the bed and went to the wash-basin to rinse his face of its paint and patches. Dipping his hands repeatedly into the water, he instructed Tom to collect the things he would need. By the time he had dried his face and hands and donned his fur-lined cloak, they were ready to depart. The only element of his disguise he retained was the long black wig to conceal his yellow hair.

They exited the inn through the yard to avoid encountering the innkeeper or his wife. Then they strode to the entrance to Plough Yard and turned into the short alley Gideon had discovered on the previous day. Here, they were forced to move forward at a snail's pace. Except for the light from a sliver of a moon and a few scattered stars that managed to shine through the thick haze of coal smoke covering the area, the alley was in total darkness. They carried no lanterns or torches to alert the neighbours to the presence of strangers, but a half-dozen dogs barked at them from behind garden walls. As far as Gideon had been able to tell from a quick glance, no one had observed them ducking into the narrow entrance to Plough Yard, but he did not know how long the dogs would need to bark before someone bothered to investigate.

Keeping one hand against the wall to guide him, he led Tom round the bend in the alley, until the feel of splintered wood touched his palm. With a hiss of warning, he stopped and turned to remove his wig. He handed it to Tom, then felt inside the leather saddlebag Tom carried for his blue mask and cape. He donned them both, before accepting the tricorn Tom extended. He had little need of a hat, but the brim, though cocked, would still provide a shadow over his face.

Gideon wiped his palms on his breeches. After two long days of waiting, it was thrilling to be doing something, at last.

"Wait for me here," he whispered, "and do not worry. I shall be in and out as quickly as possible."

"What do you want me to do if a cry is raised for the Watch?"

"Circle round to the front and direct the crowd towards Fleet Street. I will make my way back to the inn by way of Holborn. But if Mrs. Kean was correct, I doubt that any cry will be raised. If there are Jacobite secrets in the house, Burchet will not dare call the Watch."

With Tom's whisper to "mind where he stepped," Gideon tried the gate. When it proved to be locked, he got a boost over the fence and landed quietly on the other side. He paused until his eyes made out the shape of the building and consulted his memory. Then, carefully and quietly he made his way around the outdoor privy to the right-side corner of the house, where he had noticed chinks in the plaster abutting one support.

He felt up the side of the timber and found not only chinks for his hands and feet, but a stout wooden peg that had worked its way partially out over the years. Holding onto the peg with one hand, he used the other to grasp for a gap in the plaster and started his cautious climb, creeping upwards one finger-hold and toe-hold at a time. In this painstaking way, he eventually arrived at the middle story, which he recognized by the jointure between two timbers. These provided him with a narrow ledge on which to rest. He paused for a full minute before edging along it until he felt the framing for a window beneath his hand.

As he had hoped, the window had nothing but a shutter as a cover. The older, more modest houses had been built without the expensive luxury of glass. When he clung to one of its panels to feel about for a latch, the shutter swung outward, nearly dislodging him from his perch. Scrambling, he regained his balance, opened the panel, and hoisted himself over the window ledge.

The threatened fall had set his heart to pumping, but he was pleased to find that the shutter had not been locked. Burchet—or his housekeeper, if he had one—must not have thought it likely that a burglar would attempt to enter by the upper story. Gideon knew of the aversion the French had to sleeping in a room with all the windows closed.

He could see much better now, for a fire had been banked in the hearth. The glow from the embers was strong enough to show him that he had arrived in a kind of office, which must once have been a bedchamber. A desk, a chair, and a chest used up half the space, while the rest seemed devoted to the storage of papers. Along one wall, shelves made of planks had been placed to hold registers, and a few more littered the floor. Against another wall stood a cabinet with pigeon holes, with papers poking out of some of them. On the wall behind the desk, bundles of papers hung on strings. These would most likely have something to do with Burchet's trade.

To find what he was looking for, Gideon would need more light. He felt his way to the door, where he expected to find a candle.

His hand immediately fell upon a shallow dish, resting on a stand by the door. He took it over to the fire and, using a live coal, lit the candle it held. He brought it back and held it in one hand while opening the desk with the other. Finding a few letters in French, he leafed through them, but found nothing suspicious at first. Then, digging at the back of the drawer, he discovered Burchet's copy-book and sat in the chair to study it.

Here was the evidence he had sought. Gideon's pulse raced as he worked his way through the copies of a dozen or more letters that Burchet, presumably, had written to someone in France. The letters professed to be concerned with a business affair. Large sums of money were mentioned, but the source of them was vague. In one letter, Burchet appeared to be asking how large a sum his correspondent expected him to raise. In another, it was he who pledged to raise some twenty thousand pounds or more, but the letter did not reveal the purpose of the money.

The letters had been written to an Abbot Butler of Cambrai in France. The name Butler alone was enough to raise Gideon's suspicions because it was the name of the former Duke of Ormonde. The duke, once one of the most powerful peers in Great Britain, had been stripped of his lands, his titles, and numerous honours for plotting to put James Stuart on the throne. Now, he lived as an exile in Paris, like his father who had fought for Charles I. The Butlers were an ancient Irish family, tracing their lineage back to Charlemagne. They had always been loyal to the Crown. Converting from the Roman Catholic Church to the Church of Ireland had cost the last duke the affections of his family, but it had made his descendants very wealthy. Still, the majority of that name would have retained their Catholic faith, so it came as no surprise to discover that one was an abbot. And, as Catholics, they would be even more dedicated to James Stuart.

Other letters in Burchet's desk had been directed to D'Aulmay de Coulange, still others to Mr. Harvey of Combe, two men Gideon knew to be Jacobites. The most suspicious thing about them was the use of initials in the place of names. From the context of the letters, Gideon thought that M.H. might refer to Mr. Harvey, D.D. to the Duke of Ormond, and M.B. possibly to the former Lord Bolingbroke, who had been the Pretender's Secretary of State.

He searched through the desk again and found a few more letters, written over a year ago and bearing Mr. Harvey's signature. In these, numbers instead of letters had been used to disguise the names. From the context, Gideon believed that 22 stood for the Duke D'Aumont, 6 for the late King Louis XIV of France, who had supplied the Pretender with arms and ships for his invasion, and 8 for the Pretender himself. Number 9 seemed to refer to King George, but Gideon could not guess as to the meaning of 24000 or 14.

In the end, it did not matter. He had ample evidence that Burchet, if not a spy, had been engaged in raising money for the Jacobite cause. He might also have acted as a messenger between Lord Wragby and the Pretender's men in France, sending letters under the pretext of business between himself and someone being helped by Abbot Butler.

He studied the last letter in Burchet's copy-book to search for a reference to any current plot but saw nothing in it to alarm him. Neither did he find any reference to Lord Wragby or his friends, nothing to help him uncover a motive for the viscount's murder.

Disappointed, he returned the papers to the desk and got ready to leave. He did not bother to hide the traces of his presence, reasoning that if Burchet did notice them, they would act as a warning. It was foolish to keep evidence of his treason lying about.

The sound of a tread on the other side of the door made him freeze. He must not have heard the opening of the front door or the steps on the stairs. But the house had stood, perhaps, for hundreds of years. Its timbers would be so aged and hard that they would scarcely give.

Instead of fleeing, Gideon blew out the candle and placed it on the desk. Then, quickly moving to the window, he drew his sword and stood, just as the door was flung wide.

At first, nobody entered. Then, a head peeked around. The dark silhouette of a man, his arm raised with a cudgel, appeared in the doorway. The Frenchman must have seen the glow of his candle and realized that an intruder was inside.

Gideon did not wait for Burchet's charge, for the cudgel looked thick enough to disarm him. Instead, he said quietly, "I am not here to rob you, but if you do not put that weapon down, I may be forced to use violence. Why don't you step inside the room, so we can have a chat."

"Who are you?" Burchet did not obey, but stood with his cudgel raised. He did not sound alarmed.

Gideon supposed that a man who would engage in treason when the penalty for it was a gruesome death must have steely nerves. He took a firmer grip on his sword.

"I am a friend of Lord Wragby's," he said. "I am trying to find his killer."

Burchet lowered his cudgel a few inches, but he did not come in. "Well, you will not find his killer here." He spoke with only a slight French accent, as if he had spoken English for years.

"He used you to send messages to James at Avignon, did he not?"

Burchet took a few steps forward to peer at his desk, the condition of which could be made out in the glow from the dying coals.

"So, you have been through my papers. Then you will have seen that there is nothing in them concerning Lord Wragby's death."

"Yes, but I wonder if any of his more clandestine activities could have driven someone to kill him."

Even in the dark, Gideon detected Burchet's shrug, a peculiarly French gesture that never ceased to amuse him. "You will have to ask that of someone else, monsieur. It is really nothing to do with me."

"And it did not worry you to lose a confederate in this manner?"

"If I am to be honest with you, monsieur—and considering that sword in your hand, I should be—no, not at all. Lord Wragby had an image of himself and his importance to his Majesty that was not—how shall I say—of the most precise. He played at spying, as an actor plays upon the stage."

"You do not think it possible that one of your other confederates killed him to silence him? I know he could be indiscreet."

Burchet gave an exaggerated nod. "This is possible, yes, but if it is so, no one has informed me of this intention." He paused, then asked politely, "Have I answered all of your questions, Monsieur-with-the Mask?"

Gideon found himself liking this curious agent. "I believe you have for now."

"If for now, then forever, for I assure you that my answers shall never change."

Burchet had rested his cudgel against the door jamb, so Gideon sheathed his sword and bowed. "I shall leave you then, monsieur. I would suggest, however, that you burn some of the papers I discovered in your desk. Your copy-book would be of great interest to the authorities, and if they were to read it, I fear you would not be permitted to live much longer."

"Who's to say whose book that is, monsieur? It was not written in my hand, which can easily be proved. If you looked at my work upon on the wall, you would see that for yourself."

Gideon wondered what to make of this statement, which Burchet had spoken with the utmost certainty.

It was his turn to shrug. "As you say, then. *Au revoir, monsieur.*

Bonne nuit."

He thought of asking Burchet if he might use the stairs and front door to leave the house, but realized he would be forced to remove his mask and cape in the street. Besides, such an exit seemed unworthy of the conversation that had passed between them. So, with no more ado, he climbed back out of the window and, finding his finger-holds again, edged back along the swollen timber until he reached the corner. Then, he lowered himself like a cat down the trunk of a tree until the ground seemed close enough to drop without risking a fall. Landing safely, he crossed the small garden and, finding the latch on this side, let himself out of the gate.

Instantly, Tom appeared at his side. "You were in there a long time, my lord."

"A bit longer than I intended. Hand me my wig, and let's get out of this alley. I will tell you what I learned over a mug at the Red Hart."

Who has the vanity to call you friend,
Yet wants the honour, injured, to defend;
Who tells whate'er you think, whate'er you say,
And, if he lie not, must at least betray . . . .

CHAPTER XIII

In the morning, Gideon received a message from Sir Francis that Lord Charters would be willing to meet him at the King's Head that evening at ten o'clock. Unwilling to waste time at the Red Hart all day, he sent Tom home and walked the streets to familiarize himself with this area of London. He knew it could pay to know its exits and alleys in case he found himself in the position of having to flee.

He first revisited the neighbourhood of St. John's Gate—much less sinister by daylight, with the bustle of ordinary traffic and a great deal of building in progress in St. John's Lane. North of the gate, in what should have been the centre of the former priory, there were rows of new houses of three stories with flat brick fronts. At the end, however, where the court widened into a square, he discovered remnants of older houses.

A large shuttered house on one side and the shell of a burned-out church on the other reminded Gideon of an incident he had heard of. A few years back, when he was travelling abroad with his tutor, his father had written to say that the old priory church of St. John's, then being used as a Presbyterian meeting house, had been gutted by a High-Church mob. The riot had arisen in response to the arrest of a Tory clergyman who had preached on the threat to the Church of

England posed by nonconformists. The rioters had burned the church pews in front of the mansion across the square, which belonged to the Whig Bishop Burnet. Although deploring the violence, his father had written of the tumult with barely suppressed glee. Bishop Burnet had since died. His house, with its imposing pediment, appeared to be empty, but the large garden in its forecourt showed signs of being kept.

The ancient church must originally have been a more imposing structure. The Dissolution had seen it much reduced in size. It stood hemmed in by tenements on the south and a house on the north. Gideon had recently seen an advertisement offering the building for sale or rent.

The City of London was full of such histories; but he reminded himself that he was not here to be a tourist. He made note of the alley at the rear of the square, which could carry him into Clerkenwell Green and back to St. John Street, should he need it. Then he retraced his steps past Smithfield to study the streets between Newgate and St. Paul's, in preparation for his meeting that night with Lord Charters.

As he walked, he was distracted by pleasant thoughts of Hester and the prospect of seeing her on the morrow. He looked forward to the spring when he hoped their investigation would be concluded, the thaw would make the Channel safer to cross, and they could finally live together.

He was happily engaged in these musings when the stench from Newgate Market jolted him back into an awareness of his whereabouts. As the nearest market to the cattle sales at Smithfield, it carried the freshest beef and pork in town, but the waste from its many butchers tainted the air. The roast beef at the King's Head that evening would be tempting as long as the wind did not carry the odours from Newgate Market eastward.

Deciding that he had explored the streets enough, and feeling hungry in spite of the stench, Gideon turned back towards his lodgings with the intention of stopping to eat in an ordinary on the way. He passed beneath Newgate and had reached the Old Bailey when the people in front of him parted to reveal an apparition.

A man, in his fifties perhaps, was parading towards him down the street, a sword at his side and a long silver staff in one hand. Gazing about with a proprietary air, he strolled as if the street were his kingdom and the pedestrians his subjects. As he passed, he tipped his tricorn hat to Gideon, who noticed that the head of the man's staff had been cast in the shape of a crown.

A question from a nearby pedestrian elicited the response that the man with the staff was the notorious Jonathan Wild, the greatest thief-taker in the City of London. Gideon paused to gaze after the man, who turned into the Old Bailey. Seeing Wild reminded Gideon of the advertisement he had seen for the snuffbox, which had appeared again in last night's *Evening Post.*

So. That puffed-up specimen was the infamous Jonathan Wild, who was said to have nabbed so many thieves. His was an unsavoury business at best, since a person could be hanged for stealing just a modest value of goods. Wild had looked harmless enough until Gideon had looked into his eyes. Something in their depths had sent an unpleasant shiver down his spine.

But thievery was not Gideon's immediate concern. A growl from his stomach reminded him of his current needs, so he put the thief-taker out of his mind and started planning how to extract useful information out of Lord Charters.

That evening found him seated with Lord Charters and Sir Francis Lichfield at a table at the King's Head. The panels on the walls were very dark and the air was thick with smoke from the fire and the patrons' clay pipes. A burning strip of cloth in a dish of animal fat provided the only light for their table, and it routinely spit.

Sir Francis had greeted Gideon with shifty-eyed nervousness and presented him to Lord Charters, who had acknowledged him with the merest sketch of a bow. It was evident that he considered this meeting beneath him and had come with the greatest reluctance. Nevertheless, he had condescended to take a seat and to be treated to a glass of brandy.

Before he could take a first sip, Gideon raised his own glass, and asked, "What toast do you propose, my lord?"

Lord Charters rightly took this for a challenge. After checking over his shoulder, he irritably replied, "Why to the king over the water, of course."

"To the king over the water!" Gideon repeated with more force. They raised their glasses and took a swallow. "You will forgive me," Gideon said, placing his down, "but in the current circumstances one cannot be too careful."

"That is precisely why we never should have met," Lord Charters growled. "I do not know what your business is, but I should think that last year's defeat would have put an end to planning for the moment. Regrettably, of course, but nevertheless . . . ."

"Does that mean you have lost faith in the cause?"

Lord Charters looked down his nose. "Do not presume to question my loyalty to his Majesty. You forget your place."

Gideon bowed his head. "Forgive me, my lord; my ardour is to blame, as well as frustration over our recent defeat. I am here to tell you, however, that his Majesty will never give up his righteous quest. His agents still work hard on his behalf. You must have had some knowledge of this through your friendship with the late Lord Wragby."

Lord Charters waved a hand. "Yes, Phillip let on what he was about, but I thought that it all came to naught when he ran through his allowance and was forced to come home," he scoffed. Friend or no, having already come into his own inheritance, Lord Charters could afford to sneer at Lord Wragby for being dependent on his father.

His reference to Lord Wragby's business in France confirmed Gideon's suspicion that Lord Wragby was the "young fool" Lord Stair had referred to, the gentleman James had employed as a go-between with the Landgrave of Hesse to promote a marriage with his daughter.

Gideon nodded. "You are correct with respect to that business, my lord. But did you not know that Lord Wragby still maintained a correspondence with his Majesty?"

Lord Charters's eyes darted to his friend Sir Francis, who shifted uncomfortably. He turned back to Gideon. "I may have been aware of it, but I fail to see why it should be a matter for my concern."

"Why, quite simply, my lord, the loss of your friend and his endeavours is a great loss to his Majesty. If King James is to know the status of his hopes in England, a substitute must be found—preferably with as good connections as Lord Wragby's."

Lord Charters leaned back on his stool as if wishing to distance himself from the conversation. "Such a person may be difficult to find."

"His Majesty relies on a friend of Lord Wragby's to take his place, someone who Lord Wragby told him can be trusted. You are one of the people he mentioned, my lord."

Even in the dim, flickering light, Gideon could see that Lord Charters blanched. "Phillip had no right to volunteer my services, or indeed, even to speak of me in such a role."

Gideon acknowledged this with a nod. "And he did not, of course. He had no notion that he would be murdered and his service to his Majesty lost. He merely spoke of the two of you who were loyal to the cause. Now, however, given the current situation, James naturally requires one of you to step forward to assume his duties."

"Well, you may tell his Majesty for me that as greatly as I deplore his situation, present circumstances forbid my deeper involvement."

Gideon fixed Lord Charters with a glare, hoping to convince him of his anger. "You would turn your back on your king at this juncture? Was Lord Wragby's faith so misplaced?"

Lord Charters leapt to his feet, his hand on his sword hilt. "How dare you question my loyalty or my courage! I never pledged myself to Phillip's intrigue. He guarded his secrets and only mentioned them to raise himself in our estimation whenever he felt that his friends did not admire him enough. I never said I would—"

"Forgive me, my lord!" The tavern-keeper appeared suddenly at Lord Charter's elbow. "An urgent message has arrived for your lordship." Turning his back on Gideon, he whispered something in Lord Charters's ear.

As he did, Gideon noticed that a number of men were hastily leaving their tables. Alarmed, he stood and said, "What is it? What is happening?"

Lord Charters's face had lost its colour again. "Come, Lichfield," he said to Sir Francis. "We must get away from here."

"What has happened?" Sir Francis had got to his feet. His eyes darted left and right in their sockets.

Ignoring Gideon, Lord Charters said, "The Ambassador from Sweden has been arrested and his papers seized. We must not be discovered here."

Shocked, Gideon made to follow them, but Lord Charters rounded on him, "You see what risks you have asked us to take! If our names turn up in those papers, I shall know who to blame!" Turning on his heels, he hastened from the tavern with a panicked Sir Francis in his train.

Gideon waited just a few moments before exiting the King's Head. Using the alleys he had scouted that morning, he returned to the Red Hart, maintaining a sedate pace. If anything were sure to alert the authorities to his guilt, it would be to run.

As he walked, he pondered the tavern-keeper's news. In his life, he had never heard of an ambassador being arrested. Surely to do so was to contravene diplomatic protocol. It would break any treaty that existed between Great Britain and Sweden and could easily lead to war. To have ordered such a drastic measure, King George must have been convinced that a great betrayal had occurred.

Only one thing could account for it: King George's spies must have learned of a plot between the King of Sweden and the Pretender. The fact that Lord Charters had instantly perceived a danger to himself made it likely that he had at least been told of the possibility of an alliance. For all his pleas of ignorance, it looked as if he knew more of the Pretender's business than he was willing to let on.

But Lord Charters was not the only person who would be affected by this development. With a sinking in his chest, Gideon realized that his and Hester's plans would have to change. He retreated to his room at the inn, shut the door, and paced while cudgelling his brain.

⌀

At breakfast, a messenger arrived with news for Lord Hawkhurst. Harrowby opened the note and scanning it said, "Good God!"

"What is it, Cousin?" Hester asked. With Mary, she and Harrowby made up the only three at table, both Isabella and her mother preferring to take their morning chocolate in bed. She paused with her cup halfway to her mouth, expecting to hear something trivial, but put her cup down when Harrowby replied,

"It's a message from Lord Sussex. The King has ordered the arrest of Count Gyllenborg! He was taken into custody at eleven o'clock last night!"

Seeing the shock on Hester's face, Mary asked, "Who is Count Gyllenborg?"

"The Swedish envoy. It says here, *'The King having receiv'd reiterated Advices, and uncontested Proofs, of many very dangerous Practices which have been carried on and managed for some Time past by Count Gyllenborg, Minister of the King of Sweden here, and which clearly tend to foment in his Majesty's Dominions a Rebellion among his own Subjects, which was supposed to be supported by foreign Troops—'"* Harrowby raised his head from the paper he was reading. "Egad! He has been plotting with the Pretender to invade us!"

He hurried to down the last of his chocolate before rising from his chair. "I must get dressed to discover what further news there is!"

"But what does it mean?" Mary asked. "Are we to be invaded?"

"I do not think so," Harrowby called back as he left the room. "I believe the plot was discovered in time, but this will give rise to all sorts of havoc, I fear."

Mary turned to Hester. "What does he mean by that, Hester? If the plot was discovered in time, then why should there be havoc?"

"Because one does not arrest a minister from a foreign country. I assume he means that this arrest will put Sweden and Great Britain at war, unless the King's ministers can justify his action to Sweden's satisfaction. But King Karl has been bellicose, to put it mildly. He's amassed a large army, just when others are being reduced."

"Are we in any danger?"

Hester gave her cousin a reassuring smile. "I doubt if anyone in this family is, but we must see what develops. When I am out this afternoon, I will pick up other newssheets."

"Are you sure you do not wish me to accompany you to Jeremy's?"

"No, thank you, my dear. I believe he has personal business to discuss. I shall take you with me another time."

Meeting her brother was the excuse Hester had invented to see St. Mars. When she entered the nave of St. Martin's-in-the-Fields, her heart alive at the promise of seeing him, she found him pacing the aisle. Worry and anger were written on his face. He came quickly to meet her and enfolded her in a tight squeeze as if unwilling to let her go.

For a blissful moment, Hester rested against him, relishing the feel of his muscular chest and arms. Then she pulled back to peer up into his eyes. "What is it, my dear?" Though evidently glad to see her, he showed clear signs of dismay.

"Have you heard of the arrest that was made last night?"

"Yes, the Swedish ambassador. What is there about it that worries you?"

"I have spent the morning listening to conversations in the City. The merchants take it as given that this will put us on a path of war. It may be that the King of Sweden is prepared to invade. At any rate, that is what King George must believe, and he will take immediate steps to prepare for the country's defence. That means recalling the troops and seamen who were recently discharged. All shipping between Great Britain and Sweden will cease, and the Channel will be full of English ships."

Hester saw where this must lead. "So, it will be harder for us to cross?"

He nodded regretfully. "Much more dangerous, I'm afraid."

She looked into his eyes and saw how deep his disappointment was. "My darling, if you wish to risk it, I shall go with you."

He firmly shook his head. "No, I am not going to subject you to that kind of risk. We shall just have to see. Meanwhile, I shall have to find us a better place to meet. Otherwise, I shall not be able to tolerate the wait. I've waited too long to be with you already."

Hester put her arms about his waist and laid her head on his chest. "I, too, my love. Whatever place you find for us, I shall find a way to come."

He kissed the top of her head. "At least I can hold you in here without fear that a priest will discover us, but holding you only sets up desires that I cannot fulfil."

A smile curled Hester's lips. In her wildest dreams she had never imagined that St. Mars would want her this much. The knowledge was highly gratifying. She was not without similar wishes herself; most of her days were spent in dreaming, it seemed.

Eventually, they nestled together in a pew and their talk turned towards the discoveries they had made in the mystery of Lord Wragby's death.

"I have spoken with Sir Francis Lichfield and Lord Charters, but I cannot claim to have gained their confidence, especially the latter's. He came reluctantly and grew angry at my suggestion that he replace Lord Wragby in the Pretender's service. But I know he maintains contact with Jacobites. Someone brought him the news of the ambassador's arrest."

St. Mars went on to describe his conversations with the Jacobite suspects. Then, he told her about his discoveries in the house in Fetter Lane.

"My! How much you have accomplished! I fear I have very little to report."

His grin was wistful. "I was hoping that a quick resolution of James Henry's problem would get us away that much sooner, but it appears it will not."

Hester squeezed his hand. "But the sooner we have solved the mystery, the readier we shall be when our opportunity comes." Reverting to their suspects, she asked, "In your conversations with Lord Wragby's friends, did you get a feeling for any motive that one of them might have had for killing him."

"No. It does appear that he was more deeply involved in the Pretender's affairs and that he kept some secrets from them. Lord Charters was expressing annoyance about that when we were interrupted, but my impression was that he felt Lord Wragby boasted of his involvement chiefly to impress his friends."

"That agrees with my impression. He delighted in being the centre of attention and in causing a scene."

"But that is hardly a motive for murder."

"No, but perhaps Lord Charters or Sir Francis was afraid that his indiscretion would put them in peril. It would have been impossible to silence him. I told you how he disparaged King George at Hampton Court on Coronation Day. His father's friends were beside themselves over the chance that he would be overheard."

"Then, perhaps they had a stronger motive than Lord Wragby's friends."

Hester slowly shook her head. "I do not think so. Lord Ireton's friends might be embarrassed by such talk—even distressed—but with Lord Ireton's patronage, they were unlikely to be accused of being traitors. If Sir Francis or Lord Charters were implicated in any way, they would surely be arrested, as so many in their party have been"

St. Mars agreed. "Have you ruled out Ireton's friends as suspects, then?"

"No . . . at least, not Sir Horatio Allenby. He seems almost desperate to cast blame on James Henry, which suggests he may be trying to conceal his own guilt. Of course, he may simply be currying favour with Lord Ireton, who remains convinced that James Henry murdered his son."

"And Lord William Silsbee? I hear he is politically ambitious."

"Lord William has not called on us, but he has carried out one of Lord Ireton's more despicable errands." Hester told him about Lady Wragby's eviction from the house she had occupied with her husband and her subsequent need to seek the protection of her father.

"Poor girl," she concluded. "She seems genuinely to mourn her faithless husband. It would be hard to understand the reason for her loyalty when he treated her so coldly, but I suspect she blames his father for coming between them. Her memories of Lord Wragby are of a very attentive lover, which I suppose he was before he tired of her."

"Is it possible that either she or her father is responsible for Lord Wragby's death?"

"I cannot believe so, when she had nothing at all to gain. As long as he was alive, she had at least a house to inhabit and perhaps some hope of reconciliation. Now, she has nothing to her name."

"Except the freedom to marry someone else."

Hester smiled, but shook her head. "Spoken like a man. And who do you suppose will marry a widow with no dowry to speak of? Certainly not another aristocrat, even a mad one. No, she was better off as Lady Wragby, even if her husband never visited her . . . or maybe especially because he never visited her."

"Was Lord Wragby truly mad?"

'Mary and I have discussed that. He could certainly behave irrationally, but to me his behaviour seemed more like that of a rebellious—perhaps neglected—son, seeking attention wherever he could get it. I imagine his father was very strict, and perhaps the only way Lord Wragby could get his attention was to misbehave."

St. Mars nuzzled her neck. "That sounds like a rare bit of wisdom. I shall have to show you my worst tendencies so you can tell me who to blame for them."

Tickled from her head to her toes, Hester giggled. She squirmed against him until he stopped, clamping his arms so tightly about her that she could no longer move.

"Ah, love, you mustn't do that," he said huskily, "or I shall not be responsible for my actions."

The desire in his voice inflamed her own. "Oh, my dear, I wish we could escape."

He moaned. "Let's just not speak of it until it is safe to plan, else I'll go mad with frustration. Lord Wragby's behaviour will be nothing compared to mine, and you'll have no one to blame but yourself."

She sat up indignantly. "Me? When I invited you into my bed? If I had not, you would have been so forbearing that we might still be playing at courtship."

That provoked a devilish grin. "Yes, and imagine my surprise to discover that you were such a wanton hussy! I was terribly shocked."

"Well, I am glad to see that you have recovered."

"Have I? I fear not. I am very afraid that you will continue to fascinate me as long as we both shall live."

Hester was so overcome by this speech that she could think of nothing to say. She took his face between her hands and kissed him deeply.

They sat with their foreheads touching until she said with a sigh, "I shall have to go, you know."

"Yes. But I shall send you word where to come next. And then be prepared to spend an hour, at least. More if you can manage it. We can never have enough time together."

The tremor in his voice promised that the next time she saw him, it would be for much more than a cuddle in a church pew.

On the way back to Hawkhurst House, Hester stopped a boy selling copies of the *Daily Courant*. It had no further news about the Swedish envoy's arrest, but there was one piece of news that caught her eye.

We hear the Marquis of Ireton is ill of the Small-Pox.

Her burst of elation was quickly suppressed. It was a grievous sin to wish for anyone's death, and more people succumbed to the smallpox than did not. Hester would not allow her wishes to stray so far, but his illness should give her more time to prove James Henry's innocence.

She hurried home with the news, where Mary received it with less restraint. "Then James Henry can come home! I shall write to him straight away."

Hester held her back. "Do not forget that he must obey his master's orders. And Sir Horatio may still take it upon himself to lay charges. We do not know his motives."

"But surely, he will be far less likely to pursue the issue with Lord Ireton ill. He will not be visiting him—no one would be so foolish as to expose himself to the smallpox."

"Unless he has already had it, in which case he is no longer susceptible."

This gave Mary pause. Disheartened, she said, "Should I not inform James Henry, then? I would not wish to put him in peril."

She looked so forlorn that Hester sighed. "I shall leave that to your judgement. But you might mention that he is not out of danger, yet."

The girl agreed and went off to write a letter to her lover. With a pang, Hester wondered what other trials the two would face, even if James Henry were to be cleared of blame. They still had Mary's mother to convince, and in terms of difficulty, Mrs. Mayfield ranked at least as high as both the smallpox and an accusation of murder. Maybe higher than the two combined.

"Away, away! take all your scaffolds down,
"For Snug's the word: My dear! we'll live in Town."

CHAPTER XIV

Over the next few days, the newssheets were full of rumours about the Jacobite conspiracy. News came from Avignon that the Pretender, who was supposed to be sailing for Italy to comply with the decree of exile, had been declared too indisposed to travel. The Whig press speculated that his true design was to set out for a different place entirely, and that he had prolonged his departure in the hopes that his conspiracy with the King of Sweden would result in an invasion of Great Britain.

As he had done in other times of heightened security, Harrowby ordered the ladies in his family to refrain from penning any letters or writing in their journals. "For," he cautioned, "you do not know if an innocent remark will be misconstrued as treasonous."

They had gathered with Isabella and Mrs. Mayfield in the drawing room before setting out for their evening's amusements. Mary, who had not been in London during the recent rebellion, and had not yet posted her letter to James Henry, protested. "But why should his Majesty suspect anyone at Hawkhurst House of treason? We could not be more loyal than we are. Surely that is a caution that should apply just to Tories and Jacobites."

Harrowby was completely ignorant of her motive for wishing to conduct correspondence, but to Hester's surprise, he replied approvingly, "That is correct in theory, my dear, but even his Majesty's most loyal subjects can be misunderstood when the threat is immense. I am pleased, though, to hear your earnest protests of loyalty and advise you to repeat them loudly and often whenever you are at Court."

Hester thought it best to qualify his advice. "We shall certainly abide by your wishes, Cousin, but I think Mary should be sparing in her remarks on politics. It could appear suspicious for a girl her age to express herself publicly on such matters, especially if she starts to comment on subjects upon which she has previously been silent."

Harrowby stared until, light dawning, his eyes grew round. "Ah, the lady should not protesteth too much? Is that what you intend with your advice, Mrs. Kean?"

"Indeed, my lord, you put it most . . . originally."

He beamed, but said modestly, "Not I, Mrs. Kean. That was Shakespeare I was quoting."

"Indeed, sir? Well, there you have the advantage of me. But the phrase is most apt in our current situation."

"Well, I have no plans to write at all," Isabella declared. She was playing with the lace frills at the end of her tight sleeves. On entering the drawing room, she had begged them to admire her new overdress, embroidered with roses and adorned with tiny pleats that fell from the back of her neck to the floor.

Since, in Hester's memory, Isabella had never once put pen to paper, the only surprise in her comment was that she had bothered to make it. Mrs. Mayfield, too, pledged not to indulge in an activity to which she applied herself only in moments of direst necessity. Both ladies employed Hester to read and write their missives for them, but they seemed to have forgotten this fact.

"Excellent!" Harrowby said, after obtaining these promises. "Then, I foresee no reason for concern."

It had escaped his notice that Mary had not agreed to his request. Hester made a mental note to speak to the girl later about the need to omit any reference to the King, the Pretender, or the current crisis in her letters to James Henry. By now, most people were aware that the government was reading all correspondence sent through the Post, and in the last crisis many personal papers had been seized. Hester herself would have to be careful to use a messenger for any note to St. Mars, but there would be nothing in their few words to each other to concern the ministry.

Not long after the security of his family had been resolved to Harrowby's satisfaction, everyone except Hester took carriage to go see the new farce, *Three Hours after Marriage,* which was written by three authors, including Mr. Pope. It was rumoured that the female characters had been based upon persons of worth. The *British Gazetteer,* in its *Weekly Journal,* had indignantly condemned the piece for its abuse of the ladies, blaming Mr. Pope in particular and going so far as to call his physical deformities a curse from God and to warn people that they should hold no society with him. Hester, who had met the poet and liked him, in spite of his being both a Papist and a Tory, would have liked to go to the play to see if she could recognize the ladies who had been mocked, but though offered a seat in Harrowby's box, she had pled the need for solitude.

Her aunt, though usually an adversary, had proved an ally in this instance, for it ill-suited her sense of consequence for a dependent like Hester to be accorded the same privileges as herself. Too, Hester had no doubt she would use the occasion of the play to introduce Mary to potential suitors. Mary would never be receptive to her mother's choices, but Hester thought it would do her no harm to meet other gentlemen whose qualities she could compare to James Henry's. Dreading the scenes that would surely ensue when her aunt discovered the romantic feelings between him and her daughter, Hester had to hope that Mary might form an attachment to someone else. It would hurt to see James Henry disappointed in love. He was more deserving of happiness than most men, but if Mrs. Mayfield could not be made to agree to the match, as Hester was certain she would not, then he was already doomed to disappointment.

The moment Hester heard their coach depart the courtyard, she put aside these thoughts. She went to her bedchamber to fetch her hooded cloak. Then, down in the hall, she buckled wooden pattens to her shoes, for the streets were very muddy, and without any word to the servants, left by the front door. She trusted that by now the footmen's friendship for her was strong enough to give them no cause to inform their master or mistress of her comings and goings. If anyone did inform them, she was prepared to say that she had been called to her brother's house because his wife was sick. To spend a few hours with St. Mars, she was prepared to lie as convincingly as an errant husband.

She had received a note the day before with the address of a house in Little Windmill Street. She had written back immediately to say that she could meet St. Mars while her family was at the play. Now, she left by the gates and found the hackney coach he had said would be waiting for her at the entrance to Bear Alley.

Prepared to make the trip alone, she was delighted to find St. Mars waiting for her in the coach.

When, after climbing in, she expressed her surprise, he said, "I did not want you to come unaccompanied in the dark. The streets are far from safe."

She thanked him with a kiss, reveling in his protection. "Tell me, then, where are you taking me?"

"Not to a church, I'm afraid. I hope you will not be too disappointed. If you are, you shall have to consider this an abduction."

"Well, if you are hoping for a ransom, you should have abducted a wealthier female."

"Oh, I shall exact a payment, never fear." A deep note in his voice made his meaning quite clear.

With a tremor in her own, she said, "Now, you mustn't tease me. Where are we going?"

He put his arm around her and gently squeezed. "To a small house, quite near to here. Before I saw you last time, I sent Tom searching for lodgings to rent. We were lucky to find a place that you can reach quickly, on a street that is not so fashionable that either of us should have to worry about being recognized."

If she was seen, Hester knew it would be disastrous. If Mrs. Mayfield got word that she was secretly meeting a gentleman, even if he was not known to be St. Mars, she would insist that Harrowby throw her out of the house. For a moment, the prospect of disgrace made her heart leap into her throat, but she calmed herself with the knowledge that she would never be destitute. St. Mars would take her into his home, and as soon as possible, they would sail for France.

The coach had been making its way north, lurching over muddy streets. The noise of jingling harness and hoof beats from other carriages steadily diminished as they left the busier streets, heading towards the outskirts of town. Now, they turned onto a quiet street and pulled to a stop. St. Mars opened the door and stepped out before turning to hand Hester down.

She found herself before a quiet row of small houses. Though it was dark, the quarter looked respectable. A tension of which she had not even been aware suddenly left her, and she realized that unconsciously she had expected a neighbourhood like Covent Garden. She laughed at the fear she had nursed, albeit unwittingly, of living the life of a courtesan.

"Why do you laugh, my dear?" St. Mars asked. He had paid off the driver and was ready to lead her up the short steps. "I know it is small, and it is barely furnished. There was simply not enough time. But Katy and Tom have done their best to make it comfortable."

She smiled and took his arm. "It is much more to my taste than my lurid fantasies, I assure you."

Relief was in his answering laugh. He pulled her close. "Then, let us see if we can live up to the more lurid of them once we are inside."

An hour later, they lay sated in each other's arms. Hester had never before experienced such unrestrained passion, but here, as St. Mars had intended, they could give full rein to their love with no fear of being seen or heard. The room was furnished sparsely, yes, but it had a comfortable bed, a pair of chairs, a glowing lantern on the floor, and a dressing table with a mirror and brushes. A washstand with a basin and a pitcher considerably filled with water occupied one corner.

There was, in short, everything she would need to repair the damage to her hair and clothes from an interval of lovemaking that had left her warmed and beaming like a lazy cat stretched out in the sun. She felt as wrung out as a mop—but a very happy, floating mop—with some kind of liquor drifting through her veins. Idly, she wondered what had become of her clothes, for she could hardly remember anything that had happened after St. Mars had said, "Let me help you off with your cloak."

With a moan of satisfaction, he stirred beside her, leaving the spot where he had flung himself, so as not to crush her while he recovered, to pull her to him again. Then, they lay back to front like a pair of nesting spoons, basking in happiness.

Eventually, St. Mars said in a low voice, "I have been thinking that we should marry, but I cannot see how we can do it here or how we can get to the Reverend Mr. Bramwell. We could ask Tom to bring him here, but I cannot be sure that he does not blame me for my father's death. We never had a chance to speak after my arrest."

"Then, I suppose we shall have to wait until we go abroad and can find a Protestant minister."

"That is not what I want. I want us to live here as husband and wife, and when we travel abroad to go as husband and wife, not as man and mistress. I do not wish for you to be treated as less than a wife, not even once. It will be bad enough to be married to an outlaw without having to suffer indignities from insolent people."

She was touched that he had given so much consideration to her dignity and confessed to herself that it would be hard to maintain if the nature of their relationship were ever called into question.

"Then what do you suggest? Going to Scotland?"

She felt him shake his head. "No, that would be nearly as dangerous as crossing the sea. Scotland is heavily fortified against the rebels and more troops will be moved there immediately."

"What, then? Shall we resign ourselves to wait? I can, if necessary."

"I had rather not. There is always a chance that you will become pregnant, and I want all our children to be born into marriage." He was silent for so long that Hester could feel a tension building up between them.

With an idea of what he wished to propose, she prompted. "St. Mars?"

He released a pent-up breath. "Would you agree . . . to a Fleet wedding? It is not what either of us wants, but it is not as scandalous as it seems. The marriage would be legal, and besides . . . it's the only solution I've been able to think of."

At this last confession, Hester had to laugh. She rolled over in his arms to see him. He had thrown off his black wig, and not fearful of exposure in the dark, had not applied the white paint and patches that obscured his looks during the day. The glow from the lantern lit his face sufficiently for her to see the blue of his eyes and the fairness of his hair. She took his face between her hands and kissed him long and lovingly before saying, "That is reason enough for me, as long as you can find a real clergyman to marry us. That is my only requirement, that we can be certain no impostor has led us through our vows. I shall be very happy to be your wife."

They spent another hour together before Hester got up to go home. They had agreed that they would be married as soon as St. Mars found the priest and she was able to escape the house in the evening.

In the coach again, she mentioned the item she had read in the newssheet, reporting the illness of Lord Ireton. "Of course, he may recover, in which case, James Henry will still be in danger, so we must persevere in our search for the real killer."

"Now our temporary needs have been met, I will devote myself more to the investigation."

"As shall I, I hope, if I can just find a means of questioning Sir Horatio and Lord William."

After seeing Hester out of the carriage, Gideon ordered the driver to take him to the horse ferry at the bottom of Market Street, where a few watermen's wherries were also docked. In the spring, the ferry would be filled with people crossing to enjoy the Spring Garden at Vauxhall, but on a winter night, it was quiet.

He hired a waterman to row him across the Thames and gazed lazily at the twinkling lights of lanterns floating across the river. Then he walked in the dark to the house where he lived with Katy and Tom.

In the kitchen he was greeted by a roaring fire and the enticing odour of cooking apples. He noticed that his servants were careful to hide their curiosity. Katy was doing her best to restrain a smile, and Tom fought a blush. They knew where their master had been and what he had most likely been doing. It had been necessary to take them into his confidence to find and fit up the house. Tom had demonstrated his disapproval by grumbling about the risks involved to both his master and Mrs. Kean if they were seen, but Gideon knew that his real objection had been concern for his master's morals and for Mrs. Kean's reputation.

Gideon was happy to put his mind to rest by informing them that Mrs. Kean had agreed to marry him in the Fleet as soon as he could find a legitimate priest. This announcement only partly mollified Tom.

"It's good you're planning to do what's right, but that it should come to this! The heir to my old master, married in the Fleet! T'isn't right, my lord, and you know it."

"It is not what Mrs. Kean deserves, but she agrees with me that it will be best to be married.

"Besides, if anything should happen to me, then she will be able to inherit my property, whatever that turns out to be." He had not discussed this reason for wishing to marry with Hester, but Gideon had long had it in mind. He might be captured and hanged at any moment, and he wanted to be sure she was provided for.

Tom understood this logic. "But how can you be truly married without using your real name?"

"I do intend to use it." At Tom's exclamation, Gideon held up one hand. "From what I hear, we shall be in and out of the Fleet in a matter of minutes, and no one is likely to recognize my name as long as I do not give them my title. My name has not appeared in the newssheets as such for a year or more, and I doubt the prisoners in the Fleet are regularly treated to the newspapers. If anyone should happen to make the connection between Gideon Fitzsimmons and the outlaw St. Mars, I am confident we shall be long gone before the authorities can be alerted."

Tom was forced to be satisfied. He nodded, and Gideon was preparing to go up to his bedchamber when the child Tom and Katy had taken in entered the room. Busy with his own affairs, Gideon again had been surprised to see him when he had returned from his stay at the Red Hart.

The child was still mute, but under Katy's gentle treatment, he had lost a great deal of his fear. Tom had given him chores in the stable, and he seemed happy to do them. He had obviously come to trust both Katy and Tom and no longer jumped at the slightest sound. Tom even found it possible to correct the boy's errors, as long as he used a tempered voice.

Now, as the boy drew near the fire to warm his hands, he gave a wet cough and started to spit.

With an eye to his master, Tom stopped the child in time. "No, not here," he said, taking the boy by the hand to draw him into a corner. "If you need to spit when you're in the house, you find yourself a corner, like this one. That's right. Then, you take the toe of your boot just so, and you rub your spit into the ground." He watched as the boy copied him, then patted the curls on his head. "There. Now you know the way to go about it."

The paternal note in Tom's voice stirred Gideon's memories. It was the same he had heard every day until he had learned all that Tom had to teach him. It appeared that Katy was not the only person in his house who had developed a fondness for the boy. So far, Gideon had seen no evidence that Tom and Katy were able to produce a child of their own.

He had said nothing recently to Tom about the boy, intent as he had been on arranging the house for Mrs. Kean, but now he told him to accompany him upstairs to question him about his plans for the child.

Seating himself in the only chair the room had to offer, he said, "Still no notice of a missing boy in the newssheets? Are you certain?"

When Tom swore that he had not let a day go by without checking the advertisements, Gideon admitted that he had seen nothing either.

"It is very strange. A child like that must have been a valuable servant to someone. It makes no sense that his master would not try to recover him, unless he's dead or too ill to do so. And even then, one assumes that anyone wealthy enough to possess the boy would have other servants to see that his disappearance was reported."

Tom grimaced, but his look was hopeful. "It's been a good month or so since we found him, my lord. It don't look as if anybody's going to claim him, so he might as well stay here. Me and Katy can see that he's no bother."

Gideon frowned, concerned more for Tom and Katy than for the boy. "It's not that he's a bother, but should we not place an advertisement ourselves, saying that a boy has been found."

"No! Please, Master Gideon, don't do that! If whoever owned 'im don't care enough to put a notice in the newssheets, then I'd say it was just the boy's good luck. It's plain as day that somebody did somethin' to scare the words right out of 'im. He won't talk to me or Katy yet, but when he don't know I'm listenin', I've heard 'im speak to the horses.

"He just needs a little peace and quiet. Once he gets over whatever was done to 'im, maybe he'll tell us hisself who done it. Then he can say if he wants to go back or not."

"Very well," Gideon rested his elbows on the desk. "You and Katy can decide what's to be done with him. I shall be busy enough trying to catch Lord Wragby's killer and finding an ordained cleric to read the Order of Marriage in the Fleet. Mrs. Kean insists that she will not be married by an impostor."

Tom grinned, but his relief over the boy was palpable. "I told you she was a proper lady, my lord."

"As if I needed anyone to tell me! Away with you now. I need to think about what I must do next."

He watched Tom leave to return to the kitchen, but his thoughts did not immediately turn to the suspects in Lord Wragby's murder. Gideon had no wish to return an abused boy to his master and was nearly as relieved as Tom and Katy that no advertisement had been posted. Still, it was more than just a little odd that the boy should be allowed to escape his employer without a single word in the news.

Perhaps he had run away in some other town and had managed to make his way to London on a boat. That was an idea that they had not discussed. But people in the country were always placing advertisements in the London newspapers for lost dogs and horses, and for runaway apprentices, so why not for this boy? Something about the situation felt suspicious, and the lack of a notice rang a chord in Gideon's brain. He could not recall it at the moment, but he felt sure there was a similar question floating somewhere in his head.

Well, he would just have to wait for it to surface. He had a murderer to catch and a wedding to plan. With a broad smile, he thought of the pleasure he and Hester had given and received in each other's arms and of the promise of more to come.

℘

On Monday, Hester and Mary went for a walk in St. James's Park. The weather was cold, but the sun was shining brightly enough to draw a great many people out of doors. Mary had treated herself to a ride early that morning, but she was willing to accompany her cousin on her exercise.

Enthusiastic walkers, they declined the use of chairs, and making their way down Portugal Street, entered the King's garden at the public entrance across from Hyde Park, where the soldiers were encamped. The gatekeeper readily let them in, before turning away an orange-seller who had followed them from Dover Street.

This portion of his Majesty's large park had none of the formality of the area close to the palace, which was laid out in the Italian style with parterres, walks, and ponds. Here, strollers could enjoy a more natural setting. In the spring, the King's deer would be grazing in the woods, but at this hour in winter, they were hiding.

There were soldiers here, too, officers out for a stroll, ogling the ladies who passed. When two raised their hats to Hester and Mary, they walked closely together and ignored them. They were not afraid of being accosted, for the soldiers knew they would be severely disciplined if they caused any trouble this close to the palace. Queen Anne had laid down strict rules for the park, which were still being enforced. No mean people, beggars, carters, pedlars, dogs, or annoying boys were allowed into the park. The only coaches admitted were those bearing the royal livery and the only person permitted to ride in the park had been the Queen's gardener. No one was permitted to walk on the grass, but must remain on the gravel walks.

Hester and Mary had not been strolling long, when they spied a large retinue heading their way. Soon, it became apparent that not only the King, but the Prince and Princess of Wales, were taking the air. They were attended by a vast number of nobility and gentry and cheered by the public. All the officers stopped ogling the women to salute.

Hester recalled the story she had heard about King George's reaction to seeing the public in St. James's Park. "This is a very odd country," he had said in French. "The first morning after my arrival at St. James's, I looked out of the window and saw a park with walls and a canal, and was told they were mine. The next day, the ranger of my park sent me a brace of fine carp out of my canal, and I was told that I must give five Guineas to the man for bringing me my own carp out of my own canal in my own park."

The anecdote had said as much about England as it had about the courts of Europe, where no one dared enter a king's garden uninvited. She was grateful she lived in a nation where the people had more rights. It would be hard to leave England, but if that was what she must do to be with St. Mars, she would. With a touch of melancholy, she reflected on all she would miss. She suspected that St. Mars felt the same way at the thought of turning his back on his home, but he had accepted that he had no choice.

Hester and Mary interrupted their own exercise to curtsy as the royal party strolled to the end of the park and turned to make its way back to the Palace. After giving them room to pass, Hester and Mary followed in their wake.

They had not recently had any chance to discuss Lord Wragby's murder. Hester had returned from seeing St. Mars on Saturday evening in time to avoid any questions about her absence, and she had concealed her glow of happiness by questioning the others about the play. It had come as no surprise that whatever satire the playwrights might have intended, none of Hester's family had caught it. In fairness to Mary, she was not acquainted enough with the persons parodied in the piece, and Hester admitted that she, herself, might have missed most of the references, too. As a rule, she avoided the worst gossip.

The next day, her family had attended church together at the Royal Chapel, where Harrowby had the honour of carrying the Sword of State before his Majesty. The Bishop of Carlisle preached before the Royal Family, and the Bishop of London administered the Holy Sacrament. The mark of the King's favour had bolstered Harrowby's confidence so much that he had behaved very gallantly to Isabella that evening.

Now, Hester and Mary walked arm in arm for warmth. Mary was silent, looking sightlessly out at the lime trees that lined the gravel walk. Hester attributed her low spirits to James Henry's troubles. As soon as the crowd that had gathered to see the royal procession drifted away, she remarked upon Mary's cast-down look, ending, "We shall have to discover Lord Wragby's murderer if James Henry is ever to be out from under this cloud."

"But what can we do, Hester? I have tried and tried to think of a way to help, but nothing I think of is within my power to execute. I can hardly call upon Lord Wragby's acquaintances to ask if any of them killed him."

"No, but we can at least reason out a motive. That will be a step. Then, if we discover a plausible one, we can seek someone's assistance." Hester knew that she could not always reason clearly when she was with St. Mars, so it would help to talk things over with Mary.

"Whose assistance? Harrowby's?" Mary's tone expressed strong doubt. "I doubt he would take an interest in anyone's troubles but his own."

Hester had not had Harrowby in mind, but all she said now was, "Do not forget that Harrowby does have an interest. James Henry is a valuable servant who would be very hard to replace. No matter what Harrowby says to deny it, he knows this. But let us leave that out of our discussion for now. Since the murder, I have been convinced that Lord Wragby's killer must be one of four gentlemen."

Surprised, Mary stared at her, and Hester said, "You recall the morning we visited St. Paul's, and I had that dizzy spell?" She described the threat she had heard and how Mr. Wren's revelation of the "whispering gallery" had made her realize that whoever had uttered the words must have been in the gallery at that moment. "Then, when we learned that Lord Wragby was strangled, exactly as in the threat, I felt certain that he was the one for whom it was intended."

"But that must have been weeks before the murder. How could you recall whom you saw?"

"Because as soon as I understood that the voice could have come from anywhere along the gallery, I took note of the men who were present. No one left while we stood near the top of the stairs, and of the men I saw, only four could have known Lord Wragby well enough to make such a threat: the two who were with him, Sir Francis Lichfield and Lord Charters and the two who were with his father, Sir Horatio and Lord William Silsbee."

Mary eagerly accepted her reasoning and begged her to go on.

"Since the murder, I have learned a bit more about Lord Wragby, including things that might explain why someone would wish to kill him."

At Mary's incredulous look, Hester said, "I know he was insufferable, but it is one thing to detest a man and entirely another to kill him. If being insufferable were the only reason for killing him, however, does it not make sense that the offended party would simply have called him out? These are gentlemen, remember. They have pistols and swords with which to settle an offense. Strangulation is an act that must be hidden. There is no honour in it."

"True, but there must be a great deal of anger or hatred."

Aware that her cousin was right, Hester nodded as she mused. "But the voice I heard was so cold. If there was any anger in it, it was carefully contained. The speaker might just as well have been planning an execution."

Mary shuddered. "Who among your suspects would be capable of such a thing?"

"I wish I knew. My experience of them is too slight to guess. We do know, however, that Lord William Silsbee showed some kindness on one occasion, when he stopped Lord Wragby's footmen from beating James Henry."

"Yes, that was good of him, but then he did inform poor Lady Wragby that she would have to leave her house, so he must be capable of some coldness, at least."

"But, remember, she said he had the grace to look mortified."

Mary scoffed. "Yet he did his patron's bidding. I call that cowardice. Perhaps Lord William is too much of a coward to have met Lord Wragby in a duel."

Hester pondered this as she looked out over the park. The trees were leafless and the ground was brown, as infertile as her ideas at the moment. They had nearly reached the far side of the park, so she suggested they turn back.

As they headed the other way, she said, "We both heard Lord Wragby's assertion of his loyalty to the Pretender, and I have since learned that he did more than merely boast of it." She told Mary about the house she had seen Lord Wragby enter and that it belonged to a Jacobite agent.

She lowered her voice to ensure that no one could hear. "His two friends, Sir Francis and Lord Charters, may also be spies, in which case they might have feared that Lord Wragby would expose them out of carelessness. He seemed to have no fear of arrest, perhaps because of his father's influence, but his friends could have been under no such delusions. If ever he revealed their loyalties, they would lose all."

Mary stopped to look at her queerly. "How do you know these things, Hester? What have you been doing?"

Hester tried not to blush, but she could not contain her smile. "I promised, did I not, that we would not have to do this alone? That there was someone who would help us?"

Mary studied her. "You were not speaking of Harrowby? Then, perhaps this friend of yours can investigate the people that we cannot."

Hester turned and resumed walking to cover her unease. "He can question some of them, yes, but not all. He would not be safe approaching Lord Ireton's friends. That is why you and I must put our heads together to think how to learn more about them."

She was grateful that Mary did not ask to know why this was so. Perhaps, conscious of the secret she was keeping herself, she had learned to respect others'. To Hester's amazement, falling into step beside her, she changed the subject.

"What do we know about Sir Horatio Allenby?"

"Only that he is diligent in carrying out Lord Ireton's wishes." Hester reminded her of Sir Horatio's visit to Hawkhurst House when he had tried to get James Henry dismissed.

Mary frowned. "Hester, it seems that Lord Ireton's two servants— for I hesitate to call them friends—are both so eager to please him that I do not see why either would risk his patronage by murdering his son."

"Unless they thought that Lord Wragby posed a danger to him. At the celebration on Coronation Day, I got the impression that they had had to be his minders on more than just one occasion. Perhaps his boast of allegiance to James Stuart within the walls of King George's palace was simply the last straw, and one or both of them decided to rid their master of a son who was not merely an embarrassment, but a serious danger."

"If one of them did, he will be desperate to conceal his act from Lord Ireton."

"Which will be easy for as long as Lord Ireton is ill, but if he recovers, I have little doubt that he will take up the pursuit of his son's murderer again. Then, it will become even more imperative for the killer to cast blame on James Henry. Perhaps all we can do at this point is watch to see if one of them becomes more zealous in that regard. If he does, we must find a way to plant a seed of doubt in Lord Ireton's brain."

"How?"

Hester shook her head. "We will not know how until we see the direction the threat comes from. But something will occur to us. We are likely to encounter them all at Court over the next few months, so we must be prepared to speak to them whenever a chance arises."

"I know what I shall do," Mary said with spirit. "I shall tell them all what a shame it was to evict Lady Wragby from her husband's house. That will be very impertinent, and my mother will cringe in mortification, but I will not care about the consequences if they force her to stop her matchmaking. You should have seen the wastrels and pimply youths she presented to me at the play! Much more of that, and I shall happily court disgrace with every word."

Hester's reaction to this statement was mixed. On the one hand, she was happy to see that Mary's spirits were lifting. On the other, she wondered how far the girl would go to escape her mother's control.

Elope to Scotland with James Henry?

As they reached the end of the park at Portugal Street and turned towards home, Hester had to smile. As easily as she could see Mary on her way to Scotland, she found it impossible to imagine James Henry in the carriage with her. He was more likely to wait until all of Mary's prospects had been exhausted before presenting her mother with his suit. James Henry had never been one to throw caution to the wind.

Then, Hester thought about the pledge she had just made to St. Mars.

Would anyone who knew her believe that she would agree to be married in the Fleet? A shot of worry flew through her. It was one thing for her and St. Mars to elope. They had a place, a safe place to go. If James Henry and Mary eloped, he was certain to lose his position. They could live at the house the former Lord Hawkhurst had given him, but how well would they live? Was his property large enough to sustain them? Hester feared it was not.

But this concern must take second place to the more immediate danger to James Henry's life. And they would not even know how great that danger was until they knew if Lord Ireton survived the smallpox.

What walls can guard me, or what shades can hide?
They pierce my thickets, through my Grot they glide;
By land, by water, they renew the charge;
They stop the chariot, and they board the barge.
No place is sacred, not the Church is free;
Even Sunday shines no Sabbath day to me . . . .

CHAPTER XV

Despite the public show of confidence and unity by King George and the Prince and Princess of Wales, the trouble between Sweden and Great Britain grew with each day's news. The *British Gazetteer,* which was supported by the government, reported all the measures being taken to strengthen the country against the possibility of invasion. Expresses were sent to Scotland to alert officials there to have a watchful eye over the coast and land passages. No one would be allowed to dock or to pass through that country without giving a good account of himself, and the City of Edinburgh, important to the Jacobites, was to be surrounded with troops.

All the captains of ships coming into Edinburgh were examined, upon which it was learned that a few well-known Jacobite lords had met there with an emissary from the King of Sweden before sailing on a mission to speak directly to King Karl, on orders from the Pretender.

As the merchants and stock jobbers St. Mars had overheard had predicted, an embargo on shipping was imposed. A general embargo in this nation of merchants could not be supported long, but it was lifted and then reinstated temporarily while his Majesty's bill to ban all trade with Sweden worked its way through Parliament. A plan to move all the troops in and around London to Blackheath was suspended, and a great press was put on to man his Majesty's ships to ready them to meet the Swedish fleet. A squadron with twelve or more ships than usual was provisioned to sail for the Baltic and to cruise off the coast of Scotland.

As the news of a planned invasion passed through the kingdom, many Jacobites took heart. Riots erupted again at Stamford, and at Oxford, where the Tories held sway and the memory of past battles lingered, the Heads who had recently sent an address of loyalty to King George reported suffering the resentment of the university and being threatened with expulsion.

An advice from Amsterdam reported that at the request of Great Britain, the government of Holland had arrested Baron von Görtz, a kind of "grand-vizier" to the King of Sweden who, learning that he was being sought, had tried to escape in the guise of a merchant. Upon his arrest, the baron confessed to being the projector of the intended invasion of Great Britain, boasting that he, himself, had provided ten thousand arms and other necessities for the purpose, believing it in the best interest of his master the king.

Alarmed by the plot, the government at The Hague put off the reform of its troops, a benefit that had been expected as a result of the recently-signed Triple Alliance. All the Protestant governments had been put on guard.

In England, just days after the newssheets had reported that an amnesty for the rebels still in prison was being considered, new arrests were made for treason.

In London, there were grumblings over the embargo. As a rule, however, the merchants were Whigs and supported King George. The Jacobites in the City had been suppressed after last year's riots and, with soldiers occupying London, they remained silent.

This included the two whose acquaintance Gideon had worked so hard to make. Sir Francis and Lord Charters refused to reply to his messages asking to meet with them again. He had worded the messages with care. No suggestion of treason tainted them, but still, both gentlemen ignored them.

Gideon doubted that Hester had had any more success. The discovery of the plot had thrown Londoners back into a state of anxiety, just when it had seemed that peace had been achieved. Until the government knew how far the plot had progressed, members of Parliament would be too busy with the King's requests to devote time to the pleasures of society. This meant that Hester would have few opportunities to investigate Lord Ireton's friends.

Wary himself of being captured in the search for Jacobites, Gideon stayed away from the haunts he had visited. His prudence was rewarded when he read in the *Evening Post* that the owners of both the King's Head and the Duke of Albemarle's Head had been taken up by King's Messengers. The newssheet said that they had been questioned and released, but their arrest proved that the government's agents knew that both taverns were Jacobite meeting-places. They had helped Gideon make the connections he needed, but he would never set foot in either again.

He would have been terribly frustrated by the lack of progress if not for the house in Little Windmill Street. Hester managed to meet him there again on two occasions. In the meantime, with Tom's help, he scouted the Fleet, looking for an ordained priest to marry them. As many marriages as were performed there—and they numbered in the thousands—it had not been easy to find an honest clerk.

At their last rendezvous, Hester had asked him how such clandestine marriages could be legal.

As they had lain together, he had traced her features with his finger, explaining, "For some reason buried in legal history, clergymen in the Fleet Prison cannot be prosecuted by the government—at least not for fulfilling the duties of their calling. So the Marriage Act cannot be enforced there. It is the only place one can be wed without the reading of banns, which you and I must not risk, or by a special license, which I would not be able to obtain under my legal name."

"Are there many clergymen in prison?"

He could tell the idea distressed her. "Not that many, no. But even priests can fall into bad habits—drinking or gambling, I suppose—and find themselves too deeply in debt to pay their bills."

"Are we to be married in the prison chapel?"

"No, you should not have to enter the prison itself. Most of the weddings are performed in nearby taverns or inns, as long as they are within the Liberty of the Fleet. The ministers pay for a day pass to conduct their business outside. A few may still perform weddings inside the prison, but if they do, their warders extort too much of their earnings.

"The reason I have not found anyone to marry us yet is that the business is so lucrative that a great many impostors have turned their hands to it. Even some turnkeys, I understand."

Hester eyed him askance. He chuckled and kissed her on the forehead. "I promise, you shall not be married by a turnkey! I cannot guarantee the sobriety of the priest who will recite our vows, but he shall be a priest!"

She tapped him in a playful rebuke. He laughed again and wrapped her in his arms.

Lying on top of her, he whispered, "Are you having second thoughts?"

With a tremor of pleasure, she smiled. "I gave you my word and I shall not take it back. But will we ever tell our children how we were married?"

"Ye gods, no! Not if we ever want them to obey us!"

They had made love again before Hester had to leave. He had promised to find a priest before seeing her again. He had sent Tom to discover what he could of the different marriage taverns, but Tom had come back defeated. Gideon had no choice but to examine them himself.

The stroke of nine o'clock that evening found him wandering the streets between Fleet Lane and Ludgate Hill outside the Freedom of the City of London. This area east of the Fleet ditch was one he had never explored. The lanes were so twisted and narrow as not to deserve the appellation "street." The taverns, inns and coffee houses were ancient, having been spared from the Great Fire. Upper stories in wood and daub projected so far into the lanes as nearly to meet overhead, and in front of every house, it seemed, some hawker was touting the virtues of his marrying chapel. The Cock and Acorn, the Horseshoe and Magpie, the Shepherd and Goat were only a few of the dozens of places Gideon saw. Now, he understood Tom's difficulty. There was nothing he could use to test the legitimacy of the cleric inside.

Since he was unaccompanied by a woman, Gideon was spared the worst importunities, but again and again he observed the arrival of a poor couple who were instantly surrounded and overwhelmed by competing interests, then swept into whichever tavern had the strongest advocate. The Hand and Pen was a popular name for a marrying house. Gideon was sure he had passed three of them already. The Rainbow Coffee House at the corner of Fleet ditch had a reputation outside the area. Its claim to fame this evening was that it offered the best wedding reception in the Liberty.

Young couples, fleeing the disapproval of their parents, were easily lured in by fake promises. Poor Huguenots who could not afford the fees the Church of England would demand handed over their half-crowns to any impostor who had dressed himself in the robes of a clergyman and professed to keep a register.

At one point in his wanderings, Gideon found himself outside the prison, itself. The stench from the ditch beyond where all its waste was tossed was nearly overpowering. A coal-heaver—judging by the amount of soot on his clothes—was standing beneath one of its brick arches, assuring passersby that the Reverend Mr. Mottram could perform their ceremony at the cheapest price.

Spying a gentleman who, in his black wig and face paint with a sword on his belt, appeared more prosperous than any other likely customer in sight, he quickly attached himself to Gideon, promising he could be married in the finest room the Fleet had to offer.

"T'is the Lord Mayor's Chapel, an' I swear to yer lordship that ye'll not find a better appointed room fer yer nuptials."

Dubious as he was, Gideon thought that perhaps he should examine the facility. Hester had asked if they would be married in a chapel, so he ought to see if the man's claims were valid.

Following him through the arched portico, Gideon was instantly struck by the number of prisoners either standing or wandering aimlessly within the prison walls. The taproom was evidently in the cellar, for men in rags emerged with full mugs in their hands. Gideon was ushered up a short flight of steps, on each of which some poor beggar was sitting as if not knowing what to do with himself.

The sounds echoing off the walls were more distressing than deafening—doors slamming, women pleading, children crying—for many of the debtors' families would have been forced by impoverishment to move in with them.

Gideon had already made up his mind not to bring Hester into the prison, but he carried on to see the room the man had touted. He was glad when they turned into a nearby door, where a man in clerical garb was performing the rite to unite a very young couple. As, his job finished, the coal-heaver left Gideon inside the door, he took a look about. The room was certainly not a real chapel, just a space that had been furnished with a few chairs and cushions. A coat of arms had been stuck upon the wall, consisting of a chevron argent, charged with three roses between three crosslets. Certainly, some effort had been made to give the place a legitimate air.

Spotting a new customer, the cleric sped up his proceedings, and soon the pair was declared man and wife. They were hustled to a table where stood an open register and inkwell. While the couple added their signatures, the cleric excused himself to speak with Gideon.

Introducing himself as the Reverend Mr. Mottram, he asked, "Have you not brought your betrothed with you, sir?"

"I told her that I would make inquiries first."

"Ah, yes, the ladies can be very timid about such things. I hope you will assure her that every attention to her delicacy will be observed."

Gideon asked him about his qualifications and could find nothing suspicious in his replies. The school he named was certainly one that could have prepared him for the Church and he gave the date and place of his ordination.

Next, Gideon asked to see his register. Mr. Mottram took him to see it, promising to supply the happy couple with a marriage certificate and crown stamp. He excused himself again to write something beneath the signatures that had just been added and to wish the young couple every happiness.

They were very young, Gideon observed, likely too young to be married without their parents' consent. As the cleric was bidding them goodbye, Gideon stooped over the register to see what he had written—*Hi non nupti fuerunt fed obtinerunt Testimonium propter timorem parentum.* In essence, he had written that the couple was not married, but had obtained this private ceremony for fear of their parents.

Gideon doubted that either of the two had been able to interpret the Latin. The cleric had taken their money and deceived them, taking measures to protect himself from any repercussions.

Mr. Mottram rejoined him with an apology for the interruption.

Having witnessed enough, Gideon was ready to leave, but Mr. Mottram took hold of his sleeve. Employing a confidential tone, he asked Gideon to assure his bride that any detail that concerned her could be accommodated on the spot. "If there is any concern about the date of your union, rest assured that it will be recorded exactly as you both wish."

It took Gideon a moment to comprehend what the man was suggesting. Then it came to him. Mr. Mottram was offering to antedate the marriage in case his bride was pregnant. He might be a real clergyman, but he was little better than a fraud.

By this time, Gideon was so convinced he was dealing with a scoundrel that he found himself amused. With a pleasant smile, he bid Mr. Mottram good day, and promising to deliver the messages to his intended, took himself back out of the Fleet. He left, intending to tell Hester all about his adventure, but, given that her father had been a clergyman, Gideon was not positive she would find Mr. Mottram's tricks as diverting as he did.

The noxious odours from the prison followed him as he quitted the place. He knew they must have permeated his clothes. Realizing that he was no closer to finding a priest to marry him and Hester, he gave up for the evening, hoping a better solution would come to him.

℘

Throughout the month of February, the need to defend the country interfered with hopes for the social season. The King was too absorbed with urgent matters to provide entertainment at Court. As was his habit the first two years of his reign, he dined mostly in the company of his mistress, only occasionally honouring the Duke of Newcastle with a visit. The Prince and Princess of Wales did attend the plays from time to time, but the evening assemblies were few and small.

Not only did this make it impossible for Hester to investigate Lord Ireton's friends, it meant that she had to devise ways to keep Mary and her mother apart. Fortunately, in the evenings, Mrs. Mayfield could often find a card party, and as long as she could gamble, she was diverted enough to neglect her daughter's future.

Hester and Mary took walks every day in the park and ran errands for Isabella, seizing any excuse to escape the house.

Hester was pleased one day to read an item in the newssheets that gave her an idea for an outing. It seemed the Regent of France had made a gift of two horses to King George, said to be the most beautiful horses ever seen. Nothing would entertain Mary better than a chance to view superior horseflesh, so the afternoon after the announcement appeared they received permission to visit the King's Mews.

The entrance to the Great Mews was just north of Charing Cross, scarcely a half-mile away. For this excursion, they wore pattens. Both the Haymarket through which they must pass and the mews themselves would be littered with mud and muck. They bundled up in fur-lined cloaks against the cold and set out.

Walking as briskly as they could on their raised soles, they soon were nearly to the gate. On the corner at Charing Cross, they passed an old menagerie which advertised a "collection of strange and wonderful creatures from all over the world." Mary was not too old to be distracted by the promise of seeing things as wonderful as a "Monstrous Female Creature that was taken in the Woods in the Deserts of Ethiopia in Prester John's Country, the noble Picary (which is very much admired by the learned), the noble Jack-call, the Lion's Provider, which hunts in the Forest for the Lion's Prey," or the "strange, monstrous creature, brought from the Coast of Brazil, having a Head like a Child, Legs and Arms very wonderful, with a Long Tail like a Serpent, wherewith he feeds himself as an Elephant doth with his Trunk."

Hester let the girl read the proprietor's claims, but she had no intention of going inside. If Mary really wished to see the odd creatures, she could return with one of the footmen, who would enjoy the show as much as she would. Hester had seen enough of such exhibitions with Isabella and Harrowby to know that, while the creatures might indeed be curious enough to arouse one's interest, they were invariably caged in the greatest misery. Whether or not one believed that lesser mortals had feelings, she had no doubt that they deserved better treatment than they received.

Fortunately, Mary was discouraged by the shabby air of the place and the vulgar behaviour of the people who emerged, laughing and mocking the poor creatures inside. With a grimace, she turned back to continue the journey with Hester. At the gate, the guard admitted them without any trouble. Indeed, they were not the only people whose curiosity had brought them to the mews today. A stream of visitors preceded them along the narrow entrance to the Great Mews. When they arrived at the spot where it opened into the mews itself, a veritable crowd had gathered up ahead, hoping to catch a glimpse of the famous horses.

Hester and Mary crossed the vast open yard, which was flanked on both sides by rows of stalls. Both inside the stalls and in the yard, grooms and coachmen dressed in the royal livery were tending to their charges with curry-combs, brushes, or picks for the horses' hooves. A blacksmith in the corner was hammering out a shoe, and the jangle of harness and an occasional whinny added cheer to the bustle. In a special stall, Hester caught a glimpse of one of the royal coaches, gleaming with gilt.

She and Mary carefully negotiated their way past the dung that the boys with shovels had not yet collected, until they reached the gathering at the other end of the yard. From here another entrance led from the Great Mews into a smaller one called the Green Mews. As they waited their turn to be admitted, a disappointed murmur went up, and they learned that the King's new horses were not yet on public display. His Majesty had invited just a few of his subjects to see them today.

"I'm sorry, Mary," Hester said. "I had hoped that we might catch a glimpse of them, but maybe we will another day."

"That's quite all right. There are plenty of fine ones to see." Mary was trying to peer into the passage to Green Mews, when she suddenly grasped Hester by the elbow. "Look who is coming out! Is that not Lord William?"

Hester, who had turned to go, glanced back and spotted him emerging from the passage. "Yes, I believe it is."

"Do you think we could approach him?"

Though Hester dreaded the thought of putting herself forward— she was not at all certain that Lord William would acknowledge them—she decided to be bold. Before Lord William could escape, she took hold of Mary's hand and led her directly into his path, forcing him to stop.

He looked up with a start, and for the first time Hester got a good look at his face. He seemed much thinner and paler than the last time she had seen him. The rims of eyes were red, as if he had been missing sleep. She could not tell if he recognized her, but as his gaze darted to Mary and back to her, his nostrils slightly flared.

"Good day to you, Lord William," Hester said, as Mary and she made deep curtsies. He responded with a polite bow, so she continued, "We were hoping to see his Majesty's new horses, but we were told that they would not be on view today. Did you see them?"

"Yes, his Majesty was kind enough to invite me to have a look at them. They are truly splendid. The Regent of France could not have made the King a gift that would please him more."

As Lord Ireton's protégé and a Whig Member of Parliament, it was not surprising that he had received a special invitation.

"Well, I suppose we shall get to see them another day."

Before he could excuse himself and move away, Hester continued, "I hope you will forgive us for accosting you, but perhaps you re-member my cousin and me." She gave him their names and reminded him of their relationship to Lady Hawkhurst. "The truth is that we both have wished to thank you for your kindness to Mr. Henry, Lord Hawkhurst's receiver-general. We do not know how seriously he would have been injured if you had not stopped his attackers."

His reaction amazed her. Fear widening his eyes, he recoiled, then stammering, he said, "I beg you will not speak of it. It was nothing."

He moved to step around them, but Mary said quickly. "On the contrary, my lord, your action was of the utmost importance. You must persuade Lord Ireton that Mr. Henry did not murder his son!"

He turned a ghostly white. For one second, Hester thought that he might faint. Then, taking off his tricorn and using it to shield his face, he mumbled his excuses and fled. Mary and Hester stared after him, their mouths agape.

Finally, Hester said, "Have you ever seen such odd behaviour? He could not have been more frightened if we had threatened him with pistols."

Mary turned helplessly. "Was it my fault, Hester? Should I not have spoken so bluntly? I know you would have introduced the subject more adroitly, but I was afraid he would escape."

"No, it was not your fault. You were a bit importunate, but he was already afraid. He was desperate to get away the moment I mentioned Mr. Henry."

Taking Mary's arm, she started to walk back across the Great Mews. "Why would the very mention of Mr. Henry make him want to turn and run? Did you notice how ill he seemed? I am convinced that something is seriously wrong."

"He could be afraid of being discovered." As she walked beside her, Mary remembered to take care where she placed her feet. "Maybe it was he who killed Lord Wragby, and he is terrified that Lord Ireton will find out."

Hester considered. "That is possible, but perhaps his conscience is troubling him over something else. What if he knows who committed the murder but dare not say, whether it was himself or a friend? He did look afraid, but also unwell, as if he had not slept in a long while."

"Well, if he does know who did it and is letting Mr. Henry take the blame, then he deserves to be sick!"

Hester sighed. They had reached the gate to the mews and exited at Charing Cross. Opposite the menagerie they had passed, a crowd had gathered to watch the antics of Punch at the booth of the Italian puppet-master. Ignoring the performance, Hester replied, "I wish I could feel that we had accomplished something by speaking to him, but we may merely have put him on guard. It would surprise me if he let either of us come near him again."

She proposed taking a walk through Spring Garden, which she had not seen since the fire, and Mary agreed. They turned at Drummond's Bank to walk towards Whitehall. Amidst the pedestrians milling about, Hester heard the unmistakable sound of Scottish burrs. Though hard to decipher, they still conveyed enough for her to detect a disgruntled mood.

Shushing Mary with a raised finger, she signalled for her to pay attention to the conversations. Raised in the North, as Hester was, Mary was no stranger to Scottish accents. As they passed two men who had exited Drummond's Bank and were making their way towards the British Coffee House—a place many Scots gave out as their postal address in London—Hester overheard them complaining about the government's attempt to force Mr. Drummond to hand over his books for examination. They were evidently proud that he had stood up for his depositors and refused to comply.

The Crown would be looking for evidence that the bank had sent money to the Pretender. It was rumoured that he had borrowed from Drummond's for his last invasion, and the patriotic Scots had rushed to transfer their money there.

The Scots' conversation was just another reminder for Hester that the government was rooting out all the Jacobites in the kingdom and of how careful St. Mars must be that his activities were not detected and misunderstood.

Mary was too absorbed with her own concerns to eavesdrop for long. When Hester whispered to her what the men had said, she changed the subject. "Can you not ask your friend to speak to Lord William about Mr. Henry?"

"No, not yet." The last thing Hester wanted was for Lord Ireton or any of his friends to become aware of St. Mars. "I hope that will not be required. First, I must think about what you and I can do."

They continued past a cluster of taverns and shops offering the same kind of tasteless amusements that they had seen at Charing Cross. Then, seeing the Admiralty up ahead, they turned right into Spring Garden, which was just east of St. James's Park.

Inside, they found a quiet space with no traffic to disrupt their talk. Along the path stood a row of leafless trees with early wood anemones pushing up between them. It was too early for most flowers, but along the hedges Hester spied yellow Celandine in bloom. Not eager to return to Hawkhurst House, she and Mary decided to prolong their stroll. Since their plan had been to see the horses, they would not be expected home soon.

It did not take them long to come across the burned chapel set amidst charred trees. They stopped to gaze at the forlorn sight.

"I wonder what started the fire," Mary said.

Hester shook her head. "I have not heard much about it. I assume someone was careless with a flame."

After a moment, she added, "You know, this is where James Henry was the night that Lord Wragby was killed. I saw him just before Harrowby sent him out with the footmen to help fight the fire."

It was Mary's turn to sigh. "If he had just been at Rotherham Abbey or at any other of the Hawkhurst estates that evening, he would never have been suspected of the murder."

"Yes, but there is nothing we can do about that. Lord Wragby must have been killed in one of the alleys leading from here. I wonder what he was doing."

"I thought you believed he was visiting a mistress or a brothel."

"How could I know? We do not even know at which hour of the night he was murdered. But, yes, I have always assumed he was indulging in some vice." Hester thought for a minute, then said, "But what if he was on a different sort of errand? What if he was meeting another Jacobite or someone else who had lured him here?"

Mary's ears perked up. "That could be worth finding out." Her face fell. "But how can we?"

"I suppose we could try speaking to his valet, if only we knew who that was. Perhaps Pierre would know."

"But then, what? Could we speak to him?"

"Perhaps . . . or we could engage Pierre to do it! He can be very helpful at times—even crafty."

The two cousins looked at each other and beamed. Mary laughed out loud. "I vow, Hester! You are good at this sort of puzzle, you know."

With a smile stretching her face, Hester responded, "This is terribly immodest, but I have to agree."

On the evening of the first of March, in honour of the thirty-fourth birthday of the Princess of Wales, a splendid ball was given at St. James's Palace. Earlier in the day Hester's entire family had witnessed the general celebration. Isabella and Harrowby had gone to Court to congratulate the Princess along with a huge company of nobility and gentry. Attendance at the ball, however, was limited to the number of people who could be seated, so Hester, Mary, and Mrs. Mayfield were left at home to entertain themselves.

Not at all pleased to miss an evening at Court, Mrs. Mayfield made use of Harrowby's absence to vent her spleen on her niece and her daughter.

Hester's turn began the moment they returned to Hawkhurst House after observing the fireworks. As they entered the hall and started to remove their cloaks, Mrs. Mayfield said, "I have words to say to you, Hester. I should have known that you would serve me an evil turn, and after all that I have done for you, too!"

"What have I done to offend you, Aunt?" Hester had no idea.

Mrs. Mayfield removed a folded piece of paper from the pocket in her skirt and shook it in her niece's face. "You cannot tell me that you were unaware of this! You, who have nothing better to do than read the newssheets!"

Hester reached for the paper, but her aunt was not finished.

"I shall know how to thank you, never fear! Just wait until my lord hears what you have done. You will not be able to twist him to your liking again, not when he reads how abominably you have used me." She turned to storm up the staircase, and mystified, Hester and Mary followed.

"Aunt Mayfield, I can promise you that whatever you have read, I have never purposely harmed you. There must be a misunderstanding, but if you do not let me see what the paper says, I will never know what has aroused your ire."

"You shall see! And, Mary, you will not think so highly of your cousin after you have read this."

In the dark, they followed her into the withdrawing room, where a footman was hastening to light candles. A second servant was making up the fire, which had been banked, awaiting the family's return.

Mrs. Mayfield took a seat in the gilded armchair nearest the fire, and Hester and Mary found other chairs. Without a clue to the cause of her anger, Hester's heart sank. If there was anything she disliked, it was a scold from her aunt.

"Bring that candle to Mrs. Mary." Mrs. Mayfield directed the first footman, pointing an accusing finger at her daughter, as if she were an accomplice. She handed Mary the paper. "Now, Mary, read that second item on the right side of the page and you will see how wicked your cousin is."

Throwing Hester an apologetic glance, Mary leaned towards the candle on the table beside her, searched for the item, and read. "*Hereby is detected the famous Anodyne Necklace sold at the Sugar-Loaf in the Strand: Beads made of Dead People's Sculls.*"

Hester nearly blurted out a laugh, but she restrained herself as Mary read on, *"A rare Artifice! a choice Preface or Introduction to a Belief of Romish Takes! No wonder the Relicts of their Saints are held in such Estimation, when the Sculls of indifferent Persons can effectually remove all manner of Ailments in Old and Young, and be instrumental in the Cure of Clap and Pox. Charming Doctrine of Dr. Chamberlen!"*

Mary would have stopped there, but Hester begged her to go on.

"But that the Dr. may avoid any Odium for the future recommending the same, the said Necklace, with Additions, is given GRATIS, for only buying the Specifick Tincture most effectual for Children's easy cutting Teeth, Convulsions, Fever, Rickets, Obstructions, and other Ailments incident to them, price 5 s. Sold only at Mr. Barnet's and Mr. Pratt's abovementioned."

"You see, Aunt," Hester said, "I did read the advertisement, but saw no reason to call it to your attention because it is obviously an attempt to steal Dr. Chamberlen's trade, which has been so successful."

"Successful, hah! That necklace you bought for me has done nothing to cure my toothache!"

"I meant that the sales of his necklace must have brought him a great deal of money. If the necklace did not work as he claimed, then, I am very sorry, but you, yourself, asked me to procure it. I merely read the advertisement to you. And you have had such a miserable time with your teeth that you decided to try it. But my point is that the very same mountebanks who have condemned the necklace, offer it to their customers in nearly the next sentence.

"And," Hester continued before her aunt could object, "if you will let Mary read on, you will see the original seller's response." She nodded to her cousin, and Mary quickly continued.

"Any Person that pretends to know what the Celebrated Necklace recommended by Dr. Chamberlen, for Children's Teeth, &c. is made of, is entirely mistaken, it being a Secret known to none but the Author: So that to insinuate to the World that it is made of This or That Matter, to render it Odious, is a Notion so inconsistent with the Art of Physick . . ."

As Mary read, her mother continued to fume, but did not interrupt. Hester did not know if that was a good sign or not.

". . . yet some Persons think it very worth their while to Counterfeit it, and assert, that they dispose of the VERY SAME, and yet, at the same time rail against it."

Believing she had now made her case, Hester thanked her cousin and said, "You see why I did not call it to your attention, Aunt? If you doubt my intentions, further down in the advertisement the author suggests that anyone with doubts is free to call on Dr. Chamberlen at his House in Great Suffolk Street, where he will try to satisfy all comers of the success of the necklace. Perhaps, if you were to visit him, he could allay your concerns."

"It is not I who should visit him! I have much more important things to do with my time. You should go."

"I will gladly run any errand you wish." Since this would give her an opportunity either to see St. Mars or to question Lord Wragby's valet, Hester spoke truthfully.

She had already spoken to Pierre about Lord Wragby's valet and learned that the man had found a new employer in Jermyn Street. How Pierre had become informed of this was a mystery in itself, but everyone knew that servants gossiped with one another. Hester supposed that their gossip was little different from the talk at Court. Only the subjects would be different.

Now, Hester had to think of a way to approach Lord Wragby's

man without causing a scandal or getting the poor man dismissed.

Her aunt had been embarrassed by her explanation, for clearly she had not read the offending newssheet herself. Someone else must have told her about the "dead peoples' skulls" without bothering to inform her of the rest.

She abruptly dropped the subject and with barely a breath in between started criticizing Mary for having wasted all her chances to find a new husband.

Mary responded heatedly, and within seconds they had erupted in a row.

Hester did what she could to mediate, assuring her aunt that there would be many new opportunities for Mary to meet gentlemen, once the King determined that he had done enough to make the country safe. "Then all sorts of assemblies will be held, and you shall have no more to worry about."

That was the worst thing she could have said in front of Mary, who stared at her as if she were a traitor. "I do not care one jot if Mama worries! I have no intention of marrying anybody simply because she wishes it. I have a very good idea of what I want, and I shall have it, if I have to embarrass you all to get it!"

Mrs. Mayfield gasped. "Ungrateful, spiteful child! I don't know where you got such a horrible, defiant nature. But, make no mistake! You will marry where I tell you to, or I will see that my lord puts you out in the street. That is where disobedient girls meet their ends, and when that happens, do not think that I shall mind. I shall be happy to wash my hands of you!"

Fortunately, before Mary could respond, a footman came in to say that Mrs. Mayfield had a visitor, a person she had met at Court, who was as avid a gambler as herself. Before the lady was shown up, Hester and Mary made their escape. Mary wished to follow Hester to her chamber to vent her temper further, but Hester told her that she had heard enough spite for one night and that she preferred to go early to bed.

"Mary," she said wearily, outside her cousin's door. "I wish you would not bait your mother. You know that you cannot be so assertive with her."

"Better to be assertive than deceitful! I refuse to let her think that I shall subjugate my happiness to her greed. It is time she realizes that I will never be forced."

"Would it not be better to wait until an actual threat to your happiness arises? If one ever does, you can deal with it then, and you will have my full support, but this incessant arguing will not break down her resolve. It might drive her to do something truly objectionable."

"Objectionable? Hester, how can you be so blind? You are wrong if you think she will ever agree to my wishes. She has no real affection for me, nor I for her. In fact, I hate her with all my heart, and I am just as eager to be rid of her as she is of me." With that, Mary went into her room and slammed the door, leaving Hester more discouraged than she had felt since St. Mars's return.

She could not wait to see him, to feel his arms around her. For a moment, she closed her eyes and tried to imagine him here with her, but Mary's anger had hurt her too much to be instantly dismissed. If Mary, her only real friend in the family, stayed angry with her, then perhaps she should leave now.

But, if she did, who would clear James Henry of suspicion? Hester knew that she must not complain of Mary to St. Mars. He had been reluctant to assist his half-brother. If he believed that Mary did not merit their efforts, if he came to think of her as no worthier than the rest of the Mayfields, he might decide to give up their investigation.

Mary did deserve their help, as dangerous as it might be for both of them to go after a murderer. The trouble was that she had inherited some of her mother's less-desirable qualities, not that Hester would ever tell her she had. She could be a bit wild, wilful, and truculent, but underneath her heart and mind were good.

All she needed was a steady hand, someone with an even temperament to inspire her with a desire to overcome her faults. Someone precisely like James Henry.

Now, if they could only prove James Henry's innocence, that would be one hurdle conquered. Then, perhaps *he* could be the one to deal with Mrs. Mayfield.

Whether in florid impotence he speaks,
And, as the prompter breathes, the puppet squeaks;
Or at the ear of Eve, familiar Toad,
Half froth, half venom, spits himself abroad,
In puns, or politics, or tales, or lies,
Or spite, or smut, or rhymes, or blasphemies.

CHAPTER XVI

The very next day, on 2nd March, the *British Gazetteer* published a summary of the correspondence seized from Count Gyllenborg's house, which revealed the extent of the Jacobite plot.

In letters dating back to the previous autumn, Count Gyllenborg, the Swedish Ambassador, and Baron von Görtz, a German at the King of Sweden's court, had discussed the ships that would be needed to transport men and arms to Great Britain to overthrow King George. The Pretender had promised sixty thousand pounds sterling to be used as the Swedish king saw fit. The Swedes believed that much more money would be needed, since to overcome the British navy would require several ships of sixty to seventy guns. The letters revealed that even before receiving the money Baron von Görtz had arranged to purchase six ships of this size, armed and rigged, to be delivered at the beginning of March, when the harshness of winter would have abated to give the invasion a greater chance of success. To forward this plan in the greatest secrecy, in October the King of Sweden had granted von Görtz plenipotentiary powers. He was prepared to commit up to twelve thousand Swedish troops, and ships to carry everything they would need, except horses, which he counted on obtaining in England.

Count Gyllenborg's task was to ascertain how much support they could expect to receive from the English, who, the Pretender's agents promised, were prepared to rise *en masse*. They claimed that animosity towards King George ran so high that the malcontents needed only a body of regular troops to which to attach themselves. As with the previous rebellion, however, Count Gyllenborg found that the principals in the Jacobite faction would pledge the money that was needed only after seeing assurances from the King of Sweden, in his own hand, that he would assist them.

At one point in the correspondence, Baron von Görtz stated that James Stuart had asked permission to move his residence to Sweden; but the baron had responded in the strongest terms that such a move would be the same as declaring war by the sound of a trumpet and would absolutely wreck their plans.

He and Count Gyllenborg discussed the English concerns of a threat to the Church of England. There was little support for returning the country to the Roman Catholic Church, and James Stuart's refusal to convert from that faith had always been the greatest obstacle to his kingship. This led to a suggestion by von Görtz that they should make their interests known to the English people, for the King of Sweden intended to preserve English liberties; but Count Gyllenborg's arguments for the utmost secrecy prevailed. If the Dutch got wind of the planned invasion, they would likely declare war upon Sweden in support of their ally King George.

The plot was so well advanced by the moment of Count Gyllenborg's arrest that Baron von Görtz had advised him not to worry about raising money. It was clear that he believed the Jacobites' claims that the English people would welcome an invasion to restore James Stuart to the throne, and that such matters could be resolved once their victory was achieved. The Count agreed, adding that they should take advantage of the current discord within the ruling party, which might bring some of the Whigs to the Pretender's side.

One of the most disconcerting statements in their correspondence was that Lord Mar, who had instigated the Jacobite rebellion nearly two years ago, had a cousin, a Scotsman, who was physician and privy counsellor to the Russian tsar. This doctor reported that the tsar had a mortal hatred for King George and sympathy for the Pretender and that he wished to see James Stuart restored to his throne. The suggestion was that the tsar would be willing to enter the conflict on Sweden's side.

The Russian troops had not yet left their winter quarters in Mecklenburg. If what the doctor said was true, they would be in a position to attack Hanover.

Reading this intelligence in the newssheet, Gideon thought it was no wonder King George and his government had reacted so decisively. Every boat or ship that looked the least suspicious was being boarded. Smugglers had been caught sailing up the River Forth just past Edinburgh. As much as Gideon longed to be living with Hester in France, he was glad for the prudence that had made him postpone their departure.

For now, the house in Little Windmill Street would have to suffice. Their moments together were the happiest he had ever spent. Compared to the loneliness of the past nearly two years, he was in heaven.

And now there was no urgent need to find a permanent home for Tom and Katy. That could wait.

The revelation of the Swedish plot made him eager to resume his investigation of Lord Wragby's Jacobite friends. Neither Sir Francis nor Lord Charters had been taken up by the Messengers, which meant that neither of their names had appeared in the Swedes' correspondence. This was of questionable significance, since both emissaries had apparently been too cautious to put the names of their supporters in writing. Gideon tried to recall the letters he had read in Burchet's house, but as far as he could remember, they had dealt only with raising money. The writer—presumably Burchet, even if the handwriting did not match his—had not seemed aware of the Swedish plot. His connections were in France, and there had been no reference to support from any other quarter. This might indicate that neither he nor Lord Wragby had been aware of Count Gyllenborg's plans.

Lord Charters and Sir Francis had both ignored Gideon's requests to meet again. If Gideon were to rule them in or out as suspects, he would have to run them to earth.

Tom had discovered where they lodged. Both resided in the area northeast of Covent Garden and frequented the hummums and brothels in that area. In that, they were like most other gentlemen of their age. Tom had reported, too, that occasionally on Sundays, they dined with a group of friends at the Greyhound Tavern in Bury Street, near St. James's Square. He had not seen them go to any of their former haunts where Jacobites met.

Gideon decided to visit Lord Charters at his lodging to question him in private about the murder of his friend. The worst that could happen would be that he refused to receive him. Gideon doubted that Lord Charters would notify the law of the appearance of a Jacobite spy on his doorstep. He would have a hard time explaining why "O'Brien" had come to call.

For three nights, Gideon made the journey to Lord Charters's house without finding him in. He had no more success with Sir Francis. Frustrated by the length of the trip from his house on foot, on his third attempt, he rode one of his horses, taking the horse ferry from Lambeth.

Finally, as he dismounted in front of Lord Charters's house, he saw him emerge in the company of Sir Francis.

Neither man had spotted him, for the horse stood between him and the house. Gideon had to make a quick decision: whether to confront them in the street or follow to see where they were going. He had just made up his mind to trail them, when Sir Francis hailed a hackney cab and the two gentlemen climbed in.

Gideon waited until the hackney had turned the corner before remounting Looby. He followed at a sedate trot. The fact that the two men had chosen to ride rather than walk suggested that their destination lay at some distance away, so he was not surprised when they led him past Lincolns Inn Fields, along Holborn past the town ditch, and up beyond Smithfield. He was taken aback, though, when they turned up St. John's Street and into St. John's Lane, where the hackney set them down at St. John's Gate. If they were going to meet other Jacobites at the Duke of Albemarle's Head, they would be taking an immense risk. The owner of the tavern might have been released, but government spies were surely watching his establishment for any sign of Jacobite activity.

As soon as the two men disappeared through one of the doors cut into the blocked-up gate, Gideon dismounted and beckoned to a street urchin to come hold his horse. He gave the boy a silver coin and promised him another if he saw that Looby came to no harm. Since Looby was generally docile, Gideon did not worry that he would prove too much for the boy. His doubts about his quarry's destination did worry him, however. If they were not headed to the tavern, he could lose them at any moment.

He hastened to pursue them through the gate. On the other side, he was rewarded by the sight of two figures in gentlemen's clothing, making their way across the open square, the heart of the former priory. They had engaged the services of a linkboy, whose torch illuminated their silhouettes, making it easy to distinguish them from others in the square.

As Gideon trailed some thirty yards behind, he became aware that these two were not the only gentlemen converging on the square. A few others, also wearing powdered wigs and tricorn hats, seemed to be heading in the same direction. As they approached the north end of the square, the two he was following hailed the other group. The gentlemen in front turned to wait for them. Then, together they carried on, speaking in normal tones.

At first, Gideon thought that they might be going to meet other Jacobites, and that instead of using their previous meeting place, they could be heading for the tavern on the corner of Jerusalem Court. As far as he had seen, there was nowhere else for an assembly.

Then Gideon, who had slowed to let them get a safe distance ahead, realized that a half dozen sedan chairs had been set down outside the former priory church, and that ladies were being helped out of them.

Now, he wondered if he should turn back. If this was just a social gathering, it clearly was not a meeting of Jacobites. There was nothing clandestine at all in their behaviour. On the contrary, they were noisy enough to attract the attention of the residents in the square. The keeper of the tavern came out to see what all the jollity was about as the ladies and gentlemen, laughing and chattering, followed the linkboy to the door of the old priory church on the east side of the square.

The church should have been empty. It was derelict because of the fire, which had left it gutted. Gideon was surprised, therefore, when Sir Francis, Lord Charters, and their friends followed the linkboy inside. Curious, Gideon decided to keep after them since something extraordinary was about to take place.

As he opened the door to the nave, he tried not to make any noise. Fortunately, the group was making so much of its own that the creak of the door attracted no notice. The hollowed-out church was completely black inside, making it easy to hide. As he softly closed the door behind him, their voices echoed loudly round the space. The church had the familiar musty smell of old, abandoned buildings, mixed with a faint odour of charred wood and something else that Gideon could not identify.

The linkboy led them to the northeast corner of the church under the vestry, where some lanterns had been lit and set upon the tile floor.

Sir Francis paid the linkboy off, then turned to lead the group down a narrow stone staircase, along which, apparently, more lanterns had been placed. As Gideon moved through the shadows, unseen by the returning linkboy, he heard the men's and ladies' laughter echoing up the stairwell. When he reached the top of the stairs, a strange acrid smell met his nostrils and he had to suppress a sudden cough.

Near the base of the stairs, he paused to peer around the wall. Lord Charters's friends had entered the old crypt, where they were raucously greeted by other ladies and gentlemen already seated at a long board. The board had been set for a meal. With the party just arrived, they numbered some twenty or more persons. In addition, a dozen servants stood ready to serve them. The newcomers were ushered into the empty chairs, as they exclaimed over the setting, which without exception they declared to be perfect.

Gideon was grateful for the darkness, relieved only by a row of lanterns placed along the wall of the bay where the party was seated, and the neighbouring bay where servants were busy concocting a meal. Glancing at the faces round the table, he recognized a few. If not for his disguise of blackened brows and dark wig, they might have been able to name him, as well. Fortunately the crypt was so enormous that he was able to sneak past them to a third bay from which to observe the proceedings.

The acrid smell he had noticed in the stairwell was even more pronounced down here. Looking around, he discovered that it emanated from a brazier which had been set up deeper inside the crypt. A servant in livery was tending the coals and stirring a pot from which the noxious fumes arose.

Lord Charters seated himself at one end of the long table. A vacant chair stood at the other. After the company had been served with wine, Lord Charters called them to order. "Let us make a toast to our president." He raised his glass in the direction of the empty chair. "To the president of our brotherhood—" then, recalling the presence of ladies, he added—"and sisterhood. I give you the Prince of Darkness!"

"To the Devil!" All the others raised their glasses and took a sip.

"To Satan!" A gentleman called out another toast, and they drank again.

Amidst the laughter that followed, Lord Charters called for order. "Sir Francis Lichfield and I have called you to this special meeting of the Brotherhood of the Damned in honour of our departed friend, Phillip, Lord Wragby, best known to you all as the Father. Speaking as the Son, and for Sir Francis, the Holy Ghost, I ask you to lift your glasses again."

In a soberer mood, the party toasted Lord Wragby, some calling out, "To Phillip!" but an equal number exclaiming, "To the Father!"

"To our ambassador in Hell!"

This drew prolonged laughter and exclamations of agreement. Lord Wragby, it seemed, had promised them that whenever he was summoned before St. Peter, he would choose Hell over Heaven. Evidently the whole party—or club—had pledged to join him thither, no matter which one of them should happen to die first.

"May he enjoy the inferno and all its temptations!"

"And the pleasures of the flesh!"

"Down with the Church and its minions!"

To each of these toasts, the members responded with more drinking and cries of encouragement.

The sombre mood, which had affected the gathering at the mention of their lost friend, had quickly vanished. By now, the members had drunk so much that they were all in a jolly frame of mind.

"Shall we elect someone to take Phillip's title?" one of the ladies asked.

Lord Charters waved an airy hand. "I shall leave that to our patriarchs, prophets, and martyrs to decide. But first, we should sup." He beckoned the servants to begin serving. A selection of cold meats was passed around, offered under the names, "Devil's Loins," "Breast of Venus" and other titillating titles.

By now, the purpose of the meeting had become all too obvious. These were not merely atheists, but blasphemers, brought together perhaps by Lord Wragby to mock the Christian faith. The women, whom Gideon had first supposed to be harlots or mistresses, were actually ladies of quality.

The stench from the brazier made sense, too. If the president of the club was the Devil, then the fires of Hell should be filled with burning sulfur. It was an easy detail to provide, and much enjoyed by the company, who complimented Lord Charters and Sir Francis on achieving the perfect atmosphere. Apparently, they had never met in this crypt until now, but if ladies were to be included, the club could not gather at either a tavern or a coffee-house. A more proper meeting place had had to be arranged.

Looking about, Gideon had to admit that they had found the perfect setting for their meeting. Unlike the church above, the crypt appeared to be in a good state of preservation. It consisted of four bays, separated by stout columns, which still retained their moulded capitals and bases. The two bays the party occupied were of Norman style, the other two old English. Openings for pointed windows flanked the western bays, indicating that at one time, the crypt had stood aboveground, but now they were blocked up with stones. The central avenue of the crypt was about sixteen feet long and twelve feet high.

The eeriest feature of the place was a wall against which stood rows of ancient coffins. They had been turned up on their ends four and five deep. Covered in dust, and so old that some of their ends had fallen off to expose the skeletons' feet, they lent a rare sense of the macabre.

As Lord Charters called out for a servant to pass the "Holy Ghost Pie," Gideon felt that he had seen enough. There was nothing here to learn about Lord Wragby's murder or either of the two suspects. The nature of the club and its gatherings might say a great deal about its members, including Lord Wragby, but it had not illuminated any motive for murder.

When the servants were all busy serving the guests, their faces turned away, Gideon stole quietly through the shadows along the wall, back up the stairs, and out into the night. He took a deep breath, glad to be out from under the pall of brimstone, even if the air of London was full of soot.

There were worse things than soot.

A few days later, when Hester managed to get away, she met St. Mars in Little Windmill Street. After they had made love, and were curled up together, he told her about his visit to the Reverend Mr. Mottram. The story made her laugh; but she was disappointed to hear that he had not found a priest to marry them. The discouragement in St. Mars's voice led her to change the subject and soon they were bringing each other up to date with their activities.

Knowing that her own contribution was unlikely to be as great as his, Hester began by telling St. Mars about her confrontation with Lord William Silsbee.

"So you think he feels guilty about something he has done?" St. Mars asked, when she had finished.

"Or else, because of something he knows. I could not tell which. And he seemed afraid. I would say that Mary and I had frightened him by bringing up Lord Wragby's murder, except that we did not. We only thanked him for stopping Lord Wragby's footmen from beating James Henry."

St. Mars's frown was pensive. "It does seem strange, I'll admit. Is Lord Ireton still threatening Harrowby, if he doesn't dismiss James?"

The news of Lord Ireton's recovery from the smallpox had duly been reported in the newssheets.

"That is unclear," Hester said in reply to St. Mars's question. "Isabella had to dance with him at the Palace ball, and something he said nearly sent her into hysterics. When she came home, she was not very coherent on the subject. I doubt she was paying much attention to his conversation until his manner turned threatening, because she has to concentrate very hard on the steps. She said that, as he escorted her to her chair, he pinched her arm so tightly, it hurt. Harrowby had seen Lord Ireton invite her to dance and had taken it for a conciliatory gesture. That relieved him, so he was not watching when Lord Ireton told her to pass along his message."

"And the message was . . . ."

At a loss, Hester raised her brows. "That is where Isabella's story becomes vague. She said he might have said that he would call Harrowby out. But would a gentleman deliver a challenge in that manner?"

St. Mars laughed. "I doubt it. Perhaps he said something to the effect that he would consider Harrowby accountable for his servant's misdeeds. Essentially, the same message he sent by Sir Horatio."

"Well, it's still monstrous! It's a wonder Isabella did not fall into hysterics in front of his Majesty. The Prince of Wales had danced with her very early in the evening—a sure sign of his regard. Harrowby was so pleased to see it, and Isabella was enjoying her triumph until Lord Ireton spoiled everything for her. She had to retire to the room set aside for ladies and tell the servant to bring her cold compresses for her neck. She was still shaking when they came home."

St. Mars had nothing to say about the incident, so Hester continued with her idea that Lord Wragby might have been lured to Spring Garden. She asked if he thought it possible that one of the other Jacobites could have lured him there to kill him.

"Of course, it's possible, but I am beginning to doubt that either Sir Francis or Lord Charters was actively involved the plot." He told her about following them to the bizarre meeting of their club and his sense that they were much too enaged in the pursuit of pleasure and nonsense to participate in any plot to overthrow the King.

Hester listened to him with a growing feeling of distaste. "That must be the club Sir Marmaduke mentioned, the Brotherhood of the Damned. What a childish display! I can just imagine Lord Wragby sitting there with them, hoping that word of what they were doing would get back to his father. But I suspect that with a parent as strict as Lord Ireton, the only blows his son could land would have to be indirect."

"I did not see anything to suggest a motive for murder. I am afraid we shall have to concentrate on Lord Ireton's friends, as unlikely as that may seem."

Hester expressed her disappointment that neither of Lord Wragby's friends appeared to be a likely suspect, but added, "I still have the feeling that he must have been lured to his death. I would like to ask Lord Wragby's valet if his master received any note in the day or two before his murder that could have invited him to the place where he was slain. Pierre knows who his employer is now. The problem will be how to speak to him without embarrassing myself."

"You don't wish to be seen chasing after a valet? Never fear, my love. That sounds like a perfect task for Tom, unless the valet is too superior to speak to a groom. But what makes you believe Lord Wragby was lured to the spot?"

"It was a strange place to be late at night without either friend or servant in attendance. The only other times I'd known him to go anywhere alone was to see Mary or to the Frenchman's house."

"Tell me again where he was murdered. I do not think I know."

"It was in a narrow street, leading from Spring Garden."

Resting against St. Mars's arm, Hester felt him give a start.

"Which spring garden? At Vauxhall or Charing Cross?"

"Charing Cross. Is there anything significant in that?"

"There may be. Just a moment, let me think."

Hester turned her head to observe him. He was lying with the back of his hand across his brow. She could feel some new excitement building in him.

He removed the hand from his face and turned to meet her gaze. "When did the killing take place?"

"Do you mean which hour of the clock?"

"No, the day. Can you recall the actual date of the murder?"

Hester thought briefly. "Yes, it was the same night as the fire, when the chapel at Spring Garden was burned down. Harrowby sent James

Henry and the footmen to help fight the blaze, you see. That is one reason why James Henry is suspected—he was known to be quite near the place where Lord Wragby was killed. No one can swear that he never left the fire."

"And do you know the date of the fire?"

"Yes, sorry, my dear. It was the second of December. I remember, because that was the first Sunday of Advent."

In a burst of excitement, St. Mars slapped the mattress. "I knew something about it was odd!"

"About what?" Excited herself, though she did not yet know why, Hester pushed herself up to face him.

He turned to prop himself on one elbow. "This may sound far-fetched, but I have been puzzling over an advertisement I've read several times in the newssheets since we came to town. I saw it again today.

"It states that a jewelled and enamelled snuffbox was found in the vicinity of Spring Garden at Charing Cross on the night of 2 December."

"My love, I fear you have lost me."

He laughed, and rising to a sitting position, pulled her to his side. "Well, let us see if I can find you again."

With Hester nestled happily in the crook of his arm, he said, "Do you not think it odd that no one has claimed such a valuable object? Yet, no one has since the first week of December."

"Ah, now I see. You think that perhaps the murderer dropped it and cannot claim it without revealing that he was there on the night of the murder."

"That was precisely my reasoning . . . though I suppose Lord Wragby could have dropped it himself."

"No, now wait. If the snuffbox did belong to him, he would often have been seen using it. You know how gentlemen are. They are always showing each other their toys."

"Humph! Are we? My love, have you forgotten that I am a gentle-man?"

Hester tapped him on the hand. "You know I do not mean you. You are a superior member of your sex. I mean the vain sort, like Harrowby."

"Was Lord Wragby as vain as my cousin?"

Hester sighed. "I do not really know. Still, I can imagine him show-ing a new snuffbox to his friends, or at least offering them a pinch of tobacco from it. If the snuffbox in the advertisement is as magnificent as it sounds, I'm sure his friends would have remarked it. And, then, do you not think that they would recognize the description and re-trieve it from the person who found it?"

"I should think his father would, at least."

"But those two were almost never together. I doubt that Lord Ire-ton would know what any of his son's toys looked like."

"Very well. So, my theory could be correct."

"It certainly bears investigating. Would it be possible to retrieve the item?"

He squeezed her to him. "Without a doubt. Just leave that to me."

After exchanging all the details they needed, Gideon put Hester in a hackney coach and went to the livery to retrieve his horse. Turning the new information through his mind, he rode down to the Millbank and took the horse ferry across the Thames, barely conscious of his journey.

He could get Tom to question Lord Wragby's former valet, but he did have doubts that the man would speak to a groom. Valets did not normally consort with outdoor servants, and it might take Tom an in-ordinate amount of time to cultivate a speaking acquaintance with the man. If Gideon were to approach the valet himself, perhaps with the prospect of employment to tempt him, any information he had might be extracted more quickly.

Gideon had just thought of a way to accomplish this when he reached his house. He directed Looby to the stables and dismounted in time to hand the reins to Tom.

"Mrs. Kean's in good health?" Tom asked, as usual.

"Yes, thank you, Tom. I shall tell her you inquired. We had a great deal to discuss, and I may need to ask for your assistance again."

"Yes, my lord." With a sigh, Tom turned to lead Looby to his stall.

Gideon peered after him through the stable door. The boy, whom Tom and Katy had decided to call Sam, was sitting in the hay, petting Argos, but he instantly jumped up to fetch the curry comb and brushes. The sight of his eagerness made Gideon smile. Then, while Tom unsaddled the horse, he watched to see what Sam would do next.

The child waited for Tom to hang the saddle and blanket in their place. Then, to Gideon's amusement, without a word Tom carried a stool into the stall and set it down next to Looby. The boy climbed upon it and immediately set to work grooming Gideon's horse. The scene evoked another memory of his childhood, and for the first time he marvelled that a man like Tom with so many fears and worries— disease, foreigners, the dark—could instil such confidence in a frightened child.

Of course, Tom did not lack confidence around horses. He knew them in the way he knew his own body. And they trusted him. Many times, Gideon had seen him soothe the most skittish mount. He supposed that restoring this young boy's sense of security must not be much different from calming a startled horse.

They still had not seen any advertisement about a missing page in the newssheets, Gideon reflected, as he turned to go to the house. By now, it might be safe to assume that they never would.

Still, it was very odd.

Gideon halted. It was as odd as the fact that no one had claimed a valuable snuffbox.

That was the echo that had been lingering just out of his hearing. These two very different, but similar deviations from the way people usually behaved. The failure to reclaim very valuable property.

Gideon suppressed a new wave of excitement. The two things occurring—or rather, not occurring—could be just a coincidence. But they were rare enough, and remarkable enough, to merit investigation.

Gideon was about to go back to the stables to ask Tom a question, when he recalled that Katy could answer it just as well. Thinking it better not to raise the subject in front of Sam, Gideon continued into the house, where he found Katy sewing by the kitchen fire.

"No, please, do not get up," he said, when she put down her sewing to fetch his meal. "Dinner can wait. There is something I need to ask you."

Katy slowly lowered herself back down, her eyes opening wide.

"It's about Sam," Gideon said. "When did you find him exactly?"

The question made her ill at ease. Her face fell, as if she had been dreading this moment, and she swallowed, before answering, "It was in December, my lord."

"Can you be more precise? Do you recall the date or which day of the week it was?"

Katy shook her head. "No, my lord. I've never paid that much mind to the calendar."

Gideon smiled to reassure her. "But you do go to church most days. Can you remember if you found him in Advent or Christmastide?"

She brightened immediately. "Oh, in Advent! I'm sure of that. He had already been with us awhile before Christmas."

The excitement that Gideon had suppressed threatened to engulf him now. But he needed to make sure. "When you went across the river that day, did you hear about the fire at Spring Garden—the one at Charing Cross?"

Katy looked confused. "Yes, we did, but what does that have to do with Sam? That happened a few days before we found him."

Gideon took in a deep breath. That was it. The dates corresponded, just as he had hoped they would. But Katy was plainly ruffled, so he hastened to relieve her mind. "I do not think the boy had anything to do with the fire, but something else occurred that night. You and Tom both have thought that something frightened Sam—so much, perhaps, that he has refused to speak. Did you not tell me—or maybe it was Tom—that when you found him, he was frozen and starving?"

Katy nodded. Her brow was still wrinkled, but at least she knew that he was not accusing the child of setting the fire.

"My lord, I wish you would tell me what these questions are about."

"I will. I will tell you and Tom both, but I need to think first. You must not worry, though. If I am correct, it is doubtful that anyone will come forward to claim the boy."

A smile spread across her face. "Thank you, my lord!" Greatly relieved, she bounced out of her chair. "Should I get your dinner now?"

Gideon laughed. "Yes, I'm ready to eat, but, please, do not celebrate just yet. And say nothing to Sam. I shall have to make sure that what I'm guessing could be correct."

She bobbed him a curtsy. "Yes, my lord."

But Gideon could see that her hopes had been raised and that, if he was wrong, it was going to be even harder to take Sam away.

He had better be correct.

But why insult the poor, affront the great?
A knave's a knave, to me, in every state:
Alike my scorn, if he succeed or fail,
Sporus at court, or Japhet in a jail,
A hireling scribbler, or a hireling peer,
Knight of the post corrupt, or of the shire;
If on a Pillory, or near a Throne,
He gain his Prince's ear, or lose his own.

CHAPTER XVII

That night, when Sam had gone to sleep on his pallet in the kitchen, Gideon called Tom and Katy upstairs into the small parlour to talk about his theory.

When he had first bought the house, Gideon had sent Tom to a bailiff's auction at the house of a bankrupt gentleman to furnish his own as quickly as possible. His purchases had included a few small tables and straight-backed chairs, only one of which had been set in Gideon's bedchamber, where he ate, slept, and thought. The rest had been placed in this tiny parlour, which he seldom used.

Earlier that evening, he had instructed Katy to light the fire in the room to take off the chill. Now, as he poked at the logs, the temperature was tolerable. Here, gathered round the fire, they could discuss Gideon's notion without the boy's overhearing.

After instructing both of his servants to sit, Gideon explained why he had asked Katy about the day the boy was found. He told them about the advertisement for the snuffbox that no one had claimed, and why he thought the two things, the unclaimed snuffbox and the boy for whom no one had advertised might be tied to the same event.

They agreed, it was strange that no one had tried to recover either the snuffbox or the boy, especially when both appeared to have been lost about the same time.

"But what would either of them things have to do with the fire at Spring Garden, my lord?" Tom asked, revealing that Katy had repeated their conversation.

"Perhaps nothing at all. The fire may simply be a coincidence. But something else took place on the night of the fire, and the boy may have witnessed it."

With both their gazes fixed on him, Gideon said, "That was the evening that Lord Wragby was murdered. And the next day someone found the snuffbox in the area, near Spring Garden at Charing Cross. The only reason I can fathom why a man would make no attempt to retrieve such a valuable article is because he does not wish it to be known that he was there right before the object was found. Either because he set the fire—and I believe that was determined to be the result of an accident—or because he was involved in the murder."

"And you think Sam saw the killing?" Katy and Tom were both shocked.

"I think it possible, yes. The timing is right, and again, no one has claimed the boy. Of course, I could be wrong, but I have reflected on nothing else since I came back this afternoon, and no other explanation makes as much sense.

"If Sam came from outside London, his employer would still have advertised here for his return. There would be no other way to locate a runaway servant, and just to let him go would result in too much of a loss. And if his master lives in London or Westminster, why else would he not try to retrieve him, unless he had something reprehensible to hide?"

Gideon studied his servants' expressions, illuminated by the glow from the fire. Both were struggling with his reasoning, which he had had most of the day to consider, and they were obviously anxious about how it would affect the boy.

"He is still not speaking? Not even to you, Tom?"

Tom shook his head. "No, my lord, and if he thinks I can hear him, he don't even talk to the horses."

"But he can speak? You do know that?"

"Yes, my lord." At Gideon's steady look, Tom said earnestly, "But

I don't think you can ask him anything, my lord! He's not ready to talk."

Katy added her pleas. "Sir, please don't ask him to tell you what he saw! He's still too afraid to tell us his name. He's very young, my lord, and if he did see anything like a murder, it's no wonder he's scared."

Gideon took a deep breath and tried not to let his frustration show. "Very well, I shan't. I'll try to find Lord Wragby's killer without involving Sam, but if I cannot, we may need to question him. And, if we come to that point, if need be, I shall let you do it. But do not forget that Mr. Henry's life may depend upon finding the murderer."

Tom looked chastened by the reminder, but a glance at Katy strengthened his resolve. "Yes, my lord. Let's see what else you can do first, and we'll try a bit harder to get Sam to talk to us. Maybe if we can get him to open his mouth about something else, the rest'll come a mite easier."

With this agreed, Gideon retreated to his bedchamber while Tom and Katy extinguished the fire. Gideon understood their concern for the boy. Deep down, he was proud of them for taking in the waif, not as a servant, but as a child. Not many people would have taken the trouble for a homeless boy, much less a black one.

It was frustrating, true, not to be able to question a person living under his own roof, who might have the answers that had left him and Hester in such a quandary. But there was the snuffbox, and that was something he could start on the very next day.

The following morning found him in his black periwig, and heavily made up, taking a waterman's boat across the Thames. He landed at Blackfriars Stairs and strode up Water Street towards the Old Bailey.

The advertisement for the snuffbox had instructed the claimant to leave a description in writing for Jonathan Wild at the Blue Boar Inn in Little Old Bailey Street, with word of when he would call there again. Gideon had written a note, describing a snuffbox in much the same terms that Wild had used—a box with enamel and brilliants. He knew enough about snuffboxes to guess at a few more details. Gentlemen's snuffboxes were usually made of silver with pique ornamentation or embellishments in tortoise shell, mother of pearl, wood or horn. One with enamel work and diamonds would be quite rare, so he assumed the metal used would be gold. Since the Huguenots, who were most expert at painting enamel, had made a specialty of floral designs, he ventured that flowers would figure somewhere in the image. The brilliants were likely to be affixed to the rim of the lid. So, Gideon had added those details to his description.

Arriving at the Blue Boar Inn and going inside, he looked around for Jonathan Wild, the famous thief-taker he had seen walking down the street. Wild did not appear to be here, but Gideon's survey of the room detected a number of unsavoury-looking individuals, who studied him out the corners of their eyes. In his expensive periwig and *justaucorps,* he must look like ripened fruit, ready for picking. He put his hand to his pocket and was relieved to find his purse still there. He would have to remember to guard it from pickpockets while he was in the area.

Except for, perhaps, a keener interest in a stranger come into their midst, the patrons of this tavern acted much like those of any other drinking establishment. As soon as they had finished making an assessment of him—discouraged, no doubt, by the hand clapped over his pocket and the sword at his belt—they went back to whatever business his entrance had disturbed. The only real difference was in the covert nature of their perusals.

After leaving his note with the tavern-keeper, Gideon decided to take a hackney coach to King's Square, where Hester had told him Lord Wragby's valet had found new employment. Though the distance was not too far to walk, some of the streets he would need to take would be muddy and unpaved. He walked only a short way before finding an available coach.

King's Square had been built on Soho Fields on land granted to the Earls of Portland and Leicester, but despite their intention to build houses as grand as those in Bloomsbury, the location had never been as attractive to the aristocracy as St. James's Square. Over the past thirty years, Soho had been settled by a community of Protestants expelled from France, who had established a Huguenot church. Some of the aristocracy and gentry did reside there, but the area was not considered fashionable by Court society. Gideon was not familiar with the valet's new employer—one Sir Roger Digby, according to Pierre—but it did seem that the valet had come down in the world after serving the heir to the Marquess of Ireton.

With time on his hands, Gideon told the driver to set him down in Frith Street, so he could approach the square on foot. He immediately felt the influence of France, from the Calvinistical clothes worn by some of the women to the men's plain attire and the sound of French pronounced on the streets. He spied some Greek and Italian immigrants, too, though they were vastly outnumbered by the French, who had flooded into England, desperate and resented for their strange ways.

Strolling down the street, Gideon passed a number of fine artisans' shops, as well as houses where silk was woven. In one, through the window he glimpsed a group of elderly women making lace. Even the smells from kitchens wafting towards him spoke of a different diet than would be eaten less than half a mile away. The aroma of freshly baked bread was welcome to his nostrils for it moderated some of the more pungent odours of the street.

In polite French, he inquired about the house of Sir Roger Digby, and eventually found a resident who could point it out to him. Noting a few landmarks, he committed them to memory to relay to Tom. Then, checking his timepiece, he decided it was time to see if Jonathan Wild had received his message.

This time, when he entered the Blue Boar, he noticed a distinct change in the mood of the place. Silence seemed to reign, the only sounds being the dull clunk of mugs on wooden tables and the hasty steps of the drawers as they rushed to fill orders for beer. A whisper or two did reach his ears, but the voices remained low, even when uttering a simple request for a pint. The patrons did not assess Gideon as before. Their furtive glances were directed not at him but at the closed door in the far wall of the room, as if at any moment a serpent might emerge from it.

Gideon crossed to the counter and asked the tavern-keeper for Jonathan Wild. The man dropped what he was doing to lead him to the dreaded door, where he softly knocked and, after a moment, was directed to enter. He motioned for Gideon to proceed and turned back to his duties.

Opening the door, Gideon espied a man seated alone at a desk, built upon a dais in the centre of the room like a throne, the man whose presence in the Blue Boar had instilled such caution. He wore a collarless coat over a contrasting woollen vest with numerous small buttons unfastened to his waist to reveal a linen shirt. His head was covered by a round hat, which resembled a turban except for a knot that graced the top and a soft brim turned up at the edge. Leaning against the desk beside him was a silver staff, the top of which was engraved in the shape of a crown. He had a short face with a wide, flat nose, a deeply furrowed brow, and baggy lids above and below bulging eyes.

Recognizing the man he had seen on the street, Gideon approached the desk, affecting a hesitant air. He had given some thought to the manner he should present, alternating between arrogant and fearful, and settling finally upon nervous. He reasoned that anyone claiming an object that was clearly not his would have ample reason to worry that his lies would not be believed. If he could not convince Wild that the snuffbox was his, he would have to construct a more convincing story as he felt his way along. If nothing else worked, he would pretend that he was acting on behalf of someone who did not wish to be named.

Jonathan Wild stood at his approach and made a sweeping bow, undoubtedly practiced at great length. It combined just the right degree of arrogance and subservience to place him on a level somewhere between his inflated notion of himself and the image he cultivated as a devoted servant to the rich victims that he and his brethren bilked.

"Mr. Jonathan Wild?" Gideon asked, as if he did not already know.

"Yer servant, Mr. . . ."

"Digby. Sir Roger Digby." Gideon saw no reason to invent another alias, so he used the first name that popped into his head. He had not put a signature on the note he had left with the tavern-keeper. "I've come to collect the snuffbox mentioned in your advertisement, don't y'know."

"Ah . . . yes." Wild turned to his desk to pick up Gideon's note and, frowning as if he found something troublesome about it, studied it minutely. Eventually, he raised his eyes to Gideon and gave an ingratiating smile. "Please sit, Sir Roger." He indicated the spindly wooden chair with a sagging leather seat that stood in front of his desk. "And before we get down to business, I'll have my usual fee—five shillin's. And then we can talk about yer property."

Gideon was not going to baulk at five shillings. He reached into his pocket and dropped the coins into Wild's outstretched hand, imagining how much the thief-taker must make in a year at this rate.

After Wild had stowed the money away, he sat behind his desk and took hold of his silver staff. "Now, ye've come for the snuffbox, and if ye can prove it's yers, ye'll have it straight away. But before I can give it to ye, ye'll have to describe it a bit better than ye did."

Gideon had taken the chair, but he decided to bluster. "But I already gave you the details! They are in that note!" He had hoped that, having waited so long for the item to be claimed, Wild would be eager to dispose of it and would not wish to prevent a transaction from taking place.

Wild spoke smoothly, "Yes, but ye see, ye only gave me what I put in the paper. To be sure that the snuffbox is yers, I must hear more about it."

Gideon hemmed and hawed, before eventually confiding, "Well, the truth is, you see, that the snuffbox is not actually mine. It belongs to my uncle. He lost it on his last visit to London. Went to Spring Garden, y'know, to look for a bit of company. Had no idea where he'd dropped it until he saw the bit you placed in the newssheet. He doesn't receive them regularly, y'know, which is why he did not ask me to reclaim it until recently."

"Ah . . . yes." Wild nodded as if Gideon's story made perfect sense. "I wanted to ask why ye didn't come forward till now."

"I just got the letter from him yesterday. You see, he recognized your description at once, but he didn't write me any more about it than what I put in that note in your hand."

"He didn't describe the picture on the lid?"

Something in the way Wild leered made Gideon say, "No, but I think it had a woman in it."

Wild looked up sharply, but his eyes gave nothing away. "What makes ye say that, Sir Roger?"

"Oh, I seem to recall catching a glimpse of it—when he was offering me a pinch of snuff, don't y'know—but I could be mistaken. I often am. Not much one for noticing things, don't ye know." Gideon babbled like a man who could not be expected to remember anything of use.

Wild was studying him, as if trying to make out how much money he could extract from this idiot. "Maybe there's some other reason why yer uncle didn't describe the box?"

His question threw Gideon for a loss. Was Wild hinting that there was something about the box that the owner would not wish known? Or had Wild arrived at Gideon's theory—that it could have been dropped by the murderer?

He tried to gain a hint to Wild's meaning so he would know what reaction to feign, but the thief-taker was adept at hiding his thoughts. Wild was watching him closely. In the end the only response Gideon could think of that would not betray his ignorance was more bluster. "What do you mean to insinuate, you knave?" He half-stood, his right hand on his sword. "I did not come here to have my uncle abused! If you do not intend to return his property, then say so directly, but I shall know the reason why!"

"'Ere now!" Alarmed, Wild tried to appease his visitor. "Don't draw yer tayle! I'm sure yer uncle's a boman-cove, and I don't mean t' nip'un." In his haste to undo the offense, he had slipped into thieves' cant, exposing his true self. He had too much to lose by offending a member of the gentry. His reputation for finding "lost" property was the basis for his trade, his bread and butter.

"Well, what did you mean by it, eh?" Bluster had worked so well that Gideon kept it up.

"All's boman, I tell ye! That's 'well' to you." Wild regained his composure. "It don't make deuce t' me if he wants to put a doxie on his snuffbox. Ye'll have t' tip me some gelt for it, though. That's a rum snuffbox, that is."

Doing his best to hide his surprise, Gideon pretended to be placated by the rogue's explanation. He raised his nose to indicate that he would not discuss his uncle's taste and resumed his seat.

"How much will you ask for it?"

Wild made a false show of giving this consideration, when he must long ago have determined how much he would ask for the box. "I take half of what it costs to replace it. That way, I can give a snack t' the cove what found it, and yer much better off than havin' t' buy a new'un like it.

"I'll give it t'ye fer ten Guineas."

Gideon did not try to hide his wince. It was a huge sum, and he could not even be certain that it would provide him with the clue he needed. Still, if the snuffbox was as magnificent as described, it should be worth twice the amount. If it proved worthless to the investigation, he should be able to recover his money by selling it.

"I shall have to see it first. I cannot hand over such an extraordinary sum before making sure that the snuffbox is as you say it is."

With the prospect of so much money coming his way, Wild quickly agreed and, taking a ring of keys out of his pocket, got up from his desk to step over to a large chest. He unlocked the chest and lifted out a strong box, which he proceeded to unlock as well. During this process, he threw an occasional glance over his shoulder to see if Gideon was peeking at his hoard. He took out a small object wrapped in paper and, after putting it in his pocket, locked up his strong box and then the chest.

Returning to his desk, he unwrapped the paper and presented its contents to Gideon with a bow, a leer spread across his face. The reason for his expression became immediately clear.

The bottom of the box appeared to be made of pure gold. The base of the lid was silver and its rim was circled with brilliants, as Gideon had guessed. To his untutored eye, the diamonds appeared to have been cut by an expert from Antwerp, for they shimmered in the light.

But the feature that raised Gideon's eyebrows was the enamel painting on the lid. Two figures were portrayed: a black page in livery and a beautiful woman with one breast completely exposed and a hand placed invitingly beneath her partially-raised skirt.

The face of the woman was so well rendered that Gideon suspected it was a portrait. Her pose was so scandalous that she had to be the owner's mistress.

At first, the presence of the page in the painting had excited Gideon's interest, but he could not say that the boy in the image was the one Tom and Katy had rescued from the streets. The painted child could have been any black boy of an early age, with the rounded features of a young child. The artist had made no effort to portray him as an individual, perhaps not even seeing him as such. His interest, and presumably the desire of his patron, had been to capture the woman's face.

With a nod, Gideon acknowledged that the snuffbox in his hand was the one he had sought. He brought out his purse and counted ten Guineas into the thief-taker's hands. Wild, who must have expected to receive a draft on a bank, was so astonished by the pile of gold coins that he stared at them for a long moment. Then, he examined each one for signs of clipping and tested the legitimacy of each with his teeth.

When his examination was complete, he made Gideon a deeper bow and ushered him from his office, asking that his respects be conveyed to "Sir Roger's" uncle.

Before exiting Wild's office, Gideon placed the snuffbox deep inside his vest pocket. Guarding it from the Blue Boar's patrons with a hand clamped over the flap, he strode out of the tavern and quickly made his way home. He glanced over his shoulder several times to see if a pickpocket or footpad was following, but when none appeared, he assumed it was because Jonathan Wild had rules that his fraternity must follow. It could not be good for business if one of his agents robbed the same person twice.

As Gideon was rowed back across the Thames and upriver to Lambeth, he thought about what he had learned.

The image of the black page on the snuffbox was not enough to confirm his suspicion that Sam had witnessed the murder of Lord Wragby; but the presence of the page did suggest that the owner of the snuffbox had such a servant. The artist's rendition of the child's features was so poor that it was at least possible that Sam was the one who had posed with the owner's mistress.

The woman was not anyone Gideon knew, unless the artist had taken liberties with her features. Gideon was of the opinion that few portrait-painters captured their subject's real look, certainly not most of the popular artists at the English Court today. Their subjects looked very much alike, their features moulded to the fashionable ideal, which recently, for ladies at least, resembled a bird. That was what most of their customers seemed to want.

Still, despite the lack of attention to the boy's face, the enamel painting had been executed by a talented hand. The woman did not look like the fashionable portraits Gideon had seen. She was beautiful, but one should expect the mistress of a wealthy gentleman to possess extraordinary beauty. That was what she had to sell.

Gideon wanted to show the snuffbox to Hester to see if she recognized the woman on the lid. He wondered if she would be scandalized by the provocative pose, but considering the passion in their lovemaking, he somehow doubted she would. He was more disturbed by the thought of showing the picture to Tom who, he suspected, would be horrified to see it.

The dull clunk of oars in their locks and the soft lap of water against the wooden sides of the boat provided a soothing music for his thoughts. He pondered how to make use of the snuffbox to identify the murderer. It was possible that it had belonged to Lord Wragby. Gideon agreed with Hester that if it had, all his friends would have seen it, at least the men. It was not something that a gentleman would show to a lady, but it was such a splendid piece of work and the subject was so enticing that most men would want to flourish it in front of their friends. If Gideon were to do that with each of their suspects, their reactions should tell him a great deal.

By the time Gideon's boat reached the stairs at Vauxhall, he had decided on a course of action. First, he would show the snuffbox to LordWragby's friends. If neither knew it, he would know to focus his investigation on the two who had visited the gallery of St. Paul's with Lord Ireton on the day that Hester had overheard the threat.

Lord Ireton's threatening behaviour to Isabella at the ball had thrown both her and Harrowby into a serious quandary. Isabella was terrified of encountering the marquess again and demanded that her husband accompany her every time she left the house. With the King expecting attendance in the House of Lords to prepare the country's defenses, this meant that she was often obliged to remain at home, sometimes until too late at night for any entertainments. Unused to denying herself the smallest pleasure, she eventually accepted the escort of Lord Kirkland and Sir Marmaduke in Harrowby's stead, though neither relished the prospect of defending her against one of the best swordsmen in the country.

Harrowby was once again presented with the choice of facing Lord Ireton or giving up his valuable steward, who not only acted as receiver-general for his rents, but oversaw the management of his extensive estate—which he had not been raised to manage and would not have the slightest clue where to start.

As usual, it fell to Hester to remind him of this, which she did while trying not to make him feel his own ignorance. Instead, she pointed out that he would be forced to abandon his duties in Westminster to travel to all his properties, to give up the pleasures of London for the discomfort of bad roads, the complaints of his tenants, and the dreariness of travelling alone.

Fortunately, Harrowby had no illusions about the romance of travel or any desire to expand his knowledge of the Hawkhurst estates. The picture Hester painted of his life without James Henry, at least until he managed to find someone as trustworthy, terrified Harrowby even more than the possibility that he would have to meet Lord Ireton at dawn—perhaps due to its certitude. He opted for a plan of action that she suggested wherein he would do his best to avoid Lord Ireton's threats by clinging to the Prince of Wales.

Though King George and his son had made a brief demonstration of unity, it was well known at Court that the Prince of Wales was continuing down the path he had started even before his father had left England for Hanover. He and the Princess had set up their own court within St. James's Palace, which was now frequented by the Whigs opposed to the King's new ministers. Ever contrary to his father's wishes,

Prince George cultivated the support of the politicians who had broken with the King, whether over the appointments he had made or the bills that he pushed on Parliament.

Recalling the warning Lady Cowper had given her on Coronation Day, and aware of the turmoil within the Whig party, which Count Gyllenborg had referenced in his letters to Baron von Görtz, Hester advised Harrowby to confine his Court visits to the Prince of Wales. Lord Ireton was one of the King's men and unlikely to visit the Prince. This was not a wise course for Harrowby over the long run—it could never be wise to side with a prince over a king—but in the short run it might save Harrowby from a terrifying encounter.

Harrowby was not at all averse to her suggestion, having always preferred the society of the lively Prince and Princess to the dull German King.

The other place he must be certain to avoid was Lord Ireton's coffee-house. Every gentleman spent his mornings at his favourite coffee-house, and the patronage of these was often determined by political party. Fortunately, Harrowby had never been a member of the famous Kit Kat Club of which Lord Ireton was a founder. As long as he continued to frequent the St. James's Coffee-House and ventured nowhere else, he should be safe.

So, for the moment, James Henry's position had once again been preserved. Lord Ireton's threat, however, made Hester acutely aware of her failure—hers and St. Mars's—to identify Lord Wragby's real killer. They had been too wrapped up in their own happiness to devote their minds fully to the problem that must be solved.

At St. Mars's insistence, Hester had turned over the task of questioning Lord Wragby's former valet to Tom. That left her with no clues to pursue. As much as she disliked going to Court, she decided that spending more time there was the only way she was likely to gain any useful information. Mrs. Mayfield was always eager for Mary to display her beauty where a possible husband might see her, but she did not wish to be tied to her daughter. She was agreeable, therefore, when Hester suggested that she could take Mary to the Palace to pick up the current gossip and perhaps bring her to the notice of new acquaintances.

Once Hester had explained her plan to Mary, the girl was willing enough to go. The last thing Mary wished was to be left at home to suffer her mother's abuse. The following morning, then, they dressed in their finest day gowns with silk skirts over hoops, contrasting stomachers, elbow-length sleeves trimmed with lace, delicate kerchiefs and lace caps. Robed like this, they would be admitted to the courtyards of the Palace, where they were certain to encounter courtiers eager to gossip.

They rode to the Palace in chairs to spare their shoes from the mud caused by a rain the previous day, and were set down at the Tudor gate. Passing through to the first courtyard, they spied a number of ladies coming and going from the stairs that led to the new suite of rooms for the Princess of Wales. After more than a year of attending Court, Hester had learned which ladies might welcome a conversation with her and who would not. Often it was the least likeable person who was most desperate to repeat the rumours she had heard to a person of no consequence like Hester, though the Princess and a few of her ladies were always cordial to her. She looked around for Madame Schultz, one of the German ladies who loved to gossip and could be counted upon to need a willing ear, but did not see her among the ladies crossing the courtyard.

It did not take long for Hester to notice that the temper in the courtyard today was unusually sombre. Hushed voices, hurried steps, and a few reddened eyes told her that something unfortunate had occurred. Before she could ask anyone what was wrong, one the younger ladies in the Princess's service hurried over to them. Lady Mary Capell, sister to the young Earl of Essex, was a bubbly girl with few pretensions. About the same age as Hester's cousin, she had always been friendly, in spite of the difference in their rank. Now, with tear-filled eyes she ignored their attempt to greet her with a curtsy and said, "Have you heard the dreadful news? Lord William Silsbee was murdered last night!"

Hester's heart leapt into her throat. For a moment she could not breathe.

After a moment of stunned silence, Mary voiced their shock. "Where? How?"

"They say he was assaulted by a footpad in Lincoln's Inn Fields. He was found . . . stabbed . . ." Lady Mary's voice nearly broke on the word. ". . . quite late last night when a resident crossing the square spied his corpse. He was carried into the nearest house, but it was too late to save him. All his pockets had been turned out, so it must have been a robbery."

"Does anyone know why he was there?" Hester asked. Her mind was awhirl with theories. It was possible that Lord William had been killed in the course of a robbery, but she could not believe it.

Lady Mary gazed at her strangely. "Not that I have heard, but he must have gone to visit a friend."

"Of course," Hester said hastily. "That was a foolish thing to ask, but it is such a terrible shock. We were speaking to him only a few days ago. What a tragedy!"

Lady Mary tearfully agreed. She told Hester and her cousin that Lord William had always been a good friend of her brother's.

As she went on to praise his fine qualities, Hester listened with only half an ear. She was convinced that Lord William had been murdered by the same person that had killed Lord Wragby, and she thought she knew why. It had been evident to her that Lord William knew something about Lord Wragby's death, and that the knowledge had frightened him. He must have known, or at least suspected, who the murderer was. His conscience had been troubling him. Any clergyman's daughter would have recognized the guilt Hester had seen on his face.

Had Lord William confronted the killer, or had his sickly demeanour revealed his suspicions? Had he had to be silenced?

Hester experienced a pang of guilt for having confronted the young man. Had she and Mary made it harder for him to live with what he had known? Had Mary's plea for James Henry driven Lord William to confess what he suspected to the killer? If so, then Hester and she were partly responsible for his death.

"Oh, here is Lady Cowper!" Lady Mary exclaimed. "Perhaps she will be able to tell us more."

Hester turned to see Lady Cowper, looking distressed and exhausted, coming from the stairs to the Princess's rooms,.

Seeing her condition, Hester would not have bothered her, but Lady Mary was too wrapped up in her own grief to notice another's distress. She hurried over to Lady Cowper, asking, "Are you leaving, Lady Cowper? I thought you were in waiting this week."

Hester and Mary followed a few steps behind and arrived in time to hear Lady Cowper answer, "Yes, but our mistress has given me leave to go home. She noticed how upset I was, though I did try to hide it. I shall be better after a few hours' rest."

"You must have been terribly upset by the news we've just heard." Hester made the baroness a curtsy. "We should not keep you from your bed."

Lady Cowper sighed. For a moment, she seemed too tired to leave. "Yes, it was horrible. Lord William was on his way to visit my husband, you see. He had written earlier in the day to request a private meeting. Usually my lord would have gone to the House, but the letter said his business was of vital importance to the realm, so my lord agreed to the meeting and remained home. When Lord William did not appear, he did not know whether to be angry or concerned, but after a half-hour or so, my husband decided he could wait no longer.

"It was a shock to discover that the poor gentleman had been murdered within sight of our windows." She shuddered. "If his corpse had not been discovered in the dark, we might have seen it ourselves this morning. As it was, we heard a great hue and cry sometime after midnight, and neither of us could fall back asleep. The news was simply too dreadful."

"And you have no idea what Lord William's business was?"

"No, but my lord believes that it must have had something to do with the Jacobites. Why else the secrecy and urgency?"

"Is it possible that whatever he meant to impart was the reason for his murder, and that it was not the result of a robbery?"

Lady Cowper's gentle eyes turned fierce. "If that was the reason, then the Pretender will have even more to answer for!"

Hester had forgotten that it had fallen to Lord Cowper to preside at the trials for treason. It was a duty that no one could want, but he had not been able to refuse King George's request to act as Lord High Steward at the trials of the Jacobite peers. Lady Cowper had confided to Hester how much the stressful duty had cost her husband's health. It was no wonder that another death that might be laid at the Pretender's feet would arouse her ire.

Having learned as much as she was likely to, Hester urged Lady Cowper to seek her rest. She curtsied again, and wishing the lady-in-waiting a more peaceful repose, bid her good day.

As soon as Lady Mary Capell left them to pour out the shocking news to others, Hester pulled her cousin aside. "I think we have heard enough. Shall we go?"

Mary agreed and turned to accompany Hester out of the Palace, saying in a lowered voice, "Hester, I cannot believe that Lord William's death is a coincidence, can you?"

"No. I believe he had decided to confide what he knew to Lord Cowper, and that the murderer guessed his intention and followed him to their meeting. He would not have wanted it to take place."

"But why would Lord William go to Lord Cowper and not just to a magistrate?"

Hester waited to answer the question until they had passed through the gate and there were no ears close enough to hear. "I cannot know for certain, but I imagine he was afraid to speak to a magistrate before he consulted a person with more experience. I do not know if Lord Cowper was a particular friend, but he is generally respected, and he is, after all, the Lord Chancellor. If anyone can give good advice on how to proceed in a criminal case, especially one concerning the murder of an aristocrat, it would be he. He is also a Whig, and if Lord William did know the identity of the murderer, I think we must assume that he is a Whig, too."

"Well, it must be Sir Horatio, then! He is the only one left."

Hester refused to discuss the matter more until they arrived at Hawkhurst House. After a few minutes' wait, they were able to secure the use of two chairs. If not for the mud, she would have much preferred to walk; but, despite the rudeness of the chairmen and the clumsy ride, she welcomed the few minutes alone to reflect.

Could Sir Horatio truly be the murderer? After she revisited her list of suspects, a kernel of doubt entered her mind.

What was it that Lord William's note to Lord Cowper had said?

That the business he needed to discuss was of importance to the realm. To Lady Cowper, this had meant that it had something to do with the Pretender. And the planned invasion? Had Hester been wrong, and the information Lord William had to convey had nothing to do with Lord Wragby's murder but, instead, concerned the Jacobites? The death of Lord Wragby could not be described as a great loss to the kingdom, but he had been an agent for the Pretender. In his sometime-role as Lord Wragby's minder, could Lord William have learned of some treason that Lord Wragby or his friends had intended to commit?

If that was the case, he might still have been Lord Wragby's murderer. Then, who in turn would have killed Lord William? Someone who had to guarantee that Lord Wragby's treason remained a secret? That raised Hester's suspicions of Lord Wragby's friends again, even if they did spend their time in nonsensical parodies of church rites. Was it not possible to be entertained by blasphemy on one hand and commit treason on the other?

Her thoughts had been so overturned by Lord William's killing that she could not make sense of anything now. She had to discuss it with St. Mars. She would think up an excuse to leave the house and send him a note as soon as she knew when she could get free.

What? armed for Virtue when I point the pen,
Brand the bold front of shameless guilty men;
Dash the proud Gamester in his gilded Car;
Bare the mean Heart that lurks beneath a Star . . . .

CHAPTER XVIII

Gideon received Hester's note that evening, asking him to meet her early on Monday morning. He would not have time to question Lord Wragby's former valet, but he could try to put two of their suspects to a test.

He had recalled a piece of information that Tom had picked up while following Sir Francis and Lord Charters. He had seen them meeting their friends for dinner on Sundays at the Greyhound Tavern in Bury Street. It might be worthwhile to see if he could waylay them on their way to the tavern, while Tom watched Sir Roger Digby's house for a glimpse of his valet.

Aware that his errand near St. James's Street would place him in greater peril of being recognized than his night-time forays into London, Gideon applied even more paint to his face than usual and took special care that his blond hair would not escape from beneath his black wig. It was becoming more fashionable to coat gentlemen's wigs with powder, but since the object of his wig was to disguise his fair colouring, he wore it without.

With only this one task in mind, and nothing else he could accomplish that day, Gideon decided to make his journey by boat and foot and to leave his horses at home. He had exercised Penny that morning, taking her out on the country roads between Lambeth and Kennington. He could take Looby out later, if Tom was still not home by nightfall. The length of the days was steadily increasing and soon would equal the hours of night. It was hard to welcome the spring when one felt so much safer in the dark.

Gideon instructed his waterman to row him all the way to Hungerford Stairs, where he did not expect to encounter any of his acquaintance. Since the market there had burned down, the area around it had become relatively quiet. From there, he wove his way through the streets to the Greyhound Tavern, avoiding Pall Mall, which would be thick with strollers on a Sunday afternoon.

He had to imagine the route his quarry might take on the way to meet their friends, but it would have surprised him to find that either Sir Francis or Lord Charters had risen to meet the dawn. Like most gentlemen, they would have stayed abed until it was time to dress, which could take some time. This meant that they would most likely approach the Greyhound from home, and they would be among the walkers parading on Pall Mall.

Arriving in Bury Street well before the fashionable hour for dinner, he positioned himself on the corner of King Street to have the best chance of intercepting them if they came from St. James's Square, the Palace, or the old paved alley that joined King Street to Pall Mall. He had no intention of entering the Greyhound and running the risk of meeting someone he knew face to face.

His wait was tedious, especially when he had to ignore the stares of passers-by—some of whom he knew—who wondered why any gentleman would choose to loiter on a street corner. He would have liked to lower the rim of his tricorn, but knew it was better not to look afraid of being seen. Finally, he caught a glimpse of two familiar figures coming towards him from the direction of St. James's Street, and he set off to meet them. They must have walked the length of Pall Mall to the Palace before turning back to meet their friends.

In just a few moments, Gideon reached them and moved to intercept their path. The dismay on their faces when they perceived him struck him as comical.

"Good afternoon, my lord," he said, making a sweeping bow to Lord Charters, "and to you, Sir Francis. What good fortune to encounter you like this." He was tempted to add that they did not look quite as happy to see him, but restrained himself. In his limited experience, few spies had a sense of humour.

Sir Francis's eyes flew wildly about as if he feared to find King's Messengers lurking all around him. Lord Charters stepped close to Gideon, and whispered harshly, "What can you mean by this? Have we not made it perfectly clear that we have no wish to talk to you?" He reached for his sword, but discovered he had not worn it, no doubt because today was Sunday.

"Perfectly clear," Gideon replied easily, "but I could not leave town without bidding you both goodbye. And there is one piece of business that we have not finished."

Now, Lord Charters, too, tossed glances over his shoulder at the gentlemen passing them in the street. "Not here, you fool! You must be aware, we're just steps from the Palace!"

Gideon was gratified to see how nervous he was making them. He had waylaid them in a busy place, so that no one passing could fail to notice them. "Ah, yes, how foolish of me. Then, perhaps you would like to take our conversation to a less public spot?"

"Not now!" Lord Charters hissed. When two passing gentlemen glanced up in surprise, he moderated his voice. "You shall have to make an appointment with my secretary." He tried to brush past Gideon and Sir Francis followed.

"I'm afraid that just won't do. But never mind, I shall accompany you to your destination."

Emitting an angry growl, Lord Charters abruptly halted. Having to stop suddenly to avoid running into his friend, Sir Francis cursed under his breath. After exchanging a desperate glance, they turned to keep Gideon from walking up Bury Street to the Greyhound, where their friends would see him.

"We will give you five minutes, but not a second more." With a jerk of his head, Lord Charters signalled for Gideon to follow. He turned into King Street and crossed to enter the old paved alley.

It was a long passageway, narrower even than most alleys, a perfect place for Gideon to try out his plan. As soon as Lord Charters judged that he had led them far enough to be safe from passing eyes, he rounded angrily. "What is so important as to risk all our lives? Do you not realize how serious the situation is now?"

His manner unconcerned, Gideon reached into his pocket for the snuffbox. He held it out where both men could see it, before saying, "I should not worry, if I were you. No one here has ever seen me. If you will act as if I am an acquaintance up from the country, no one is likely to take any interest.

"May I offer you a pinch?" he asked, as if his intention were to give their meeting an innocent appearance. Before opening the lid of the box, he searched their faces for a reaction.

Lord Charters glanced at the box and waved it impatiently away. The image caught Sir Francis's eye, but after taking a second glance at the lady's pose, he merely leered. He waited for Gideon to open the lid before helping himself to a pinch of tobacco, then placed it on his sleeve, sniffed it, and sneezed.

Lord Charters glared at his friend with disgust. "You are wasting our time," he said to Gideon. "Your minutes are nearly up. What was so important that you had to force this conversation on us?"

Satisfied that his question had been answered, Gideon said, "I wished you to know that I shall be returning to the Continent. If you have any message for his Majesty, I shall be happy to deliver it."

Lord Charters gaped. "That is all? For that, you waylaid us in front of the Palace? If I had my sword, I swear, I would happily run you through!"

"No, of course, it is not all. I hoped you had reconsidered my request, or at least had thought of someone who might be willing to act for his Majesty in place of your murdered friend. But, since it appears you have not, I shall take my leave. I warn you, however, that his Majesty, though very generous to those who are loyal, is not quick to forgive those who are too cowardly to serve him." Gideon delivered this condemnation with as much scorn as the Pretender's gentlemen would have used in the circumstances.

Lord Charters was so irate that he took a threatening step forward before remembering that he was not wearing his sword. Sir Francis uttered a credible imitation of the growl his friend had earlier voiced.

"Gentlemen, your servant." With a sneering bow, Gideon turned his back on Lord Wragby's friends to head into Pall Mall. He would have preferred to avoid it, but now that his question had been answered, he had no desire to be spotted with men the government would already suspect of being Jacobites.

Now, he did pull his hat lower on his brow and raise the collar of his cloak. It was still chilly enough in March that no one should find it odd if he felt the cold. He stepped out into Pall Mall and followed it to Cockspur Street, keeping his gaze on the ground and walking at an unhurried pace, until Charing Cross was behind him and he could breathe more easily.

Tomorrow, when he saw Hester, he would have some useful bits of information to share. And judging by her summons, it seemed that she would, too.

✿

The next day, Hester could arrange to be away for only a brief period. A few warm kisses were all they allowed themselves before, sitting comfortably against the head of the bed to exchange their news.

Hester went first, telling St. Mars about Lord William's murder and wondering aloud if the message he had intended to deliver to Lord Cowper was about the treasonous activities of either Sir Francis or Lord Charters. "If whatever he had to divulge was so important to the realm, then it must have been about the Pretender or one of his agents, surely. Doesn't this mean that Lord Wragby's friends should be the object of our attention?"

St. Mar was frowning. "I am not so sure. Last night, I showed them the snuffbox I told you about, and neither exhibited the slightest reaction. I thought it possible that it had belonged to Lord Wragby, if not to one of his friends, but that is clearly not the case. I still believe it belonged to the murderer, though."

"So you retrieved it! How?"

St. Mars told her about his negotiation with Jonathan Wild. Hester listened in rapt admiration, thinking to herself that there was nothing he could not do.

"What a despicable specimen he is!" St. Mars finished. "When I see that our authorities allow him to use his criminal enterprise as our system of justice, I'm appalled by the corruption in England."

Hester sympathized, but did not wish to be distracted. "What makes you certain that this snuffbox is a clue? And may I see it? Do you have it with you?"

St. Mars surprised her by laughing. Freeing his arm from behind her, he reached into his vest pocket and extracted a jewelled box.

The first thing that struck Hester was the opulence of the piece, the glitter of its brilliants and the colourful enamel. The next was the pose of the woman on the lid.

Hester recoiled slightly and raised her eyebrows. "Oh, my! Is this what gentlemen put on their snuffboxes?"

"No, my dear." St. Mars put on a pedantic tone. "Very few gentlemen can afford a snuffbox like this. The diamonds alone cost a pretty penny, and the enamel work is of the finest quality. And we haven't even taken into account the gold."

She reproved him with a look, but felt dimples forming in her cheeks. "My dearest lord, you know perfectly well what I meant, and I was not referring to the object's cost."

St. Mars chuckled. "Yes, I know. But the fact that the box is so expensive is relevant. I've asked myself which of our suspects could afford an expensive toy like this. But I wished to show it to you, to see if you recognize the lady."

Hester studied the woman's face. "No, I cannot say that I number her among my friends."

He laughed again. "*Touché.* I deserved that for teasing you. Of course, I did not expect her to be a bosom friend of yours, but if she is the murderer's mistress, I thought you might have seen her—riding with a gentleman in the park or at the opera."

Aware that their time together would be short, Hester stopped playing. She gave the picture another look before ruefully shaking her head. "No, I'm afraid not. But what does make you so sure that the snuffbox is a clue to our mystery?"

"I could be wrong, but I cannot help believing that it is. The two things were so odd that the explanation would almost have to be some violent event. And now, I've discovered that the timing was right. Both the snuffbox and the boy were found just after Lord Wragby's murder. It would be a strange coincidence, indeed, if two calamitous incidents, each involving a very wealthy person, occurred in the same vicinity on the same night . . . especially two that required keeping a secret at great expense."

Hester was doing her best to follow, and almost had, but something he had said still confused her. "You said, 'two' things. I remember the ad for the snuffbox that was never answered, but what was the second thing?"

He looked at her in surprise. "The boy!"

"My dearest love, of what boy are you speaking? I have never heard you mention a boy."

He rolled his eyes, but his impatience was not with her. He explained that he had rehearsed so many conversations with her in his head that he did not always know which ones had taken place and which he had just imagined. He went on to tell her about a young black boy Tom and Katy had found down by the Thames just a few days after Lord Wragby's murder.

"Since then, we have been expecting to see an advertisement asking for his return, but just like the snuffbox, no one has claimed him."

St. Mars told Hester, they had guessed that the boy must have witnessed something that had shocked him into silence. They both knew how fashionable it was to have a black page, and how improbable it was that the boy had come from anywhere other than an aristocrat's household. "And what could make anyone abandon such an expensive acquisition as that?" He shook his head. "No, I am convinced that both the child and the snuffbox belonged to the murderer. I even wonder if he did not pose for the artist with the killer's mistress."

By the time St. Mars had finished explaining, Hester had begun to agree. "If the child was the murderer's page, then he should have seen the snuffbox."

St. Mars gave a grimace. "Yes, but the boy is refusing to speak. Tom says he has heard him talking to the horses when he thinks no one is listening, but he will not utter a word to us, even to Katy. I doubt we could get him to name his master. He is too afraid."

"Poor child!"

"It is possible, of course, that he belonged to Lord Wragby. Did you ever see a boy like that in his service?"

Hester tried to remember, but she was forced to shake her head. "Of course, he might have employed a page we never saw, but why would anyone have such a servant and not make use of him? Lord Wragby enjoyed parading his retinue, so I think I would have seen his page, if he had one."

"What about Lord William or Sir Horatio?"

Unable to answer, she shook her head. "Either could have had one, but I am in no position to say. I usually saw them in Lord Ireton's company when they would not have brought their servants with them. And I have seen them so infrequently that I cannot know. There were so many pages in attendance at Hampton Court on Coronation Day that one could have been attached to either man, and I would not have known."

Then, recalling another instance, she said, "I do recall that Lord Ireton had a young page in his train when I saw him in St. Paul's."

After a moment's thought, St. Mars turned to her with a question in his eyes—a question she could read. The same notion had flittered through her head the moment the words had left her mouth.

"No." She firmly shook her head, unwilling to accept the idea. "That would be inconceivable."

St. Mars understood—even agreed—but still he frowned. "Are you certain? Should we not at least consider the possibility?"

Hester kept shaking her head. "That idea is so contrary to a divine universe that I do not see the point." Distressed by the very thought of their new suspicion, she clasped his hand. "We should focus on what we know to be reasonable."

"Very well." St. Mars seemed willing to turn from this new direction to his thoughts. "I suppose what I shall have to do first is find a way to show the snuffbox to Sir Horatio. If it was his, or even Lord William's, he should react violently."

"I wish there were some way that I could do it. I hate to think of you approaching anyone with such good connections to the authorities."

St. Mars teased her. "You could always take up snuff."

She smiled. "Yes, but I would raise more than a few eyebrows if I pretended to own that snuffbox."

"True. You might even be arrested. On second thought, I advise you not to do it."

"You are too kind, my lord."

"Not at all. I live only to serve you."

It was said in jest, but Hester heard a deeper sincerity in his words. Her thoughts turned wistful. "I do not suppose that you have found a clergyman to marry us?"

Instantly, his manner changed from teasing to rueful. "No, my love, but I will find a way, I promise." Then, as if a solution had popped into his brain, a smile spread across his face. "No sooner said than done! I do not know when it will take place, but I have thought of something that may work. I shall set it in motion today on my way home."

Hester was buoyed by the cheer in his voice. She knew he had not given up on their marriage, but she did not wish to be married by a fraud. No matter how much she and St. Mars both wished to be wed, he had found no one else to officiate.

"What are you going to do?" she asked.

"As soon as possible, I shall question Lord Wragby's valet, but first I shall find a means of showing the snuffbox to Sir Horatio."

She tapped him playfully on the shoulder. "You know very well what I was asking about, and it was not about our suspects."

"Ah . . . but you must allow me to surprise you. For a marriage to be happy, there should always be a few surprises."

"If that is so, then you must never complain when I come home from the shops with new clothes and trifles."

"Egad! The woman is dangerously clever! Come here, closer, and let's make better use of our time."

On his way back to Lambeth, Gideon altered his usual route to stop by the Fleet Prison to speak to the clerk of the Fleet Chapel. A few coins lighter, but elated at having a plan, he continued on his way until he reached his house across the Thames.

As he walked, he gave thought as to how to approach Sir Horatio. The best way to strike up a conversation would be to meet him in his usual coffee-house. The problem with that, of course, was that, in a coffee-house patronized by Whigs, which it was certain to be, Gideon might run into not only his cousin but also members of the government who would be happy to see him hanged.

Of all the pleasures London had to offer, the one Gideon missed the most was the daily visit to a coffee-house. The coffee-house was where an Englishman sat down with other men, usually of similar tastes or politics, and read the newssheets while sipping his morning beverage. The rules of each house were much the same. In the confines of the establishment, all men were equal. As long as they paid their penny at the bar, they could take any seat and speak to anyone. No one had to cede his chair to a man of higher standing.

It was a pleasure Gideon had taken for granted until it had suddenly been denied. Drinking coffee alone simply did not provide the same satisfaction. He would never have set foot in a Whig establishment while his father was alive, and now the fear of being recognized would remove any hope of pleasure, but unless he could think of a better place to meet Sir Horatio, he would need to brave his coffee-house.

It would make sense to send Tom to watch Sir Horatio to see which of his habits Gideon could exploit. Having decided to do this before reaching home, Gideon then turned his mind to Lord Wragby's valet.

That morning, before Gideon had gone to meet Hester, Tom had given him an account of the valet's movements over the previous day, as well as other useful information he had managed to ferret out. The valet's new master, Sir Roger, was a man who had made his fortune in the City. He was a successful draper who had won the custom of the aristocracy because of the elegant materials he was able to import. His success had allowed him to become an alderman and a knight, to purchase a house in King Square—a desirable location for anyone who made a living selling silks and satins—and to employ the services of a valet. It made sense that a man who made his living from the clothing trade would choose to have a valet to impress his neighbours, but in order to maintain the success of his business, Sir Roger still had to work in his shop. His best customers insisted upon his personal service, when patrons of an inferior shop might be fobbed off with the attentions of a clerk.

The result was that Sir Roger's valet, a young man named Rawson, found himself unsupervised for a good portion of the day. Having waited upon an aristocrat of Lord Wragby's status and spendthrift habits, Rawson had managed a much greater wardrobe than his new employer required. Now he was able to finish his work in less time, leaving him with idle hours to fill. Tom had discovered that he frequented the White Horse Tavern, not far from the square where he lived and worked, and it was there that Gideon directed his steps the next day.

With Katy's help, he had taken great care in dressing, making sure that his coat fit his shoulders to an inch, his silk hose was sparkling clean, the lace at his cuffs flowed over his wrists like water, and the paint on his face was thick enough to proclaim him a fop.

He and Tom arrived outside the White Horse shortly after three o'clock, about the hour when Tom had followed Rawson to the tavern. Gideon sent Tom in to see if the valet had arrived. He emerged less than a minute later and crossed the street to where Gideon waited.

"He's in there, my lord, sitting by hisself at a table in a corner by the fire. You'll know 'im as soon as you see 'im. He's the only one in the whole place dressed fancy like a valet."

"Good. I'll meet you back at the house." With a nod, Gideon sent Tom on his next task. He would perform the same kind of reconnoitre outside Sir Horatio's lodgings until he learned something of that gentleman's habits.

Gideon strolled across the street and into the tavern, where he paused to raise a handkerchief to his nose. He surveyed the room with distaste, until his gaze lit upon a man he took to be Rawson. With every eye in the tavern following him, he called in a nasal voice to the man behind the bar and ordered two pints of "his best" to be delivered to the table in the corner, which he indicated with a flick of his lace. Then he sauntered across the room, taking elaborate care not to let the skirt of his coat brush against any of the patrons. Arrived at Rawson's table, he seated himself across from the valet, who stared at him in astonishment.

"You are Rawson, I presume." Gideon did not wait for the man's acknowledgement before proceeding. "I was advised that I might discover you here."

Before Rawson could ask whom he had the honour to address, the tavern-keeper arrived with their beer. Gideon used the interruption to avoid answering any questions, and continued, "I always admired the way Lord Wragby was turned out, don't y'know, so I made inquiries to discover where you had found new employment. I would have tried to engage you sooner, but when Lord Wragby died, I was away in the country, and I only recently learned of the tragedy, don't y'know.

"A shame, of course!" he said, cutting Rawson off. The valet's mouth was still hanging open, but when it seemed he might speak, Gideon said, "Well, drink up, man! Mustn't let the bubbles go flat."

As if noticing the mug in front of him for the first time, Rawson sat up with a jerk and did as he was told, taking half the mug at a gulp. He had the air of a man who had already consumed a number of drinks, making Gideon wonder how long he would manage to hold onto the position Sir Roger had given him.

"They say your master was murdered somewhere near Spring Garden. Is that right?"

"Yes, that is where he was found."

Shaking his head over the loss, Gideon displayed what he hoped would be taken for a natural curiosity. "How did he come to be alone there at such an hour?"

"I do not know . . . forgive me, but were you acquainted with my former master?"

"Well, naturally! But, then, everyone knew Lord Wragby, did they not? I could not claim to be a close friend, but we did frequent the same coffee-house. So you have no idea why he would be out by himself without any servants to guard him?"

"No. Occasionally, he would go out without an escort. Usually not at night, but sometimes during the day."

"Want another?" Gideon pointed to Rawson's mug, which he had emptied.

The valet's eyes opened wide with pleasure. He had to be thinking that the gentleman across from him, whoever he was, would make a very liberal employer.

He nodded, and Gideon called to their host to bring another beer. He waved off a second for himself, having barely touched the first, but he downed a few sips.

After daintily wiping his lips with his handkerchief, he said, "Well, I never go abroad at night without at least one companion. There is greater safety in numbers, don't y'know. But, perhaps someone asked Lord Wragby to meet him?"

Rawson's tongue had been amply loosened by drink, and having no obligation to his former master now, he seemed willing to discuss Lord Wragby's habits.

"Someone may have, I don't know. He did receive a message earlier that day. It was waiting for him when he came home to change for the theatre that evening."

"Did you see it?"

"No, not after it was opened, but I did spy it earlier when it was lying on the salver."

"So you do not know who wrote it? You did not recognize the hand?"

Fortunately, by now Rawson had drunk too much to notice how pointed Gideon's questions had become. "No, but he often received letters that he would burn. That's probably what he did with that one."

"Hmm. Curious! What an extraordinary thing to do with one's mail!"

"Oh, not the letters that came in the post. These were things that messengers would bring."

"Ahh . . . that explains it. A *billet doux!* He wished to protect the lady's reputation."

Rawson frowned. He wavered on his bench. "No, though I did not recognize the hand, it was clearly not a lady's."

This was plainly all Gideon could expect to get out of Lord Wragby's former valet. He had hoped to learn the identity of the person who had lured Lord Wragby to his death, but it was reasonable to assume that a magistrate would already have asked that question.

Before leaving, he reached into his pocket and brought out the snuffbox. Holding it so Rawson could see it, he waited until the man's eyes focused before opening it and taking a pinch of snuff.

As if in answer to a command, the church bells rang the half-hour. "Oh, dear me!" Gideon gave an artful start. "Can that be the time? I must hasten away." Taking his purse out of his pocket to leave money for the beer, he got hastily to his feet. Then, forestalling any question Rawson could formulate in his bemused state, he said, "Well, that must be all for now. I shall see what can be done to free you from Sir Roger, though it shall have to wait till the next time I am up in London."

With a wave, he hurried out of the tavern. Then, in his normal rapid stride, he covered the street to the next corner and turned in case Rawson got it in his mind to follow.

Though satisfied that he had not given Rawson cause for suspicion, Gideon was much less satisfied with the outcome of their conversation. He had not managed to learn the name of the person who had lured Lord Wragby to Spring Garden, or truly even if such a person existed.

He had discovered, however, that the snuffbox had not belonged to Lord Wragby, for once his fuzzy eyesight had cleared, Rawson, though amused by the image on the box, had not revealed the slightest flicker of recognition. As Lord Wragby's valet, he would have seen every one of his possessions. No, if the snuffbox had belonged to anyone connected with the murder, it would have to have been the murderer himself.

And round the orb in lasting notes be read,
"Statesman, yet friend to Truth! of soul sincere,
In action faithful, and in honour clear;
Who broke no promise, served no private end,
Who gained no title, and who lost no friend;
Ennobled by himself, by all approved,
And praised, unenvied, by the Muse he loved."

CHAPTER XIX

It took Tom a few days to discover which coffee-house Sir Horatio Allenby frequented and the hour he was most likely to visit it. When Gideon heard Penny's whinny, announcing Tom's return, he went down to the stable and lounged atop a wooden box to listen to Tom's news.

His announcement that Sir Horatio frequented the St. James's Coffee-House came as no surprise, but it did raise Gideon's pulse. Of the coffee-houses known to be frequented by Whigs, the St. James's was the most dangerous place for Gideon to be seen. His cousin Harrowby went there every morning, as did most of the powerful Whig politicians. So regular were the customers of a coffee-house that a newcomer would always be remarked. Footpads and highwaymen had been known to visit these establishments to pick out likely victims, so strangers were scrutinized. Even with his wig and thick paint, Gideon would run the risk that a fixed stare would expose his features to someone who could recognize the outlaw Viscount St. Mars.

He was girding himself to brave the Whig coffee-house when Tom's next words offered an alternative.

"There's another place he goes, my lord. Just about every night, he goes to White's Chocolate House."

Gideon sat up abruptly. "To White's? Now, there is something in-teresting."

"Is it, my lord?"

"Yes, it means that Sir Horatio is a serious gambler. Of all the gam-bling establishments in London or Westminster, the stakes at White's are the highest."

"At a chocolate house, my lord?"

Gideon laughed at his servant's doubt. "Chocolate may still be served at White's, but other beverages are, too. It may have started out as a place to buy a morning chocolate, but over the past several years it has changed into something less innocent. Many a great fortune has been lost over a hand at White's."

"Then Sir Horatio must either have a lot of money to lose or good luck at cards." As he talked, Tom had unsaddled Beau and now was combing him down.

"Or, there is a third possibility."

"Indeed, my lord? And what would that be?"

"He could be a card-sharp, a cheater. And if he is, he could have had a different motive for killing Lord Wragby." Gideon stood and brushed the straw off his breeches. "There's only one way to find out. Tonight, I shall have to pay a visit to White's, myself."

∅

While Hester waited to hear what St. Mars's investigations would uncover, every prediction he had made about the risk of escaping to France was confirmed. The King commanded all officers in the army to report to their posts. The Admiralty called on all ships' officers to return to their ships. A general embargo against Sweden was imposed. Even if Hester and St. Mars managed to free James Henry from sus-picion, they could not leave the shores of England until the current crisis was resolved.

There was nothing Hester could do but try to distract Mary from her misery. Exposure to other gentlemen at their social engagements had done nothing to weaken her attraction to James Henry. If any-thing, the men she encountered only served to magnify his good qualities. Hester could not blame the girl when she thought of the men Mrs. Mayfield had paraded before her daughter—or rather, forced Mary to parade for.

Marriage for its own sake had not been the fashion for many years. No matter how pretty and lively a girl was, unless her suitor had immediate need for a fortune, which only she could supply, she would have no serious suitors at all. With few exceptions, the gentlemen Mrs. Mayfield pursued considered marriage no less a punishment than leg shackles in Newgate. A wife might deprive a fellow of his "gentlemanly" pursuits: drinking, gambling and whoring. Even if a gentleman needed an heir, he would still hold out for the highest bidder for the position of brood mare.

If he wanted a companion for tenderer moments, he could easily set up a mistress, the advantage being the ease of disposal when her attractions ceased to please.

This attitude was so prevalent as to promote a repugnant arrogance in the comportment of young aristocratic men, which a girl with spirit and intelligence like Mary could only find insufferable. She was observant enough to detect their sneers, which her mother chose to ignore. Mrs. Mayfield had tricked one aristocrat into marrying one of her daughters, but she would never succeed in that mission again.

To a girl in love, James Henry's absence of several weeks seemed like eternity. It had not helped that he had not written. Hester tried to convince her cousin that it would be improper for him to do so without her mother's permission, but after weeks of his neglect and her subjugation to poor examples of manhood, Mary had started to doubt if his affection for her was real.

The situation changed very suddenly.

Hester had just returned from running an errand for Isabella when Will, the footman, greeted her with the news that during her absence James Henry had arrived at Hawkhurst House and had asked for a private meeting with his lord.

In a near-whisper, he added, "Lord Hawkhurst was not happy to hear that Mr. Henry had returned without his leave, but he did agree to see him."

Hester's immediate thought was that James Henry must have

grown impatient with the injunction to stay away, and that rather than wait to be sent for or apply for permission to resume his duties, he had decided to plead with his master instead. As she sat down in the hall to take the pattens off her shoes, she asked quietly, "Does my aunt know that Mr. Henry is in the house?"

Will grinned. "I doubt she knows, mistress, or the place wouldn't be so quiet."

Tempted as she was to smile in agreement, Hester said, instead, "And my cousin Mary? Has she been informed?"

With a shake of his head and the suggestion of a wink, Will said, "I thought maybe you would be the best one to tell her, Mrs. Kean."

Hester thanked him and, after removing her cloak, went upstairs to prepare herself for the fireworks that were sure to erupt if both Mary and her mother heard of James Henry's arrival. She knew that Mary would never forgive her for keeping his presence a secret. At the same time, she thought she should discover the purpose of his visit before making the girl aware. It was possible that James Henry did not wish to see her, in which case the news that he was here would only cause Mary pain. And, if he left as quietly as he had come, it was possible that Mrs. Mayfield would never be informed of his visit.

Hoping to preserve the peace, Hester had not allowed for the gossip that floated upstairs on the lips of the maids. Within a very short time of her return, first Mary, then her mother came rushing out of their respective bedchambers. Mary's face was all aglow with eagerness, while Mrs. Mayfield's was as dark as a winter storm.

Encountering Hester between her chamber and the door to Harrowby's dressing room, where she was waiting in the hope Pierre would emerge, Mary hurried to her. "Is it true, Hester? Has James Henry come? Why did you not fetch me instantly?"

"I just learned it myself a few moments ago," Hester hedged, "and decided I had better confirm it before raising your hopes."

"So, it is true? He is closeted with Harrowby?" Mary's face fell. "I wonder why he did not come to speak to me first."

"Mary, you know how grave an error it would be for Mr. Henry to offend his lord. If he is going to keep Harrowby's support, he must behave properly in every respect." Hester continued, "I doubt he had

Harrowby's permission to come to town, and I hate to think how angry Harrowby would be if he discovered that his servant had disobeyed his commands and then not come immediately to justify himself."

Hester had barely finished speaking when Mrs. Mayfield found them. The sight of them, lurking together outside Harrowby's rooms, made her cheeks grow so red as to look in danger of exploding.

"There you are! I might have known! Planning and plotting to go around me to throw yourself at that man!" Though her initial words had been directed at them both, the final ones were definitely meant for Mary. "My mind has not changed. I still refuse to allow you to see him. And I shall tell my lord just what I think about allowing that murderer into this house."

"Careful, Aunt," Hester said, through tightened lips. "Are you certain that would be wise?"

"When it comes to being wise, Miss Prim, who thinks so much of herself, then we shall just have to see. But I know who's to blame for Mary's failure to get a good husband. It's you and Mr. Henry who have put common ideas into her head. I would have found her a great husband long before now, if not for you two."

"Like Sir Edward Moss, who intimated that he would be happy to set me up as his mistress, if I was so inclined, or Lord Elston, who has to have his meat minced for him since he's lost nearly all of his teeth? No, thank you, Mama. I am not interested."

Mrs. Mayfield gave a huff. "Why, I am sure that is nothing but a pack of lies! As if Sir Edward would ever behave so rudely to a sister of the Countess of Hawkhurst! And so what if Lord Elston has lost a few teeth? He still has most of his sense, and I hear his estate earns a good four thousand per year."

Their voices had steadily risen until this last assertion came out as a screech. Hester tried to hush Mary before she matched her mother's loudness.

The door to Harrowby's dressing room opened, and Pierre emerged with a look of severe disapproval. *"Madame! Mesdesmoiselles!* If you please! My master refuses to be disturbed by this bickering. 'E 'as given Pierre 'is command that you are all to return to your bedchambers until 'e summons you into 'is presence. And 'e does not wish to 'ear one word from any of you until that moment. You 'ave understood, *oui?*"

Mrs. Mayfield was outraged to be dismissed at the hands of a servant, but she did not dare disobey Harrowby's orders. With a glower at Mary and Hester, she turned on her heel and stormed off.

Mary heaved an unhappy sigh. Her hope of seeing James Henry after so long a wait had been thwarted. She did not know whether Harrowby would give his permission for them to see each other.

Hester had sent her aunt away with a look that must have expressed at least some of her disgust. She knew that she would be made to pay for it later; but her chief concern was for Mary, on whose lips she could see protests forming. She took Mary's arm and said, "Come, Cousin. We shall have to do as we are bid. We live here on Harrowby's sufferance, you know, and we mustn't be foolish."

The summons came scarcely an hour later, when a footman knocked on Hester's door to tell her that his lord wished to see her and Mrs. Mary in the withdrawing room. They went down feeling a mixture of trepidation and discouragement, but ready to hear whatever Harrowby had to say, and determined not to let Mrs. Mayfield undermine his trust in James Henry.

They were both surprised to find James Henry standing just inside the door with a look of eager anticipation. His gaze immediately fixed on Mary, as if to drink in every feature of her face. The happiness that lit her eyes on seeing him was reflected in his. He hastily stepped forward to take her hand.

Hester, who had been ignored, but did not mind in the least, looked to Harrowby for an explanation. He was holding a glass of wine and beaming as if he had just heard the most entertaining joke.

"Come in, come in, Mrs. Kean! Do not fear that I shall bite. I have just been chatting with Mr. Henry here and it seems we have occasion to celebrate."

"Indeed, my lord? What occasion?"

"Now, now . . ." He coyly shook his head. "You mustn't be impatient. We must wait for one other person to join us before we raise our glasses. It is really too bad that Isabella is not here to celebrate with us, but she went to the Palace, and I find I cannot wait any longer to tell the rest of you the good news."

He reached to a tray that had been placed on the table beside him, and handed Hester a glass. "Mary," he called to his sister-in-law, "come take a glass of wine. We must be ready, you know, when the time comes for toasts."

Mary stepped over to retrieve the glass he held out for her, confusion written on her face. She and James Henry had exchanged a few whispers, but it seemed he had not enlightened her as to the thing they were to celebrate. His smile suggested it was something that had made him very happy, but he had to let his lord have the pleasure of imparting it to everyone else. Mary looked as if a butterfly were trapped inside her chest, but as she could not imagine receiving what she wanted, she could not allow it to take flight.

In the next moment, Mrs. Mayfield appeared, her cheeks flushed with indignation. She took one look at James Henry and drew herself up, "What is the meaning of this, my lord?" she asked Harrowby. "What is this person doing here? I thought you had banished him from your presence, and I certainly do not wish to have my daughter exposed to a criminal!"

This speech, intended to remind Harrowby of the danger of giving his protection to James Henry, had the opposite effect of increasing his delight. With undisguised glee, he said, "Then that is very unfortunate, madam, for your daughter is to be married to him!"

A gasp of joy escaped Mary's lips. She instantly shifted her gaze to James Henry, who with glistening eyes smiled down at her and said, "That is, if you will have me for your husband."

"Yes—" Mary stepped towards him, but her mother interrupted.

"You cannot do this, my lord! You have no right!"

"No, I do not," Harrowby said, with a giggle, "but someone else does. Tell her what you told me, Mr. Henry."

By now, Mary had reached James Henry's side and taken hold of his arm to gaze up at him in wonder. He returned her loving gaze before, ever polite, he respectfully addressed her mother.

"It occurred to me that with Mr. Mayfield's decease, the legal guardianship of his children would most likely reside with his eldest son, Mr. Dudley Mayfield. So, I called upon your son and presented

him with my suit to marry your daughter, Mrs. Mary. He was naturally surprised by my request, but since we had met last year, he gra-
ciously received me, and over the course of a few meetings, he granted
me permission to pay my addresses to his sister."

With his hand covering hers, he looked down at Mary. "And if you
have no objections, he and I have arrived at an agreement. Everything
is settled between us. You have only to say if you would prefer to be
married from here by special license or from your brother Dudley's
house."

The look on Mrs. Mayfield's face was one Hester would never forget. Her aunt had hoped to benefit from binding Mary to a wealthy
gentleman with a title. Instead, she had been outsmarted and outma-
noeuvred by a man she despised. Her comeuppance could not have
been more greatly deserved, and Hester could not deny herself a moment of satisfaction.

But her deepest feeling was of happiness for the joy of two of the
people dearest to her. James Henry was a good man, who deserved to
be rewarded, and Mary, who already had the gifts of intelligence and
wit, would only improve in temperament through love and admiration for him.

"Shall we toast to the happy couple?" With another giggle, Harrowby raised his glass.

Hester had no doubt that his merriment arose entirely from the
unexpected pleasure of dealing his mother-in-law a blow. He had been
made to suffer as a result of her unrealistic ambitions for Mary. If not
for Mrs. Mayfield's attempt to foist her daughter onto Lord Wragby,
none of his fear of Lord Ireton would ever have come about. It was
certain to return, but for the moment he could revel in Mrs. Mayfield's
discomfiture.

She was struggling to recover her composure. The wind had been
knocked out of her sails, and no whiff of deliverance had arrived. She
could not question Dudley's right to decide the fate of his sisters and
brothers. His apathy towards his siblings had allowed her to do with
them as she liked, but once reminded of his duty, he must have taken
great satisfaction in asserting his authority. Hester recalled that Dudley had always dismissed his mother's goals for Mary as too ambitious

and destined to fail. No doubt, he had rejoiced in the opportunity to prove himself right. And, Hester supposed, James Henry had been as persuasive and as firm as a suitor could be.

While Harrowby made a toast to the engagement, Mrs. Mayfield stood in stony silence, the only clue to her feelings a pair of widened nostrils. When the toast was concluded, however, she refused to raise her glass, and said, instead, in a tone of wounded dignity, "If you will excuse me, my lord, I should like to retire to my bedchamber."

"By all means, madam! Feel free to remain there as long as you like!" Harrowby lifted his glass in her direction before tossing its contents down his throat.

With no evidence of sharing his triumph, Mary watched her mother depart from the room, but aside from a suspicious dampness in her eyes, she did not allow her mother's churlishness to spoil her own happiness. She smiled up at James Henry, who clasped her hand as if he would never let it go.

Hester hastened to give them both congratulations and kissed each on the cheek. Neither could doubt the sincerity of her wishes.

After drinking a few more toasts, Harrowby did recall the unresolved issue of Lord Wragby's murder. He advised the couple strongly to be married from Dudley Mayfield's house and to be quick about it. "I cannot have you staying here for long," he warned.

"We shall do whatever pleases my lord," James Henry said, "but with your permission, I should like to stop in town for just a few days to attend to some of your lordship's business that should not wait. I promise that no one of any consequence will learn of my presence."

"If the business is that important, then very well. But I will expect to see you gone in no more than a few days. Mary, you are not obliged to leave now—the roads are still too rough—but no doubt you will wish to return to Yorkshire as soon as the weather improves."

Mary agreed. She looked as if she would have been happy to ride north with James Henry immediately, but she was not so foolish as to consider that an option.

Harrowby took himself off to his coffee-house a short time later, leaving Hester alone with the couple. She would have left them alone, but James Henry, sobering, asked her to stay a few minutes with Mary while he explained the arrangements he had made on her behalf.

"If your mother were inclined to hear me," he said to Mary, "I would have gone over them with her, but since she is not, I will feel easier if another family member who has your best interests at heart is here to approve."

Mary would have waved off any need to explain, but James Henry insisted. So, after he stoked the fire in the withdrawing room, they drew their chairs near it and sat down.

"First, I must apologize for not coming to you immediately on my arrival, but I knew my lord would look more favourably on my request if I went directly to him. Besides, I had to know if my employment was still secure before asking you to be my wife.

"You will be pleased, I hope, to learn that he has no plan to dismiss me. I shall keep my post as his receiver-general, so my income, which is very generous, will continue as it has been." His face clouded momentarily. "Of course, until this wretched business of Lord Wragby's murder is solved, I shall not be able to carry out my duties in the way I have. I shall have to be circumspect in my trips to London, but I see no danger in our living at my house in Kent. You do understand that I must travel every few months to collect my lord's rents, do you not?"

Mary laughed at his worried look. "Yes, my love, I do, and I shall be riding with you as often as you allow."

He did not have to say how much this response pleased him. The glow in his eyes said it all. Hester knew how lonely James Henry had been. Now he would have a companion on his travels, one moreover who would enjoy every mile they rode together.

He went on to tell her how much he had settled on her in the marriage contract Dudley's lawyers had drawn up. Mary protested that since she had no dowry, there was no need on his part to make her a settlement. But Hester joined James Henry in affirming that a settlement should be made in the event James Henry's death left her with children to raise and her own widowhood to support.

"It is not much, I assure you, but at least in that instance you would not starve. And, though I asked him for nothing save the assurance of employment, my lord has promised to make you a gift of a thousand pounds. I know you will add your thanks to mine for his generosity."

Surprisingly touched by Harrowby's gesture, Mary assured him that she would express her gratitude at the first opportunity.

Knowing Harrowby better than Mary did, Hester could easily imagine how his conversation with James Henry had gone. Still fearing Lord Ireton's wrath, he would not have been happy to see his servant; but as soon as James Henry explained his errand, making it clear that he had approached Dudley because Mrs. Mayfield would never have given her permission to the match, Harrowby had seen a way to do her an evil turn. Mrs. Mayfield had always expected that he would provide her daughter with a dowry, and in hoping to catch a titled husband for Mary, she would have cajoled and wheedled him for a much larger sum. With James Henry as her suitor, Harrowby must have figured that in disappointing his mother-in-law, he could afford to make Mary a modest gift. No wonder he had giggled throughout his toasts.

But the important thing was that Mary and James Henry were to be wed, and they were certain to be happy.

Now, all she and St. Mars had to do was prove James Henry's innocence, and they would be safe, as well.

※

That night at ten o'clock, as Gideon arrived outside White's Chocolate House on St. James's Street, he was grateful for the clouds that obscured any view of his features from the gentlemen on the street. Once he was inside the club, he hoped that the shadows cast by candlelight would also help to shield his face from penetrating stares.

Gideon had never been inside White's, though it was located near Hawkhurst House at the Piccadilly end of St. James's. His father's friend, Robert Harley, Earl of Oxford, had condemned the place as the bane of the English nobility, for the number of fortunes that had been squandered within its walls. In spite of the strictures issued by many prudent and prominent voices, White's had flourished. The late Queen Anne had promulgated various acts to try to rid her kingdom of vices, including gambling, but the task had proved impossible. No one who engaged in vice was willing to report on the businesses that made their living preying on the weak. Now, gambling was not only tolerated, but encouraged, at the Court of King George, where the Hanoverians indulged a passion for cards. Gideon had never been bitten by the urge to wager his all on the deal of a hand, but a knowledge of card games had been an essential part of his education as an aristocrat.

The house he now approached was meaner than others on the street. Cheaply built, it had not been made to accommodate the number that crossed its threshold. The front porch sagged, and, beneath the flaking paint, Gideon suspected there was rot. The whole area between here and the City of London was full of faro-houses—Greek shops—and other gaming-houses, with a cluster round Covent Garden. Perhaps, they looked even meaner than White's, whose patrons were limited to the high and mighty, but in the end, as the poet John Gay had said, it was just another den of thieves.

Several chairmen blocked the entrance, leaning against the house to sleep until their masters were ready to go home. Gideon picked his way through them and pulled on the bell.

The door was opened, releasing a powerful odour of perfume. The servant who had opened it, seeing a gentleman he did not know, asked his business. Taken aback by this unexpected greeting, Gideon said that he had come to play. When it appeared that he was not to be admitted, he extracted the fat purse from his pocket and assured the man that he had the wherewithal to bet. He was told that so many gentlemen came there every night that Mrs. White had decided to admit only those who played there regularly.

This was such an unusual policy for a chocolate house that for a moment Gideon was taken aback. Then, refusing to leave without making a serious attempt, he asked if there were not a ticket he could purchase for the privilege of entering. The man hemmed and hawed until Gideon reached into his purse and slipped a gold coin into his palm. After just a moment's hesitation, the servant agreed to make an exception this once and bowed him in.

Inside, Gideon found a dark room with a dozen or more tables covered in baize, each lit by a single candle. Crowded round them were gentlemen in full-bottom wigs and satin coats. Wreaths of smoke from a roaring fire thickened the air. As his eyes grew accustomed to the fog, he could make out the expressions on the players' faces, ranging from poorly-concealed elation and feigned indifference to desperation and despair. Joyful or downcast, everyone wore the same look of intensity. The mood in the room was one of deadly earnest. There was not a newssheet to be seen in the place. Nor at this late hour was anyone engaged in idle conversation. Waiters moved silently about the room, refilling the players' glasses.

Francis White, *né* Francesco Bianco, the owner of White's, had died while Gideon was touring abroad, leaving his widow to run the house. Gideon spied a woman of middle age, serving chocolate behind the counter at the end of the room, and assumed her to be Mrs. White. She wore the high lace cap favoured by the coffee-women, but still observed a measure of propriety by remaining behind the bar and leaving the interaction with her customers to the man at the door.

He hastened past Gideon to confer with his mistress in a low voice, placing the Guinea Gideon had given him on the counter for her to see. The frown of disapproval that had appeared on her brow quickly cleared, and she bestowed a smile on Gideon with a regal nod. After another brief conversation, the servant returned to Gideon and offered to find him a seat at a table.

Gideon's eyes had been sweeping the room in the hope of spotting Sir Horatio Allenby. Spying him at the second table from the door, he told the servant that he would prefer to join that one. Fortunately, a place soon opened up, so the servant led Gideon to the vacated chair, and after asking his name, introduced him to the other players as Sir Robert Mavors.

The players with few remaining coins in front of them greeted him with a nod, their minds burdened by the size of the sums they had lost. Those who appeared to have played at least some winning hands were more inclined to spare the newcomer a glance, but they quickly returned their attention to the banker who was shuffling the cards.

It was a testament to his regular play that Sir Horatio had been designated banker at the table. In front of him stood stacks of golden Guineas, alerting Gideon to the level of stakes played. After sitting down, he extracted a number of coins from his purse, having determined in advance the amount he was prepared to lose in his quest for the truth. Fortunately, as games of chance went, faro gave a punter better odds than some.

Sir Horatio lost no time in setting up the next game. The deck was already in the box and the first card discarded by the time Gideon had gathered his coins.

"Gentlemen, place your bets."

In the first deal, all cards on the layout carried the same odds except the value of the soda card. With no superstitions to guide him, Gideon scattered a few Guineas evenly over the layout, but he noted that most players were not governed by odds. They each had their favourite cards and stacked their coins accordingly. With King George's head staring up at them from a dozen different spots on the table, Sir Horatio first dealt the banker's card, the Queen of Clubs, and placed it to the right of the box, then the player's card or *carte anglaise* to the left.

Already, the players who had laid greater bets on the queens suppressed a groan, as Sir Horatio collected their coins. Gideon had placed one coin on the ten and was the only gentleman at the table to receive a Guinea to match his wager. Since he did not subscribe to the notion of a lucky number, he removed his new Guinea from the ten and placed it on the two.

Sir Horatio did not find it necessary to call for the next bets to be placed. Every man at the table had followed the movement of coins across the baize and was ready for the next draw. Watching the players out the corners of his eyes, Gideon could not understand their fascination for the game, but he supposed there must be something mesmerizing about it. He found the play boring when there was no skill involved. Even games that involved tricks and skill held little attraction for him. He had much rather be outdoors riding his horse at a gallop, jumping a hedge, fencing with swords, or even reading than suffering the worry and shame of wasting his inheritance on a game.

Gideon hoped that tonight he would learn something to make his losses worthwhile. As intent as the players were on the cards, his only chance of gaining Sir Horatio's attention would be between games, while he was shuffling the deck before placing it back into the box. If Gideon could not catch the man's eye at the end of this game, then he would have to sit and play through another before trying again.

As the number of cards in the box decreased, he prepared to execute his move. The players at the table had hardly taken their eyes off the board to sip their drinks, though the greatest losers among them drank deeper than the others. He wondered if one could estimate a man's losses by the redness of his eyes.

Finally, Sir Horatio called the turn. Those who still had money to risk nervously placed their coins on the board. The increase in tension was palpable. The man to Gideon's left unconsciously jiggled his leg. The neighbour on his right murmured something that might have been a prayer. Even Sir Horatio betrayed signs of stress as he moistened his lips.

Gideon refrained from betting, certain that no one would notice his omission except, perhaps, the man who held the bank and who stood to win the most on the final draws. Instead, he reached into his pocket for the snuffbox.

The final three cards were drawn to a chorus of groans and one sigh of satisfaction. As Sir Horatio collected from the losers and paid the one winner, Gideon raised the lid of the snuffbox, holding it so that the image of the woman and the black page would be in Sir Horatio's line of vision. He helped himself to a pinch a snuff, then offered the box to his neighbours on either side.

As he had hoped, his gesture was big enough to capture Sir Horatio's attention for just a moment. That was enough to make him take a second, longer look. At first, as he took in the image on the box, his eyes widened. Then they narrowed before flying to Gideon's face.

It was as clear a sign of recognition as Gideon could have hoped for. What he did not see was any sign of panic. Sir Horatio studied his visage as if imprinting it on his memory.

"That is a very charming toy," he said, frowning. "Where did you get it?"

Gideon shrugged. "I do not recall. It may have been a gift. Or it is possible that I picked it up here in town." He held Sir Horatio's gaze a moment longer than was comfortable, then offered him a pinch of snuff.

When the man refused and resumed shuffling the cards, Gideon returned the snuffbox to his pocket. He sat through one more game before thanking the gentlemen round the table for a pleasant evening and leaving White's.

If anyone thought it strange that he should leave after only two games, they gave no sign, too engrossed were they in their play to notice much else. The only exceptions were Mrs. White and the man at the door—whose expressions said they wondered why he had come— and Sir Horatio Allenby, who betrayed a glimmer of anxiety. Gideon left with the impression that if Sir Horatio had not been trapped as the banker, he would have followed.

His mission accomplished, Gideon could have gone home, but an instinct prompted him to wait to see what Sir Horatio would do. He looked round for somewhere to linger long enough for fifty-two cards to be dealt in pairs and wagers counted and paid after each. If Sir Horatio did not appear after the next game, then Gideon would take himself off.

The bagnio not far down the street seemed as good a spot as any to wait. The difficulty would be in distinguishing Sir Horatio from another gentleman in the dark. Gideon took up a position just to the left of the bagnio door and leaned against the wall, as if waiting to meet a friend. He kept his hat tipped down to shadow his face and ignored the men and women who passed through the door on their way to the hot and cold baths.

Waiting had never been his forte. If he had planned to tail Sir Horatio, he would have brought Tom with him, but he was becoming impatient with the investigation and his lack of progress. Sir Horatio's recognition of the snuffbox was the first sign Gideon had received that he might be drawing close to an answer. So, he smothered his impatience and stayed where he was.

He did not have long to wait. Almost as soon as he had reckoned that the next game could be finished, allowing his quarry some minutes to extricate himself from the banking duties, a figure who might be Sir Horatio emerged from the door of White's and turned in his direction. Careful not to draw any attention, Gideon slowly straightened and prepared to follow. He did not know if the man was Sir Horatio, but he took the chance, reckoning that if Lord Ireton's friend did not leave White's at this juncture, he might as well retire.

He was frustrated by not having a view of the man's face as he trailed him down St. James's Street towards Pall Mall. Then, as the man passed the St. James's Coffee-House, a fortuitous thing occurred. He glanced sideways to peer into a window just as he passed beneath Michael Cole's famous Globe Light, which hung outside the house, and Gideon saw that his gamble had paid off.

From there, it was easy to keep track of his quarry for Sir Horatio walked directly to his destination without another pause. After passing a dozen or more houses and shops, he turned left to enter St. James's Square. He knocked at the door of one of the grandest houses and was soon admitted by a servant in scarlet and gold livery.

When he saw which house the man had entered, Gideon's heart started to race. Even as late as most gentlemen stayed awake, the hour of midnight or later seemed unusual for a social call. Wondering what it meant—that Sir Horatio had felt compelled to visit Lord Ireton at this hour—Gideon headed for home.

Perhaps the snuffbox *had* belonged to Lord Wragby, and Sir Horatio merely wished to inform his patron about seeing it, in case the stranger who had appeared at White's had been involved in his son's murder. It did seem strange that neither of Lord Wragby's friends nor his valet had recognized the box, but perhaps he had not possessed it for long. It could even have been a gift from his father.

If such were the case, then Gideon was no closer to identifying Lord Wragby's killer than he had been before he had bought the box from Jonathan Wild. And, he noted with a grimace as he made his way to the Thames, Lord Ireton would be sure to take a keen interest in the man who had it.

All the more reason to make haste to the river and hire a waterman to row him home.

Could laureate Dryden Pimp and Friar engage,
Yet neither Charles nor James be in a rage?
And I not strip the gilding off a Knave,
Unplaced, unpensioned, no man's heir, or slave?
I will, or perish in the generous cause:
Hear this, and tremble! you who 'scape the Laws,
Yes, while I live, no rich or noble knave
Shall walk the World, in credit, to his grave.

CHAPTER XX

Gideon got very little sleep that night. His rest was disturbed by an anxious feeling, a deep knot twisting in his guts as if he had eaten a piece of rotten meat. He could not escape the feeling that something grossly unnatural had occurred, but his nature waged a defensive war with his mind, refusing to go where his imagination wanted to lead.

Then, at dawn, when he had given up on the prospect of sleep, a niggling detail he had noticed and dismissed as unimportant finally registered in his brain. Leaping out of bed with a muttered, "What an idiot I've been!" he hastily dressed and went downstairs to speak to Katy.

The aroma of cooking bacon announced that she and Tom were ready to break their fast. They always woke before he did, and after the late night he had put in, she would not have disturbed him at such an early hour. The surprise that both his servants felt on seeing him was reflected on their faces. Normally, Gideon would not have liked to interrupt their morning, but his question was too pressing to wait.

Before raising it, he asked, "Where is Sam?"

Katy exchanged a worried glance with Tom before saying, "He's gone outside to collect the eggs. He does that for me every morning, my lord."

With a nod, he walked over to her, and said gently, "When I first came home from France, I noticed that he was wearing a new suit of clothes. Did you make those for him?"

An evasive look came into her eyes, but she replied, "Yes, my lord, I did. The clothes he had on were dirty and torn, and so wet that I feared he would catch cold."

"What did you do with those clothes?"

Again, Katy cast a glance her husband's way. Looking back severely, Tom nodded, as if he had told her that this would happen eventually.

With a sigh, she said, "I washed them and mended the tears, in case he should ever need them, my lord."

"May I see them, please?"

Resigned now, she went into the room off the kitchen, which she shared with Tom, and returned carrying a small, tidy bundle of clothes. Gideon took them from her and spread them across the table; but he did not have to do this to see that their scarlet and gold matched the livery he had glimpsed last night. There was no mistake. The boy had been wearing the Marquess of Ireton's livery.

"Why didn't you show these to me before?" Gideon asked.

It was Tom who answered, taking whatever displeasure his master might feel onto his broad shoulders. "We reckoned that whoever owned the boy was that brutal to him that we didn't want to send him back. But if the man had advertised, my lord, I promise we would have returned him. We were just waiting for the news to come, but when it didn't, it seemed like providence, my lord."

"Didn't you recognize the livery?"

Tom vigorously shook his head. "No, my lord, I swear! It's not one I've ever seen before. If I had known who the boy's master was, I would have told you."

Even if Gideon could believe that Tom would lie to him, he had to accept his story. He, himself, had not been familiar with Lord Ireton's livery until he had seen it on the servant last night. His father and Lord Ireton had always been political enemies. Lord Ireton had never set foot inside Hawkhurst House, nor had the former Lord Hawkhurst ever visited him.

"In truth, my lord, by the time your lordship come home, we'd forgotten all about the boy's clothes. Or—" with a guilty look at Katy— "at least, I had."

Katy had been hanging her head throughout this discussion. Gideon handed the clothes back to her.

"You can put them away again before Sam sees them. He might be upset if he does." Meeting Katy's startled look, he added, "And if my theory is correct, you may be able to burn them soon."

Now Tom gave a start. "Whose livery is it, my lord?"

"It belongs to Lord Ireton."

Deep confusion came over Tom's face. It echoed the doubts that had kept Gideon awake half the night. "The murdered gentleman's father, my lord? But why wouldn't he want to get the boy back?"

Before Gideon could reply, the door to the yard opened, and Sam entered, beaming as he held up the eggs he had found. A cold morning current of air followed him inside, but it was not responsible for the chill descending Gideon's spine.

Katy had hastily hidden the clothes. Now, she welcomed Sam back with forced cheer, praising him for doing such a splendid job. Gideon could not help noticing how much the boy's manner had improved. The look of perpetual fright was gone. Gideon guessed that it would not take much to bring it back, and he had no appetite for being the one to resurrect it. But patience was a luxury where men's lives were concerned, and the murderer had already struck twice.

He sat down at the table and called the boy to him. Sam came readily, used enough to Gideon by now not to be in mortal terror of him. Gideon first admired his basket of eggs and ventured to pat the boy on the shoulder.

When he saw that this was welcome, he said, as gently as he could, "Sam, I need to show you something. It's something I found. All I need you to do is tell me whether you've seen it before, and if you know who it belongs to. Then, you can go be with the horses, if you like. You can live here with Mr. and Mrs. Barnes as long as you are happy. You are not in any trouble. Do you understand?"

Grasping the seriousness in Gideon's tone, the boy tensed, but after seeking reassurance from Tom and Katy, both of whom assured him that he would come to no harm, he turned back to Gideon and nodded.

Gideon reached into his pocket and brought out the snuffbox. He had no sooner introduced it to Sam's view than the boy emitted a sound halfway between a gasp and a sob. Katy immediately stepped forward and put her arm around his shoulders, but he made no attempt to run away.

"So, you have seen this box?" Gideon asked.

The boy nodded.

"Did it belong to your master?"

Sam hesitated, before admitting this with another nod.

"Remember, Sam, I promised you can live with us. I will not send you back to your master . . . but I need to know. Did this snuffbox belong to Lord Ireton, and did he drop it when he strangled his son?"

Tom and Katy both gasped. Such an unnatural act had never occurred to them. They were as shocked by the notion as Gideon and Hester had been. That was the reason both Hester and he had refused to entertain it sooner. All their eyes were on the boy, who gave a great shudder in Katy's arms, but who now with a tremulous sigh, almost of relief, said, "Yes."

That a word had issued from his mouth was nearly as astonishing as the information he had to impart.

Gideon smiled at the boy. "Thank you, Sam. That is all I needed to know. Now, would you rather spend time with the horses or eat some of those eggs you found."

The boy considered his choice for a moment before pointing to the door. Evidently, he had used enough words for now. Katy released him and gave him a nudge, but said, "I'll come find you, soon as your eggs are ready."

With a dazed look, as if he had just escaped from a fire and was astonished not to feel any burns, Sam went outside.

"Maybe I'd better be sure he don't run off, my lord," Tom said, gazing anxiously after the boy.

"If you wish, but I think he will be all right." Knowing what a trial the past few minutes had been for both his servants, Gideon gave them a smile. "Now that we know the truth, our work is certainly cut out for us."

"Why do you say that, my lord?"

Gideon answered with a sigh even more audible than the boy's. "Because I do not know how we are to prove that Lord Ireton is the murderer. It is going to take more than the testimony of an escaped page and the evidence of a dropped snuffbox to convince any magistrate that the King's favourite aristocrat killed his own son."

In response to his urgent summons, Hester met St. Mars at the house in Little Windmill Street.

He wasted no time before telling her what he had confirmed, and the shock of his information took her breath away.

Hester had seen cruelty. She had witnessed the results of greed and desperation and many earthly sins, but the notion that a father would cold-bloodedly set out to murder his own son made every part of her recoil. She had disliked Lord Wragby intensely. She had been shamefully relieved that Mary no longer had to fear him. Now she wondered how much of his character had been twisted by having a soulless man as a father.

Seeing the distress in her eyes, St. Mars enveloped her in his arms. She wrapped hers around him and held on tightly until the wave of revulsion passed. Then, they lay together on the bed, for once too riveted on the problem facing them to indulge their passion.

"If Lord Ireton is the murderer, then how on earth are we to expose him?"

St. Mars gave a rueful laugh. "That is what has worried me since I first discovered it. We cannot take our evidence to a magistrate. I doubt there is one in the City of Westminster, or in the entire country for that matter, who would dare risk taking on one of the King's favourite courtiers. Only a fool would risk it. And if Lord Wragby were his father's only victim, I'm not sure if I might not suggest at this moment that we forget all about his crime."

A moment passed before Hester caught on to his meaning. "You are speaking of the murder of Lord William Silsbee? Do you know that Lord Ireton was responsible?"

"Who else would have had a motive for killing him? You said that Lord William was showing signs of being troubled by something—

perhaps, his conscience. If he was with Lord Ireton in the gallery at St. Paul's, he might have heard the threat Ireton made about his son. Even if he did not take it seriously then—and who would?—after Lord Wragby was murdered by that very method, he must have recollected the threat. Later, he would have seen the advertisement for the snuffbox in the newssheets and, knowing it to be Lord Ireton's—there cannot be another like it—he would have come to the same conclusion we did, only much quicker. He would have noticed the absence of Lord Ireton's snuffbox and, perhaps, the loss of his page. He might even have commented on the absence of the boy.

"Whatever he did to alert Lord Ireton to his suspicions, we shall probably never know, but I suspect that Lord William, being an honourable man, decided he must take them to the Lord Chancellor. Again, being honourable, he might first have confronted his patron with them in the hope that he could explain them away. When Lord Ireton could not or would not, Lord William would be faced with the same dilemma we are now."

Hester could not deny the argument he had made. Even if Lord Ireton's son had been his only victim, she would have pressed to expose his killer, but Lord William's murder made it even more imperative. "But how are we to do it? The notion of trying to convince Lord Cowper that a powerful member of his party has murdered two young gentlemen makes me tremble."

They discussed various means of revealing Lord Ireton's crimes, but no private meetings or anonymous letters would be certain of convincing the King or Parliament. In the end, they agreed that somehow they must expose Lord Ireton in front of enough witnesses, including the Lord Chancellor, Lord Cowper, and, if at all possible, Lord William's father, the Earl of Rutherford.

"Now, all you have to do is gather them in one place simultaneously," St. Mars said lightly, "and you can leave the rest to me."

Hester gave him a chastening look. "Oh, that is all, is it? Then, why not the House of Lords?"

When he seemed to consider this seriously, she said hastily, "No! I forbid it! You would never be admitted to the chamber, and getting back out would be impossible. I do wish to bring Lord Ireton to justice and to relieve James Henry of suspicion, but never at the cost of your life! You must promise me that you will never set foot in that place!"

He laughed, and she saw that he had only been teasing. "Very well, I promise. But I wasn't jesting about getting those people to a place where I can force Lord Ireton to expose himself. And if the venue offers me a way to escape afterwards, it would be much the better."

Still worried more about his safety than bringing Lord Ireton to justice, Hester could scarcely think. The situation seemed impossible. How could she, with no influence, and St. Mars with a price on his head convince two of the most powerful men in England of a third one's crimes?

St. Mars was musing aloud. "It will have to be somewhere public and well-lit, for we can only bring it off at night. Spring Garden? No, that's much too large a space. We must be certain that our witnesses are close enough to hear Lord Ireton confess. But I will need an exit in case things go badly."

"But how can we lure them anywhere?"

"That will be the easy part. I will send them each a note guaranteed to draw them. For Lord Ireton, I shall offer to restore his snuffbox and to keep silent for a price. For the Lord Chancellor and Lord Rutherford, I'll promise to expose the murderer of Lord William Silsbee."

A notion had come to Hester, but she hated to reveal it for fear of the danger it would pose to St. Mars.

He read a new idea on her face and said, "What? You will have to tell me, you know. We have no other choice."

Hesitantly, she said, "I did read a notice for a masquerade that is to be held at the opera. Most of the aristocracy should be there. Even the Prince of Wales may go."

"But that is perfect! I can wear my Blue Satan disguise. I have worn it to a masquerade before, and no one was the least suspicious. In fact, if I recall, Harrowby even expressed his admiration of the tailoring."

That was true. Moreover, at a masquerade, St. Mars could remain masked, which would give him a much better chance to escape.

They discussed how to recognize Lord Ireton in the crowd. Once that question was answered, Hester said, "And I shall make certain that Lord Cowper and Lord Rutherford are positioned where you need them to be."

It was St. Mars's turn to protest. He was not keen for her to be there, but Hester was adamant that she must be. They argued about it briefly, but Hester won by saying that he would find it impossible to keep her from coming when he was busy with Lord Ireton. St. Mars frowned and told her she was a disobedient minx. Then he rolled on top of her and showed her just how she deserved to be treated for her impudence.

Afterwards, when they lay quite satisfied in each other's arms, Hester told him about James Henry's surprising return and the scene that had taken place in the withdrawing room at Hawkhurst House.

For a moment, St. Mars was speechless. Then he laughed. "Well, I suppose I should congratulate him on outwitting your aunt. I find it hard to imagine James Henry in the role of determined suitor, but I suppose love can inspire wonders."

"Yes, he genuinely loves Mary, and she him. I believe they will be very happy together." A wicked impulse made Hester add, in a casual tone, "I doubt he would have acted with as much resolution in order to marry me, but then I had no need to ask anyone's permission."

St. Mars stiffened. Not a hair on his head stirred when his eyes sought hers. "Am I to understand that he wished to marry you?"

The temptation to be coy fled the moment Hester felt the darkness of his gaze. "No, my love, he did not truly wish it; but he did have the goodness to make me an offer some months ago. He was distressed by the way my aunt treated me, and being lonely himself and having respect for me, he offered marriage as a salve to both our problems."

St. Mars huffed. "Very gallant! That is more like what I would expect from James Henry."

Hester scolded him with a glance, but she had to laugh at his pique. which her vanity was pleased to attribute to jealousy more than resentment. "Yes, and I was very grateful for it, I assure you, almost grateful enough to accept. But I did not like to take advantage of his kindness when he might eventually find happiness with a woman he truly loved—as now he has—nor did I think it fair to impose on his goodwill when my heart was firmly committed to another."

This assurance mollified him, but still he took her firmly in his arms. "Well, thank God, someone showed some sense!" The strength in his hug told her that he understood how close he had come to losing her. After a few seconds, he asked, "Was that why you were so distant with me last spring?"

"Yes . . . and no. I thought that you had decided to go to France and not come back. I was trying to protect my feelings. But, for a brief while, I had persuaded myself that his offer was the only chance I would ever have for a home and family of my own. In fact, when we parted after Tom's and Katy's wedding, I had made up my mind to accept him, and it was only when he requested my answer that I realized I could not marry him."

"And all that, when I thought I had made my love for you painfully evident." Chagrined, he shook his head. "But I should have said something sooner, even when I believed you were rejecting my advances. To think what my cowardice almost cost!"

"You could just as well accuse me of being the coward. It is true that I did not always respond to your flirting, but I could not believe you meant it seriously and I was afraid you might think me loose." Hester nearly added, I was afraid that you might ask me to be your mistress, but she realized that this would hurt him. St. Mars was an honourable man. He would never have used her unfairly. It was her own lack of confidence that had led her to question his motives.

She was relieved when a chuckle emanated from deep in his throat. "You, my dear, loose? If you ever had a tendency to wantonness, you managed very well to hide it. I shall never get over the astonishment of discovering how willing a lover you can be, but as I am certain you reserve all your passion for me, I make no complaint." His subsequent actions assured her that his discovery had made him very happy, indeed.

But they could not indulge in mindless bliss for long when such an enormous challenge faced them. Before many minutes had passed, they returned to planning the act they hoped would trick Lord Ireton into revealing his crimes.

At Hawkhurst House, the few days before the masquerade ball were hectic, as everyone meaning to attend had to come up with a costume. In an especially generous mood, Harrowby purchased tickets for all the members of his family, Hester and James Henry included. Naturally, most of the servants' efforts went into sewing new costumes for Harrowby and Isabella, who had decided to go as a Turkish sultan and his dancer or Roxana, both in rich red fabrics with a large turban for the earl and a tight vest for Isabella to accentuate her voluptuousness.

Mrs. Mayfield commanded Hester's needle to make her a dairymaid's gown, which would have been more appropriate for a girl Mary's age. Somehow, between fittings and stitching, and under the pretext of needing to purchase more ribbon, Hester managed to escape long enough to pay an important visit to Lady Cowper.

By the day of the ball, there was just enough time to sew each of the remaining three attendees a domino. James Henry's cape was black, as customarily worn in Venice. Mary's was a becoming blue. And, to help St. Mars identify her among so many revelers, Hester chose white. Her hood and mask, worn with the long cloak, were also white. The impracticality of this choice would guarantee that few, if any, like it were worn.

The ladies caught a few hours' rest in the afternoon, for masquerades started very late at night. At the appointed hour, as they were dressed and ready to descend the stairs, Mary asked Hester if she did not fear that her costume would quickly become soiled.

In reply, Hester took her quietly aside. "I need to wear something easily distinguishable."

When Mary would have teased her about meeting a lover, Hester forestalled her. "Remember when I told you that someone would help us reveal Lord Wragby's murderer? Well, tonight he means to expose the killer, but we may need your help."

"I'll do anything, of course! But why can you not just—?"

"If we are successful, you will see why it has to be done this way. But I will need you and James Henry to help me ensure that the men who need to witness the unmasking are near enough to see it. We must stay close together."

Mary had been excited to attend a masked ball with her intended, where intimate behaviour would go unremarked, but she swallowed her disappointment to assure Hester that they would stay nearby her and alert.

"And you must take care not to let James Henry interfere." Hester impressed this upon her cousin. "My friend will be acting to prove his innocence, but it may not be apparent at first."

Thoroughly sobered now, Mary promised to do as she asked.

Within a half-hour, the chairs that carried them from Hawkhurst House were setting them down in front of the red brick arches that gave entrance to the King's Theatre in the Haymarket, where they were immediately surrounded by a costumed crowd. It was clear from the laughing and jostling that this would not be a tame occasion, for it was well-known that a masquerade offered its guests a chance to misbehave. With St. Mars's safety pressing on her mind, Hester was at pains to keep together with her family until their tickets were presented at the door and their costumes approved, for no one was admitted to a masquerade without a disguise.

Inside, the scene was chaotic. Though she had been to a few of Mr. Handel's Italian operas here, this was the first time Hester had attended a masquerade presented by Mr. Heidegger, known to London society as the Swiss count. He had lately taken over management of the theatre, and to make it more profitable had promoted the sort of masquerade the Venetians enjoyed at carnival. Now that Hester had caught just a few glimpses of the wildness she was likely to see all night, she understood why they were becoming so popular.

In the crowded theatre she could not identify any of her acquaintance. Anyone with a ticket and wearing a costume would be admitted, so she had no way of knowing if the nymph who was hanging on the satyr's arm to her right was his wife, his mistress, or even a common whore—indeed, even if she was some other man's wife. The room was awash in colour and patterns to dazzle the eye. As Hester struggled to make sense of the scene in front of her, the figures resolved into a strange meeting of dairy maids, harlequins, monks, cooks, and Turkish dancers. A jester brushed by her, the bells on his cap jingling. The conical hat of an Etruscan vied for attention with the high-crowned Geneva of a Puritan.

The theatre itself had been altered to accommodate the crowd. The floor of the pit had been raised even with the stage to create a space for dancing. An orchestra was set up at the back of the stage—the walls of which were draped in painted cloth—and it was playing a reel. While, several years ago, the ceiling had been lowered from Mr. Vanbrugh's original construction to improve the sound, still the voices of a hundred or more people echoed through the cavernous space. Widely spaced pairs of Corinthian columns adorned each side, each pair framing a statue on a pedestal.

The room was brightly lit by an enormous round chandelier suspended from the centre of the ceiling, with a row of smaller chandeliers running along each side. Tables had been set up against each side of the pit with the boxes rising above them. Servants in long powdered wigs stood behind the tables, serving drinks, while others handed down fresh supplies from behind curtains draped in front the boxes. In the corners of the pit, more tables were laid with trays of pastries.

Hester had just finished taking this all in when her aunt announced in a carrying voice that she would be in the card room if anybody wanted her. She saw Mrs. Mayfield making her way across the pit to the door that led to rooms on the west side of the theatre. Hester was relieved not to have to worry about what her aunt might do when St. Mars's plan was unfolding.

She did not see St. Mars. Nor could she imagine how he would know Lord Ireton from any other man present—or how she would help him to do it for that matter. Nevertheless, she tried to make out distinctive features that might give a clue to the identities behind the masks. Deciding to make a game of it, she enlisted Mary's help, while James Henry went to get them all refreshments.

"The only thing I know," Hester said to her cousin, "is that Lord Cowper will be wearing a black domino, but so will a quarter of the gentlemen here. Still, I cannot believe he will engage in any frolics, so we should look for a black domino standing apart or in conversation with other gentlemen." She had to raise her voice to be heard over the din in the room.

"Will Lady Cowper not be with him?"

"No, for it is her turn in waiting, and the Princess does not care for masquerades. She is supping at Richmond tonight with the Countess of Grantham. The Prince may be here, however, and if he is, Lord Cowper might be near him."

"Then, perhaps, we should move through the crowd and listen for the Prince's voice."

At a loss, Hester was about to agree when she spied a group of three black dominos, standing near a pair of columns on the east side of the theatre. One of them had a long straight nose and a dimple in his chin, features belonging to the Lord Chancellor. She was subtly pointing him out to Mary, when James Henry returned with a servant bearing drinks and sweetmeats on a tray.

They stood drinking and eating, while the revels went on around them. Then, raising her voice to be heard above the music, Hester asked if they did not wish to dance and declared her intention of finding a quieter spot in which to stand. "I shall see how that niche over there suits me," she said, indicating a shallow space near the group of black dominos. "If it does not, I shall make my way around the floor until I find a comfortable spot."

James Henry objected to leaving her alone in the crowd, but Mary understood what Hester wished to convey. If the gentleman she had spied was not Lord Cowper, she would keep on with her search.

"I will keep you in sight," Mary promised, "and if you should need us, you must signal."

Grateful, Hester nodded before, holding her glass close, she pushed her way past a boisterous set, which included a Spanish *señorita,* a baker, and a red-robed cardinal, to approach the three black dominos. They had now been joined by a fourth figure, splendidly garbed as a Turkish sultan. Hester did not need to hear his German accent to recognize the Prince of Wales who was flanked by a pair of guards.

A closer look at the gentleman with the straight nose and the dimpled chin convinced her that she had found Lord Cowper. She positioned herself at a discreet distance from the men and sipped at her wine, while searching the room for Blue Satan.

The minutes crept past at a tortoise's pace, as she stood waiting. Through the crowd, she watched Mary and James Henry execute the steps of a reel, the music for which she could hardly hear above the laughter and chatter in the room. She was aware of masculine stares directed her way, for it was unusual for a lady to stand all alone in a crowded room. She hoped to escape their attentions by ignoring them, but eventually a big man, dressed as a woman, loomed over her and in a drunken voice asked, "Do I know you?"

It was the proper way to approach anyone at a masquerade, but Hester could not like the way he leaned drunkenly over her or the smell of stale wine on his breath. She replied, "No, sir," and driven from her spot, circled the room, keeping one eye on Lord Cowper and the other on Mary and her betrothed.

"Do I know you?" A male voice came over her shoulder, but this one made her smile. She turned gratefully to find a familiar pair of blue eyes sparkling through a mask. A tall, straight figure in a blue satin cape, he wore his fair hair tied back in a queue, with a tricorn hat pulled low over his brow.

"Thank, Heaven! I had almost given you up."

"Sorry, my dear, but the only sure way for me to know Lord Ireton was to follow him here. I've been waiting outside his house for the past two hours, and he has just now condescended to grace us with his presence." Looking just past her, St. Mars nodded towards another black domino. "That is Ireton, and I dare not take my eyes off him for more than a few seconds, or I'll lose him in this crowd. Have you managed to locate Lord Cowper?"

"Yes, he is standing with the Prince of Wales along the wall to your right. The Prince is the Turkish sultan."

St. Mars sucked in a deep breath. "So . . . we are to have a royal audience. Very well, my dear, there is no time like the present."

He gave her hand a quick squeeze and left to cut through the crowd.

With her heart pounding in her ears, Hester watched him approach Lord Ireton from behind, speak a few words in his ear, and offer him a pinch of snuff from the enamelled box. She saw the figure in the black domino stiffen, and imagined the indignation that must have swept through him. Then, as quickly as St. Mars had approached the marquess, he slipped back into the crowd to make his way towards the entrance to the theatre.

It seemed clear that Lord Ireton had been unprepared for such a sudden manoeuvre. Taken by surprise, he hesitated a moment before following the blue satin cape. As he did, he raised a hand in a beckoning gesture and a second black domino came out of the crowd to join him. They paused and conferred for a few seconds. Lord Ireton pointed to the retreating back of Blue Satan, before the two black dominos thrust their way through the revellers to catch him.

Worried about the danger the second man might pose, Hester desperately searched for Mary. When she could not see her amongst the dancers, she felt close to panic, but soon she saw her leading James Henry through the crowd.

As soon as she reached Hester, Mary asked, "Is everything quite right? You look agitated."

"Yes—no. I cannot be sure. The friend I told you about has just sprung his trap. Lord Ireton is trailing him, but he is not alone. He signalled to another gentleman—possibly, Sir Horatio, but I could not tell. If there are two men after my friend, I fear they may be too much for him."

James Henry heard most of her speech, enough to know that something involving Lord Ireton was afoot. "Lord Ireton is here? Then, perhaps we should go."

"No! We must stay in case he needs us." Hester saw St. Mars lead Lord Ireton out of the room and wondered if they should follow. But St. Mars had said nothing about leaving the theatre. According to their plan, she was to find Lord Cowper and, if possible, the Earl of Rutherford, and get them to witness the exposure of the killer. She had to assume that St. Mars would lead Lord Ireton back to the spot where Lord Cowper was standing.

"In case who needs us?" James Henry asked, frowning.

Hester ignored the question, which she could not answer at any rate, and said instead, "We need to place ourselves close to Lord Cowper. He is standing over there." She nodded in the baron's direction. "Come with me, and please, be quick."

Trusting Mary to follow, Hester fought her way through the masqueraders again to stand near the group that included the Prince of Wales and Lord Cowper.

Arriving just behind her, James Henry recognized the Prince's voice. "Is that . . . ?" he said, indicating Prince George with a tilt of his head.

"Yes, and if I am not mistaken, Lord Rutherford is the gentleman to his right." Whatever St. Mars had promised the earl and Lord Cowper in his notes, it seemed they had found each other and were waiting for his promise to be fulfilled.

The wait was straining Lord Rutherford's patience. So recently bereaved, he would not have attended the masquerade if not for St. Mars's note. He stood stiffly beside the Prince, his posture barely concealing the turmoil he must be feeling. If not for the presence of Prince George, Hester doubted he would have waited this long to see if his son's murderer would be revealed.

The noise in the room was so loud that Hester could not make out the words the Prince and his companions were saying. If not for the German emphasis of his speech, she doubted James Henry would have picked him out.

James Henry was speaking to Mary in low tones. He must be asking why they had moved to stand by Lord Cowper.

Hester was close enough to her cousin to hear her reply, "All I know is that we should trust Hester. She is trying to help us. We must be patient."

Hester was trembling from her head to the tips of her toes in anxious anticipation. She did not know how much longer their witnesses would be content to wait. Worse, still, was her fear that Lord Ireton and his confederate had managed to overpower St. Mars. Aware of Lord Ireton's renown as a duellist, she had already worried about a confrontation. Now, knowing he had an accomplice—and how ruthless he could be—she was afraid that no sense of honour would prevent him from the worst kind of treachery.

She was watching the entrance to the room, praying for St. Mars's return, when a movement behind her and a gasp from the people facing her made her turn around. A curtain had fallen from a box in the second tier above her to reveal two figures in a desperate struggle. St. Mars in his Blue Satan disguise was fighting off the attack of a black domino. His back was to the pit, the back of his knees pressed against the front of the box. His opponent was leaning into him, their swords locked at the hilt. Hester guessed that St. Mars had purposely torn down the curtain and, in that moment, Lord Ireton had seized the advantage.

The box they were in was too far above the pit for anyone to stop them. The crowd fell mostly silent, mesmerized by the two men fighting for their lives. A dozen people pressed forward for a closer view, but the Prince's guards, weapons drawn, forced them back. Lord Cowper, Lord Rutherford, and the Prince of Wales were riveted upon the action in the box and near enough to hear.

The swordfight must have been raging for some minutes, for both combatants' brows were covered in sweat and they were heavily panting. The curtain and the raised voices in the theatre must have muffled any noise from their fight.

After an initial gasp, Hester held her breath, praying that St. Mars would not be injured, until he managed to break the other man's hold. With one great push, he threw Lord Ireton off. The older man tumbled backwards over a chair, which had been knocked on its side. More chairs lay scattered about the box, evidence of their struggle.

With his chest heaving, St. Mars spoke while Lord Ireton scrambled back onto his feet. "Your Highness, Lord Chancellor, my Lord Rutherford—here is your murderer! Lord Ireton, will you take a bow?"

Another gasp went up from the crowd, followed by cries of outrage. With a start, James Henry whispered to himself, "St. Mars?"

"He lies!" Lord Ireton lunged, but St. Mars parried his thrust.

"Your friends would prefer to believe you," he said, "but they must be permitted to hear the evidence. Would you lay down your sword, so that my friends and I can present it?"

"I will kill you!"

The clang of their swords' meeting rang again and again, as St. Mars parried every move. He was fighting defensively, saving his breath for speech.

"Killing is your preference for settling disputes, I know. And my death would surely silence me, but others are aware of your crimes, Lord Ireton, and you cannot possibly silence us all—as you did poor

Lord William Silsbee, when he confronted you with his suspicions."

Out the corner of her eye, Hester saw a black domino—Lord Rutherford—give a violent start. Someone quickly put out a hand to restrain him.

"With your permission, your Highness . . . ." Lord Cowper stepped forward, as the Prince of Wales gave a nod. "You spoke of evidence. What evidence do you possess?"

A frenzied assault by Lord Ireton prevented St. Mars from answering immediately. Lord Rutherford, Lord Cowper, and the Prince exchanged troubled looks, which Hester interpreted—If the marquess is innocent, why will he not allow us to hear his accuser?

When his energy began to flag, Lord Ireton called out, "Allenby! Come here! I need you!"

The second black domino entered the box. Hester's heart gave a lurch of dismay. Sir Horatio tried to reach St. Mars with his blade, but Lord Ireton was in his way. His thrusts were too hampered to be effective.

St. Mars made a quick series of lunges, which forced both his adversaries to retreat. After beating them back, he turned and leapt over the short wall into the next box, ripping away its curtain in the same fluid motion. Then, finding his feet, he turned again to face Lord Cowper.

"Here," he said, reaching into a pocket for the snuffbox. "This was found near the place where Lord Wragby was killed the morning after his death." He tossed it down to the group of black dominos, and Lord Rutherford caught it. "That was made especially for Lord Ireton. He dropped it on the night he strangled his son, which witnesses had heard him threaten to do."

Next to Hester, James Henry drew in a sharp breath. Now, he understood what this demonstration was about.

Lord Ireton shoved toppled chairs to both sides to reach the front of the box where the fight had started. "That is ridiculous!" he spat. "I had given the box to Phillip. He must have dropped it when he was attacked."

"You gave your son a snuffbox with a painting of your mistress and your page on it? What an odd thing to do."

"You cannot prove that I did not!"

"No, but my lords, I ask you, after his son's death, why did Lord Ireton make no attempt to retrieve his box when it was repeatedly advertised by Jonathan Wild over three months? Does it not seem more probable that the box is his and that he feared the discovery that he was with his son that evening?"

Lord Rutherford had shown the snuffbox to Prince George, who nodded. "Yes, I haf seen this box in your possession, my Lord Ireton."

Furious now, the marquess made the grave mistake of snapping at the Prince of Wales. "It still means nothing." He was frustrated by his inability to silence the man dressed as Blue Satan. Wildly waving his sword, he slashed at the curtain entangling his feet. He tried to cross the wall that St. Mars had leapt, brandishing his sword, but the point of St. Mars's was always there to prevent him.

"What other evidence do you have?" Lord Cowper called out. In truth, as St. Mars had said, the snuffbox alone would never persuade Lord Ireton's peers and friends in the House of Lords that he had committed so heinous a crime.

"I have a witness who watched him squeeze the life out of his son." St. Mars fended off Lord Ireton's increasingly vicious slashes. "Lord Ireton's page witnessed the murder, my Lord Chancellor, and, terrified by what he saw, ran away. Perhaps, Lord Ireton can explain why he never placed any advertisement to recover his runaway page?"

The marquess gave a furious cry as he tried to silence his tormentor. He missed the looks the witnesses exchanged. It was clear to Hester that the logic St. Mars had employed was finding receptive ears.

"And you say that someone heard him threaten to throttle his son?" Lord Cowper pressed.

"Yes, my lord. In the gallery of the dome of St. Paul's Cathedral."

At these words, James Henry, who had been riveted to the action in the boxes, turned to stare at Hester. She felt his gaze upon her, but did not turn to meet it.

"Another lie! There was no one else near me!" In his rage Lord Ireton had lost control. He seemed unconscious of how damning this statement was.

"Sir Horatio Allenby was near you, was he not? And Lord William Silsbee. Lord William, at least, must have heard you, but I doubt he realized that you meant it. No decent person would have believed it. Not until your son was strangled, when he must have started to wonder. And his doubts tortured him, so that he finally had to speak. He confronted you, did he not, and when you admitted to murdering your son, he informed you that he was honour-bound to inform the Lord Chancellor? That is why you waylaid him in Lincoln's Inn Fields and murdered him, too."

Covering his eyes, Lord Rutherford issued a painful moan.

Lord Ireton ignored him to shriek at St. Mars, "I will uncover who you are and make you pay for this! How dare you challenge me? Do you not realize how powerful I am? Why, the King would be lost without me!"

Prince George gave a bark of laughter. *"Mein Gott!* When my father hears that—" He did not need to complete his thought.

Lord Ireton seemed finally to realize that his audience was no longer on his side. His eyes raked the peers and the Prince who were frowning up at him in condemnation. "Phillip was a fool and an embarrassment. Any father would be ashamed of such a son. And his Majesty will thank me for disposing of him. My lords, do you realize, he was spying for the Pretender? Yes, indeed, he was, and when I learned of it, that was the final straw. All his life, he had been a disappointment to me, and it was my duty to punish him. I simply wished to do it in my own way, so that no stain would attach to my name."

He treated the Prince of Wales to an arrogant sneer. "Your father will thank me, your Highness. Just see if he does not."

Prince George turned angrily to his guards. "Seize Lord Ireton and take him to the Tower. It shall be my duty to inform his Majesty that his most trusted subject is a foul murderer." The satisfaction in his tone left Hester in no doubt of how much he would enjoy delivering the news to his father. Lord Ireton's hatred for his son was not something likely to engage the Prince's sympathy.

Lord Ireton cursed Prince George's impudence. He turned to escape from the box, before the guards scaling the tier of boxes in front of him could reach him; but Sir Horatio, who had seen that the battle was lost, quickly switched allegiances and held him back from the door at sword point. Lord Ireton stormed and raged at all of them, but he was eventually overcome.

The quiet that had seized the crowd now broke, as dozens of voices erupted at once, first in whispers then rapidly increasing in tone. Within seconds, the theatre was as noisy as it had been before the first curtain had fallen, as if what they had watched was nothing more than an entertaining performance.

Hester looked up at St. Mars's box in time to see his blue satin cape disappearing through the door at the back. Then, and only then, did she take a deep breath. Her energy had fled. She felt as limp as a dishcloth.

Lord Cowper, his hand on Lord Rutherford's shoulder, gazed up as if to speak to the man who had come dressed as the highwayman Blue Satan, but St. Mars was safely gone.

Mary took her cousin by the arm. "You did it, Hester!" She turned to address James Henry. "The man in the blue cape is a friend of Hester's, and they have been working to prove your innocence."

James Henry stared at Hester, but said nothing. He was too stunned to speak.

When he recovered from the shock of seeing his half-brother and absorbing the enormity of what had been done for him, she knew he would have questions, but she was too drained to deal with them now. Pleading exhaustion, she begged to go home.

"But what about your friend?" Mary asked, looking about her. "Shouldn't we stay to pay our thanks?"

"He has already left, but should I see him, I will thank him for you."

"And you must thank him for me, as well."

Hester looked up into James Henry's face and was pleased to see a penitent smile.

If, after all, we must with Wilmot own,
The Cordial Drop of Life is Love alone,
And SWIFT cry wisely, "Vive la Bagatelle!"
The Man that loves and laughs, must sure do well.
Adieu—if this advice appear the worst,
E'en take the Counsel which I gave you first:
Or better Precepts if you can impart,
Why do, I'll follow them with all my heart.

EPILOGUE

In the course of the next week, James Henry learned about the friendship that had grown between Hester and St. Mars. She told him how they had solved the mystery of his father's death but had not had the evidence to prove it. Listening with Mary, he also heard how the half-brother he had accused had helped Hester piece together the clues that led to Lord Ireton's arrest.

Harrowby—who had witnessed the marquess's undoing at the masquerade, but whose brain had not accepted the gentleman in costume as his nemesis Blue Satan—declared himself delighted to have his receiver-general freed from all suspicion of murder. He gave James Henry permission to return to his full duties without fear of retribution. Nevertheless, he still urged Mary to be married from her brother's house to avoid any unpleasantness in his.

Mrs. Mayfield, who had missed the excitement, intent on her wagers, was made to admit that with respect to murder, at least, she had misjudged her future son-in-law. This did not mean that she was reconciled to Mary's match, but James Henry could be grateful to be spared any further calumny of that sort at her hands.

Near the end of the week, Hester received a message from St. Mars, informing her that he had found a legitimate priest who would marry them in the Liberty of the Fleet and asking her to name the date and time when he should come to fetch her.

The affair of Lord Ireton and its resolution had nearly driven any thought of a wedding from Hester's mind, but St. Mars's note brought on a rush of excitement that banished every memory of the fear she had endured that night at the Haymarket. After consulting Mary and inventing an excuse for Isabella and her aunt, she wrote back with the information he had requested, sorry only that paper and ink could not convey the depth of her willingness.

Three days later, she approached the waiting hackney coach at the corner of Piccadilly and Eagle Street, where she had asked St. Mars to come. Before she could reach it, the door flew open, the step fell down and his hand appeared to help her in.

She had not seen him since the night of the masquerade and found herself overwhelmed with relief. They hugged each other tightly, not needing to speak to express the joy that the day would bring. When they pulled away after a few kisses, St. Mars knocked on the roof of the coach to let the driver know that they were ready to go.

The first hints of spring were in the air. A strong wind the night before had blown away the worst of the soot from all the coal fires. The sun was struggling to provide a bit of warmth.

Hester had dressed her hair with special care and worn her favourite pink gown. Her cheeks felt as if they were glowing.

St. Mars had left off the most concealing features of his disguise. He had to wear the black wig to cover his fair hair, but he had foregone the thick white paint and had limited his patches to two.

When Hester asked why he had not disguised his face, he replied, "I wanted to make sure that you would know your own husband. I cannot have you going off with any painted and patched scoundrel that might offer to marry you today."

"Very wise. But tell me, how did you come to locate a genuine priest among so many imposters?"

"Ah, you would like to know my secrets. Well, if you will pardon my boasts, I will tell you. I bribed the clerk of the Fleet Chapel to inform me immediately when a presentable clergyman was next condemned to the Fleet. He did, and I met the Reverend Mr. Whitfield two days ago, at which time he promised to remain sober and to perform our ceremony in exchange for my discharging his debts. I have spent the past two days doing so, and Tom has visited Mr. Whitfield every day to ensure he was living up to his side of the bargain. That is to say, that he visited the taproom no more than three times per day. We did not wish him to die of thirst, after all."

Hester shook her head in admiration. "I shall be marrying a man of exceptional skill. Thank you, my love. I hope, this will not cost you too much."

"Every penny will be worth it if it makes you happy, but no, the poor man's debts are not exorbitant. I only hope he can manage to stay solvent henceforth, but my ability to help him further will be limited."

Their carriage slowed to a walk, and peering through the glass, Hester saw that they had arrived in the neighbourhood of the Fleet. It was necessary to move slowly for all the pedestrians. A group of drunken sailors, clutching women to their sides, staggered down the street. Hawkers called to them, offering them the cheapest wedding to be had in the liberty. Competing "chaplains" and chapel owners clamoured for their trade, and above every other house hung a sign whose symbols suggested something about marriage.

St. Mars laughed at her widening eyes, but still he asked, "Are you certain you wish to go through with this?" His voice was light, but his look was serious.

"Perfectly, my dear. Just as long as we never have to live here or in any other prison. So you must promise me never to be caught, for I should have to move in with you if you were."

He took her hand and pressed it, just as the hackney rolled up before the prison doors. As St. Mars helped her out, Hester spied two figures waiting behind him and hoped that she had done the right thing.

After looping her arm through his, St. Mars turned and froze. Mary and James Henry were standing outside the prison doorway, Mary beaming and her beloved pale.

"Sir Robert, I believe." With coyness in her voice, Mary moved forward to greet them. She clasped their hands and kissed them each upon the cheek. "Sir, I hope you will not object to witnesses, but I could not allow my favourite relation to be married without a family member to support her."

St. Mars found his voice to thank her for her coming. Her friendliness had obviously pleased him.

"I, too, hope not to offend you with our presence—mine, at least. But we were invited by your lady, and if you will accept my most humble apologies and my gratitude for all you have done for me . . . ." James Henry faltered, as he awaited St. Mars's response.

Throughout this brief speech, Hester did not breathe, but a sigh escaped her when St. Mars extended his hand to the brother he had never truly known. "We have both been wrong, but I hope our failures will remain in the past."

The clasp they exchanged was more than Hester had ever hoped for.

"Now, to wed!" St. Mars said, dispelling the awkwardness.

"With your permission, I should like to give Mrs. Kean away," James Henry said.

"Mrs. Kean?" St. Mars deferred the answer to her.

"I will be honoured."

With that St. Mars turned and instead of taking them into the prison, led them across the street to the sign of the Bel Savage. Hester was conscious of dozens of people calling from every doorway, of competing vendors elbowing to reach them, of many defeated expressions at the custom lost. On a normal day, she would have been dismayed by the raggedness of their clothes, by the meanness of the houses, by the clamour for business that she could not give them, but today was not like any other. Today, her life would change. She would be married to St. Mars.

He led them into a parlour, where a blazing wood fire threw out a pleasant warmth. Tom and Katy were waiting there in the company of a clergyman dressed in threadbare robes. They broke out in broad smiles at the sight of their master leading Hester into the room; then Tom gawked to see the other couple behind them.

"Hello, Tom." With a warm smile, James Henry extended his hand. "I had a notion I would find you here."

"Mr. Henry!" Tom was almost speechless when he shook the other man's hand. "I never thought to see you again, sir. But it's good that you're here."

"And this is your wife?"

As Tom presented Katy to his former master's receiver-general, Hester was greeted by the clergyman. Mr. Whitfield welcomed her and St. Mars with reverence—due undoubtedly to his gratitude for St. Mars's paying his debts. He apologized for the surroundings, but told Hester that this inn appeared to be the quietest place in the liberty for nuptials, provided the whole inn had been hired. He assured her that his register was valid and that everything concerning her marriage would be legal, not only in the sight of God but in the government's eyes.

Throughout these pleasantries, St. Mars fidgeted beside her, impatient to start. Now, he called for Mr. Whitfield to begin the proceedings, and the clergyman called for silence.

He had a pleasant voice that took Hester and St. Mars through the ritual. In a blur, it was over, and Hester heard herself proclaimed, Mrs. Gideon Fitzsimmons. They both signed Mr. Whitfield's register and thanked him. Now, at least, he would be free to return to his former life. Hester wished him well and expressed her hope that there would be no return of his difficulties.

She turned to receive a kiss from Mary. Tom and Katy eagerly welcomed her as their mistress.

Then, James Henry took her hand and kissed it. "My earnest wishes for your happiness, Lady St. Mars."

Until these words left his mouth, Hester had never once thought that now she would be a French viscountess, the wife of the *Vicomte de St. Mars*. Dazed, and a bit frightened by the realization, she was scarcely aware of the hasty goodbyes, the invitation Mary extended to St. Mars to her wedding this summer in Yorkshire, and Tom's and Katy's waves, as St. Mars hustled her out of the inn and into the waiting hackney.

"My Lady St. Mars, will you spare an hour or two to consummate our marriage?" St. Mars raised her hand to his lips, awakening her desire. "I would carry you away with me this instant, but until the embargo is lifted, we shall have to go on as we were."

"Yes, my dearest lord, I can and I will. If necessary, I will gladly invent a feeble excuse for my absence, in exchange for your most ardent attentions."

"You will not mind your aunt's strictures?"

"No, nothing she says can ever hurt me again. I plan on being much too dizzy with happiness to be bothered by pettiness or spite. Nothing short of death or destruction is likely to rattle me now."

THE END

AUTHOR'S NOTE

A few years ago, when touring St. Paul's Cathedral, which for some reason I had ignored on my previous trips, I learned about the Whispering Gallery. This instantly suggested the plot of a mystery.

Every author of historical fiction has to choose how to bring history to life. My approach has been to use mainly fictional characters and to weave their stories through the actual events on a day by day basis. Modelling some of my characters after real historical figures, however, provides me with credible plots for the early Georgian era. I know that when I read historical fiction or see a historical film, I always want to know how much of the story is true, so here is my account.

In this book, the character of Lord Wragby was modelled on Philip, Duke of Wharton, the first and last of that title, whom Pope called, "the scorn and wonder of our days." I fictionalized his character for the simple reason that he was not murdered in 1716, but Lord Wragby's scandalous, extravagant, treasonous, blasphemous, and cruel behavior were all taken directly from Philip Wharton's early words and deeds.

Philip Wharton was the founder of the infamous Hell-Fire Club. Some readers will be familiar with the legend of a later club identified with the same name and said to belong to Sir Francis Dashwood, at which orgies and Black Masses were supposed to have taken place. According to my reference, *Hell-Fire Duke* by Mark Blackett-Ord, this later club never used the name Hell-Fire, and the reported orgies were an invention of Sir Francis's political enemy John Wilkes. The original Hell-Fire Club satirized the Church of England, and its members were blasphemers. This was scandalous enough for the second decade of the eighteenth century when it was founded. I borrowed details from the club—its purpose, regular meeting place, and rituals—renamed it the Brotherhood of the Damned, and described a fictional meeting in the crypt of the old Church of St. John's Priory, deeming it an ideal, macabre site for such a group to gather.

Jonathan Wild, of course, is a historical figure. In early eighteenth

century London, in the absence of a police force and when harsh punishments were the only deterrent to crime, Wild devised an ingenious
way to work the system to his benefit. Understanding that returning
stolen property for a fee was a safe and profitable alternative to being
hanged for theft, he gained control of the London criminal community by fencing stolen goods back to their owners. The property was
advertised as either lost or found and returned "with no questions
asked." The owner paid Wild his expenses for advertising plus half
the value of the stolen object, which Wild split with the thief. If any
criminal tried to operate without cutting Wild in, he would turn him
over to the law for a large reward. Over time, this playing for both
sides eventually led to his downfall. The character of Peachum in *The
Beggar's Opera* was inspired by Wild, but also understood to be a dig
at Sir Robert Walpole.

The original for my character Burchet was a man who was tried for
treason in the Old Bailey in January, 1717. Francis Francia, a French
Jew from a successful commercial family, but long-time resident of
London, had been baptized a Christian in his native Bordeaux, according to custom at the time. It is not clear why he developed Jacobite sympathies, but under the cover of his correspondence with a
relative of the Duke of Ormond over a matter of business, Jacobites
in England passed letters to and from the Pretender's agents in France
from 1713 to 1715. Acting on a tip, Lord Townsend intercepted letters from France addressed to Francia and obtained a warrant to search
his house, where a copybook was found to contain more treasonable
correspondence. It was the custom in those days for men to create a
copy of the letters they wrote for their records. I used the code found
in Francia's letters in my description of Burchet's papers.

The evidence should have been enough to hang Francia, but he
was too wily for the government. First, he disguised the handwriting
in his copybook, so he could claim that the letters were not written
by him. The prosecution had no way to prove that they were. Next,
using a new right, he examined the potential jurors and struck thirty-
four names to come up with a panel of Tories, who would be more
sympathetic to his cause. Lastly, he embarrassed Lord Townsend, who
had examined him in prison in view of two other inmates, who could

not overhear their conversation. At the end of his examination, Francia complained that he was starving, as he had not brought enough money with him to pay for food. Moved to charity, Lord Townsend reached into his pocket and handed him coins. In his trial, Francia claimed that Townsend had tried to bribe him and brought in the two prisoners to testify that they had seen Townsend give him money. The jury eventually brought in a verdict of innocent, and the spy, Francis Francia, went free. His trial left me with the impression of a clever man who stayed cool in the face of danger.

The best (and virtually only) account of the early years at the court of George I is the *Diary of Mary, Countess Cowper, Lady of the Bedchamber to the Princess of Wales*. This is why I have chosen to use her as a character in my books, and I have tried to relay her comments and opinions faithfully. It was something of an aside to my plot to include the week-long labour of the Princess of Wales, but I hope it serves as an illustration of the conflicts between the English and Germans at court and a reminder that no amount of power or privilege can shield people of any era from tragedy.

With so few references for this period, the newspapers have become my greatest resource. During the months covered by *Whisper of Death*, the keepers of the Duke of Albemarle's Head and the King's Head were taken by the King's Messengers for questioning, giving me two locations where Jacobites met. Also, the Reverend Mr. Mottram was arrested for performing fraudulent weddings in the Fleet Prison, and the particulars of his scams were reported. Other details of London, its streets, buildings, citizens, etc., were gleaned from many factual sources.

I am constantly amazed by the way history repeats itself and how issues we deal with today find their parallels—often their precursors—in the few years of the eighteenth century covered by my novels. I include them perhaps more than I would if they did not resonate so strongly, but it is never my intention to comment on the politics of our day. These books are meant to entertain, and I hope they do.

Finally, for those who have not read my previous books, I have used the abbreviation Mrs. for mistress, as even single ladies were called in those days.

LITTLEWORTH from STOCK MARKET

A WEDDING IN THE FLEET. (*From a P*